Born and bred in Dundee, Kev_ _Glasgow where he works as a sports journa_ _ _he Daily Record and Sunday Mail. He is married to Thanyalak and is the proud father of Jennifer. Moristoun is his first novel.

*To my special girls Thanyalak and Jennifer. Everything I do in life is for you.*

Kevin McAllion

# MORISTOUN

AUSTIN MACAULEY
PUBLISHERS LTD.

A CIP catalogue record for this title is available from the British Library.


ISBN 978 1 78455 284 8 (Paperback)
ISBN 978 1 78455 285 5 (eBook)


www.austinmacauley.com

First Published (2016)
Austin Macauley Publishers Ltd.
25 Canada Square
Canary Wharf
London
E14 5LQ

# Acknowledgments

Thanks to Jennifer for the motivation to get the book finished before her arrival and to June for her support and encouragement throughout her pregnancy. My mum Susan was also a massive help during the book's creation, giving feedback for every chapter I wrote. I owe a huge debt to my former colleague Roddie McVake for his proof reading, corrections and support when reading a first draft. I'm also hugely grateful to my best friend Brian Stewart and Adrienne Chalmers for taking the time out to read the first draft in full and giving me their impressions.

# Chapter One:

# Defender of the realm

Buchan prided himself on giving clients his full attention but it was hard not to let his mind wander as Hogg babbled away while fidgeting in his seat. Condemned men rarely show grace under pressure but Hogg's reaction to the most grievous of predicaments was particularly pathetic.

"There must be something you can do!" he said to Buchan at the end of an interminable bout of self-pity. "Can't you check The Book again? There has to be some way I can get out of this."

Unfortunately for Hogg, there were no crumbs of comfort Buchan could throw at him. Hogg held a Q45 form in his hand and only the most inept of prosecutors could fail to secure the sentence that would banish the accused from Moristoun.

"Who are we facing in court?" he asked Hogg. "It should tell you the prosecutor's name near the bottom of the form."

Hogg's sweaty palms unfolded the piece of red paper and his eyes scanned the page for a few seconds before finding their target.

"Your case will be heard by Lord Bane on July 6," said Hogg as he read from the letter. "Public defender Buchan will handle your defence and chief administrator Farqhuar will lead the prosecution."

Those words were every bit as disastrous for Hogg as the ones that would eventually tumble from the lips of Lord Bane. Farqhuar was the sharpest of Moristoun's bureaucrats and Buchan was no match for him, especially when the odds were so heavily stacked against the accused. Hogg had committed a Category A offence and no amount of courtroom chicanery could save him. Buchan's role in this case, therefore, was little more than ceremonial.

"Farqhuar is the last man you want to see when you're standing in the dock," Buchan said. "I'm afraid we stand little chance of winning. I can only recommend you make the most of your last few weeks here because your new home is going to be far from pleasant."

"Can't you plead insanity or use some other trick to get me off the hook?" said Hogg. "We still have a couple of months to prepare my case."

Had such an option been available, Buchan could have certainly built a convincing case for madness as Hogg was being tried for attempted murder, the most idiotic of crimes in Moristoun. How anyone on the island could delude themselves into thinking their own hands had the power to control life and death was beyond Buchan. Their very presence in Moristoun proved such a belief was wildly misguided. It was a point he put to Hogg, who broke down in tears as he finally accepted the hopelessness of his situation.

"I've been so stupid," he sobbed. "But I just couldn't help myself. That arsehole McCall had been pushing my buttons for years and I finally lost control."

"Control and patience are the very virtues you need to survive here," said Buchan. "Anyone who has read The Book would know that."

"The Book? Who has time to get through that? It would take decades to read every page."

"It only took me 14 years actually," said Buchan. "And that's nothing in the grand scheme of things. Time is the one thing we Moristounians have in abundance, something you of all people should appreciate."

"Are you seriously suggesting we should all read that bloody thing? I had to give up after just one page. It was incomprehensible."

"Like I said earlier, it's all a question of patience. If you're not prepared to put a bit of time and effort in then you won't be rewarded."

"Where's your reward, then?" said Hogg. "You're still stuck here like the rest of us."

"I'm using the system to engineer my exit but it will take time," replied Buchan. "It's the only way out, with the obvious exception of following your own exit strategy. However, I think you'd agree that remaining in Moristoun is far preferable to the fate that awaits you."

This brutal truth sparked another bout of sobbing and Buchan decided it was best just to sit back and let Hogg give free rein to his emotions. The crying was soon brought to a halt, however, as a knock at Buchan's door was followed by the entrance of an impeccably dressed figure who was carrying a cane. The sight of Hogg blubbering like an infant clearly amused Buchan's visitor, who addressed the tragic figure as if he were a puppy who had just soiled the Persian rug at his country mansion.

"Pull yourself together, Hogg!" he said. "These pathetic waterworks won't impress Judge Bane. If you're looking for sympathy you'll be sorely disappointed."

He then turned his attention towards Buchan and said: "I hope this isn't the path you plan to go down in court. Such a shameless display would demean both you and your client."

It disappointed Buchan that Farqhuar could think he would stoop so low but he was in no position to take his courtroom adversary to task. His own freedom was linked to maintaining Farqhuar's favour so he remained calm and addressed his superior with due respect.

"I can assure you Mr Hogg will handle himself with the dignity and grace the court expects," Buchan said. "He's just a little upset after discovering his case is a lost cause."

"Of course it's a lost cause," replied Farqhuar. "The stupidity of the morons in our midst never ceases to amaze me. This is the third attempted murder in the last year. Why do these idiots persist with such a pointless pursuit?"

Buchan was every bit as baffled as Farqhuar and could only point to the ignorance of those too lazy to study The Book. However, there was one man in the room who could provide a more detailed answer so he invited Hogg to expand on the reasons for his mindless act.

"Frustration builds up inside when you're stuck on this miserable island for as long as I have been," he said. "It's hard to hold back your anger and you just lash out. I'm only human."

Buchan felt like correcting the grammatical mistake in that last sentence but such pedantry would have been harsh as Hogg's words summed up the situation perfectly. The point also wasn't lost on Farqhuar, who turned to Buchan and said: "Indeed, where would we be without the many flaws of humanity? It's what keeps you and I so busy."

Buchan nodded in agreement as he was certain Farqhuar's visit had nothing to do with crushing the already fragile confidence of Hogg ahead of their meeting in court. The presence of the accused was just a pleasant coincidence for Farqhuar; he was here to add to Buchan's workload with another case. Hogg found this out seconds later when his meeting with the defence counsel was brought to an abrupt halt by the most withering of dismissals.

"Run along now, you wretched rat," Farqhuar told Hogg. "The Council can't have vermin like you wasting the time and talents of Buchan – we have far more important business for him. Get out of my sight before I add intense physical pain to your emotional torment."

Farqhuar's choice of animal for his disparaging remark was apt as Hogg cowered in fear of the cane pointing in his direction before scurrying out of the office. Buchan felt sorry for his client as Hogg made that undignified exit but Farqhuar was right when he claimed devoting time to this case was futile. It would only distract him from helping someone who could actually be saved, not to mention himself.

"What do you have for me?" he asked Farqhuar as the chief administrator wiped Hogg's sweat off the chair with a handkerchief before taking the weight off his feet.

"It's one of your favourites – a Q99," replied Farqhuar. "Another miserable wretch is planning to join our community and The Council would like you to stop him. Immigration is getting increasingly out of hand. We're running out of places to house them."

"Hogg's house will be free soon," said Buchan. "And Miss Sanderson has finally passed to the other side, as well. They may be flocking in but some are also making their way out."

"Not enough to maintain the equilibrium unfortunately. The avarice of the buffoons running the show on the mainland has whipped up quite a storm and the flotsam and jetsam are washing up on these shores with disturbing regularity."

Buchan had to admit the last few years had been exceptionally busy but he was hoping his own tireless work on behalf of The Council would bring perpetual peace closer to his grasp. Adding another Q99 to his list of successful cases would be a step in the right direction so he quizzed Farqhuar further about his salvage operation.

"This one will provide a stern test of your abilities," Farqhuar said. "James Patrick McSorely has managed to cram more than his fair share of misfortune into the last 30 years."

The scale of Buchan's task was then laid bare as Farqhuar provided a detailed biography of Moristoun's latest prospective citizen. Some light relief was provided by the brief chapter that dealt with McSorely's sexual embarrassments but, that apart, it was an unremittingly bleak tale. Buchan was proud of his success rate when it came to Q99s but it would take all of his ingenuity to avoid a failure that would haunt him just as much as his first bungled assignment.

"Do you think you will able to handle this one?" said Farqhuar. "It would certainly increase your standing with The Council if you managed to convince McSorely bringing his pathetic life to an end might not be such a good idea."

"Well, I've never shied away from a challenge," replied Buchan. "How long do I have to prepare a strategy?"

"It could just be a matter of hours, unfortunately."

"A couple of hours! Your department is supposed to keep a close eye on cases like this to make sure we can act early whenever things threaten to get out of hand. Did the grim reaper's repeated presence at family gatherings not set off any alarm bells?"

13

"Don't address me like I'm some kind of idiot, you impertinent twerp. We've been maintaining surveillance and up until now we've been satisfied he wasn't a serious risk."

"So why is he now just hours away from ending it all?"

"I'm afraid it has been a particularly bad day. The fickle hands of fate have delivered slap after slap to his face and he just can't take any more punishment."

"But how am I supposed to convince this McSorely not to kill himself if I can't even speak to him?"

"You'll need to set up a meeting somehow then use all of your charm to talk him back from edge. Cold calling appears to be your only option – here's his phone number."

As Buchan picked up the piece of paper with McSorely's number scrawled on it, his mind searched for an alternative solution. He hated speaking to people on the phone because the subtle nuances of body language didn't come into play. Years of courtroom dealings with undesirable characters had taught him everyone was capable of lying through speech but only a select few could force their body to be implicit in the deceit. To truly understand this troubled character, Buchan would have to meet him face to face but calling McSorely at this delicate point would only spook him into speeding up his departure from the mortal realm. Piquing his curiosity and rekindling a passion for life would be far more productive so Buchan took the brave step of defying Farqhuar and suggesting a more modern form of communication.

"I think McSorely would respond more readily to a bit of mystery," he said. "I want to send him a link to that website I've been working on with one of my other Q99s. It's perfect for cases where you need to buy a little time. It helps to postpone the suicide and gives me the chance to set up a face-to-face meeting. The site is a little unorthodox but it might just work."

Farqhuar was intrigued by this mention of Buchan's website as he recalled the many strings he had been forced to pull at Council HQ to secure internet access for his lackey.

"I hope this website is worth it," he said. "Plebeians such as yourself aren't supposed to have access to all the wonders of technology. You're here as a punishment, remember. I had to use my considerable influence to get you connected and I will be far from amused if you have been wasting my time."

"Computers are an essential tool of the trade now," said Buchan. "People of McSorely's generation live most of their lives in a virtual world. How am I supposed to relate to him if I can't take a peek into that baffling realm? I've had to learn a whole new language in the last three months."

Farqhuar had to admit Buchan had a point as his patience now regularly snapped during induction meetings. The dictionary that sat on his desk was falling to pieces due to the number of times it had been launched at "slavering illiterates" so he could understand Buchan's need to immerse himself in the patois of these cyber Scots.

"Very well Buchan, let's see what you and the odious swine McKeown have come up with to connect with these uneducated boors," said Farqhuar.

As Buchan took Farqhuar on his virtual tour of Scenic Suicides.com, beads of sweat began to form on his forehead. As a novice in the world of computers, Buchan had relied heavily on the technical expertise of his mainland partner in crafting the website. Had McKeown stuck to his brief of design and maintenance, this wouldn't have presented Buchan with much of a problem but he also considered content as a major part of his duties, adding many an embellishment to the words emailed to him. Every time Buchan logged on, he seemed to find some new dark aside hidden away somewhere and he could only wonder what hand grenade was waiting to explode on Farqhuar's first visit to the site. It was hard to tell when the chief administrator was in a foul mood as a scowl rarely disappeared from his face but Buchan was still braced for a bollocking when Farqhuar finished his tour and turned towards him to deliver a verdict.

"You don't need to be a master of deduction to spot the dirty hand of the Paisley pervert in this creation," said Farqhuar. "Is this how you have been keeping that reprobate McKeown busy?"

"I appreciate it's rather unorthodox for a man of your refined tastes but the website has been working wonders with McKeown's rehabilitation. The stimulation of his creative side seems to be having a palliative effect on his depression."

"Warped might be a better word than creative when it comes to some of his childish attempts at humour but I have to admit you have a point. The people I've assigned to McKeown's case no longer consider him to be a high risk. Maybe this kind of approach might actually reap rewards with other contemptible characters. Have you tested this website out on anyone?"

"Not yet. It hasn't been suitable for any of my recent Q99s but McSorely might fit the bill."

"Yes, he's a twisted little character, isn't he? This website could be right up his street. And it's not as if we have much of a choice. Let's send him an email and see how we get on."

It was now just a matter of composing the paragraphs that would reel McSorely in – a task that proved difficult for Buchan as only a handful of his original words had survived McKeown's latest sub-editing session. Buchan's mind went blank as he tried to sum up the concept in just a few sentences but his writer's block was cured when Farquhar brandished his cane again and urged him to get "a bloody move on". Buchan didn't need a second invitation and his best stab at an imitation of McKeown's cyber prose saw the following message flash up on his screen:

"Are you thinking of killing yourself? Has it all become too much to bare? Are you tired of a world where idiots are splashed across our TV screens and treated like gods? If the answer to any of these questions is 'Yes' then maybe we can help you. We all have to die someday, so why not beat the Grim Reaper to the punch and pick your own way to bow out? And do it in style. Don't go for something lame and predictable like slitting your wrists or popping pills. That's suicide for losers – kill yourself like a winner with Scenic Suicides. We can give you the tools to be katapulted off a cliff at one of several breathtaking locations in the Highlands of Scotland. And we'll take care of all the paperwork that arises out of your death – drafting and notarising a will, writing a suicide note and any other special requests. Don't delay, visit scenic suicides.net today!"

Farqhuar demanded a look at the email before its despatch and lectured Buchan for a couple of sloppy spelling mistakes prior to giving his official authorisation.

"Too much to 'bare'?" he raged. "Are we dealing with people who have an irrational fear of taking their clothes off? And catapult is spelt with a C not a K, you buffoon! You're supposed to be a man of the law, Buchan – the least we should expect of you is the ability to string a sentence together."

Buchan considered blaming his mistakes on overexposure to the shocking grammar of McKeown and others fluent in Facebook but this clearly wasn't a good time to mount a defence of his literary capabilities. So he merely shrugged off Farqhuar's abuse and made the necessary corrections before clicking the button that would hopefully lead to him making the acquaintance of James Patrick McSorely.

# Chapter Two:

# McSorely is pushed to the edge

Fate had conspired against McSorely to such an extent that even the bedside radio was now mocking him, fuelling his insomnia with a 4.23 a.m. blast of Night by Jackie Wilson. That this song marked the nadir of the soul singer's baffling foray into a parody of an opera tenor was bad enough but the lyrics were chipping in with an additional volley to the testes.

"Night, here comes the night," warbled Jackie as he exercised his lungs to something approaching full capacity. "Another night to dream about you. Night, each lovely night. The only time I'm not without you. Once more, I feel your kisses. Once more, I know what bliss is. Come dawn, my darling, you're gone. But you come back into my arms each night."

McSorely had naively thought turning the dial towards Clyde 2 before crawling into bed would have protected him from such torment. With a stream of hits from the 60s and 70s on the playlist, he figured he was unlikely to encounter any numbers that would conjure up memories from his own miserable 30 years of existence. Like most of McSorely's calculations, however, it had proven miles off the mark, the error on this occasion coming from his failure to factor in the inherent bitterness of regional disc jockeys forced to work the graveyard shift.

Since assuming control of the airwaves at 4 a.m., the lowlife whose name already escaped McSorely had subscribed to the "I'm going to make each and every one of you fuckers suffer every bit as much me" doctrine favoured by so many of his contemporaries. For those who thought he couldn't top the unmitigated misery of a Lulu double-header to kick off proceedings, he had pulled an ace out of the sleeve by inflicting Cliff Richard's Congratulations on greater Glasgow and beyond. With a flair for sadism that was fast approaching show-boating, the man behind the mic followed that treat up by inviting Tiny Tim to take another Tiptoe Through The Tulips. The fare had become so awful by this point that it was beginning to take on kitsch value for McSorely but the DJ then had to spoil it by turning gay to Night and making it personal. Conjuring the demon of Sarah – and five months to the day since he lost something even more precious to him, the ability to sleep – was an insult too far. He couldn't take much more of this; it had to end.

Thoughts of suicide had first surfaced a week into his living nightmare as the prospect of eternal sleep began to seem much more alluring than anything the material world could offer. The idea scared McSorely as much as it tempted him, though, an understandable by-product of his Catholic education. What if the zealots at St Andrew's were right and damnation awaited him rather than a right good kip? This dilemma merely added to the thousands of other questions that raced around inside McSorely's head every night and denied him a pleasure most people took for granted. Of all the miseries that had assailed him, it was insomnia that had pushed McSorely closer to the edge. Now it was threatening to topple him over the cliff completely, so it was time to call the one man capable of pulling him back from the brink.

McSorely silenced Jackie Wilson as the song reached its climax before using the same hand to flick the switch that brought a shimmer of light to this darkest of nights. He then clambered out of bed and pulled on his dressing gown before plucking his mobile phone out of the toy monkey that served as its own resting place. McSorely punched in a number that had become all too familiar then sat down to await an answer. After three or four rings, hours of solitude were finally broken by human contact as a cheery voice said: "You're through to the Samaritans. How can I help you?"

It was way too cheery, though, lacking the sincerity and gravitas of the man who regularly convinced McSorely life was worth living. The tone also seemed to suggest it was either a woman or a eunuch, something which required a surgical procedure it was hard to envisage his guardian angel agreeing to.

"Can I speak to Paul please?" said McSorely. "He usually works the nightshift, doesn't he?"

"Oh, I'm afraid Paul no longer works here. I'm his replacement, Cindy. Maybe I can help you?"

Silence was all that greeted Cindy for a few seconds as the latest blow to McSorely's psyche was processed. He eventually ended the impasse by asking about Paul's whereabouts but that only brought more misery.

"Oh, it's a terrible story," said Cindy. "When one of my colleagues came in for the morning shift yesterday she found Paul slumped on the floor in a pool of blood. Went at his wrists with a kitchen knife, apparently. I guess all those depressing stories finally got to him."

"No, no ... he can't be dead," said McSorely. "Paul was the only one who truly understood me."

He then started to sob, providing Cindy with something of a test on just the third call of her Samaritans career but she tried her best to retain a professional veneer.

"There, there ... let it all out love. A good cry never hurt anybody. You let those tears come and we'll talk when you're ready."

Tears came much more readily for McSorely than sleep and he let loose for a couple of minutes before composing himself. Cindy then seized the initiative and tried to pull McSorely towards her comforting bosom.

"You'll have to forget about Paul," she said. "He's gone. But I'm here now and I'm a professional too. I'm sure I can help you get over what's bothering you."

McSorely very much doubted this and wasn't slow in relaying his concerns over Cindy's suitability for her new post.

"Well, you haven't got off to the best of starts," he said. "Your opening gambit was revealing my one friend and confidant had just topped himself. It's hardly textbook counselling."

This punctured Cindy's confidence somewhat but she tried her best to mount a defence of her capabilities.

"Honesty is always the best policy," she said. "Lies get you nowhere. We all lose loved ones and it's about how we react."

"Oh, I've lost plenty of loved ones, don't you worry about that," said McSorely. "I'm a dab hand when it comes to grief. The only problem is I now have nobody left."

Upon hearing this news, Cindy invited McSorely to open up about the loss of nearest and dearest but he decided against unburdening himself to a stranger whose initial offerings hinted that she was the intellectual inferior of a trained chimp. Conversation, even with such a simpleton, nevertheless remained a more agreeable option than returning to bed with only Satan's personal DJ for company, so he decided to fill Cindy in on the misfortunes he was more comfortable talking about. By the time the poor Samaritan had learned of the two Labrador puppies who had chased bouncing balls into the path of a Range Rover, Cousin Elsa's heroin addiction and subsequent descent into prostitution, the unscrupulous colleague who had engineered McSorely's sacking by directing his company laptop to amputeesexorgy.com, the disastrously phrased expressions of teenage love that had forced Spanish pen pal Maria into a hasty move from Madrid from Valencia, and the fact McSorely was a season-ticket holder at Albion Rovers, she was close to tears herself.

"Jesus, you've had it hard, haven't you?" was all Cindy could manage when it came to summing up the ill fortune that McSorely considered minor league compared to the real heartache he was keeping in abeyance. "I don't think I'm ready for a caller like you yet. Can you ring back when Karen clocks on at 10?"

McSorely, though, was in no mood to listen to another well-meaning but fatuous counsellor, so he hung up before bursting into tears again. Although a job with the Samaritans was clearly not Cindy's true calling and she would soon join

McSorely among the massed ranks of the unemployed, he had to admit she was right about one thing – crying did make him feel better. He had felt like killing himself when Cindy had passed on news of Paul's passing and such a scenario may well have unfolded had his old counsellor not persuaded McSorely to rid his house of any paraphernalia that might have aided a suicide attempt. Pills were conspicuous by their absence in McSorely's medicine cabinet, each piece of cutlery was now plastic, the oven was not gas but electric and his Philishave stood little chance of inflicting substantial damage to his wrists. He still had the option of tipping a toaster into the bath but McSorely couldn't be arsed rooting around in his cupboard for the extension leads that would ensure a supply of electricity from the kitchen. It also seemed an unnecessarily violent way to bid the world farewell and Luke Skywalker's suffering at the Emperor's hands before his dear old dad intervened had taught McSorely an important childhood lesson that electrocution was a fate to be avoided at all costs. A more serene death held far greater appeal and McSorely had the option of popping down to Sainsbury's at 7 a.m. and investing in the pills that would take him on his final journey. That was still two hours away, though, and the therapeutic powers of a good greet had lifted some of the gloom associated with Paul beating him to a knockout punch. He still lacked proof that life was worth living, though, so McSorely turned on his computer in search of something to cheer him up.

Swatting aside the temptation to seek succour in the female form was always a Herculean task whenever McSorely was faced with his Google homepage but the Catholic guilt that accompanies such surfing would have only pushed him towards more melancholy. So McSorely instead logged on to Facebook to see if any of his online friends could provide him with a reason to keep faith with humanity. These virtual acquaintances were a mixture of former St Andrew's alumni, old work colleagues, fellow Albion Rovers diehards and a South Korean student who provided stiff competition in games of online Scrabble. Cousin Elsa also had a Facebook page but McSorely stopped visiting when it became clear she had started using it to advertise her wares. That move may have lost the page McSorely's patronage but Cousin Elsa was unlikely to shed any tears about that after gaining 9,456 new admirers.

The unabashed vulgarity of Cousin Elsa's Facebook flyer was at least a more honest and entertaining exhibition of society's decay than the banal posts McSorely had to sift through before finding something he considered even mildly amusing or informative. The latest offerings were particularly lowbrow, mainly because it was Saturday night and saddos across the land couldn't wait to inform the world of their latest insights into X-Factor and Strictly Come Dancing. Reading these critiques on what was essentially a lavishly funded pub karaoke competition usually acted as compelling evidence that suicide was the only option but McSorely pushed on in the belief he might still find something that restored his faith in humanity. That theory was soon shot down, however, as the rest of the day's posts provided further proof that life in 21st century Scotland had about as much substance as a speck of moon dust. Narcissism and schadenfreude were the overwhelming themes as McSorely's acquaintances queued up to offer testimony in what was becoming an overwhelming case for suicide.

"Just bought my new 42-inch plasma," wrote former class-mate Mark Jones. "Can't wait to hook it up to my Xbox and massacre some civilians on Modern Warfare 3!"

"Nine goals for the Kevmeister at fives today," wrote Rovers fan Kevin Reilly. "Albion should sign me up – I'm the Messi of Coatbridge."

"LOL! Check out this video," urged McSorely's next-door neighbour Paul Franklin, an invitation he decided to decline as the title of the YouTube clip – "EPIC FAIL!!! Skateboarder breaks jaw" – revealed it was something too tasteless for even You've Been Framed to consider.

And so it continued, post after post, human beings using the precious right of free speech to prove they don't actually have anything worthwhile to say. The only glimmer of goodness in this ocean of vanity and greed came from the

Scrabble-playing Korean, who was seeking sponsors for a half marathon in aid of cancer research. It was all too much for McSorely and with one move of his mouse, he closed this window on a dystopian world for the last time.

Only one thing could now halt McSorely's determination to push ahead with his imminent erasing – and that was a win on the £8million lottery rollover. Society had come to the conclusion that money can't buy you happiness but McSorely would have appreciated the chance to at least put that theory to the test. He had bought a year's worth of lucky dips nine months ago yet it had thus far proven to be as wise an investment as betting the house on a sub-prime mortgage derivative seconds before capitalism's house of cards was torn asunder by Hurricane Karmic Vengeance. Further proof of McSorely's bad luck was provided by the fact his £52 stake had yet to yield even a £10 prize and the prospect of pocketing a cheque from Camelot now seemed every bit as mythical as the medieval legends the lottery organisers had appropriated for commercial gain. However, there was still one last chance for McSorely to pluck Excalibur from suicide's stone and take his place at the round table of the modern elite – loathsome millionaires whose wealth and influence was every bit as ill-deserved as that afforded to the ancient kings and noblemen born into privilege. Virtual winners in the lucky dip were informed of their rise in status via email so there was a sense of excitement when McSorely logged on to his hotmail account and learned his only new message had been sent by the National Lottery. Visions of reclining on a sun lounger at a beachfront mansion far from Caledonia's tundra flashed before McSorely's eyes but he was soon blinded by another poke in the sockets from reality.

"We are delighted to inform you that your numbers this week – 3, 6, 11, 14, 21, 33 and 39 – have won you the prize of £10. This amount has now been deposited into your account. Congratulations. Thank you for playing the National Lottery."

For McSorely, this hollow victory was worse than finding out it was time to chuck another virtual ticket in the recycle bin. Teasing him with the prospect of a jackpot win for a few seconds was unnecessary cruelty after the night he had just endured, akin to a sodomite repeatedly flicking the ear of his victim while singing Justin Bieber numbers. McSorely was definitely going to buy those pills now, although he still had over an hour to wait until Sainsbury's opened its doors.

While his eyes were diverted to the bottom of his monitor to check on the time, a new message was flying across cyberspace to McSorely's inbox. This was an unusual occurrence as the precious few social contacts McSorely made these days normally came via Facebook while any junk mail was intercepted by the filters. So it was with more than a hint of curiosity that McSorely returned to his inbox to see who was trying to contact him. That curiosity then turned into bewilderment as McSorely learned the email had come from a company calling themselves Scenic Suicides and was entitled: "Are you thinking of killing yourself?" For a moment, McSorely thought biology had finally triumphed over psychology and he had drifted off into the long-lost world of his dreams. But a quick slap to his face soon dispelled such a notion and another look at the screen confirmed that was indeed the subject matter of the message. Paul and his dim-witted successor were the only ones whom McSorely had informed of his darkest desperation and it seemed unlikely either had a hand in the email's despatch. Paul was too scrupulous and honourable to cash in on the misery of his callers by hawking their personal details to the vultures who clutter junk mail folders, while Cindy was so bad at her job she had even forgotten to ask McSorely for his name. The idea of her using sophisticated tracking technology to uncover McSorely's IP address, hack into the computer and pilfer his personal details was beyond belief, especially as just 20 minutes had elapsed since their conversation. McSorely guessed this would be an insufficient period of time for her to recite the alphabet, never mind devise such a complicated scheme. The email, therefore, was either a staggering co-incidence or an act of God. McSorely didn't wish to incur the wrath of the man upstairs by deleting his communiqué just moments before a potential gamble with his eternal fate so he decided to open the email and see what destiny had in store.

His initial appraisal was that the message looked too dull and uninspiring for someone who counted the Northern Lights and Great Barrier Reef amongst his many creations. If this message did indeed come from God, he needed to invest in a better graphic designer, or an intelligent designer, to humour the red necks from America's Bible belt. But as McSorely began to read the email, he became more and more convinced there was a hint of divine intervention about its composition. Upon reaching the end of the message, all McSorely could do was sit there in shock. Although every logical bone in his body screamed out: "It's just a coincidence you muppet!", McSorely's mind drifted towards the supernatural as many more questions joined the traffic jam of imponderables inside his head. There was surely some higher power at work here, why else would popping pills be deemed as "lame" and a "loser's way out" just moments before McSorely was about to embark on that course of action? After much consideration, he decided there was only one option. He had to visit that website.

A slideshow greeted McSorely as he logged on to Scenic Suicides and it started off with pictures of inner-city poverty from Glasgow and Edinburgh. Junkies cooked up, 14-year-olds pushed prams around while smoking fags, Old Firm fans laid waste to each other, children with venom etched across their faces beat up the ginger loner on his way home from school and a Job Centre queue snaked round a street corner past a series of 99p shops and bookmakers – all to the background music of Frankie Miller's Caledonia. These scenes of urban devastation soon gave way to a series of stunning Highland landscapes, however, as Frankie began to reach a crescendo. The slick presentation, quite at odds with the spartan email that had enticed McSorely to the site, then ended with the quite brilliant slogan: "Scotland – it might be a shithole to live in but what a place to die!" This maxim reeled McSorely in further and he spent the next hour exploring every area of the site. McSorely soon began to realise he hadn't put enough thought and planning into his suicide as the site flagged up several issues he had ignored. He hadn't seen the point in writing a will as there was nobody he wanted to leave his earthly effects to. Scenic Suicides, though, alerted him to the folly of this decision by pointing out: "If you die without leaving a will, your entire estate will go to the next of kin."

In McSorely's case, this was Cousin Elsa and he knew the pawn shop would be the only beneficiary when she turned her inheritance into drug money. That would also make him an accessory to her own rapidly approaching death and cause further spiritual harm if he was dragged in front of a heavenly court. Something, therefore, had to be done. The only problem was McSorely didn't have a bloody clue what course of action to take. Thankfully, Scenic Suicides had the answer:

"If there is no one you want to benefit from your death, make sure you have nothing to pass on. Sell all your possessions, treat yourself to a memorable final day on God's green earth and give any remaining cash to charity. Everyone's a winner, with the obvious exception of your bitter, spurned relatives. But you probably despise them anyway, so why not enjoy one final laugh at their expense?"

McSorely liked the sound of that, especially the "memorable final day on God's green earth". A shudder ran through his body when he realised what his last 24 hours would have amounted to had the email not diverted him to Scenic Suicides – breakfast of half-stale toast, two hours of football escapism in his role of Manchester United supremo on Football Manager, 90 minutes of bitter football reality as Albion Rovers lost 3-1 to Alloa at Cliftonhill, dinner of a Greggs steak bake and some oven chips, an evening spent watching two entire series of Red Dwarf on Dave, virtual frustration as defeat at Stamford Bridge cost his United side the title, release of aforementioned virtual frustration at a series of pornographic websites, hours of insomniac insanity, conversation with a Samaritan simpleton, Facebook's confirmation that life wasn't worth living, death by paracetamol. Hardly the stuff of legend and it certainly couldn't compare with being catapulted off a cliff in the Highland sunshine just 24 hours after blowing wads of cash on a series of indulgences. McSorely had to admit he was just an amateur when it came suicide, it was time to put his death in the hands of the professionals.

He made a conservative estimate of his assets and came to the figure of £8,000 – more than enough to paint Glasgow red. Now all he had to do was set the garage sale in motion and figure out what to spend the proceeds on. This was not a matter to take lightly because McSorely knew he would only get one shot at his final day on earth, unless he joined the ranks of those poor souls who ended up in a hospital bed instead of the morgue after their suicide attempt. This was unlikely in McSorely's case, however, as even Bruce Willis' character from Unbreakable probably wouldn't fancy his chances of surviving a sling shot off a Munro. Hours of thought, therefore, had to go into McSorely's final hours but the prospect of mulling over every minor detail didn't faze him. He was, after all, an insomniac. Contemplative thought was his specialised subject. Plotting the course of his farewell thrill ride wasn't the only matter up for consideration, though. He also had to compose a couple of suicide notes. Again, this was something McSorely had initially thought unnecessary, although laying a Facebook guilt trip on his acquaintances had seemed appealing when their vacuous rubbish was directing him towards the medicine aisle at Sainsbury's. He couldn't really explain why he wanted to top himself and there was always a danger his words would be misinterpreted. McSorely felt sorry for the legendary writers who now found their work under the microscopic eye of literary critics desperate to justify their own meaningless existence by finding hidden meanings in the works of authors with a far greater literary flair. While his note was unlikely to end up on the desk of the Times literary editor, he knew the only person who would receive a copy – the lucky girl who had narrowly avoided becoming Mrs McSorely – would probably scrutinise it for hours in search of answers. McSorely was worried phrases like "I never felt comfortable" and "nobody really understood me" would be misconstrued as an admission he was a latent transsexual but Scenic Suicides pointed out silence would only lead to even more slanderous speculation.

"Failing to explain the reasons behind your suicide is a dangerous path to go down. Don't give your enemies the ammunition to say: 'He always looked a bit guilty when he told me he was an animal lover. I'm now beginning to think he meant that literally.' Or 'Someone told me he'd been impotent for years. It can't have been easy walking around with a burst balloon flapping between his legs.' Take command of your legacy by outlining why you are taking this brave step. That way you can absolve any loved ones of blame and settle some old scores with those who helped make your life a misery. And don't worry if you can't string two words together – our skilled team of writers will help you draft an eloquent and touching note. We can even throw in a few jokes if you're a fan of black humour."

Someone with a personal history as harrowing as McSorely's couldn't fail to see everything through black-tinted spectacles but jokes would have only made Sarah believe she was the victim of a distasteful wind-up. Besides, he had always prided himself on a good command of the written word and McSorely wanted to make sure the only person he still carried any affection for – his relationship with the Albion Rovers players was every bit as inconsistent as the team's form – received a heartfelt explanation. Once again, this task was something to which McSorely had to devote the many free hours insomnia granted him. It had to be tweaked and caressed until any doubts and nuances had been removed.

Picking the scene of his spectacular descent to death proved to be much easier. Slideshows of the most popular places were available at the click of a mouse and when McSorely saw the view from the summit of Ben A'an, his mind was made up. The piercing azure of Loch Katrine provided the centrepiece for this glorious Highland landscape while mighty mountains framed the backdrop. The idea that something as beautiful as this could share the same creator as the flawed, damaged soul staring at it on a computer screen seemed absurd to McSorely. Still, he had to concede it wasn't

29

impossible. After all, did Ben Elton not write both Blackadder Goes Forth and We Will Rock You? There was also the modern-day output of the Rolling Stones to take into consideration and even Bob Dylan – that great defier of Trainspotting's Sick Boy theory – had sullied his reputation by recording a Christmas album. Maybe God, therefore, had just lost his creative spark after that difficult second album. If there was a divine being still putting in 24-hour shifts on the production line then McSorely chose to view his suicide in practical terms. He was just returning damaged goods to the warehouse; maybe God would learn from his mistakes and make sure the latest model didn't have the same design flaws. For there was no turning back now – Scenic Suicides had emphatically earned themselves a new customer.

There were more amusing asides on the registration screen and McSorely enjoyed a chuckle when the drop down menu "Reasons for suicide" gave members the chance to choose "none of your bloody business", "that fucking Rubik's cube" and "the shame of my sexual attraction to marsupials". Some of the disclaimers McSorely had to tick before becoming a fully-fledged member also provided plenty of mirth, with one proclaiming: "I consent to my name and image being used in a tasteless testimony to help Scenic Suicides make even more money" and another reading: "Scenic Suicides can sell my personal details to disreputable companies who will hound me remorselessly. Yes, I am interested in Viagra, investment opportunities in Nigeria and no-strings-attached sex with someone in my area."

This was then followed by several paragraphs of legalise protecting the company from any criminal proceedings and potential civil lawsuits. McSorely found the jargon hard to follow at first but eventually managed to work out how the staff of Scenic Suicides avoided a stretch in prison. Basically, they were just a "legal consultancy service" who had a side-line in selling giant catapults. What the customer then chose to do with said catapult was none of their business. There was clearly a mad genius at work here and McSorely looked forward to meeting him. So he clicked on the "complete registration" button at the bottom of the page and set the wheels the motion.

# Chapter Three:

# The Tortured Souls of Moristoun

It was happy hour in the Tortured Soul and the denizens of Moristoun had gathered to wash away their worries in the traditional manner. These 60 minutes of supposed gaiety were usually played out to the soundtrack of Patsy Cline's greatest hits and Gail knew this night would be no different when she spotted McTavish approaching the jukebox with a two pound coin in hand. It was a ritual he performed with clockwork regularity yet the task of picking which songs to share with his fellow drinkers always seemed to stump McTavish. That £2 investment bought him 10 songs and Gail could see it pained McTavish deciding which of the 25 numbers on the CD wouldn't make the cut on this occasion. His first two selections – I Fall To Pieces and Sweet Dreams – had already finished by the time McTavish returned to the bar and picked up his pint of bitter. He then took a swig and turned to Gail before delivering the words she had been expecting: "God bless the soul of sweet Virginia Paterson Hensley." When Gail first heard this tribute many years ago, she assumed the girl in question was a long-lost love brought back to the forefront of the old man's mind by the laments of Patsy. It was only when she broached the subject of McTavish's love life with her father that she learned Virginia Patterson Hensley was in fact Ms Cline's real name. "I've never heard the poor old bugger talk about a wife or girlfriend," he told her. "If he's hiding an old scar then he obviously prefers to keep it hidden away." The thought that McTavish had spent his entire life in solitude filled Gail with even greater pity for the figure who propped up the bar night after night. She couldn't bring herself to be angry with

McTavish, no matter how many times he drove her crazy by filling the air with Patsy's most famous refrain. It was a feeling shared by almost all of the regulars and anyone who voiced their dissent by shouting "no this shite again" was soon hounded out of the pub and told their custom was no longer welcome.

While Gail didn't have a bad word to utter about McTavish, the same couldn't be said for the two reprobates who flanked him at the bar – Henderson and McCall. Their relative youth, both were in their mid to late 30s, made their dependence on alcohol all the more tragic. It also ensured their interest in Gail was decidedly more infernal than paternal and this lechery always peaked on occasions when the landlord, the man Gail called Dad and everyone else called Jimmy, wasn't around. This, unfortunately, was one of those occasions as Jimmy had left Gail in charge of the bar while he popped out to run some errands.

"How old are you now then, Gail?" said Henderson, dipping a tentative toe into flirtation's waters. "You're not a wee girl anymore, are you?"

"I'm 17, Mr Henderson. The same age I was when you asked the other day. You didn't think I'd have a birthday party and not invite you, did you?"

This quip brought uproarious laughter out of his partner a crime, the same over-the-top response one usually witnesses whenever a sportsman says something mildly amusing during a press conference and the journalists roll about the aisles as if it was one of Groucho Marx's greatest one-liners. It was hardly surprising such sycophancy seeped out of McCall as he worked for Radio Moristoun and was part of the town's tiny media community. When his mirth finally subsided, McCall chipped in with his own flirtatious remark, buoyed by the discovery Gail was in the mood to take him and Henderson on.

"Every night's like a party when you're behind the bar," he said. "You light up this place. A wee part of me dies when I step through the door and see you're not around."

"He's right my dear," said Henderson. "You're the one ray of light in our otherwise dark existence."

"I'm pretty sure Mrs Henderson won't be too happy if I tell her that," said Gail, in a bid to douse the barfly's passions before things got too heated. As usual, though, it had little effect.

"You can tell that crabbit old bastard anything you want. It's no skin off my nose."

Mrs Henderson only accompanied Henderson to the pub for Hogmanay and other special occasions so Gail hadn't acquired enough knowledge of her to gauge the accuracy of her husband's character assassination. She was sure of one thing, though. Years of listening to Henderson's torturous patter would turn anyone into a cantankerous ogre. If Mrs Henderson was indeed a crabbit old bastard then Gail perfectly understood the reasons why. Quite how Henderson had managed to acquire a spouse in the first place was more of a mystery. As editor of the Moristoun Gazette, he boasted some clout in social and political circles but obvious physical flaws should have reduced his sexual influence to that of an alopecian trainspotter.

While Mrs Henderson was no catwalk model, she was not without her charms and certainly deserved a more handsome husband than the tub of lard who regularly had to wipe rivers of sweat from his brow with a manky hanky. McCall was at the other end of repulsion's broad spectrum – a lanky streak of piss who viewed maintaining acceptable levels of personal hygiene as a chore to rival 16 years on the chain gang. His straggly beard regularly dipped into the pints he knocked back and also often trapped the crisps and peanuts he tried to count as part of his five-a-day fruit and veg requirements. This visual repugnance was allied to an overpowering smell that had forced Gail to hang Christmas tree air fresheners from the optics. It was no surprise, therefore, that McCall was one of the many eternal bachelors doomed to wander the lonely streets of Moristoun with only their many insecurities for company.

Gail took pleasure in reminding McCall of his romantic shortcomings and decided it was time to deliver another rabbit punch to his kidneys while Henderson rained slanders down on his wife. "How come you never got married, Mr McCall?" she said. "There must have been quite a queue for an eligible bachelor like yourself when you were younger."

It was now Henderson's turn to break into an unwarranted laugh and this one registered 7.5 on the sycophantic sports scribe scale.

"Oh, that's a belter," he said. "This sad specimen of a man has done more to advance the cause of lesbianism than pillow fights and Lambrusco."

"Go ahead, laugh it up," replied McCall, who was now immune to such attacks on his masculinity. "I had my chances back in the day but, unlike some people, I chose not to settle for the crushing mediocrity of marriage."

Henderson chose not to respond to this barb, as he was probably making a mental note of the insult for his own personal use in upcoming spousal slanging matches, so McCall stayed at the despatch box and continued his speech.

"I always thought someone special would come along but the weeks turned into months and the months turned into years. Then cupid shot me up the arse with a poisoned arrow by sending me to Moristoun. It's as if some sadistic cattle wrangler has rounded up the most heinous heifers in all creation and herded them on to one cursed island, present company excluded of course."

Gail tried to mount a sisterly defence of her fellow females by reeling off a list of women she considered perfectly acceptable but that met with a predictable response from her chauvinistic audience.

"Eileen McGregor?"

"Rougher than a badger's arse."

"Shelia Gordon?"

"Maggot-ridden syphilitic corpses have more sex appeal."

"Marcia MacPherson?"

"Pushing 50 and dresses like a crofter."

"Wee Monica from the hairdressers?"

"Bulldog in a wind tunnel."

"Catriona Stevens?"

"Asian hunger strikers have bigger tits than her."

"Moira?"

"You're not even fucking trying now!"

Even Gail had to admit she was scraping the bottom of the barrel by bringing Moira into the equation as she looked across to the corner and saw that empty shell of a woman fill another shot glass with the bottle of vodka that was her constant companion. However, she refused to concede Henderson and McCall might have made a valid point for the first time and pushed ahead with the search for Moristoun's hidden beauties.

"What about the Goths? Some of them would be quite pretty if they took off all that makeup."

"The Brides of Frankenstein?" said McCall. "It would be like having a go at a zombie. I'd be worried about getting done for necrophilia."

Henderson was also quick to dismiss the notion, adding: "And it's not just about looks. You want a nice girl you can have a conversation with, not someone who skulks about in silence and only raises her voice in summoning Satan."

This crass stereotype was typical of Henderson but there was a ring of truth to his words. The Goths were the only other teenage girls in the whole of Moristoun and any attempts Gail made to connect with her peers fell on ground every bit as stony as their faces. This added to a sense of isolation that had been fostered by years of home schooling. The only child Gail saw during a long and lonely adolescence was the one staring back at her in the mirror but Jimmy and his wife Brenda had tried their best to compensate by lavishing every last drop of love on their daughter. Gail could not complain that her childhood had been an unhappy one – just one starved of the joy and laughter communal play can bring. It was only when she reached her teens and started to explore every inch of Moristoun, far from the protective gaze of her parents, that Gail began to discover boys and girls of a similar age were indeed dotted about the island. This revelation opened Gail's eyes to the possibility of a new dawn in her world of loneliness but it soon became clear that death, not life, was the preoccupation of her contemporaries. Thus Gail was forced to retreat back into the cold grip of her solitude, with even the warmth of her parents and their extended family at the Tortured Soul failing to prise those icy fingers open.

The tighter that grip got, the more Gail began to wonder what her life would be like if she joined the rest of civilisation on the mainland. Every time she mentioned the possibility of flying the nest, though, it always met with the same response from her father: "You're not ready yet."

Jimmy refused to countenance the possibility of Gail leaving Moristoun until she had acquired a fully rounded education.

"The mainland's not like Moristoun," he warned her. "It's a dangerous place, full of temptations and traumas, and we won't be around to look out for you."

Gail would have welcomed the opportunity to take a trip to Edinburgh or Glasgow and form her own opinion but even this simple pleasure had been denied her. Family holidays had been limited to the islands in close proximity to Moristoun as Jimmy shuddered at the thought of leaving his precious public house at the mercy of Moristoun's "collection of reprobates". Plenty of said reprobates had lived on the mainland before pitching up on the shores of Moristoun, though, so Gail bombarded them with questions in a bid to form a clearer picture of the great beyond. It was to her great disappointment that most of the responses were negative.

"God's granite litter box," was McCall's take on his birthplace of Aberdeen. "Dreary, dispiriting and desolate – and that's just the football team. Take my advice, Gail, stay well clear."

McCall also provided her with a quote from Lewis Grassic Gibbon he felt summed up his hometown with far greater eloquence than anything he could muster. "Aberdeen, a thin-lipped peasant woman who has borne eleven and buried nine," he recited with an assurance and flair that suggested the text had been committed to memory many moons ago. "Union Street has as much warmth in its face as a dowager duchess asked to contribute to the Red International Relief."

Henderson was equally disparaging about his old stomping ground further down the east coast. "Whoever called it Bonnie

Dundee was having a laugh," he said. "It has about as much charm as an abandoned sausage supper sitting next to a pile of vomit. They should have a wee desk at the bus station where you have to hand over all your hopes and dreams upon arrival. Living there is like slowly drowning in a bucket of piss."

Even the normally reserved McTavish wasn't slow in sticking the boot into his native Glasgow when conversation turned towards the Second City of the British Empire. Midway through the chorus of I Cried All The Way To The Chapel, he escaped from Patsy's spell and told his fellow drinkers: "Oh it's a cruel city. Some of the things I saw there would bring tears to a firing squad's eyes. If you take a fall in Glasgow, it boots you on the way down and plants a size 12 on top of you so you can't get up again."

This bleak assessment went down well with McCall, who had kicked off the conversation by recalling a savage beating at the hands of some Rangers supporters, long before the task of following Aberdeen on the road became reserved for masochists and blind optimists.

"Listen to the voice of experience," he told Gail. "McTavish knows what he's talking about. Now there's a man who has lived."

Having watched McCall's paragon of vivacity spend the last decade slowly rotting on a barstool, Gail begged to differ. However, her respect for the old man trumped the burning desire to shoot McCall down in flames so she decided to mark it down as a silent victory and leave the boys to their assault on the walls of this proud city. Of all the people who walked through the Tortured Soul's doors, just one talked in glowing terms of the mainland – Buchan. He made business trips to Inverness every couple of months and regaled Gail with stories about the places she had to visit when university finally beckoned.

"It's not fair to cage a beautiful bird like you up in a place like this," he said. "You need to soar free and spread your wings. There's a whole world out there just waiting to be explored."

This evangelism for mainland life was far from the only characteristic that made him stand out from the rest of the regulars and Gail never ceased to wonder how a man like Buchan had ended up in Moristoun. He was always impeccably turned out and eschewed the town's prevailing fashion for Arran jumpers and tracksuit bottoms by wearing a shirt and tie wherever he went. Buchan also took a fastidious approach to grooming and Gail had never seen him with a hair out of place, even when he had been forced to endure a howling gale while making the two-minute walk from his office to the Tortured Soul. She could understand why a look of contempt flashed across Buchan's face whenever he looked along the bar and spotted McCall taking his beard for its daily swim. He never voiced this hatred for his fellow citizen's slovenly ways, though, because Buchan considered everyone a potential client.

"When McCall finally bows to temptation and starts setting about Stu MacDonald's sheep, he's going to need someone to represent him in court," he told Gail. "It would be unwise to let personal animosity get in the way of a professional relationship."

Buchan's drive and ambition were absent in most of Moristoun's populace, who seemed happy just to tread water as the months and years washed over them like the waves that battered the coastline. He had that rare combination of hope and energy, something which only served to increase Gail's attraction to him. She had harboured a crush on Buchan ever since puberty's cruel tricks had started to make her childhood innocence disappear. The flirtatious remarks and sensual looks she showered on him would have been lustily devoured by the likes of Henderson and McCall but Buchan was immune to her charms. "Don't be inappropriate," was the phrase he always used to nip any mischief in the bud. "I've known you since you were a baby." He liked to refer to himself as Gail's guardian angel and she had to admit Buchan always seemed to be around whenever she needed rescuing in her jousts with the two demons who would have relished the chance to ravage her. This night was to be no different and Buchan made his entrance just as Gail was losing her fight to defend the honour of Moristoun's fairer sex. The sight of him approaching the bar brought a smile back to Gail's face and she said: "You can help me out here, Mr Buchan. These two slimeballs are trying to claim every other woman in Moristoun has been … how did you put it again, Mr McCall?"

"Not just beaten with the ugly stick but relentlessly defiled with it until every last drop of beauty has vanished."

"Charming," said Buchan as he took off his jacket and scarf then draped them over the vacant barstool. "Now let me think, there must be someone on this island who could give Gail a run for her money in this hypothetical Miss Moristoun contest."

"Not a chance," said Henderson. "She's the odds-on favourite. You're as well getting the shotgun out and calling the glue factory for the rest of the runners and riders."

"Don't be so hasty," cautioned Buchan. "Did Benjamin Franklin not say: 'Take time for all things. Great haste makes great waste.'"

"It will be a cold day in hell when I start taking advice from an American," replied Henderson. "The reason the mainland is in such a bloody mess right now is because our overlords down south decided it was a good idea to start aping those bastards."

"That's certainly a valid argument but you're rather over-simplifying things, something that comes naturally for members of your profession," said Buchan. "That's an argument for another day, however, let's turn our thoughts back to finding a rare glimpse of beauty on Moristoun's grievous shores."

Silence then reigned for a few seconds before Buchan threw the name of Karen McLoughlin up for debate. "Now there's a woman who could warm you up on a cold winter's night," he said.

"Never heard of her," was Henderson's response while McCall's mind also drew a blank. Even Gail had to admit Karen McLoughlin didn't register on her radar so Buchan had to fill them in before they started to think the pub's whisky had been spiked with hallucinogens.

"That's probably because she only moved here about a week ago," he said. "She's the new librarian, which explains why Henderson and McCall have yet to bump into her. But I'm surprised you haven't heard of Karen, Gail. Aren't you supposed to be down there studying?"

Gail knew this rebuke for deviating from her studies was warranted but fended off Buchan's attack by saying: "I've been a bit busy this week. I'll pop down tomorrow and get some new books out. It will give me a chance to check out the competition."

Gail was more interested in making the acquaintance of a peer who wasn't caked in layers of monochromatic makeup, so she asked Buchan about the age of the delightful Miss McLoughlin.

"Oh, she's a good bit older than you," was his disappointing reply. "Karen's probably in her mid-30s – the perfect age for Aberdeen's most eligible bachelor."

This revelation brought a glimmer to McCall's eyes and his none-too-subtle response was to ask Buchan if he had a picture of the new beauty in their midst.

"I'm afraid I'm far too chivalrous to take covert surveillance snaps," said Buchan. "And I'm sure Karen will make a much better first impression in the flesh. Get yourself down to the library and introduce yourself. As far as I know, she's single and available."

Tomorrow was shaping up to be one of the library's busiest days in years and Gail could see excitement writ large across the faces of McCall and Henderson as news of this 100 per cent increase in Moristounian eye candy began to hit home. They quickly convened their two-man council of vulgarity and began to formulate a plan of attack, leaving Gail free to converse with the one customer she actually enjoyed listening to.

"How's business, Mr Buchan?" she asked, safe in the knowledge he always had an interesting story safely tucked away.

"The good people of Moristoun are keeping me as busy as ever," he replied. "Miss Sanderson passed to the other side a couple of days ago, so I've spent a fair bit of time dealing that."

"Oh, that's a shame," said Gail. "She was a lovely woman."

"Trust me, she's gone to a better place. As you will find out one day, leaving Moristoun behind is a cause for celebration."

"I'm sure Miss Sanderson's family didn't see it that way," said Gail, mindful of the pain that would engulf her should either of her parents be snatched away.

"She didn't have any family. Just that four-legged behemoth which masquerades as a dog."

"Munchkin? Oh she's harmless. A big softie."

"You're soft between the ears if you believe that," said Buchan. "One day that beast is going to snap and I don't want to be around when it rampages through the streets like a Pamplona bull."

"What's going to happen to Munchkin?" said Gail as her pity for the abandoned Scottish Deerhound increased with every brickbat Buchan hurled at the defenceless animal.

"There won't be much of a change to her daily routine," he replied. "Miss Sanderson asked The Council if the dog could remain at her house and they agreed, in recognition of all her good work. Muggins here is charged with the task of popping round each day to sate its monstrous appetite and stretch those telescopic legs."

"What will happen when you need to go to the mainland on business? You won't be able to take her for a walk."

"Miss Sanderson said she was more than happy to let a substitute take my place when I was otherwise engaged – which brings us nicely to the real reason for my trip to your splendid establishment this evening."

"Me? Oh, I don't think so, Mr Buchan. Much as I like dogs, I don't think I'll be able to control something as powerful as Munchkin."

"That had crossed my mind, Gail. This is a job better suited to the one man who could strike fear into the formidable canine – your father. But don't despair, as the great Lao Tzu said: "Mastering others is strength. Mastering yourself is true power.""

Gail loved these quotes Buchan casually threw into their conversations and wished he was charged with the task of handling her education instead of her mother. She loved picking the lawyer's brain and relished the rare occasions when they could converse without the intervention of clowns such as McCall and Henderson.

"I'll have a word with Dad when he gets back," Gail said. "I'm sure he won't mind helping you out. You'll certainly need someone to lend a helping hand. Those trips to the mainland are coming thick and fast."

"Indeed. I'm in one of the few fields that seems to be prospering from the global recession. I've got another trip to Inverness coming up in a few weeks' time. I'm meeting a young man from Glasgow. His name is McSorely."

# Chapter Four:

# Glasgow belongs to McSorely

In keeping with most insomniacs, McSorely could see few advantages to his condition but he had to admit it gave him a right good kick of the ball when it came to making the most of his final day in Glasgow. The activities began at 4 a.m. but breakfast would have to wait, as the first of McSorely's leaving presents wasn't due to arrive until 9 a.m. To keep his hunger at bay, he tucked into the last of the Garibaldi biscuits and scraped the final few granules out of his jar of instant coffee. As he savoured the combination of currants and pastry, McSorely hoped Garibaldis were a feature of the afterlife. Heaven would prove something of an anti-climax if there wasn't a decent provision of biscuits but McSorely had to admit his chances of sneaking through the Pearly Gates were slim. Wikipedia had informed him Catholics considered suicide a grave or serious sin so his name was unlikely to be on the guest list. Some of the salacious things McSorely had planned for later would also only hasten his slide into the fiery depths and he doubted Satan's sweet trolley would offer any comfort as a Centaur set about him with a cat o' nine tails. If Hell truly was a dwelling of the damned, the standard of biscuit wouldn't rise above the humble oatcake. There was an outside chance he might be treated to a Rich Tea on special occasions such as Hitler's birthday, Fred West's wedding anniversary and Airdrie winning promotion but even they were bound to be of the flimsy supermarket variety. This, then, was probably McSorely's last Garibaldi, a thought that elicited such a powerful sense of melancholy that he vowed to buy another packet at Central Station before making the trip to

Inverness. Bidding adieu to his prized possessions had also proven tougher than expected, especially the signed Victor Kasule top that fetched just £25 from eBay's small community of Albion Rovers fans. Anything with Vodka Victor's signature was worth at least £100 in McSorely's eyes and he could only lament the fact Idi Amin was no longer around to join the bidding. After all, nothing combined Idi's greatest passions – Uganda, Scotland, philandering and violence – better than the ill-disciplined playboy once described as "an armoured car of a winger with a cannon for a shot". McSorely sincerely hoped the recipient of this piece of memorabilia – the bidder known as Cliftonhill Bill – felt a pang of guilt about the Turpinesque manner of its acquisition and made amends by splashing out on a display case. Thankfully, the rest of McSorely's fire sale hadn't gone quite so disastrously and the £200 received from the sale of his laptop pushed the grand total to an impressive £8,432. That provided ample funds for the big blow-out and the only downside was the fact McSorely's apartment now resembled a crack house. He had left himself with just two possessions – a 50-inch plasma TV and a Blue-Ray player – and these held no sentimental value as McSorely had bought them just a day ago. Deciding which film to screen as his final cinematic treat had taken several hours of thought but McSorely eventually opted for 2001: A Space Odyssey – a fitting choice given his own journey into the unknown. McSorely had always wanted to see Stanley Kubrick's masterpiece at the cinema and the fact he had failed to achieve this simple goal was one of his many regrets. It was also a contributory factor to the collapse of his engagement as Sarah had arranged a dinner party on the night 2001 received a special screening at the Glasgow Film Theatre. McSorely made a passionate plea to be absolved of his hosting duties but this fell on ears that were not only deaf but red with rage at the cheek of his request. Such was Sarah's anger at the fact her fiancé would choose a night of cinematic solitude ahead of fine dining and sparkling conversation with her friends that she refused to countenance the possibility of postponing the party. Sarah's social soiree, therefore, went ahead as planned but the dark cloud of internecine warfare hovered over their dining table. While their guests savoured every spoonful of Sarah's Chicken Balmoral and lavished compliments on the chef, all McSorely could taste was the bitter hatred of his future wife in every morsel. The feeling was mutual as hostility wafted over the table like the acrid smell of a wild animal that had been left to rot in a suspected paedophile's wheelie bin. Sarah's smile might have fooled her friends into believing she was having a wonderful time but McSorely knew better. He could tell she yearned to break down in tears like a child who had just dropped her ice cream on to the pavement after breaking her mother's resolve with hours of relentless lobbying. Only that most baffling of human concepts, saving face in the name of social etiquette, was holding back the raging torrents but it was only a temporary dam. When the last of Sarah's cosy collection of couples had grown tired of decimating McSorely's alcoholic reserves and headed for the warmth of their matrimonial beds, the barrier blocking his fiancée's fury was removed and he was drowned in a sea of resentment. After a while, though, he became immune to the insults and his mind began to drift back towards the disappointment of missing out on that timeless combination of science fiction and classical music.

This time there was nothing to stop him from embarking on a space odyssey and preparing for lift off in front of a virginal 52-inch plasma screen was actually a vast improvement on what would have been an uncomfortable pew at the GFT. The unfortunate smell most science fiction buffs carry around with their social failings would also be mercifully absent from McSorely's final trip to the cinema, along with the comments of pseudo intellectuals who think the rest of the world should be treated to their thoughts on Kubrick's take of life's true meaning. Movie projectors also sadly lack a fast forward button, a feature McSorely was grateful his new Blue-Ray player came equipped with when he remembered the first five minutes of 2001 featured just a black screen and some eerie sound effects. He toyed with the idea of sitting through it all but decided that would make him even more of a pretentious prick than the aforementioned intellectuals he held in such disdain. McSorely was also mindful of the fact time was very much of the essence. If Kubrick had a problem with him skipping through those five minutes of artistic masturbation, McSorely was more than happy to explain his reasoning over brandy and cigars when he joined the esteemed director by a grand fireplace in the next world. Thoughts of the great beyond were never far from McSorely's mind over the next few hours and as the film slowly built to a crescendo, he wondered if a kaleidoscope of colours would flash in front of his own eyes when he flew through the Highland air to meet his destiny. He would certainly enjoy that more than the edited highlights of his own life, although McSorely hoped some of things he had planned for the rest of the day would provide an interesting DVD extra.

The first of those treats arrived within minutes of Kubrick's space foetus providing McSorely with hope that a warm amniotic sack would cushion his fall when he hurtled towards the rocks surrounding Lake Katrine. The doorbell rang and McSorely was greeted by the sight of one of Glasgow's finest chefs – Vincent Le Clerc – carrying a hamper full of comestibles. Vincent did not come cheap, his appearance had made a £1000 dent in the budget, but McSorely was sure the Frenchman would be worth every penny if he delivered on his promise of the world's greatest fry up. One look through Vincent's goodie bag was enough to assuage any doubts as McSorely feasted his eyes on a giant steak, rashers of cured bacon, wild boar sausages, organic tomatoes, expensive Japanese mushrooms and eggs that looked so golden it had to be assumed the chef had just slid down a beanstalk. It was a joy watching the master at work when he turned those ingredients into a meal that would have tested the resolve of even the most hardened vegetarian. As Vincent laid the plate down in front of him and the most wonderful smells floated nostril ward, McSorely was glad his initial plan for breakfast hadn't come to fruition. He had looked into the possibility of securing Gordon Ramsay's services, although it had nothing to do with his culinary skills as McSorely just wanted to give the obnoxious chef a taste of his own medicine. When faced with the fruits of Ramsay's labour, the smuggest of smiles and the question: "So, what do you think?" nothing would have given McSorely greater pleasure than responding with a series of debased expletives and insults. Ramsay would no doubt respond in kind but if McSorely then raised the spectre of the chef's failed football career then that shortest of fuses would blow. McSorely was hoping he could add Suicide by Chef to the lengthy list of exit options by forcing Ramsay to plunge a kitchen knife into his heart, delivering a death that would be every bit as satisfying as the one that awaited him in the Highlands. He would die a happy man if he knew Ramsay was heading for a stretch in Bar L but the plan was thwarted just a day after it had been hatched, with Ramsay's agent responding to his email with one contemptuous sentence: "My client does not make personal appearances for members of the public, no matter how much money you offer."

Those words became all too familiar as McSorely further explored the idea of exacting revenge on celebrities whose fame, wealth and influence were disgustingly disproportionate to their talent. Every worthy victim on the Celebs For Hire websites he trawled was either out of McSorely's price range or unwilling to be hired. Even Keith Chegwin, Les Dennis and Shaun Williamson ruled themselves out of the gig, despite McSorely indicating he would be willing to up his offer to £4,000. They were clearly only willing to debase themselves for a client's amusement if a certain Mr Gervais was writing the cheque. The only celebrities willing to take part were a succession of reality TV nonentities and he had no interest in handing over thousands of pounds to mock someone he had never heard of. McSorely, therefore, was forced to come up with a different way to squander his fortune and eventually decided pampering himself was a wiser course of action than petty vengeance against the clowns who turned his channel surfing into a daily trudge through effluence. The wisdom of that decision was hammered home with every mouthful of Vincent's breakfast and McSorely took so much pleasure from the meal that his body lapsed into an almost post-coital state.

"Vincent, what can I say? You're a master," said McSorely. "Your wife is a lucky woman if she gets to eat something like that every morning."

"Oh, we have coffee and croissants most of the time," he replied. "It would not be wise to eat such an unhealthy breakfast every morning. Best to save this meal for special occasions."

"You're quite right," said McSorely, whose enjoyment had been multiplied by the knowledge he would never again get to enjoy such a combination of flavours. "If you do something enough times, you'll eventually lose all enjoyment of it."

"Indeed, except sex of course," replied Vincent, an answer that was disappointingly stereotypical for a Frenchman. McSorely had been pleased to discover Vincent deviated from the standard formula for master chefs by displaying a calm exterior, commendable modesty and a tolerance for the inferior beings fortunate enough to share a room with such genius. One glib remark, though, was enough to betray the fact every man fell victim to his surroundings in some way. McSorely was a far more obvious example of this than the person who sat across from him. The ice of depression that had hardened his emotional landscape was so undeniably Scottish that a wee shop on the Royal Mile could have wrapped it in some tartan paper and sold it to the Americans for £49.99. This inability to open up and bare one's soul reared its ugly head again when Vincent asked McSorely for the reason behind his extravagant breakfast.

"Oh, it's my birthday. The big 3-0," he lied. "I've got a whole day of activities planned but I doubt anything will be able to top that meal. You've set the bar pretty high."

"Glad to have been of service," said Vincent as he stepped up from the table to signal any relationship between them would stay on a professional level. "Enjoy the rest of your birthday. Maybe I'll see you at the restaurant some time?"

"I doubt it. With the amount of money I'm spending on this birthday, I'll be eating cans of beans for the rest of my life."

Vincent responded with only a smile and a few seconds later he was gone, leaving McSorely with just 45 minutes to shower and shave before climbing into a designer suit.

McSorely had never been a snappy dresser and his refusal to bow to the brands was another reason why he was a single man again. Sarah was always trying to improve his sartorial standards and never wasted a chance to remind McSorely being seen with someone whose wardrobe was furnished with items from Primark and TK Maxx was a source of unending embarrassment. Indeed, when Sarah was reeling off the long list of reasons for leaving McSorely, crimes against fashion were high on the rap sheet. "How can I stay with someone who has no self-respect?" she said. "If you looked less like a hopeless loser then maybe people would stop trampling all over you."

At the time, McSorely was in no mood to concede his fiancée may have made a valid point, clouded as he was by anger, resentment and a desire to pull that evil, overworked tongue out of her head with a pair of pliers. He was now willing to put her theory to the test, however, and was keen to see whether his new threads would accord him greater respect. McSorely had to admit he looked much less pitiful as he stared at the mirror, although he had probably taken the metamorphosis too far by splashing out on a suit only the most conceited of stock brokers would buy. Still, if ever there was a day for largesse, this was it. That was why a stretched limo was plotting a course through the unfamiliar surroundings of Govanhill while McSorely completed his transformation from slob to snob by combing his hair for the first time in years.

Sarah's theory passed its first test inside the limo as the driver, a 50-something who introduced himself as Sam, jumped to the conclusion McSorely was heading for an important business meeting.

"Right squire, where are we off to?" he asked. "I'm guessing one of the hotels in the city centre. That's the kind of suit that means business."

"Oh, today's all about pleasure," replied McSorely. "Take me to that casino on Glassford Street."

"What's the occasion then? Is it your birthday?"

It would have been easy for McSorely to continue with the lie he had told Vincent but turning 30 seemed like a poor excuse to splash out on a limousine. So he delved much deeper into fantasy and informed the driver he was celebrating a lottery win.

"Nice one," was Sam's response. "How much did you win?"

If you're going to lie you might as well do it in style, so McSorely claimed he was the mystery winner of Friday's £23million Euro jackpot.

"Bloody hell! I've got a celebrity in the back," said Sam, whose surprise was matched only by the joy of discovering the biggest tip of his career was now within reach.

"I don't know if celebrity is the right word," said McSorely. "I told the lottery people I didn't want any publicity. I hope you can keep a secret, Sam."

"Oh, you don't need to worry about me, son. I've seen plenty of things in the back of my limo that could have landed people in big trouble but I've always kept my counsel."

Sam didn't keep his mouth shut, however, when it came to advising McSorely on what to do with his vast fortune and the driver spent the duration of their trip running through his own fantasy shopping list. He did it with such enthusiasm that McSorely hoped Sam's own lucky numbers came up one day, enabling him to move from the front seat of a limo to the back. There was a refreshing lack of envy to his words, something of a surprise given he spent every working day watching people throw money down the drain on a cheap thrill, and McSorely felt slightly ashamed his own dour demeanour betrayed a lack of excitement about his fictional windfall. He tried his best to muster some enthusiasm as Sam dropped him off and McSorely invited the driver to join him inside the casino once he had found a parking space. Gambling had never been one of McSorely's vices but he wanted to see what it felt like waging hitherto unimaginable sums on one spin of the wheel or turn of card. He had been to a casino just once before but the thrills and spills of the gaming floor proved no match for the lure of a bar that remained open until 4 a.m. The only thing McSorely had gambled with that night was how many vodka and cokes he could throw down his gullet before feeling the need to empty the contents of his stomach. He took a punt on 12 – and lost. His memories of casino life were somewhat hazy, therefore, but McSorely still clung to the notion it was an enchanting world of razzle dazzle where leggy blondes watched guys in tuxedos engage in a thrilling battle of wits with the gods of fortune.

He was somewhat disappointed, therefore, by the sight that awaited him after walking through the main entrance. There was nobody sitting at the bar knocking back a Martini, just a pensioner sipping from a cup of tea as he leafed through the Daily Record. Fellow gamblers were also thin on the ground, with three or four Chinamen huddled around the roulette table and an obese middle-aged woman straddling two chairs as she waged war on the Blackjack dealer. The only signs of activity came across to the left where a variety of tragic figures sat transfixed by the bright lights and grating bleeps of the puggy machines, feeding coin after coin into greedy mechanised mouths. Friday night at the Monte Carlo Casino it most definitely wasn't but McSorely had to concede his expectations were unrealistically high for 10 a.m. on a Wednesday morning in Glasgow. If life had taught him anything, it was to set your hopes and dreams so low that even the most mundane of treats seemed like a blessing on a par with being asked to pull the ceremonial rope for Margaret Thatcher's keelhauling by the Cowdenbeath Miners' Welfare. That mindset served McSorely well as he approached the bar and discovered his first pint of the day would have to be either Carling, Tennent's or Miller. The fact he had failed to envisage a crisp continental beer helped the ensuing pint of Scottish swill taste a little less acrid as McSorely sat down and waited for Sam to join him. He had almost drained the glass of its contents by the time Sam appeared and McSorely took his driver to task for his lengthy absence, only to be met by a steely stare and the words: "Have you ever tried parking one of those fucking things?"

It was a point well-made and McSorely tried to make up for his insolence by dropping £500 worth of chips into the chauffeur's cap that had just been placed on the bar. "Don't worry, that's not your tip," he said. "Just a wee bit of money to have some fun in here. Knock yourself out."

McSorely's own stack of chips was four times the size but he was about to run the risk of seeing it suddenly disappear. It was all or nothing on his first and last dalliance with casino gaming, freed as he was from the fear of throwing it all away.

A combination of Chinese curses and celebrations filled the air as McSorely walked over to the roulette table with Sam. The little white ball had just dropped into red 14, earning two of the oriental punters tidy profits but inflicting painful losses on the others. The consequences were particularly severe for the gaunt figure who sat to the left of the vacant chair McSorely was about to occupy. He had committed to the notion that the ball was destined to land in a black bay with far greater conviction than his attempt to grow a moustache and nervous sweat dripped down from his patchwork upper lip as he came to terms with the loss of £300. That bet proved he was the table's high roller but McSorely was about to him blow him out of the water. There were more than a few mutters in Mandarin as the newcomer pushed £2000 worth of chips on to the black diamond then sat back calmly to await his fate. The high roller took umbrage at this attempt to usurp him as the group's most flamboyant gambler and decided to make it a personal battle by placing £500 on red. That machismo only elicited further enmity, though, as the ball bobbled around for what seemed like an eternity before resting on black 22. Money meant nothing to McSorely at this advanced stage of his existence but he had to admit to a genuine feeling of euphoria as fortune smiled on him at last and he received a slap on the back from Sam in addition to £4000 from the croupier. Congratulation then turned to concern, though, as the driver watched McSorely place all of his chips back on black. However, those fears proved unfounded as the ball danced to McSorely's tune once more and dropped down on black 28 when the music stopped, much to the dismay of the irate

Chinaman who had foolishly decided to renew hostilities. The rest of the group were loving every minute of it, though, relishing the welcome diversion from their dreary daily diet of gambling. They clearly despised the big-shot compatriot who regularly tried to demean them and all three offered handshakes to McSorely following his second triumph. There was no way he could stop now but McSorely opted for a change of tactics and placed all his money on red for the third spin. The high roller had now decided siding with the man who looked like a million dollars was a more profitable course of action so he also wagered a large sum on red. That proved to be a wise move and the subsequent victory helped repair some of the damage, to the Chinaman's stack if not his pride. Everyone was now convinced McSorely was a gift from the gods and that ensured the black diamond was heaving with chips when the croupier sent the wheel in motion once more. The woman playing Blackjack had even performed the daunting task of lugging her frame across the casino floor to see what all the commotion was about. Upon hearing that McSorely was the man who never lost, she also decided to have a piece of the action and said a quick prayer as silence descended on the gaming floor. It was broken a few seconds later by cheers and McSorely had never felt so popular as hugs, kisses and high fives rained down on him. The crowd called out for more and McSorely was getting ready to oblige them before a feeling deep inside hauled him back. This time he just knew he was destined to lose and although watching his £32,000 disappear down the drain would mean nothing to him, McSorely didn't want the others to share in his misfortune.

"Sorry folks," he said. "I've pushed my luck a little too far and it's now time to step back."

"But you never lose," said the gaunt Chinaman. "You have to use a gift like that."

"All I've done is won the equivalent of a coin toss four times in a row," replied McSorely. "It could happen to anyone and the odds are heavily stacked in favour of me losing this time. So I'm walking away before the casino wins, as it always eventually does."

"Fair play to you, son," chipped in the beast of Blackjack. "It's all about knowing when it's time to quit. But, just out of interest, what would you have picked if you had played on?"

"Red," said McSorely as he gathered up his chips and started to walk away. "But don't you go putting any money on that. I wouldn't have won."

McSorely didn't hang about to discover whether his prediction was accurate as he headed to the cashier to turn his plastic fortune into hard cash, but he guessed it was spot on as groans floated across from the roulette table. Sam confirmed the news on their way to the bar, revealing that everyone except the woman had gambled on red and lost. "The Chinese are too superstitious," said Sam as reflected on their loss. "Gambling's all about numbers and luck. There's nothing you can do to influence it. Still, that guy might have been on to something when he said you had a gift. It's like you can see into the future. First the lottery win and then this. You don't fancy coming down to the bookies with me this afternoon, do you?"

"I don't think there will be any need for that, Sam," said McSorely as he handed over the 32 grand to his driver. "I'll be very disappointed if this goes anywhere other than your bank account."

Of the many transactions McSorely would make during his farewell to Glasgow, none would give him greater pleasure than surrendering all of his winnings to Sam. Although his driver went through the usual polite platitudes, McSorely could tell by the look in Sam's eyes that this was one tip he simply couldn't afford to turn down. When Sam eventually bowed to the inevitable and pocketed the wad of cash, a feeling of exhilaration that dwarfed even the thrills of his roulette triumph shot through McSorely. The joy of altruism had made a belated appearance and he suddenly regretted all those beggars and Big Issue vendors he had shunned. It was now time to make amends so McSorely headed out on to the mean streets of Glasgow searching for a deserving recipient of his charity.

It was a quest that ended almost immediately as a hobo in his early 40s, sporting stained corduroy trousers, a tattered brown jumper and the defeated demeanour of a perpetually harangued husband, approached McSorely in the Merchant City to ask if he could spare some change for a cup of tea.

"I can do a lot better than that," said McSorely. "How do you fancy going for a slap-up meal at one of Glasgow's finest restaurants?"

It was not a reply the vagabond was expecting as his many requests for money that day had met with just three standard responses – "Sorry mate", "Here's a few pennies, that's all I have" and "get tae fuck, ya dirty bastard". It took him a few seconds to weigh up McSorely's proposal and he eventually decided the man standing before him in the designer suit was one of those yuppies who considered toying with the underclass a sport every bit as splendid as chasing foxes about on horseback.

"I suppose you think that's funny?" he said. "I'm just asking for a bit of shrapnel so I can warm myself up with a brew. There's no need to take the piss."

McSorely insisted he was deadly serious but years of suffering and degradation on the streets had hammered home the impression there was no such thing as a free lunch.

"You're not one of those poofs who gets their kicks from slumming it, are you?" the tramp added. "If that's the case, you're better off ringing one of those kids who scrawl their numbers on the doors of the bogs in Central Station. I'm getting too old for all that nonsense. I can pull you off for 20 quid if you want but there's no need to seduce me with a candlelit dinner. I'd rather get it over and done with."

McSorely found it hard to imagine anyone wanting to copulate with someone whose abundance of facial hair combined with a fearsome scowl and guttural grunts to create the impression a yeti had come down from the hills to terrorise the good people of Glasgow. However, the tramp had jumped to the conclusion McSorely wanted to sodomise him with such haste it suggested such a sickening scenario was not uncommon. That only increased McSorely's pity and he kept chipping away at his new acquaintance until he relented and agreed to the lunch date.

"Where are you taking me, then?" said the tramp, before introducing himself as Gary.

"It's entirely up to you? Where have you always wanted to eat in Glasgow? Take your pick – money is no object."

"We might as well do it in style then. What's the most expensive restaurant in Glasgow?"

McSorely's previous dalliances with fine dining had been limited to the occasional meal at reasonably priced eateries on Valentine's Day so he had no idea where wealthy Weegies went to sate their hunger. Thankfully, his iPhone was much better equipped to answer's Gary question and it soon guided them to a French restaurant deep in the heart of the Merchant City.

"Never doubt the wonders of modern technology," said Gary as he inspected the menu that sat behind a gold-rimmed pane of glass on the building's impressive façade. "Your phone was spot on – these fuckers charge twenty quid for a bowl of soup."

Having regularly paid just 40 or 50 pence to the master chefs at Heinz, Granny's and Campbell's, McSorely doubted any broth could be good enough to merit such a mark-up. He looked forward to seeing if the consommé would wash away his preconceptions but it quickly became clear that pleasure would be denied him as McSorely stepped into the establishment alongside Gary. The maître d' met them with a look of terror that suggested a suicide bomber had just breezed through the doors in search of his final meal. McSorely could tell he wanted to respond to the emergency Gary's presence had caused by dousing the abomination in front of him with a fire extinguisher but the maître d' instead opted for diplomatic deceit in a bid to put out the flames.

"Do you have a reservation, sir?" he asked McSorely in a Kelvinside accent that had been finely honed. "We're very busy today."

A quick glance around the restaurant exposed this as a flagrant lie because just a handful of patrons were sipping from crystal wine glasses as they picked at the food in front of them. McSorely pointed this out to the maître d' but he refused to give up the charade and insisted several scheduled diners would soon be arriving to fill the empty tables. That simply increased McSorely's anger and he longed to send the snob sprawling to the deck with an upper cut. However, that would have only ensured several precious hours were wasted dealing with the consequences of his righteous but unprovoked attack so he decided bribery was a wiser course of action. McSorely pulled the maître d' aside for a private audience in the cloakroom and whipped a large bundle of cash from his inside pocket.

"It's pretty clear you've got a problem with my friend Gary," he said. "How much is it going to take to stop all this nonsense?"

For the sophisticated gentlemen who welcomed diners to the world's finest restaurants, this would have been considered an insult on a par with McSorely relieving himself on the stand that held their precious reservations book. This was Glasgow, though, and the social climber blocking McSorely and Gary's attempt to join the privileged at their diamond-studded trough wasn't rewarded for his work so handsomely that he could afford to overlook a decent backhander. Bowing to bribery crossed his mind for a few seconds before the threat of losing a job that provided him with such an overpowering sense of self-importance intervened.

"I'm sorry sir, but it's not a question of money," he said. "We just can't let that thing come in to our restaurant. Our reputation would be in tatters. This isn't a fast food joint sir. Those Michelin stars don't get handed out as freely as the ones McDonald's managers give their employees for remembering to wash their hands in the staff toilets."

"You can mock McDonald's all you want but even one of their boss-eyed Johnny No Stars carries himself with more dignity than a snob like you," replied McSorely. "They wouldn't turn a customer away just because he's a bit rough around the edges."

"No, they'd probably hand him an application form. I'm sure your friend matches the staff profile perfectly."

The maître d' then turned to Gary and asked: "Why don't you try getting a job flipping burgers instead of begging for pennies on the street?"

"Why don't you fuck off," was Gary's response and McSorely had to intervene to stop his dining companion from supplementing this wonderfully concise sentiment with a headbutt. As McSorely ushered Gary out of the restaurant, he was surprised to see how quickly the anger of his companion subsided. Gary reacted to their ejection with an apathetic shrug that suggested he was regularly refused entry to far less salubrious establishments but there was a look of distress in his eyes when he discovered they were now heading for a hotel instead of another restaurant. Fears of a sexual assault suddenly returned and he was not slow in relaying those concerns to McSorely, who tried his best to reassure his companion that their relationship would most definitely be staying platonic.

"Don't worry," he told Gary. "I'm just going to make you a bit more presentable so we don't run into trouble with pricks like him again."

A shave and shower for Gary would also make lunch a far more pleasurable experience for McSorely, who had been stalked by an abominable odour ever since Gary's plastic cup was first dangled under his nose. Furthermore, securing a room for the day would be another act of charity, delivering his new acquaintance from a night of suffering on the streets. When Gary learned he would be sleeping on a soft hotel bed instead of a soggy lump of cardboard, his suspicions of McSorely's intentions began to soften. Unfortunately, the same could not be said of the receptionist at the Grand Central Hotel, who looked so disgusted by their request for a room that he clearly feared the bedsheets were about to be soiled by the surprising sexual union of sharp-suited city boy and venereal vagrant. The receptionist proved far less resistant to the lure of dirty money than the stuck-up maître d', however, and the surreptitious delivery of a £100 note into his suit pocket helped ensure there was room at the inn for these two unlikely bedfellows. McSorely and Gary looked like peas from a pod, however, when they walked down the staircase together an hour later. Although Gary's £150 Topman suit couldn't rival McSorely's designer threads for style, it was still a quantum leap in sophistication from the clothes he had started the day in. An even greater transformation was evident in Gary's face, which now looked at least 10 years younger after being shorn of a beard that had fallen into a greater state of disrepair than a hedge which housed discarded fish suppers, empty cans of Kestrel and soiled copies of Razzle. But the change which McSorely noticed and savoured the most was more subtle to distant observers like the receptionist, who probably thought the man now accompanying McSorely was another wealthy pervert who had just participated in the debauched defiling of that poor tramp. It was Gary's new smell that filled McSorely with the greatest joy, the rank stench of pestilence erased by the minty shower gel the hotel had provided. Being force-fed Tunes for a couple of hours by a koala bear smoking menthols couldn't have done a better job of helping McSorely breathe more easily and he could now partake of his lunch without the fear of a nasal napalm attack.

"Where are we off to then?" asked Gary on their way out of the hotel. "I hope you're not taking us back to that prick who treated me like a piece of shite."

"Certainly not," said McSorely. "I'd give cannibalism a try before I'd hand those bastards any of my cash."

"Good for you. Anyway, I'm glad he didn't let us in because the food looked ropey as fuck. What's the point spending forty or fifty quid on your dinner when the portions are so small you need to go for a sausage roll afterwards?"

McSorely's stomach began to rumble at Gary's mention of the savoury sausage treat so he asked his travelling companion to pick a new venue for a lunch that was becoming more belated than the World War II surrender of that Japanese soldier who holed himself up in the Philippines until 1974.

"Only one venue would be fitting in the circumstances," said Gary. "I'm surprised you even had to ask. I might even ask them for an application form while I'm there."

At the start of the day, a Happy Meal would have been viewed as a bitterly ironic choice for McSorely's lunch but it now proved much more apt. A smile was also etched firmly across Gary's face as he devoured two Big Macs and slugged from the giant cup that held his Fanta.

"Now that was a proper lunch," he said after gobbling up the final French fry. "Do you mind if I treat myself to a wee ice cream for desert?"

After discovering how much pleasure could be gleaned from helping others, there was only ever going to be one answer to Gary's question. As he watched his companion enjoy every scoop of his Crunchie McFlurry, McSorely began to realise they were kindred spirits. They had both suffered more than their fair share of hardships but for one glorious day they were freed from the shackles and let loose to gorge themselves on life's little pleasures. Dining with a down-and-out at the McDonald's on Sauchiehall Street hadn't been part of McSorely's grand plan but he now realised it was infinitely more satisfying than partaking of haute cuisine on his tod. McSorely's darkest thoughts always surfaced during times of solitude and it was companionship that had helped to make his day so enjoyable thus far. McSorely wasn't so deluded, however, to consider any of his new acquaintances genuine friends. Sam and Vincent, for all their warmth and cordiality, were essentially hired help and although he had spent the last two hours in Gary's company, the only thing he could say with any certainty about the man sitting across from him was that he had never seen someone dig away at a McDonald's ice cream with such slavish dedication. To take their relationship to the next level, McSorely would have to excavate just as deeply into Gary's past and unearth the misfortunes that conspired to leave him roaming Glasgow's streets with plastic cup in hand. This emotional minefield could only be safely negotiated with the aid of alcoholic lubrication, so McSorely slipped his hand into his inside pocket to retrieve the half-bottle of Buckfast he had placed there for emergency use. After betraying his Coatbridge roots by taking a lengthy swig, McSorely offered the bottle to Gary, a gesture he quickly regretted upon realising the demon drink was responsible for sending many a poor soul on to the streets. The suspicion that this fate had befallen Gary increased when his eyes lit up at the sight of McSorely's bottle and he suddenly lost all interest in drinking the final drips of ice cream. "A wee blast of the wine? Don't mind if I do," he said. "The perfect end to a perfect meal."

As he watched Gary glug from the bottle, McSorely started to fear his plan for the afternoon – a pub crawl up Byres Road that took in some of his old university haunts – would have to be abandoned. If Gary was indeed a jakey then he would have to come up with an alternative form of mutually beneficial entertainment. Sadly, the only way to find out if his companion would turn into a slavering gobshite by the third or fourth boozer was to abandon any attempt at subtlety and hit him with the $64,000 question.

"So Gary, how did you end up on the streets? It must be quite a story."

Truer words had never been said and for the next 10 minutes Gary told a tale of loss, despair and tragedy that made McSorely's own misfortunes seem relatively trifling. Abusive parents, broken marriages and dead babies all made an appearance, as did a crippling addiction. But it was drugs that had smashed Gary's life into a thousand broken pieces, not drink. More details of his descent into the gutter leaked out over the next few hours as Gary opened his heart layer by layer on their alcoholic odyssey. By the time his story had reached its conclusion, McSorely was amazed that Gary hadn't considered suicide at some point himself. The booze had demolished McSorely's own emotional defences by now and, after coming clean about the real reason behind their chance meeting, he asked Gary why he hadn't ended it all years ago.

"You never know what life will throw at you," was his reply. "Just look at today. I started off with nothing but now I've got a brand new suit, a full stomach, a wee glow from the bevvy and a hotel bed waiting for me. Just think about what I would have missed if I'd thrown myself into the Clyde last night."

"But what about tomorrow?" said McSorely. "You'll be back on the streets and hungry again. And even if you sell that suit and buy some clothes out of a charity shop, you won't have enough money to last more than a week."

"I'll cross that bridge when I come to it. Worrying about the future is just as daft as letting the past ruin your enjoyment of life. The reason we've been having such a good time today is because we've been too busy to sit around thinking about stuff."

"But you can't run away from your thoughts forever, especially when you're an insomniac like me. No matter how much fun I have during the day, I'll always be tortured at night.

"I'm just trying to point out I think you're making a mistake. But, don't get me wrong, I respect your decision. I've heard people describe suicide as the coward's way out but that's nonsense. It takes real courage. I'm not going to stand in your way – all I can do is help make sure I give you a cracking send off."

Conversation then turned towards what Gary would do with his final 24 hours if blessed with the same financial resources, a question that left him deep in contemplative thought for a few minutes.

He eventually settled on a one-man crime spree which culminated in a bloody shoot-out with the cops that rivalled anything from Quentin Tarantino's imagination. McSorely could only marvel at Gary's ability to conjure up that spectacular demise in such a short space of time but politely pointed out he would prefer to avoid leaving a trail of destruction in his final few hours. This led Gary to enquire about what he did have planned for the final few grand in the kitty and, in the spirit of openness that had flourished, McSorely decided to come clean about the most shameful of his indulgences.

"I'm spending it on a high-class prossie," he said. "Much as I've enjoyed chewing the fat with you, I need a bit of female company for my last night in Glasgow."

McSorely had always wondered what it would feel like to make love to a beautiful woman. Just three notches had been carved on his bedpost and only the most deluded of his conquests could have considered themselves a genuine looker. His virginity had been snatched away at Daniel McGregor's epic house party but the two bottles of Merrydown the 17-year-old McSorely had consumed were probably more responsible for the landmark moment than the charms of the girl who straddled him on the McGregor parental bed, which saw more action in one night than it had witnessed in the previous two years of a decaying marriage. Karen Ogilvie was far from the most abhorrent of the few girls who fell within McSorely's sphere of sexual influence (she lacked the club foot, horrendous teeth and violent acne that marked three of her closest friends out for perpetual spinsterhood) but she was hardly the kind of girl one fantasised about. This was mainly due to an appetite that stretched her school uniform into unappealing forms but such girls can often make up for their shortcomings by approaching sex with the same enthusiasm and hunger they display when placed before the Pick and Mix at Woolworths. Karen had decided McSorely would be the recipient of her liberally scattered lust at Daniel's party and his equally progressive approach to the consumption of cider ensured he was no in position to oppose an imminent mounting on the grounds of aesthetics. McSorely's inebriated state actually helped to ensure his first sexual encounter lasted longer than the standard handful of grinds that mark most journeys from virgin to man of the world. Karen had to work hard to arouse his interest in the task at hand and it was a good 10 minutes or so before they emerged from the bedroom to knowing looks and bawdy comments. McSorely's night came to a much more premature end just moments later, though, as the sexual chemicals released from his encounter with Karen combined with the many toxins gleaned from his Merrydown to deliver a knockout blow. When he finally emerged from his resting place between Daniel's sofa and radiator, McSorely felt like a nuclear survivor taking his first steps into a post-apocalyptic world. This was mainly due to the scene of devastation before him as empty cans, bottles, fag packets and pizza boxes flowed around bodies that lay contorted in anatomically impossible positions. However, there was also a sense that he was stepping into a brave new world after shedding that most unwanted of teenage tags – virgin. While McSorely's recollection of the previous evening was hazy at best, there was one 10-minute spell he would never forget – even though it came at the peak of his dipsomania. It was as if McSorely's mind had snapped his body out of its alcoholic coma by yelling out: "Sit up straight and start taking notes. You'll need to remember this for later."

McSorely's second sexual encounter was also etched in his memory and it often emerged during his darkest hours. It came during fresher's week at Glasgow University and the experience left such a deep emotional scar that McSorely was condemned to celibacy for the remainder of his four-year degree. Once again, he had been little more than a prop in the satisfaction of a ferocious sexual appetite as a blonde approached him after last orders in the student union and rammed her tongue down his throat. This was shorthand for "the night's almost over, so you'll have to do" and McSorely was happy to accept his late invitation to the party. He may have been the speccy kid picked last in the playground but at least he would actually get to kick the ball this time and wouldn't have to stand in goal waiting for the rocket-fuelled toe-poke that would shatter his spectacles. On the short taxi trip to her flat, McSorely tried his best to find out more about the girl, whose inability to snare someone earlier in the evening became more understandable when her physical flaws were fully illuminated. The woman he was about to share a bed with had no interest in small talk, however, and the only thing he learned that could be mentioned before the watershed was her name, Sharon. Her own interest in McSorely was limited exclusively to the contents of his boxer shorts, a fact hammered home when her tongue took a break from twisting his tonsils to whisper something into his ear. Instead of relaying sweet nothings, however, Sharon went into increasingly graphic detail about the series of sordid acts that would take place behind her bedroom door. For an 18-year-old whose erotic adventures had hitherto been limited to self-pollution and a one-sided sexual sumo bout, this was worrying news. There was no way he would be able to slake the thirst of this dragon, something Sharon discovered to her fury just a few minutes later when her first attempt at gratification was stymied by McSorely's lack of stamina. Had he merely been thrown out of Sharon's lair in shame after being exposed as a premature ejaculator then McSorely may have been able to write the episode off as a colourful, albeit painful, learning experience. Sharon, though, was in no mood to show such leniency to the figure who had placed her X-rated escapades in jeopardy.

"You might have finished already pal – but there's a long way to go before I'm done with you," she growled, before telling McSorely to ready himself for round two. He was then introduced to a collection of paraphernalia that even the most imaginative of hedonists would have struggled to put to full use. McSorely could only wonder what some of the contraptions were used for as Sharon plucked them out of a box that was deceptively decorated with pictures of puppies and kittens. Unfortunately for McSorely, he was to play an active role in unravelling the mystery of which piece of this vulgar puzzle went through the round window. By the time Sharon had finished with her rituals and unlocked the dungeon's door, her plaything was on the brink of physical and emotional collapse. As he staggered out on to the deserted streets at 6 a.m., McSorely considered heading straight for a police station to report the many crimes against his person. However, the prospect of reliving his nightmare in front of a sniggering policeman, not to mention the possibility of his humiliation being dissected in microscopic detail for public consumption if Sharon was ever put in the dock, banished any thoughts of legal retribution. He would simply have to live with the horrific memories that made him terrified of the female genitalia at a time when almost all of his peers considered it their holy grail.

McSorely slowly managed to piece his shattered libido and self-confidence back together, mainly due to the sterling work of his university counsellor, who was the only person to learn of his suffering at the hands of the barbaric blonde. Summoning up the courage to approach women he actually desired, however, was a feat of bravery that remained beyond him. So he joined the growing ranks of socially inept loners who turned to internet dating in a bid to find their soulmate. After four false starts, including a disturbing dinner date with an American student whose alluring profile page failed to mention the fact she was a white supremacist, McSorely was paired with the woman who was to become his fiancée. They were the perfect match at that stage of their lives, two young professionals seeking comfort in the working world after four years of university life that remained sexually vapid for vastly different reasons. Sarah was still courting her childhood sweetheart from Manchester when she began her business degree at Caledonian University and the long-distance relationship survived for three years before her frustrated beau finally pulled the plug. This was a cruel blow for Sarah as the sporadic nature of their coupling suited her perfectly and she remained single for the next three years before beginning the virtual search for a new companion. The concept of a boyfriend appealed to Sarah more than carnal consequences of an intimate relationship and this made the timid McSorely her ideal man in many ways. Of all her internet suitors, he was the only one who seemed to show little interest in luring her to bed within hours of their first meeting. The relationship was given time to breathe over the next few months and they were one of the few young couples who could truly say they were in love when matters took an inevitably physical turn. Sarah's kindness and compassion gradually erased the spectre of Sharon from his sexual psyche and his rehabilitation as a red-blooded male was complete. This brought its own problems, though, as Sarah's innate conservatism under the sheets failed to satisfy the beast that had woken from its slumber. McSorely's simmering frustration never manifested itself in adultery but it added to the growing list of problems as a relationship that had once seemed so solid began to disintegrate. McSorely didn't want to go to his grave without fully appreciating the pleasures of the flesh so he scoured the many websites offering "escort services" to discerning gentlemen as he began to plot his final day. He was surprised at how easy it was for the wanton and wealthy to get their end away as a series of beauties were offered up within seconds of keying the incriminating words into Google. Prostitution was supposed to be illegal in the UK – one of the factors that had stopped him from conducting such inquiries just days after Sarah's departure. The other barriers blocking his on-line reservation of a ticket to Gomorrah were the possibility of contracting an STD and waking up in handcuffs to find the harlot had looted all of his possessions. Such concerns do not trouble a man with just hours to live, however, so McSorely was burdened with only fears for his spiritual safety as he embarked on his sleazy search.

He was determined to find the jewel in Glasgow's classiest prostitution ring and spent hours running the rule over potential candidates. Thumbnail pictures provided the only visual clues to the girls' beauty so McSorely studied them in microscopic detail to ensure his big night would not end in disappointment. Any call girl with a black rectangle across her face was immediately discarded, as such Photoshop censorship could mask disfigurements ranging from the cigarette burns of unhinged former clients to the glassy eyes of heroin addiction. Around 70 per cent of these ladies had chosen the comfort of anonymity over the financial benefits associated with informing punters their face was every bit as impressive as the rest of the body. But this was actually a blessing for McSorely as it narrowed down his shortlist and made the task of choosing the recipient of his custom much simpler. He was eventually torn between two exotic companions – an Argentinian called Carla and a girl from Czech Republic who went by the name of Flora. The latter tried to reel him in with the promise of "intense and passionate loving in a genuine girlfriend experience" while Carla vowed to deliver services that would leave him "breathless". The prospect of such breathtaking manoeuvres, allied to the fear that Flora's "genuine girlfriend experience" would include flagging up his many flaws as a boyfriend and the phrase "not tonight, I need to finish this report", directed McSorely towards the arms of Carla. It proved to be a wise choice as she looked even more seductive in the flesh than she did in a picture that left little to the imagination. McSorely's own capacity for fantasy was stretched to its limit over the course of the next few hours as he wined and dined Carla at a series of classy establishments. His new companion attracted just as many stares as Gary had upon his first appearance in front of the maître d' but envy and lust were the overpowering emotions from the onlookers this time, not repulsion and pity. McSorely would have normally been an incongruous consort for such a lady but his designer suit helped to create the impression Carla was indeed his girlfriend rather than an expensive purchase. Carla's professionalism even started to make McSorely doubt hard cash was the only reason for her presence across the dining table. This merely added to the wonder of an evening that came to a climax in room 321 of the Glasgow Hilton with Carla providing a demonstration of why her services came at such a high price. McSorely was expecting shame to make its scheduled appearance as his drained body reclined on the King-sized bed and placed itself at the mercy of insomnia yet again. But any chance to reflect on his contribution to sexual slavery and human trafficking was placed in abeyance as McSorely's eyelids started to close and he drifted into a deep sleep for the first time in months.

# Chapter Five:

# The origins of Gail

There was a spring in Buchan's step as he walked up the ramp at Waverley Station and prepared to feast his eyes on Auld Reekie for the first time since his abrupt departure. It was merely a coincidence his first assignment from The Council had doubled up as a homecoming but Buchan was determined to enjoy every second of the Busman's holiday. If it all went to plan, he could even spend 20 minutes or so ambling down memory lane before the 4.25 p.m. train spirited him back to Inverness. Buchan also had the option of defying The Council by refusing to return to Moristoun but he wasn't stupid enough to consider making a break for freedom. The consequences of such a course of action would be disastrous, something Farqhuar had made clear during the final briefing for his maiden Q99. Managers often make idle threats in a bid to strike fear and compliance into recruits but Buchan had no doubts Farqhuar would deliver on his promise of damnation.

"Desertion is a Category A offence. Check it in The Book if you don't believe me," he said, an invitation that was clearly a test of faith. Had Buchan headed to the library to perform that very task, it would have marked him out as a malcontent, someone who clearly couldn't be trusted. The Q99s would suddenly vanish, along with any hope of engineering a speedier departure from Moristoun, so Buchan replied: "I don't think that will be necessary. Why would anyone have reason to doubt such an honourable gentleman?"

Farqhuar had plenty of doubts about Buchan, however, and had only agreed to his request for service after years of badgering. He expected the Edinburgh assignment to end in failure, as nearly every rookie found it hard to concentrate on their first trip back to the mainland, but hoped his eager gofer would learn from the experience. However, if Buchan failed to heed the lessons and was still stalked by failure after four of five Q99s, he would simply have to accept he wasn't cut out for this kind of work. When Farqhuar relayed this information, it made Buchan even more determined to succeed at the first time of asking. So he banished any wonder at the transformation of his home town and remained focused on the job as he walked across Waverley Bridge towards Princes St Gardens. Stepping into the gardens was a source of comfort for Buchan as he fondly remembered lazy childhood afternoons in the days when this new addition to the capital's social scene elicited such a sense of wonder. Modern-day Edinburghers seemed far less enamoured with its charms as they sat leafing through newspapers and picking at packed lunches instead of appreciating the splendour of the view. Even the many tourists failed to savour the beauty of their surroundings fully as they stopped only for a matter seconds to take photographs before speeding off to the next attraction on their itinerary. Buchan was depressed by unearthing what he considered further proof of humanity's regression. Did people really prefer to snatch such a brief glimpse of these wonderful images through the tiny window at the top of their cameras instead of luxuriating in the sights, sounds and smells of the real thing? Was the sole purpose of these expensive trips from Japan and America securing enough snapshots for a two-hour slide show that would make their friends and family shudder at the very mention of Scotland's capital for the rest of their lives? If such suspicions were correct then Buchan could only fear for the future of mankind as a new millennium edged closer. His own mission now seemed much more daunting as he could understand why the woman he was about to meet felt so abandoned and isolated in a society where people were too busy to notice those in desperate need of help. If they stopped to take a proper look at the emaciated teenager puffing from a cigarette while she rocked a pram with her other hand then they would have seen someone yearning for a shoulder to cry on. But the steady procession of passers-by didn't even give the young mother a second thought so it was left to Buchan to take on the role of the Good Samaritan.

Preying on the maternal instincts of Frances Mary Barr was a key part of Buchan's strategy so he opted for the greeting traditionally afforded to mothers and their new-born children.

"Isn't she a beautiful baby," said Buchan as he sat down on the bench next to Frances and gazed into the pram at the tiny figure making such a disproportionate amount of noise. "What's her name?"

"Her name's Gail and she's not beautiful – she's an evil little fucker."

It was not the reply Buchan had been expecting and panic took a firm grip as he began to realise he might be hopelessly out of his depth. If he couldn't make this track-suited adolescent realise her daughter needed the love and care of a devoted mother then he stood no chance of proving Farquhar's pessimism about his maiden assignment had been misguided.

"I'm sure you don't mean that," he said. "How could you say such a thing about an innocent child?"

"Innocent? Can you not hear the wee bastard bawling her lungs out? She's a monster and has ruined my fucking life. Why did I let that useless bastard ever put his grubby hands on me?"

Buchan knew from his case notes exactly whom Frances was referring to – Paul Smith, an L-plate Lothario who had already managed to impregnate two of his class-mates at Leith Academy by the age of 16.

"I take it daddy's not much of a help, then?" Buchan said. "Does he ever give you a hand with Gail?"

"Does he fuck. He hasn't even met his own daughter yet. Ran away like the stupid little boy he is. A total waste of space."

Buchan was in no position to disagree as the information he had gathered about Paul suggested that while his sperm was certainly vibrant, such an adjective couldn't be applied to his general demeanour. The lustful layabout was destined to spend most of his days on the dole, rolling joints in front of daytime TV while awaiting the next race from Chepstow, and the poor Child Support Agency worker assigned to his steadily growing number of cases was about to discover just how difficult it was to get blood from the stoned. Frances, therefore, would have to shoulder the burden of financing Gail's upbringing, a terrifying prospect for a girl whose slim hopes of acquiring some qualifications had vanished with the sacking of her uterine wall. She could also expect little support from her own family as Frances was the product of a brutal union between a violent criminal and a hopeless alcoholic. Daddy was midway through a 20-year stretch in Saughton while mummy's crippling addiction was undoubtedly a life sentence. The promise of sobriety that had accompanied her inauguration as a grandmother crumbled after just 48 hours when the inevitable wetting of the baby's head saw the Smirnoff tsar reassert his authority over a revolting peasant with ideas above her station. That left Frances with no credible allies in her battle with post-natal depression and she was now preparing to run up the white flag.

Buchan's powers of persuasion were all that stood between her and a one-way ticket to his own world but his case lay in tatters after discovering he had placed too much faith in the baby as a star witness. There was nobody else to call to the stand but Buchan was determined not to write off his first Q99.

"You can't let one bad egg sour you on men for the rest of your life," he told Frances. "Plenty of nice young chaps will be interested in a good-looking girl like you."

Little white lies had been an essential weapon in Buchan's armoury during his days at the Edinburgh bar and they proved particularly productive when he could convince himself they had more than a ring of truth to them. Childbirth and the subsequent sleepless nights had not been kind to Frances and it was hard to ignore the nicotine stains that sullied both her hands and teeth. However, a glimmer of natural beauty remained uncloaked by the misfortune that had turned her into such a haggard figure and Frances may well have blossomed into an attractive young lady had fate not dealt her such a rotten hand. The bashful smile that greeted Buchan's compliment proved kind words had been at a premium during the last 16 years and shed further light on how the boy responsible for so much damage had managed to talk Frances into bed so easily. Buchan's words provided only a brief boost to her self-esteem, though, as negative thoughts resurfaced to slap down any happiness.

"Don't be daft," she said. "Look at the state of me – I'm a bloody mess. And who'd want to take on such a horrible baby? All that screaming drives me mental and I'm her mum."

"She'll calm down eventually," said Buchan. "You're both just having a rough time of it at the moment. If you can ride out the storm then things will be so much better in a year or so."

"A fucking year! I can't take five more minutes of this. You can't imagine how hard it is dealing with that brat all on my own."

That was certainly true as Buchan's dealings with children had been limited almost exclusively to the days when he was numbered among their ranks. His failure to sire a successor made empathising with Frances rather tricky but it was clear she needed some time to herself.

"Why don't you let me watch her for a while?" he said. "You can have a nice walk round the gardens and clear your head a bit. I won't move an inch, I promise."

Most mothers would have respectfully declined this offer, their scepticism of the stranger's intentions sharpened by the scaremongering of an increasingly reactionary mass media, but Frances was desperate to escape the crying that had become her daily soundtrack.

"Are you sure?" she asked Buchan. "I could do with a break, right enough."

"No worries," he replied. "You take as long as you want. I'm happy to take care of her."

As he watched Frances set off on her walk around the gardens, Buchan's optimism about his assignment started to increase. Being freed from her duties for a few minutes would hopefully lead to a vast improvement in Frances' mood, thereby pushing any suicidal thoughts from her mind. He was also hoping a bit of distance from her daughter might lead to some parental pining and waited anxiously to see when Frances would turn round to make her first check on Gail's safety. Buchan was left disappointed, though, as Frances' gaze remained firmly fixed forward – and that disappointment soon turned to concern when she reached the opposite end of the gardens and broke into a run as she climbed the stairs to Waverley Bridge. Buchan jumped off the bench in alarm and set off in pursuit of the fugitive but made just two or three strides forward with the pram before the screeching of brakes, a sickening thud and the screams of horrified onlookers stopped him in his tracks. A sense of foreboding then accompanied him as he pulled the pram up the steps and joined the spectators for this macabre addition to the street theatre programme at the Edinburgh Festival. One glimpse at the lifeless body lying in front of the Mac Tours bus provided conclusive proof of Buchan's abject failure and his desolation increased when he gazed towards the top deck of the bus and saw several tourists taking pictures of the ugly scene below. That provided an even grimmer snapshot of humanity in its most brutally honest form. Everyone within eyeshot of the late Frances Barr knew they shouldn't be gaping at her bloodied corpse but they just couldn't help themselves. Even Buchan, who liked to think he operated on a higher realm to the masses around him, remained stuck in a trance for a few seconds before Gail's howls snapped him out of it. The baby had been crying from the moment Buchan first set eyes on her but those tears now seemed more appropriate after the loss of her mother. Gail was thankfully too young ever to remember this fateful moment but it still felt cruel to expose her to such a frightful scene for even a second longer, so Buchan took the pram back down to the gardens before sitting down to ponder the consequences of his failed mission. While Farqhuar had expected events to unfold in such a grisly fashion, he had neglected to pass on instructions about Gail's fate, leaving Buchan in quite a predicament. He couldn't just abandon such a defenceless child in the gardens as that might lead to the Barr family suffering yet another tragedy if Gail fell into the wrong hands. Leaving the baby in the care of her vodka-fuelled granny seemed equally cruel, while daddy was clearly only a few steps ahead of Gail in his own emotional development. He could barely take care of himself, never mind a needy child, and Buchan didn't want to run the risk of Gail accidentally devouring one of his herbal roll-ups. He could always take the baby to a police station or orphanage but that would only lead to a barrage of uncomfortable questions. Buchan was under strict instructions not to advertise his presence on the mainland and feared he might not be able to adequately explain how the child had ended up in his possession without causing some inter-dimensional ripples. The departure of the 4.25 to Inverness was also edging ever closer and breaking what had been described as a non-negotiable curfew was also fraught with danger. After careful consideration, Buchan came to the conclusion he would have to take Gail with him through the portal to Moristoun and await further instructions. If Farqhuar had a problem with that then he only had himself to blame for failing to pass on instructions about the baby.

Farqhuar, unsurprisingly, didn't see it that way and sported a face like thunder when Buchan emerged from the portal pushing a pram. "That better not be who I think it is," he said, "because I don't seem to remember including child abduction in the job description."

"That's right, you didn't. There wasn't even a single mention of what to do with the baby. Wasn't that something of an oversight?"

"Certainly not. Your sole task was to stop Frances Barr from killing herself and you failed. The baby wasn't part of your remit."

"So I'm allowed to intervene in one life but not in another. Where's the logic in that?"

"Don't get snotty with me, Buchan. You know fine well our jurisdiction only extends to the suicidal and that howling banshee polluting the air is a little young for sullen introspection. Give it a couple of years and then we might be able to help her."

"But if we act now then there's a good chance she won't end up in the same sorry state as her mother. Why do we need to wait until she is battered and bruised before sticking our noses in?"

Farqhuar's tolerance of Buchan's impudence was being stretched to the limit and that last piece of dissent was an insult too far.

"How dare you question the rule of law," he yelled. "I thought you were beginning to understand how things worked here. Isn't that why you volunteered for mainland service? All that time spent studying The Book was clearly wasted if you are still spouting such rubbish."

Buchan realised the error of starting an argument he could never win within seconds of talking back to his superior but that mention of The Book resurrected the rebellion within him. It was the only weapon a citizen of Moristoun had at their disposal if they were brazen enough to start a fight with the bureaucrats and Buchan was sure it contained a relatively recent addendum to the chapter dealing with extraordinary cases. Farqhuar's knowledge of The Book was undoubtedly superior to his own but Moristoun's chief administrator had probably been too busy to notice this latest tweak to the text that shaped the island's governance. That opened the tiniest window of opportunity and Buchan was determined to squeeze through it. If he could succeed in outwitting Farqhuar on a matter of law it would be a considerable feather in his cap. Farqhuar would have to accept Buchan was worthy of at least another crack at the Q99s and he would also be given the chance to make amends for the wreckage of his first mission by securing a brighter future for little Gail.

Challenging Farqhuar when he was already in such a vile mood was an act of daring that rivalled repeatedly prodding a sleeping crocodile with a disturbingly short stick. Buchan, therefore, would have to choose his words carefully to avoid having his head bitten off. The only thing Farqhuar respected was the law so Buchan came to the conclusion technical terms would have a far greater effect than any emotional plea.

"Isn't there a possibility Gail might now qualify for a Q101?" he said. "The Council could grant her temporary residence rights if I make an application on her behalf."

"Don't talk such tosh," replied Farqhuar. "The Council would never let a baby stay here. Q101s are only granted in exceptional cases when the rehabilitation of a Q99 is impossible on the mainland. Temporary visas also rarely last for more than a year and it could be a couple of decades before the baby is ready to return."

"But wasn't there a recent ruling that changed all that? I'm sure I saw it mentioned when I was looking through The Book about a month ago."

"I very much doubt it. I haven't read the latest addendums but it would be extremely unorthodox for The Council to make such a change."

Farqhuar's admission of ignorance over changes to The Book gave Buchan further encouragement and he continued to press his case until securing the concession he had been yearning for.

"Very well, Buchan," said Farqhuar. "If you can find something in The Book to back up your preposterous proposition then I'll be happy to let you make an application. For the time being, though, we'll need to keep our little visitor a secret. The sight of a baby in Moristoun would cause quite a stir."

"Shall I just leave Gail here, then?" said Buchan, a question he instantly regretted as it caused Farqhuar's face to turn red once more.

"Do I look like a babysitter?" he raged. "You really are an odious simpleton, Buchan. That screaming child is only here because of your idiocy and if it's not out of my sight within the next 30 seconds I'll drop kick it back down the portal. Is that what you want?"

Only a fool would have attempted to answer one of Farqhuar's rhetorical questions so Buchan kept his counsel before wheeling the pram out of the office. His relief at escaping Farqhuar's booming voice proved all too brief, however, as Buchan's attention shifted back to the higher-pitched aural assault that had started back on the mainland. If he wanted to keep Gail's presence under wraps then he would have to bring a halt to her tears before stepping out on to Antony Street. It was a five-minute walk to the safety of Buchan's home and the journey would have to be made without attracting any attention. Remaining inconspicuous while pushing Gail's pram was a difficult enough task without the added inconvenience of the baby's screams causing every set of eyes to turn in their direction. Buchan, therefore, had to find a way of keeping Gail quiet but he was at a loss when it came to coming up with a solution. Rocking the baby in his arms while singing a lullaby had little effect, which was hardly a surprise given Buchan's chronic inability to hold a tune. He found it just as difficult to step into a clown's elongated shoes as the pulling of several funny faces failed to elicit a smile from his sole spectator while Gail was equally unimpressed by his rudimentary flight simulator. That 30-second thrill ride only made her even more upset and Buchan was on the point of giving up before his right hand brushed against the outside of his jacket pocket as he plonked Gail back in her pram. The rustle this action made reminded Buchan of the sweets he had purchased at Waverley Station to make the long trip back to Inverness more bearable. His mind had been so preoccupied by the failure of his mission and the fate of Gail that Buchan had forgotten to open the packet of Wine Gums while the train sped towards the Highland capital. It was far from a wasted purchase, though, as the sweets now provided him with fresh hope of mollifying the most vocal of babies. While Buchan was suffering from metaphorical teething troubles in his role as Gail's guardian, the child's own pain was purely literal. Her dummy had been buried at the bottom of the pram for the last four hours and this separation from the one thing she could always rely on for comfort caused Gail greater distress than the disappearance of her mother. A black wine gum was far from the ideal substitute but Gail was intrigued enough by her makeshift pacifier to bring a halt to her crying, allowing Buchan to plot his escape.

He popped a tentative head outside to check if the coast was clear and was relieved to see just a couple of stragglers on the other side of the road. If Buchan could make it to the end of the street without being noticed he could then take a sharp right on to Eastman Avenue before nipping down one of the alleyways to reach his front door. He took great care not to divert Gail's attention away from her wine gum as he dragged the pram out of the front door and Buchan congratulated himself on a job well done as their journey began without the shedding of any more tears. However, he knew he would start sobbing himself if they were intercepted before reaching the sanctuary of the alleyway so there was no room for complacency. The first part of his quest went according to plan as Gail's presence on Antony Street went unnoticed but Buchan was disturbed to see a figure approaching from the top of Eastman Avenue as he looked round the corner. However, there was too much distance between them for either of the parties to make a positive identification so Buchan decided to swap stealth for speed and darted in the direction of the alleyway before making a break for home. That ran the risk of vocal dissent from his passenger but Gail mercifully stayed silent until a frantic few minutes came to an end with the slamming of Buchan's back door. Having watched the baby react with uncharacteristic stoicism to her pram's bumpy passage over the cobbled alleyway, Buchan was hoping she would now remain quiet while he nipped out to the library to leaf through The Book. However, he learned a valuable lesson about the fickleness of children when Gail burst into tears again just as he was about the step out of his front door. Even wine gums failed to soothe her anger this time and Buchan was left with no option but to depart while Gail's sobs still filled the air. All he could do was put on one of Wagner's more obscure operas in a bid to drown out the noise and hope anyone passing by his house would consider the crying that accompanied the composition as one of the German's less successful attempts at an aria.

Buchan cursed the many hours he had spent drinking at the Tortured Soul as he forced his body into another reluctant sprint on his way towards the library. Sweat was dripping off him when he burst through the doors five minutes later and Miss Sanderson was thankfully the only witness to Buchan's panting as he approached the front desk. "Goodness me, William, you're in quite a state," said the librarian. "What's the matter?"

It was hard for Miss Sanderson to hear the reply as Buchan tried to speak while catching gasps of air but she eventually managed to work out he needed to see The Book as a matter of urgency. She was happy to facilitate his request but insisted on sitting Buchan down with a glass of water before fetching the key.

"Have you calmed down yet?" said Miss Sanderson as she returned with the key in one hand and a magnifying glass in the other. "I thought you were going to pass out for a minute there."

"I'm fine thanks," replied Buchan. "Guess I'm not as fit as I thought I was."

"Why were you running about like a maniac anyway? I've never seen you in such a hurry before."

"There's a bit of an emergency back at home. I need to return as soon as possible after checking something in The Book."

"An emergency? That sounds rather worrying. What's happened?"

"I can't tell you right now, I'm afraid, but if I find what I'm looking for in The Book I might be able to reveal the secret in a couple of weeks."

"Well, I better let you in then," said Miss Sanderson before leading Buchan across to the iron door at the far left-hand corner. One turn of the key proved enough to gain access and

Miss Sanderson handed Buchan the magnifying glass before closing the door behind him.

When Buchan had first gained access to the room shortly after his arrival in Moristoun, he was underwhelmed by the sight that greeted him. The prison cells that held many of his former clients boasted more impressive interior design than the surroundings he found himself in. The room's sole decoration was an old school desk and the only other object inside the four walls was the book that sat on top of the desk. Buchan was expecting the fabled tome to be an ornate masterpiece like the Book of Kells and was disappointed to discover it was only about the half the size of a standard encyclopaedia. His presence in Moristoun had sparked a myriad of questions, surely the answers to them and all of life's other great mysteries couldn't be contained in such a thin manuscript? All it took to banish such doubts was one turn of a page, however, as Buchan encountered a dense mass of text that was too small for the human eye to read. His swift reappearance back at the front desk brought a knowing smile from the librarian and she handed Buchan a magnifying glass before he could even tell her the nature of his complaint.

"Oh, you've got to be joking," said Buchan as he collected the magnifying glass from Miss Sanderson. "Don't you have a version people can actually read with their own eyes?"

"I'm afraid not," said the librarian. "The Council forbids reproduction of the text. This is the only way you can read The Book."

If Buchan thought he had cleared the only barrier to potential enlightenment with the acquisition of the magnifying glass, he was mistaken. The size of the text was the least of his problems, something that became clear upon his return to the room when he scanned the magnifying glass over the first page. It was written in what appeared to be ancient Greek and the only foreign tongue Buchan had attempted to master during his days as a schoolboy at George Heriot's was Latin. Some of the words the schoolmaster had drummed into him by sheer fear made an appearance during The Book's second chapter as the language shifted into Latin but Buchan wasn't fluent enough to translate any of the passages. The third chapter was equally unintelligible as it was written in Gaelic and that forced Buchan to exit the room and confront the librarian again.

"In exactly how many languages is this book written?" he asked Miss Sanderson. "I'm only three chapters in and each one has been in a different tongue. Surely it doesn't change with every chapter?"

"You need to master seven languages before you can fully understand The Book – Greek, Latin, Gaelic, Hebrew, Arabic, Ottoman Turkish and Mayan."

"Just the seven? Oh, that should be easy. Why didn't they make it a real challenge and put the last chapter in hieroglyphics?"

"Sarcasm will get you nowhere, Mr Buchan. Only knowledge can set you free."

"Are you seriously suggesting I sit down and learn seven obscure languages before trying to tackle The Book? Nobody is capable of doing that."

"Oh, you'll be surprised what people are capable of when they use the full power of their minds. I'm trying to learn Chinese at the moment and that will be my fourteenth language."

Buchan didn't need to ask which seven foreign tongues she had tackled first and asked Miss Sanderson if she could provide a brief summation of The Book's key points.

"I'm afraid I can't tell you anything," was her reply. "Revealing details of The Book is frowned upon by The Council. Each citizen has to find out for themselves. All I can do is point you in the direction of our language section. It's the last row on the right and we have a large selection of textbooks."

Miss Sanderson was hoping Buchan would heed her advice and start boning up on his Greek but he reacted like every other new arrival and walked out of the front door in frustration. The librarian could usually gauge the intelligence and character of any Moristounian by measuring how long it took for them to face up to the challenge of learning the languages and was disappointed it took more than a century for the penny to drop with Buchan. However, he made up for his tardiness by becoming a dedicated student and garnered enough knowledge of the seven languages to finish The Book inside the next 14 years. The vagaries of Moristounian law helped to ensure it was a never-ending story, however, so Buchan still had to make regular trips to the library to check on the latest addendums.

Most of the additions had little direct effect on Buchan's own fate as they were usually minor legal tweaks but the ruling handed down on February 29, 1995 was to prove of considerable importance. When Buchan first came across it four months ago, he failed to give the three paragraphs the attention they merited, mainly because they were written in Mayan, the weakest of his seven languages. He only scanned the passages briefly and didn't bother to delve any deeper when he discovered the ruling concerned agents of The Council. At this point, Buchan was still just a lowly citizen and had yet to be selected for mainland service so he skimmed over the text to get the gist of the ruling before returning to his office. A few key words had stuck in Buchan's head, however, and they now provided him with hope of pulling off a coup in his latest legal battle with Farqhuar. Locating passages in The Book was often a laborious task but no addendums had been inserted since Buchan's last trip to the library so he merely had to turn to the final page to find what he was looking for. However, a far greater challenge awaited him as he faced the task of translating the three paragraphs from Mayan into English. This time, though, Buchan devoted the full power of his mind to interpreting the ancient script and took just 30 minutes to make a decent stab at a full translation:

February 29, 1995
Final ruling on case 3290567

On December 3, 1994, Chief Psychiatrist Barrett asked The Council to rule on the link between parental suicide and future Q99s after completing his report into Carol McGhee, citizen No: D45987. Dr Barrett came to the conclusion the citizen's own suicide had been directly influenced by the distress she suffered at the age of five when her mother, Aterstoun citizen Joan McGhee, took her own life. Having witnessed a growing number of identical cases over the last 10 years, Dr Barrett believes The Council should be taking preventative action as early as possible to stop the offspring of suicidal parents from suffering a similar fate.

The Council has conducted an extensive review of every case where parental suicide has been cited as a possible influence and agrees there is sufficient evidence to suggest a direct link. Agents are therefore now licensed to intervene if they believe there is a significant risk of future suicide in the offspring of new citizens. However, great care should be taken to find a solution to the problem on the mainland. Only in exceptional cases will The Council agree to the granting of a Q101. Any agent requesting a Q101 for a child should apply through the appropriate channels. They will then have two weeks to name an appropriate guardian and build a case for temporary residence before appearing in front of The Council. The decision of The Council will then be final.

Buchan wanted to rip the page out of The Book, march back into Farqhuar's office and do his best Neville Chamberlain impression concerning the significance of the piece of paper in his hand. However, such an act of sacrilege would only ruin his chances of securing a Q101 for Gail and his confidence in winning the case could subsequently prove every bit as misplaced as Chamberlain's belief that Hitler was a man of his word. Buchan, therefore, just committed the three paragraphs to his memory before returning home to celebrate with his new companion.

# Chapter Six:

# Brenda and the baby

Brenda's journey from the greengrocers to the Tortured Soul had only just begun but her arms were already feeling the strain of transporting the raw materials for another of Jimmy's meals. Sating her spouse's hunger had always been a challenge but the task was now considerably more difficult following Jimmy's decision to attempt another stab at sobriety. Something had to replace the stout that both shaped and described his stomach so it was up to Brenda to fill the void with a steady flow of meals. The steak pie she had just purchased from the butcher's was probably substantial enough to feed a family of four but Brenda knew it would only satisfy her husband if it came accompanied by a massive plate of chips and spoon after spoon of boiled cabbage. Even that wouldn't be enough to fill Jimmy up, however, so she was forced to add a tub of ice cream and two tins of peaches to the list of items that now bulged her shopping bag. Brenda's frame wasn't suited to tests of strength but her desire to save Jimmy from the fate of many a landlord provided all the motivation she needed to ensure the messages were transported home successfully. However, the other end of Eastman Avenue still looked as depressingly far away as the end of one of Henderson's anecdotes and Brenda's heart sank as she looked up and saw the road stretch out in front of her. Thoughts of her punishing walk soon disappeared, though, as a figure appeared at the top of road pushing what appeared to be a pram. He stopped for a few seconds before making a dash for one of the alleyways but this attempt to preserve his anonymity only piqued Brenda's curiosity further. While the pram was probably ferrying illicit goods to a black market transaction in the alleyway's darkest recesses, Brenda clung to the notion it was being put to a more traditional use. She knew it was daft to think a baby could be bouncing about inside, this was Moristoun after all, but Brenda was well versed in wishful thinking. She had continued to believe God would bless her with a child until the pain of her eighth miscarriage combined with Jimmy's drunken words to crush any lingering optimism and push her over the precipice. That leap from the fifth floor of Jenners Department Store saw Brenda land in a place where visual reminders of what she had been missing out on were mercifully absent. But nobody ever escapes their demons in Moristoun, a place where every citizen is a prisoner of their psyche, so babies were rarely far from Brenda's thoughts over the next six decades. That was why she now found herself racing off in pursuit of the phantom child, an unfamiliar act of physical exertion that left the heavy smoker breathless by the time she had reached the alleyway and popped her head around the corner to check on the pram's progress. Brenda's stubby legs had made the journey in just enough time for her to witness the man reach the end of the alleyway and open the back gate to the first house he came to. Brenda waited until he had closed the gate and disappeared from view before she tiptoed down the lane to take a closer look. The gate Brenda could see from the top of the alleyway was flanked to the right by a hedge that was impeccably trimmed and when she peeked over the top she witnessed a back garden that was just as impressively maintained. There was only one man in Moristoun who paid such meticulous attention to horticultural matters – Buchan. But what on earth was he doing sneaking about with a pram at this time of day?

It was now Brenda's turn to step into shoes of stealth as she opened the gate and edged her way through Buchan's garden in search of a secluded spot that offered a decent view of his living-room window. She eventually settled behind two garden gnomes of sufficient stature to shield her from detection when Buchan appeared at the window and took a look around before pulling his curtains shut. Lawyers were, by their very nature, slaves to suspicion but Buchan's paranoia on this occasion seemed to go beyond this trademark mistrust in others. Brenda was determined to find out why he was so keen to protect the pram from prying eyes so she moved closer to let her ears do the detective work. There were few clues for the amateur sleuth to work with initially but the audio equivalent of a signed confession and blood-soaked dagger then fell into Brenda's lap when the screams of a baby burst forth from the living room. The thrill of staking out Buchan had already provided Brenda with a shot of adrenalin but her heart started beating even faster upon this startling discovery. There was a baby in Moristoun and the only thing that stood between Brenda and what she had previously considered to be a mythical entity was Buchan's back door. She yearned to kick down the door and comfort the crying child in arms that had been waiting far too long to perform such a basic maternal duty. But fear, not to mention a lack of faith in her ability to batter down the oak barrier in front of her, held Brenda back. What if she wasn't cut out to be a mother after all and the baby responded to her touch by summoning a stream of bile or soiling herself as a form of dirty protest? Such rejection would have hurt Brenda almost as much as one of her miscarriages so she remained frozen in silence until events took a surreal turn when the baby's a Capella rendition suddenly turned into an operatic duet.

This persuaded Brenda it was time to confront Buchan but she heard the front door slam just seconds after deciding that chapping on it would be the wisest course of action. By the time she had made it round to the front, the lawyer was already halfway up the road and Brenda was in no position to attempt another pursuit. Her lungs had registered their disgust at the previous burst of exercise with such vehemence that it was best not to incur their wrath again by breaking into another sprint. Brenda decided her energy would be better spent securing access to Buchan's home but a search of the many plant pots in both his front and back garden confirmed her suspicions that a man of the law wouldn't be so foolish as to leave the keys to his home within such easy reach. Brenda's frustration at the failure of her quest was heightened by the wails that continued to emanate from the house and it pained her to hear the child in so much distress. Each sob felt like a dagger in the heart and it wasn't long before Brenda joined the cast of the opera by breaking into tears herself.

She was destined to play the role of heroine, however, and Brenda eventually regained her composure after several minutes of blubbing. Although her hopes of securing a peaceful passage into Buchan's house had been dashed, forced entry remained very much an option. The back living-room window seemed to be the best point of entry and she looked around the garden in search of a weapon big enough to blast a Brenda-sized hole in the glass. Her gaze eventually settled on the gnomes she had hidden behind just minutes earlier but Brenda felt a pang of guilt as she considered ramming the smiling fisherman or friendly gardener through the window. However, Brenda was spared the Sophie's choice of picking a gnome to sacrifice as she was too weak to move either of the statues any more than a few footsteps. Although this was excellent news for the gnome community, it spelled disaster for the earthenware cat that had the misfortune to sit just a few feet to the left of the fisherman, waiting for any scraps from the fruits of his neighbour's labour. The size of the cat's stomach suggested such acts of charity were not uncommon but the feline sadly wasn't rotund enough to make it too heavy for Brenda to ferry to the living-room window. This helped propel the moggy into the world of cat burglary as Brenda hurled it through the window at the moment the baby's wails combined with a booming warble from the opera singer to help mask the crash that greeted the violent union of earthenware and glass. Brenda was relieved to hear amplified crying from inside Buchan's living room when she pulled the curtain aside to check on her handiwork. She had taken a calculated gamble on the cat landing safely on the carpet instead of on top of the pram and was happy to learn she wouldn't have to ask Buchan to represent her in an infanticide trial while she tried to explain away the gaping hole in his window. The pram was situated to the right of the room and was sufficiently distant from the point of impact to avoid any collateral damage. While the baby was destined to emerge from the episode unscathed, the same could not be said for Brenda, who was now charged with the task of squeezing herself through the hole without coming a cropper on the serrated edges. She pulled the sleeves of her leather jacket down over her hands before attempting to pull some of the shards out of the window. Only a few came loose, however, so Brenda was eventually forced to stick her head and arms through the hole before taking a tumble that left her legs and arse open to attack. Brenda could hear the foreboding tear of both denim and flesh as she dived through the air before landing on top of Buchan's sofa. Her physical pain would soon be soothed by an emotional tonic, though, when Brenda approached the pram and set eyes on Gail Barr for the first time.

While babies can be undeniably adorable when gazing at the world in wonder or drifting through the peaceful world of their dreams, most neutral observers would agree they resemble gargoyles when engaged in the act of protracted wailing. For Brenda, though, the sight of Gail's contorted face, red eyes and snotty nose was a thing of beauty and her sense of wonder only increased when she reached into the pram, wrapped her arms around the baby and held Gail's fragile body close to hers. The return of a feminine touch after several hours in the cold company of Buchan led to a noticeable improvement in Gail's mood but it wasn't until Brenda spotted the dummy at the bottom of the pram and restored the teat to its rightful place that the baby's crying finally subsided. This one simple act provided affirmation of Brenda's maternal skills and a sense of peace enveloped her as she sat down in Buchan's armchair with Gail. Decades of pain disappeared in an instant and Brenda was so overwhelmed by happiness she soon joined Gail in lapsing into the kind of deep sleep only the truly contented or blissfully ignorant can hope to enjoy. The nap was to last a mere 20 minutes, however, as Buchan returned from the library to the alarming sight of a gaping hole in his living room window. His anger at this act of vandalism was soon displaced by a much more powerful feeling of fear as his gaze shifted to the opposite side of the room and the sight of Brenda cradling Gail.

"Oh for fuck's sake," he snapped, an outburst that was audible enough for Brenda to hear over the Wagner that continued to boom out from Buchan's record player. But as Brenda woke from her slumber and opened her eyes to meet a gaze that invited her to explain what the hell was going on, she remained remarkably calm for someone who had committed such an obvious act of criminality in the house of the public defender. She even had the temerity to make Buchan believe he was the one in the wrong by lecturing him for using such foul language in front of Gail and urged him to keep his voice down in case the baby also broke of out of her nap. Having spent a large slice of his day listening to Gail test the capacity of her lungs, Buchan was happy to comply and planned to use those precious few seconds of silence to prepare for the question that would inevitably follow. But curiosity played second fiddle to maternity for Brenda and she mouthed the words that confirmed her status as the child's future guardian: "I don't know who she is or where she came from but I won't let you or anybody else take this baby away from me."

# Chapter Seven –

# The Apprentice

McSorely's mind remained riddled with doubt as he emerged from the back of Inverness station and set off in search of the Scenic Suicide offices. The enjoyment gleaned from the previous day's activities had placed his presence on the train north in jeopardy but a combination of resignation and obligation eventually forced him out of the wonderful bed responsible for lustily swallowing his insomnia. While McSorely had savoured his brief taste of an existence full of excitement and possibilities, he was also realistic enough to know he would not have the luxury of lavishing eight grand on each day. That point was hammered home when he woke from a slumber he would have gladly paid an even higher sum for. After searching through his wallet and collating all the loose change rattling around inside his pocket, McSorely was dismayed to discover he was left with just £43.20, barely enough to see him through the day never mind a new life. He was also now officially homeless, having surrendered the lease for his apartment, and didn't fancy battling Gary for Glasgow's comfiest park bench when they were both ejected from their respective hotel suites. Heading for Inverness still seemed the best course of action, especially as McSorely was keen to meet the mastermind behind Scenic Suicides. He could at least afford him the courtesy of sticking to their scheduled meeting, even though the spectacular sling shot on offer now held less appeal, and it would be a shame to waste the ticket to Inverness, a city McSorely had never set foot in. He had been instructed to take a sharp right down an alleyway on Falcon Square upon his exit from the station and this helped to ensure his first impressions of the Highland capital were far from favourable. A row of bins blocked his path on the right of the alleyway and after McSorely had finally managed to negotiate a passage he was greeted by the work of a graffiti artist who had managed to cram seven expletives, the more elaborate of which were woefully misspelled, into one sentence. This Highland scribe clearly had much to learn from his Glasgow contemporaries as McSorely fondly recalled the "Picasso was a wank" scrawl he had witnessed on a wall in Maryhill many years ago. The Spanish surrealist would certainly have appreciated the bizarre nature of McSorely's recent experiences and his life took another strange turn when he reached the last door on the left of the alleyway, the supposed headquarters of Scenic Suicides.

While McSorely wasn't expecting a firm that offered services of such legal dubiety to advertise their presence, he thought they would at least work out of an office offering some pretence of legitimacy. His contact at Scenic Suicides, a certain William Buchan, had claimed the offices were "rather shabby" during their telephone exchange but McSorely now realised that was the understatement of the year as he faced a grim exterior that would have made even a Dickensian outhouse look like the Gardens of Versailles. Two more bins, filled with overflowing detritus, were flanked to the right by a door decorated with chipped brown paint and another masterpiece from the foul-mouthed graffiti artist. That door offered access to a concrete box with no windows, a textbook example of 1970s architecture at its very worse. It looked like the sort place where the IRA would torture confessions out of suspected informers so it was with more than a little trepidation that McSorely delivered the three loud knocks signalling his arrival. Thankfully, he was not greeted by a moustachioed Irishman carrying an Armalite but an impeccably dressed gentleman carrying himself with the kind of stylish dignity McSorely could never hope to replicate, no matter how many designer suits he splashed out on.

"You must be Mr McSorely," said Buchan as he beckoned his visitor inside. "I'm sorry you had to walk down such a disgusting alleyway but this is the only place we can afford at the moment. Don't worry, it looks much better from the inside."

It certainly couldn't look much worse and McSorely was relieved to walk into a respectable, modern office space after Buchan had led him down the hall and into the first room on the left.

"This used to be the function room for the pub on Academy Street but it became redundant when they built a new lounge," said Buchan as he invited McSorely to sit down on the opposite side of his desk before planting himself in the large leather chair next to his computer. "The landlord lets me have it for just £100 a month and it's the perfect place to conduct our rather sensitive business because hardly anyone knows it's here."

"You're also just a quick dash away from the train station if you need to do a runner," said McSorely. "Have the police ever come sniffing round?"

"Oh the boys in blue are far too busy to bother themselves with us. Besides, we're a perfectly legitimate and respectable company. It's all explained on the website."

"That's right. I'm only here to buy myself a giant catapult, aren't I?"

"Indeed. That's if you still want to go ahead with this. I wouldn't feel comfortable providing our usual service if you were having second thoughts."

Buchan's words came as a relief to McSorely, who had feared the businessman sitting across from him would react with fury to the news both his time and money had been wasted.

"I've had more than a few doubts, now you come to mention it," said McSorely. "You shouldn't have told me to spend all my money on one final blow out. I had so much fun it has rekindled my passion for life somewhat."

"If that's the case then why did you bother coming all the way up here? Couldn't you have cancelled the meeting and just stayed in Glasgow?"

"I did consider that but then I'd have to deal with the consequences of my deeds in the last 24 hours."

"Consequences? Dear God, you didn't kill someone, did you?"

Murder had briefly crossed McSorely's mind when he was drawing up his list of activities, with a suicide bomb attack on the National Television Awards at the forefront of his thoughts, but it was never really a serious contender.

"No, of course I didn't kill somebody," he told Buchan. "But all that big spending has left me with just over £40 to my name and I don't have a job or a home. Killing myself is probably still a better option than begging on the streets."

"What if you found a new job?" said Buchan. "Would that change matters?"

"It might do. But there's no chance of that happening. I've been on the dole for almost a year now and it seems like 100 people are applying for every position in Glasgow. My best chance of landing an annual income of 40 grand is buying one of those Rich For Life scratch cards."

"Maybe you should cast the net a little wider," said Buchan as he delved into the drawer on his desk and produced a newspaper. "Take a look at the advert on page 19 and tell me what you think."

McSorely took the Inverness Courier out of Buchan's hand then turned to page 19 before reading out the first ad that caught his eye in the Situations Vacant section:

Are you a fun-loving party girl who has always wanted to be on the big screen? If so, send a selection of candid pictures to big Hamish and he can help make you a movie star. Must be over 17 and open-minded. Terms and conditions will be discussed at your audition. Email your pics and details to mrloverman@Hamishproductions.com.

"Tempting as that might sound, Mr Buchan, I don't think the bold Hamish will be too impressed if I send him pictures of me prancing about in my undies."

"Not that advert," said Buchan, who had always agreed with those who maintained that sarcasm was the lowest form of wit. "Look at the one below it."

McSorely shifted his gaze a few centimetres and opted for silence this time as he read from the text:

Wanted: Legal assistant. Moristoun's eminent public defender seeks a dynamic young professional to assist with the administration of his rapidly growing practice. Applicants must have excellent IT skills, an inquisitive mind and an eye for detail. A fondness for dogs is also preferable but not essential. Starting salary is £20,000 per annum but accommodation will also be provided free of charge in Moristoun. Email your CV and a covering letter to: williambuchan@moristoun.co.uk.

"So you're thinking of expanding?" said McSorely. "I take it all that stuff about a legal practice is just a front for Scenic Suicides?"

"On the contrary my dear boy," replied Buchan. "I am indeed Moristoun's eminent public defender. This little venture is just a side project. Most of my time is spent back in Moristoun dealing with legal matters but once I get an assistant I can devote more of my energy to developing the website. So, what do you say? Are you interested?"

Given that the two impediments to McSorely's continued existence were a lack of employment and accommodation, the job with Buchan seemed the ideal solution to any remaining disenchantment with the mortal realm. But McSorely's mind resumed its habitual fretting as he pondered the wisdom of placing his trust in a man who had just admitted catapulting suicidal loners off cliffs was how he spent his free time. There was also the issue of his potential new home to mull over as McSorely had never heard of Moristoun before. What if this place acted as the inspiration for the Wicker Man and his new dwelling was a straw effigy that came equipped with a wonderfully effective but potentially deadly central heating system?

"Few people have actually heard of Moristoun," said Buchan when asked for further details. "I'm not going to lie to you, it's hardly the most exciting place to live. Moristoun is the most remote of the Western Isles and few souls from the mainland ever venture out there. We're very isolated. But it could be the perfect place for you to gather your thoughts and earn a bit of money before you're ready to move back to Glasgow."

"But wouldn't you want to employ someone who's in it for the long haul? Why give the job to me if you think I'll want to leave after a few months?"

"I only placed the advert yesterday and nobody has applied for the position yet. You could help me out on a trial basis while I perform the arduous task of trying to find someone who actually wants to move to Moristoun full-time. Do you think you could handle being a legal assistant?"

"I don't have any experience but most of the things you mention in the advert apply to me. I used to work in IT and I like to consider myself an inquisitive individual with an eye for detail. I don't really understand the bit about dogs, though. What does being a dog lover have to do with being a legal assistant?"

"It's actually related to your accommodation," replied Buchan. "You will technically be the lodger of a Scottish Deerhound called Munchkin. She has just inherited the house of her dearly departed owner and I'm charged with performing the necessary administrative tasks. I've been popping in every day to feed and walk the dog but it makes more sense to have someone actually stay with the creature. Would you have any objections to that?"

McSorely had never been what you would call an animal lover but it was indifference and the allergies of both his mother and fiancée, rather than any personal fear and loathing, that had limited his interaction with the world of domesticated canines. Maybe the companionship of a dog would actually help with his own rehabilitation; there had to be a reason why so many people referred to them as man's best friend.

"I'm happy to keep an eye on the dog if it means free accommodation," said McSorely. "I'm sure something called Munchkin won't cause me too much trouble."

Anyone aware of the anatomy of a Scottish Deerhound would not have made such a statement but Buchan decided against informing McSorely about the size and strength of his new landlord. Just seconds after claiming to possess an inquisitive mind, McSorely had failed to ask Buchan a single follow-up question about Munchkin so he deserved to suffer the unpleasant surprise that awaited him upon opening the door to the beast's lair.

"Well, if you're willing to take both the job and the house then I don't see any reason why we shouldn't press ahead with the trial run. I was planning to head back to Moristoun after our meeting anyway so why don't you just come with me?"

McSorely was more than a little alarmed by the rapid escalation of events since his arrival in Inverness a mere 20 minutes ago. What had begun as a curious courtesy call had quickly turned into a job interview and he was now being asked to leave everything behind at a moment's notice to start a new life on a remote island. Things were moving rather too quickly for his liking and he wasn't slow in relaying those fears to Buchan.

"I appreciate it's a lot to take in but what do you have to lose?" said Buchan. "You've already admitted you are broke and homeless so it makes sense to at least give Moristoun a chance. If you want to go back to the mainland tomorrow, I'd be happy to arrange your transit."

McSorely had to admit the alternative option of returning to Glasgow for a night on the streets held about as much appeal as trying to facilitate in the artificial insemination of lions without the aid of an anaesthetic. He stood little chance of triumphing over insomnia for a second successive night if his body was quivering under a rudimentary blanket and his mind was preoccupied with the thought of fending off opportunistic sodomites. A soft bed in a peaceful island cottage seemed far more likely to secure another blissful kip so he informed Buchan he would be willing to accompany him back to Moristoun.

"Excellent, but I'm afraid we need to sort out some paperwork before we can embark on our journey," said Buchan as he stepped up from the desk to retrieve a bundle of forms from the filing cabinet behind him. "I need you to sign a temporary lease for the house so the insurance policy is valid. Even if you are only staying with us for one night, you can't be too careful."

McSorely was disturbed to discover the blue cover page with a large Q101 in the top right-hand corner was the first of 15 densely worded documents and betrayed another of his boasts, this time the possession of an eye for detail, by asking Buchan to provide a précis of the tenancy agreement.

"It's basically a long-winded way of protecting both yourself and the dog from financial responsibility if there are any unfortunate accidents during your time together," Buchan said. "Moristoun also has some ancient by-laws that are different from the mainland so some of the paragraphs relate to your legal rights while living on the island. You can read through it if you like or just go to the last page and jot down your signature."

Although Buchan was a little disappointed to see McSorely take the easy option by quickly scrawling his name on the final page – if he didn't have the patience to look through 15 pages how could he ever hope to cope with The Book? – it made the task of transporting him to Moristoun much easier as it ensured the apprentice's defences would remain down. However, Buchan was in the mood for a little fun, so he instructed McSorely to read one particular paragraph out loud while he returned to the filing cabinet to fetch the items that would secure a peaceful passage for them both.

"The Tenant hereby agrees to let the Landlord's attorney, Mr William Shaw Buchan, use reasonable force to ensure the

Tenant is unconscious for the duration of his journey to Moristoun. By signing this agreement, the Tenant waives any right to take legal action against the Landlord's attorney for his sedation and …"

McSorely was unable to finish the sentence as Buchan's left hand quickly covered his eyes while the right held a chloroformed rag over his mouth. That ensured the insomniac had the unfamiliar feeling of losing consciousness for the second time in just a matter of hours and another new world awaited him when he finally opened his eyes again.

# Chapter Eight –

# The Defence Rests

It was a crisp December morning on the Royal Mile but bloodlust was protecting George VI's subjects from the cold as they massed around the Mercat Cross in anticipation of their favourite form of entertainment. Nothing drew in the punters more than a hanging and the fact it was a woman making that lonely trudge to the gallows succeeded in attracting more voyeurs than usual. Jane Anderson's social standing may have spared her the indignity of an execution amid the squalor of the Grassmarket but there was to be no escape from the taunts and jibes of Edinburgh's underclass. She was a fallen woman, after all, and bilious vipers from every section of society had gathered to say their piece to the harlot who had done away with Dr George Anderson. Jane knew that only the hangman would show her less mercy and those fears were confirmed when the star of the show emerged to face her public and was showered with insults, rotten fruit and an assortment of bodily fluids. Every face was contorted with evil as Jane scanned the crowd for the one man she longed to see before facing her fate but William Buchan was busy constructing his own noose just a few streets away. He had been in court to offer secret support to his beloved when a trial that had captured the public's imagination finally reached its conclusion but, from the moment that black cap was placed on the judge's head, Buchan knew he would never see her face again in this world. Watching the woman he loved swing from the gallows after a savaging at the hands of a feral crowd was an agony he couldn't bear to endure. Joining Jane is bidding farewell to this cruellest of worlds would be far less painful and Buchan knew he deserved commensurate punishment for a mess that was mostly his making.

The mystery lover who had led Mrs Anderson to break her marital vows had never been publicly unmasked. Only the good doctor himself had learned his childhood friend was responsible for the ultimate betrayal and the rage that flowed through him after Jane's confession ensured it was a secret he would take to the grave. It was Buchan who deserved to receive the full force of Dr Anderson's fury but Jane had the misfortune to be much closer to hand and suffered several fierce blows before managing to break free and find the kitchen knife that turned her from potential murder victim into murderer. The blow that pierced her husband's heart was a clear act of self-defence but such a right didn't seem to exist for married women whose sexual self-defences hadn't proved strong enough to deflect the advances of their suitors. That made plotting Jane's escape from the gallows rather tricky as the revelation of her infidelity was the only plausible explanation for an attack that was entirely out of Dr Anderson's character. Buchan, who secretly masterminded Jane's defence by pulling the strings of the lawyer recruited to represent her in court, pondered betraying his friend even further by inventing a scenario whereby Dr Anderson had snapped after being confronted with evidence of his own sexual impropriety. Such a strategy was soon dismissed, though, as Buchan remembered his friend's crippling impotency had played a far greater role in leading Jane towards adultery than his own charisma and sexual prowess. As this thought crossed his mind, Buchan began to wonder if Dr Anderson's flaccidity might offer Jane the firmest chance of ensuring that her own body wouldn't hang equally lifeless and limp from the gallows. After years of waiting for the doctor to provide a cure for her sexual frustration, the patience of this most loyal of spouses had finally cracked and she had taken her husband to task over his erectile dysfunction. This led Dr Anderson to respond with an act of violence designed to prove his masculinity beyond all doubt and poor, fragile Jane would surely have perished had she not found the knife that freed her from his bestial hands. Buchan thought this story stood a far better chance of securing sympathy for Jane than coming clean about their affair so he instructed Jane's lawyer to proceed along those lines in court.

This was excellent news for the scandal sheets, which had already made great play of the rumours about Jane's boundless libido, and Dr Anderson gained notoriety across the whole of the UK as readers lapped up the tragic tale of the Flaccid Physician. However, Buchan's plan to use the doctor's medical affliction as a cure for Jane's legal ills unravelled as a succession of witnesses cast doubt on the character of Mrs Anderson under questioning from the prosecution. Buchan, as a close family friend, was called to the stand himself but managed to remain commendably detached from the emotions swirling around inside him. While he refused to follow the prevailing fashion of pointing an accusative finger at Jane, Buchan also did little to suggest he was in cahoots with the woman most people inside the courtroom considered to be a brazen hussy. The threat of someone else exposing him as the mystery lover remained real, however, and Buchan spent many a nervous hour pacing around his office until Jane's lawyer returned with news of the day's proceedings. But he was spared the shame of having his own reputation dragged through the mud as even the star witnesses, the maid and cook on duty when the attack took place, had missed out on the juiciest piece of gossip. While they could say with assurance that Mrs Anderson had indeed been unfaithful to her husband – what else could cause such a well-mannered man to shout "You bastard whore! I'll fucking kill the both of you"? – it remained unclear exactly who had led the lady astray. One of the other staff members, a valet whom Buchan had always treated with the utmost suspicion, expounded the theory that a series of suitors were responsible for sating the lady of the house's voracious appetite. The valet even claimed he had been asked to perform the task himself on several occasions but had politely declined out of loyalty to his master. Buchan would have relished the task of ripping this ridiculous notion to shreds in court but the pleasure of exposing the valet as a habitual liar was reserved for Jane's lawyer. That didn't prove to be such a great test of his abilities as other members of the household despised the valet so much that they seized their chance to denounce him in public. By the time they had finished settling their scores with the malefactor who considered them his social inferior, his reputation was damaged almost as much as that of the lady he had tried to besmirch. Jane was therefore spared the shame of going down in infamy as Edinburgh's classiest nymphomaniac but no amount of legal manoeuvring could remove the indelible stain of her adultery.

Buchan knew their case was doomed as the trial progressed but when he returned to the courtroom for the verdict he still lapsed into a state of shock as Jane was sentenced to death. He met the gaze of his one true love as those fateful words filled the air and felt his heart shatter as the desperation and horror on Jane's face became etched into his memory. Buchan turned to the bottle in a bid to erase that picture from his mind but such a pitiful attempt at therapy never stood a chance of succeeding. Every waking hour was dominated by thoughts of the carnage his carnal desires had created, a lust so strong it had sent both his childhood friend and the woman he loved to an early grave. Buchan couldn't even take refuge in his sleep, as Jane would haunt him in nightmares on the rare occasions when whisky triumphed over woe to break the broken man's insomnia, and his suicide soon took on an air of inevitability. Deep down, Buchan was something of a romantic so the notion of bowing out at the same time as his beloved, and in an identical manner, held great appeal. Such an act would also appease his conscience as it would be a clear confession of his role in the sordid affair that had brought such infamy down on the Andersons. Buchan didn't care about having his own name dragged through the mud as a consequence; there was nothing left for him in this world and he just wanted to join Jane in leaping into the great beyond. Whether they would emerge together on the other side remained a moot point – it certainly seemed unlikely if the word of the minister who preached to both Buchan and the Andersons every Sunday from the pulpit of St Giles' Cathedral was to be believed – but Buchan hoped God would help ensure that such a tragic love story had a happy ending. It was with a mixture of fear and optimism, therefore, that Buchan stepped on to the stool in the middle of his living room and reached up to grab the noose hanging from the rafters. As he fastened the knot around his neck, Buchan looked across at his grandfather clock and saw that three minutes remained before it would strike 11. While the ghouls at the Mercat Cross were now hushed into silence as they waited to see if Jane would plead for God's mercy in her last public address, Buchan had no audience hanging on his every word. The longest three minutes of his life were destined to be played out in silent contemplation and Buchan reflected on the unfortunate chain of events that had led him to this point before making one final plea for clemency towards the Almighty. The silence was finally broken by the chime of the clock just as Buchan was saying Amen and he hesitated for a few seconds before finding the courage to step off the stool. Buchan gasped for air as the noose tightened around his neck and started slowly draining every drop of life from his body. He closed his eyes in a bid to hasten the eternal sleep that would end his suffering but this only summoned visions of Jane suffering the same ordeal. The emotional agony associated with scenes that were far more terrifying than even his most vivid nightmares soon superseded Buchan's physical torment but he couldn't bring himself to open his eyes and end the horror show. This was his penance for the misery he had put Jane through and Buchan knew he had to suffer every second before he was allowed to leave this world and his sins behind. He watched her writhe in agony for three miserable minutes but then felt a powerful surge of happiness as Jane's body finally fell limp and a look of tranquillity replaced the terror on her face. The misery was over for Jane and the knowledge she had passed to the other side helped Buchan endure the distress of his own final few moments before darkness descended and he lost consciousness.

The vision that greeted Buchan when he awoke what seemed like just a split-second later provided a stark contrast to the soft, sensual image of Jane that had accompanied his dying breath. An intimidating figure dressed in a tuxedo met Buchan's gaze from across a large oak desk and it felt as if the man with the moustache was staring deep into his soul. Buchan feared he was facing Satan himself as a chill snaked down his spine and he assumed it was only a matter of time before he was ejected from the lavishly decorated office and subjected to a series of degrading punishments. That anxiety only increased when the man in the tuxedo stood up and towered over him. He held a cane in his right hand and Buchan feared the first punishment for his impressive collection of sins would be a series of blows on the bonce. That pummelling failed to materialise, however, as the man merely used the cane for dramatic effect while he paced around his office making his introductory remarks.

"Good morning Buchan," he said. "My name is Farqhuar and The Council have charged me with the task of welcoming you to our little community in Moristoun. You have ended up on these shores because you had the arrogance and temerity to end your own miserable existence before your time was up. Mere mortals cannot be allowed to interfere with the grand scheme of things without suffering some form of punishment.

"Your penance for trying to escape the body and mind that caused you such torment is perpetual life in the same state here in Moristoun. You will continue to feel the same sensations and emotions you experienced on the mainland but time will stand still. You will not age and death won't be waiting in the wings to offer some respite. To find a way out of here you will need to confront your demons instead of running away from them like a coward.

"I'm sure a thousand questions will be racing through your mind but I have far too much on my plate to spend more than a few minutes acting as your personal oracle. Each new arrival in Moristoun is allowed to ask just three questions to their induction officer and I urge you to think carefully before proceeding. I'm feeling in a generous mood today so I'll advise against treading the same path as one of our more dim-witted citizens, a certain Mr Hogg. His first query at the induction was: "Is this heaven?" and all I could tell him was: "No." Having witnessed the folly of asking such a closed question, you would think Hogg's next attempt would be designed to elicit an answer with far greater detail but instead he opted for: "Is this hell then?" After replying in the negative yet again, I urged Hogg to think of a question that couldn't simply be answered Yes or No and he paused for a few seconds before saying: "You're right, I need to get this last one spot on. Can I have a bit more time to think about it?" Such idiocy can perhaps be excused by Hogg's lack of education but the same luxury can't be afforded to a man of your upbringing. Hit me with your finest questions and we'll see if you are as intelligent as your case notes seem to suggest."

Buchan had found it hard to pay attention while Farquhar was making his speech because he was preoccupied with processing the fact the afterlife was neither heaven nor hell but a place called Moristoun. The few pieces of information that had stuck in his mind from Farquhar's address seemed to suggest he had landed in what the Catholics would deem purgatory but the cautionary tale of Hogg stopped Buchan from wasting his first question by asking: "Is this purgatory?" However, he was keen to glean more information about his new surroundings so Buchan tried his best to come up with an open-ended question that would hopefully lead to an illuminating answer.

"You spoke about the penance of perpetual life in Moristoun but didn't go into any detail about what this would entail," Buchan said. "How do the people here spend this never-ending existence?"

"Very impressive," replied Farquhar. "Few new arrivals have made an opening gambit that demands such an expansive answer. I can see why your legal services were in such demand. Acceptance is one of the key themes here. Everyone in Moristoun cowardly attempted to run away from both themselves and their environment instead of riding out the storm. With that in mind, The Council try to make life here as similar to your mainland existence as possible. The Council have drafted a set of laws and control the island but the task of actually policing Moristoun is left to your own ilk. We are far too busy maintaining surveillance on those who have yet to throw their lives away to keep a close eye on those who have ended up here. We haven't had a lawyer here for a long time so your arrival is actually rather timely. I'm sure you will be kept busy by some of the lawless souls who land here.

"You will find the biggest changes in your life outside of work. Despite being immortal, your body will need to be fed and maintained. Physical pain, hunger and thirst will remain your constant companion. The Council will pay you a wage to sate those demands and will also put a roof over your head but you will be prevented from accumulating private wealth. Any money made from your professional life must be returned to The Council."

"It sounds a bit like the Communism that chap in Germany is harping on about at the moment," said Buchan. "You've mentioned this Council a few times now so I think I'll trade in my second question for some more information about them. I've noticed you speak in an English accent – don't tell me that we Scots are subjugated in the afterlife as well?"

Buchan's query brought an uncharacteristic laugh out of Farqhuar and he said: "The accent assigned to both myself and all my colleagues is just one of The Council's little jokes. You Scots take so much pleasure from being ruled by your near neighbours that it would have been a shame not to continue such a state of affairs in the afterlife. Consider it revenge for nationalism, one of the most destructive curses you humans have inflicted on yourself. That 'chap in Germany' you mentioned, Mr Marx, seems to have a greater understanding of things with his internationalist approach but the Communism he espouses will be doomed to failure. Humans will always be a slave to their greed and ambition. Those who are handed the reins of power will be unable to resist the urge to abuse the system for their own personal gain; it's inevitable. Thankfully, the grubby fingers of such a destructive species will never be able to grasp power here in Moristoun. Members of The Council exist on a far higher plane and only take on human form to make the transition to this world easier for vermin such as yourself. Moristoun is run so smoothly because your lot have no effective power."

"But how can The Council possibly govern everyone who has committed suicide?" said Buchan, not realising he had just squandered his final question. "Millions of people must have taken their lives, it's impossible to fit them all into a functioning community."

"We have a growing population but it's very much under control," said Farqhuar. "Only Scottish people can end up on these shores. Perpetual existence alongside thousands of other gloomy Caledonians is further penance for nationalistic sorts such as yourself. Moristoun is one of 15 islands that house these suicidal Scots and you should just consider yourself lucky that you're not Welsh. Their place of punishment is every bit as grim but has the additional torture of choral singing."

"Are we allowed to visit these other islands?" said Buchan. "What happens if we try to leave Moristoun's shores?

"While you have impressed me with your verbal skills and inquisitive mind, it seems numeracy is not one of your strong points," replied Farqhuar. "Had you been able to count up to three, you would have noticed that your right to ask me questions expired with that little poser about how The Council deals with so many lost souls."

Farqhuar then reached into a draw under the desk and pulled out a book that he threw across to Buchan. "This little tome deals with the basics of Moristounian law," he said. "It details what citizens can and cannot do during their stay here. You will find it useful from a professional point of view but there is nothing within its pages that will unlock the real mysteries of Moristoun. Only one book can help with that task and it's housed at the library."

"What kind of book? There must be thousands of them at the library," said Buchan. "How am I supposed to know what one to ask for?"

"That sounded suspiciously like two more questions. Did I not make my policy on dealing with your curiosity abundantly clear just a few seconds ago? Your induction is officially finished and I will be terribly upset if my office is still graced by your odious presence for more than a few seconds. Make your exit through the door on the right, where Dr Barrett is waiting to conduct your preliminary psychiatric report. I'm sure he can't wait to hear all the sordid details of the pathetic affair that set you off down the path to Moristoun."

# Chapter Nine –

# Welcome to Moristoun

The journey from Buchan's desk to the toilet at the far corner of his office was only about 10 metres but it felt far further as he dragged McSorely's body across the floor. The frame of his apprentice was deceptive as McSorely's suit did a good job of concealing the spare tyre he had been cultivating with comfort food and Cliftonhill pies since Sarah's departure from the kitchen had freed him from the constraints of healthy eating. Over 13 stone was packed into his five foot 10 inches and as Buchan hauled McSorely into the toilets, he yearned for a return to the days when the development of a Rubenesque figure was limited to wealthy gourmands. After laying McSorely down on the toilet floor, he made a mental note to invest in a wheelbarrow before Farquhar added another Q99 to his workload. It was only a matter of time before the burden of obesity pushed a more dedicated aficionado of square sausage, caramel wafers and takeaway pizzas towards suicide and Buchan realised he would need some assistance if taking them through the portal was the only way to avoid permanent passage to Moristoun by more conventional means. Such cases were admittedly rare but the sight of McSorely slumped across the toilet floor provided all the motivation Buchan needed to prepare for all eventualities. Although the most physically demanding aspect of taking his passenger to Moristoun was now over, Buchan was still faced with the challenge of fitting both himself and McSorely into the cubicle marked with the sign "Out of Order". One final heave was required to hoist McSorely on to the toilet seat and Buchan made sure his new employee was balanced enough to avoid a headlong fall before turning round to lock the cubicle door. He then pressed down on the flush and waited for the required 30 seconds as they were spirited away to Moristoun's shores.

When Buchan opened the cubicle door, he was relieved to find Farquhar waiting for him in the toilet attached to his Council office. Any hope his superior would lend a helping hand in transporting McSorely soon vanished, though, as Farquhar insisted such an act of manual labour was beneath him and limited his contribution to holding the toilet door open as Buchan dragged the new arrival into the office. This soured Buchan's mood somewhat and ensured he failed to fully appreciate some rare words of praise from Farquhar's after all three figures had taken the weight off their feet. "I doff my cap to you, Buchan," he said. "I really didn't fancy your chances with this particular Q99 but, if my eyes do not mistake me, that is most definitely the pathetic figure of James Patrick McSorely slumped in my leather armchair. I take it you have the required paperwork to justify his presence here?"

Buchan was still too exhausted from the task of placing McSorely in the armchair to provide an answer, so he merely nodded before handing the Q101 form to Farquhar. But the chief administrator only took a cursory glance at the final page before shoving the form in an envelope and turning his attention back to Buchan. "I hope you realise you now have two active Q101s," he said. "That's highly unorthodox so I suggest you wrap up either of these cases as quickly as possible. The first one has still to be resolved after 17 years and I will be far from amused if McSorely's rehabilitation proceeds at the same leisurely pace."

"That's a bit unfair," replied Buchan. "You know fine well Gail is an exceptional case. It was always going to take time to prepare her for a return to the mainland and I think both myself and her adoptive parents have handled such a difficult task very well. Do you know how difficult it is to keep Moristoun's biggest secret for 17 years?"

"Oh, stop patting yourself on the back, you self-satisfied imbecile," said Farquhar. "Everyone knows speaking to a

Q101 about the island's true reality is a Category A offence. That's why a letter has already been circulated to every citizen alerting them to McSorely's presence on these shores. It's fear that has stopped anyone from opening Gail's eyes to the world around her – not your own genius. But it can't be too long before the penny finally drops and she starts to question why she's getting older and everyone else stays the same age. Time is of the essence and you will have to start making plans for her return to the mainland. Remember, if you don't act before she turns 18 then The Council will step in and take matters into their own hands."

Buchan had to admit it was getting more and more difficult to preserve Gail's ignorance of her surroundings but he shared Jimmy's fear she wasn't ready for mainland living.

"Gail's education still isn't finished," he told Farquhar. "Brenda needs more time to work on her. I'm hoping to set up a university entrance exam on the mainland but that will count for nothing if she doesn't have what it takes to pass. At this point, I'd say it's more likely McSorely will be out of our hair before Gail."

Buchan's words shifted Farquhar's attention back to the figure slumped in his armchair like an inebriated seal. McSorely's suit was no longer doing such a good job of disguising his gut and Farquhar's opinion of the new arrival decreased even further as he spotted a roll of fat peeking out from between the bottom two buttons of his shirt. Farquhar couldn't bear to have such a disgusting sight within eyeshot for even a second longer so he instructed Buchan to move McSorely through to Dr Barrett's office for resuscitation. "Remember what I said about the urgency of wrapping up these Q101s," he told Buchan as he watched the public defender resume the arduous task of moving McSorely's body. "There's a lot riding on this for you. Bringing both cases to a swift conclusion would increase your standing with The Council immeasurably. They have been keeping a close eye on your work and passage to the other side could even be your reward if a couple of Q101s are added to your CV."

Buchan had been waiting decades to hear those words and the 13-stone weight he was dragging across the floor suddenly felt a lot lighter as euphoria swept through him. It was as if he had already been transported to a wonderful new world as Buchan lost all sense of his surroundings and started to dream of joining Jane in a state of perpetual peace. For Buchan had no doubt Jane had been saved from the damnation gleefully predicted by those who had gathered round the Mercat Cross to witness her execution. The Book had taught him an important lesson about the error in trusting human interpretations of justice and spirituality. The species he had belonged to was merely an infinitesimal speck in a boundless universe and the arrogance and ignorance of the human race was laid bare in almost every page of The Book. Enlightenment only came to the tiny minority who managed to block out all the bluster and distractions to focus on life's true meaning. Buchan had never come close to finding that path during his time on the mainland but Moristoun and The Book had finally opened his eyes. Now he stood tantalisingly close to taking that final step but plenty of work still needed to be done so he snapped out of his reverie and focused again on the task in hand.

"Are you even listening to me, Buchan?" said Dr Barrett after his second attempt to ascertain the identity of the lump laying on his chaise longue had met with more silence and the same blank expression. "You look like someone who has spent the entire morning inhaling adhesives."

"Sorry doctor, I was daydreaming there," replied Buchan. "What was it you wanted to know?"

"I'd like to know who you have just dragged into my office and what you want me to do with him. I would have thought such a sharp mind as yours would have managed to work that out. It's a pretty standard response to the receipt of an unconscious individual."

"I can only apologise again. As I said, I was away with the fairies for a minute there. The man sprawled across your couch is James Patrick McSorely and he's a Q101."

Dr Barrett was upset at hearing Buchan describe his chaise longue as a common couch but the novelty of dealing with a Q101 directed him away from a rebuke. "It has been a long time since I've had to deal with one of those," Dr Barrett said as he stood up from his desk and moved towards the medical cabinet. "This will be a refreshing change from drawing up those dreary psychiatric reports but you'll have to hope my memory doesn't fail me."

"I have every confidence in you," said Buchan. "This one should be fairly straightforward – all I'm looking for is the standard amnesia and resuscitation."

"How much of his memory would you like to wipe out? Remember, once these pills work their magic, there's no going back."

"Don't worry, I've done everything by the book and jotted down the exact times. I want McSorely to remember signing his Q101 form but to forget my chloroform attack. He gave me his signature at 12.33pm and I took him by surprise two minutes later so any time between those two acts would be perfect."

This was not what Dr Barrett wanted to hear as it left him little room for error when it came to the dosage. If he got it a fraction out either way, they would have even more explaining to do when the smelling salts jolted McSorely back to life. Buchan's earlier insult about his chaise longue was still swirling around his mind so Dr Barrett decided it was now time to deliver the postponed chastisement.

"Giving me a two-minute window to work with is hardly doing things by the book!" he said. "Even if I was dealing with cases like this every day, it would be tricky getting the dosage right. Why didn't you wait a little longer before knocking the poor bugger out? Couldn't you have spoken inanely about the weather or football for a few more minutes?

"Small talk has never been my strongest suit. Besides, I wanted to have a little fun. I wrote a clause about agreeing to be knocked out and directed McSorely's attention to it in a bid to teach him a lesson about the importance of reading all the small print in any legal document. Once he had read the exact wording, I had no choice but to knock him out."

"Honestly, Buchan, you can be very childish at times. How can you teach someone a lesson about the importance of reading the small print if you then wipe their memory of that very act? Your actions had nothing to do with educating McSorely. It was all about securing an audience for your pathetic little joke. You were like a naughty schoolboy waiting for the adulation of his peers as the headmaster inched ever closer to the discovery of a chalk phallus scrawled on his office door."

There was little point in Buchan trying to defend his actions as nobody possessed a wider knowledge of his psyche than Dr Barrett. The three-hour psychiatry session that had formed part of his own induction was merely the beginning of a long professional relationship as every citizen of Moristoun was duty bound to have a biannual mental tune-up. The last two centuries had provided Dr Barrett with a detailed map of Buchan's fears and insecurities so any attempt to conceal the truth was futile. Apology, therefore, was the only course of action.

"You should be apologising to yourself," said Dr Barrett. "I expected better from someone who has read The Book. Was that nanosecond of amusement really worth all the stress you are now putting me through? And what about poor McSorely? He's the one who will suffer the most if I don't get the dosage spot on. How can you ever hope to secure an exit from Moristoun if you continue to indulge in such selfish acts?"

"Actually, Farqhuar was just telling me I stand of chance of passing to the other side if I bring my two Q101s to a successful conclusion."

"Oh, don't be so deluded," replied Dr Barrett. "Farqhuar places too much stock in statistics. Remember, he's just an administrator. The people who make the big decisions at The Council operate on a far more philosophical level. If your motivation for helping people such as McSorely is purely to facilitate your own exit from Moristoun then you will be stuck here forever. Sincerity for your clients has to be there, otherwise you're just wasting your time."

The euphoria Buchan had felt moments earlier was blown away by the doctor's appraisal of his situation. While love and compassion were the over-riding motivations behind his attempts to take Gail away from Moristoun, he had to admit he cared little about the figure flaked out just a few feet away. Pity was the only emotion Buchan felt for McSorely at the moment and he needed to work hard on striking up a relationship that would eventually lead to a genuine bond between them. Securing the trust of his new apprentice would prove difficult if Dr Barrett failed to erase the memory of his sedation so Buchan prayed the dosage was spot on as he watched the doctor slip the amnesia pill into McSorely's mouth.

Life had been full of surprises for McSorely in the last 48 hours but, as the smelling salts worked their magic and he regained consciousness, this latest twist in an increasingly strange story left him befuddled. While sudden lapses into a deep sleep were not uncommon for drunken backbenchers and snooker spectators, they were as rare to an insomniac as genuine compassion from those who so infuriatingly took their slumber for granted. That mere fact would have been enough to heighten McSorely's suspicions had he woken in the venue that played host to his unexpected bout of narcolepsy but the fact he now found himself in new surroundings only added to the confusion. There was also the presence of a strange figure in a white lab coat for McSorely's mind to compute and the only sight that provided any sort of reassurance was the presence of Buchan. It was to his new employer that McSorely turned for information as he tried to paint a picture of how he had ended up sprawled on a chaise longue and Buchan sat down next to him before delivering a version of events that contained as few blatant lies was possible.

"It's great to see you back with us again, Mr McSorely. You had me very worried for a while. There you were talking away in my office and the next second you just blacked out. It was very disconcerting. My knowledge of medical matters is limited to say the least, so I had to rush you to my good friend Dr Barrett for a proper examination. Can you remember anything about what happened?"

"Not really," said McSorely. "The last thing I can remember is accepting the job and talking about coming to Moristoun."

"Oh, that's a relief," replied Buchan as he shot an admiring glance at Dr Barrett for getting the dosage spot-on. "Dr Barrett here was worried you might have suffered some memory loss but that was exactly what we were talking about when you flaked out."

"How long was I unconscious for? And where exactly are we? It doesn't feel like I've been out for long so we can't have travelled too far."

"On the contrary, Mr McSorely," said Buchan. "You were knocked out for four hours. It would have been remiss of me as your new employer to leave you in the overworked hands of the NHS so I decided to go private. I wanted you to get the best medical attention possible and brought you all the way to Moristoun's finest physician."

"We're in Moristoun now? I thought you said it was a remote island, how could you possibly get there from Inverness in just a couple of hours."

Buchan had guessed McSorely would be smart enough to come up with such a query and had rehearsed the cover story so well that he managed to answer without even the slightest hint of hesitation.

"One of my dearest friends in Inverness is a pilot," he said. "When I informed him of our medical emergency he agreed to fly us straight to Benbecula Airport and from there it's just a couple of hours by boat to Moristoun. It's a shame you were dead to the world for the entire journey because some of the scenery is breathtaking. Still, there will be plenty of time for you to drink in the delights of our landscape once the good doctor is satisfied it's safe for you to be up and about."

This provided Dr Barrett with the cue to steer the conversation away from a story that would inevitably be stalked by suspicion. He invited Buchan to vacate his seat on the chaise longue so he could take a closer look at his roused patient then bombarded McSorely with a series of questions as he went to work with his stethoscope and ophthalmoscope to continue the charade. Inside two minutes, the doctor had established McSorely was a non-smoking heterosexual with A positive blood who liked the occasional tipple and had a weakness for meat pies but resisted the lure of narcotics. None of his bones had been broken during the games of five-a-side football that no longer formed any part of a hopelessly inadequate exercise regime and McSorely's body remained free from sexually transmitted diseases. The patient had started his answer to that particular question with the phrase "to the best of my knowledge", confirming Dr Barrett's suspicions that McSorely had recently engaged in coitus with someone of dubious moral standing. Nothing escaped his attention and the sweat that had dripped down McSorely's brow before offering the verbal clue provided ample evidence he had something to be ashamed of. Establishing whether McSorely was indeed carrying an STD held little appeal for Dr Barrett, though, and he wouldn't even have swapped an intensive three-week course of counselling an imbecile like Hogg for the task of inserting a vial down the Jap's eye of the man lying in front of him. That treat would be reserved for a GP back on the mainland if Buchan succeeded in his mission to ensure McSorely would never return to Moristoun. Having succeeded in his own task of erasing the memory of Buchan's chloroform intervention, all Dr Barrett was now obliged to do was make sure McSorely hadn't suffered any ill effects from his sedation. This was a simple assignment for someone of his talents and it wasn't long before he had turned his patient back over to Buchan for an introduction to wider Moristounian society.

Given the surreal nature of the past two days, McSorely was wondering what strange sights would be unveiled when Buchan opened the door to reveal his first glimpse of Moristoun. But he was greeted by the same uninspiring grey buildings that graced every Scottish town centre; the only thing that made Moristoun any different from a Paisley or Perth was the refreshing lack of scent marks on the walls from the big cats of global business. The Golden Arches and Starbucks siren were conspicuous by their absence and an endless succession of turf accountants weren't waging a turf war for the last few pennies of the desperate. McSorely was sure there had to be a Greggs lurking somewhere, he was still on Scottish soil after all, but every shop he saw as his eyes scanned the street seemed to be a local enterprise.

"This is Antony Street," said Buchan. "It's the main road in Moristoun and the building you have just stepped out of houses all of The Council offices. Most of the nicest shops and restaurants can also be found here and the lobster at McCauley's is simply divine. I suggest you try it as soon as possible."

"Is every business here local?" said McSorely. "I can't see branding or logos anywhere."

"We're far too remote for the big boys of capitalism to pay us any notice," replied Buchan. "And even if they were interested in setting up shop here, I'm sure The Council wouldn't allow it?"

"Why not? Wouldn't they be keen to bring more money and jobs to the community?"

McSorely's remarks brought a wry chuckle out of Buchan and he said: "It's easy to see why things are in such a mess on the mainland if you swallow that nonsense peddled by economists in thrall to Mammon. You'll find life is rather different here in Moristoun. The Council wields far more power than the politicians who are so skilfully manipulated by big business on the mainland. Everything here is designed for the benefit of the community and The Council work hard to ensure the wealth is shared around instead of ending up in the hands of shareholders sitting on a ranch somewhere in Texas."

It sounded to McSorely like he had wound up in a hippy commune but it was hard to envisage the impeccably dressed Buchan puffing from a Camberwell carrot as he sat back and let his Jefferson Airplane LP take him on another trip into consciousness expansion. He also found it difficult to believe a mere local council could exert so much power over its citizens without being slapped down by the bureaucrats of Holyrood and Westminster. But the chance to quiz Buchan further about Moristoun's governance was lost as the lawyer turned into a tour guide and bombarded McSorely with information about the buildings they passed on the walk to his lodgings. The house Miss Sanderson had bequeathed to Munchkin was located just a two-minute walk away from Buchan's office. This gave McSorely the chance to take a brief look at his place of employment, an unremarkable office space enlivened only by a series of Picasso prints on the walls, before Buchan handed over the keys to 27 Woolf Crescent in the garden Miss Sanderson had tended with devotion.

"Now, do you remember the details of our tenancy agreement?" said Buchan as he led McSorely to the front door. "Dr Barrett seemed pretty sure there was no amnesia but I want to make sure just in case."

"Don't worry, I remember our agreement well," replied McSorely. "Free board in exchange for looking after the dog. The only thing that escapes my memory is the name and breed of the mutt.

"The bold Munchkin is a Scottish deerhound. Are you familiar with such a breed?"

"I'm afraid not. As I told you before, I have limited experience with the canine world. What does a Scottish deerhound look like?"

"Oh, I wouldn't want to ruin the surprise. To find the answer to that question, all you need to do is open the door."

Although Buchan had tried his best to disguise a grin, he couldn't stop a smile from overpowering his usually solemn expression as McSorely placed the key into the lock. This aroused McSorely's suspicions somewhat but he was still genuinely shocked when he opened the door to reveal the menacing figure of Munchkin sitting upright at the end of the hall. That vision then became even more terrifying as the giant dog burst forwards to greet her visitor and McSorely emitted a pitiful yelp as he slammed the door shut and fell back on to the path. Buchan couldn't help but laugh as he watched his apprentice take the pratfall but sympathy soon displaced schadenfreude and he bent down to haul McSorely back to his feet.

"What in the name of God was that?" said McSorely as he brushed the dirt off his suit. "That's not a dog, it's like something out of Dungeons and Dragons. Do I have to roll a double six before it lets me through the front door?"

That reference was lost on Buchan, who belonged to a generation that witnessed far too many horrors in their daily existence to ever feel the need to dream up fantasy worlds of terror, but the gist of McSorely's enquiry was easy enough to ascertain. "Munchkin can be quite intimidating at first but she's really quite harmless," Buchan said. "I'm sure she was just trying to say hello. She's quite an affectionate dog. I was scared out of my wits the first time I met her but I soon discovered there was nothing to be frightened of."

"But why didn't you warn me that beast was waiting behind the door? I could have had a heart attack."

"I wanted you to learn a valuable lesson. During the interview you claimed to have an inquisitive mind but you failed to ask a single question about Scottish deerhounds before you signed the tenancy agreement. That was rather remiss of you, don't you think? You also let the dog's name influence you too much. I think the direct quote was: 'I'm sure something called Munchkin won't cause me too much trouble.' If you're going to work in the murky world of law you will need to leave all your preconceptions behind. Consider this the first lesson of your apprenticeship."

McSorely would have preferred to receive his instruction from the comfort of Buchan's office via a powerpoint presentation but had to admit the memory of Munchkin bounding towards him was likely to remain lodged in his mind far longer than any pie chart or spreadsheet. The folly of blindly penning the tenancy agreement was also now laid bare and McSorely knew Buchan would hold him in even lower esteem if he tried to weasel out of sharing his digs with a beast that reminded him of the demonic dog that ruined Rick Moranis' party in Ghostbusters. His only option, therefore, was summoning up the courage to open the door again but he looked to Buchan for advice before walking back towards the keys that were still dangling from the lock.

"How did you go about making friends with the dog?" McSorely asked. "Can you give me any advice that will fend off a mauling?"

"I was fortunate enough to make Munchkin's acquaintance while Miss Sanderson was still with us. She made sure the dog was in a relaxed mood and that made our meeting far less stressful than I thought it would be. Unfortunately, slamming a door in Munchkin's face while screaming like a baby is unlikely to induce the same sedate state. The best course of action is letting me go in alone for a few minutes to calm her down. Then you can make your entrance and have a better stab at befriending her."

McSorely was happy to agree with that plan and seized the chance to take a closer look at his new surroundings while Buchan was trying to placate the deerhound. Woolf Crescent looked like any other suburban street in Scotland but McSorely noticed a discernible difference when his ears went to work. He could make out every soothing word Buchan uttered to Munchkin behind the front door as the rest of the street was cloaked in almost total silence. The cries and laughter of children at play usually provided the audio backdrop to summer evenings in suburbia but Woolf Crescent was so quiet McSorely was expecting tumbleweeds to blow across his path at any moment. If children did indeed number amongst his neighbours then they were either locked indoors by suspicious parents or held in a trance by their PlayStation and Xboxes. McSorely hoped Buchan's attempt at psychological hypnotism would cause Munchkin to be equally oblivious to her surroundings as the door opened and he was beckoned inside once more. He was impressed to discover the dog's mighty frame no longer took up a large proportion of the hall and asked Buchan where Munchkin was now residing.

"She has a terrible weakness for dog biscuits," Buchan said. "You can use them to lead Munchkin practically anywhere. I lay a handful of them down on her bed in the living room and she's savouring them at this very moment."

As Buchan led McSorely into the living room, the new tenant was left in no doubt as to who was the boss in this house as he saw Munchkin stretched out across a king-sized bed in the near corner of the room. "That's her bed?" he said. "I was expecting her to be in one of those contraptions you see in pet shops."

"I'm afraid most pet shops don't cater for dogs as large as Munchkin," replied Buchan. "It was easier for Miss Sanderson to buy a proper bed. I would have just let the dog sleep on the carpet myself but Miss Sanderson had far more empathy for subjects of the animal kingdom. She spoiled Munchkin rotten and that's probably why the dog is so addicted to those biscuits."

Munchkin's dependence on the savoury treats was strong enough to ensure McSorely's presence had thus far gone unnoticed but Buchan knew it wouldn't be long before she wolfed down the last morsel and directed her attention elsewhere. Making the introductions while Munchkin was sated and horizontal seemed the wisest course of action so Buchan invited McSorely to join him in sitting down on the bed.

"Give her a gentle stroke on the back to let her know you're friendly," he told McSorely. "But keep your hands away from her head while she's eating. She might think you're trying to steal one of her biscuits and I doubt I would be able to repair both your hand and the relationship if Munchkin viewed you as a common thief."

McSorely knew the danger in deviating from Buchan's orders and stuck resolutely to the plan his employer had devised to ensure the dog's friendship. He succeeded for the most part, although the command to stay relaxed proved difficult as he watched those giant incisors demolish the biscuits, and within five minutes Munchkin had placed enough trust in her new lodger to permit him to tickle her belly. "What did I tell you?" said Buchan. "She's a big softie, isn't she? I'm sure you will both get along splendidly. If you feed her properly, take her for a long walk every day and give her a little love then Munchkin will cause you no distress at all."

McSorely could only hope Buchan was right as he stood little chance of continuing to fend off his insomnia while plagued by the fear Munchkin would pop into his room and devour him as a midnight snack. For peace of mind, he asked Buchan if his own room came equipped with a lock and was relieved to learn that was indeed the case.

"I'm afraid I can't show you round the rest of the house, though, because I have some business to attend to back at the office," Buchan said. "Feel free to roam around and make yourself at home. I've left my office number next to the telephone in the hall if you have any queries. I'll be there until 7 p.m."

"What about the dog?" replied McSorely. "Is there anything else I need to do?"

"Give Munchkin her dinner at around six then take her for a walk when she has finished. All her food is in the kitchen cupboard and her lead is next to the back door."

"Where should I take her? Does she have a usual route?"

"With a Scottish Deerhound, you are the one who is taken for the walk. Just let Munchkin guide you. She will stop pulling when she gets tired – that's your cue to take her home. The whole experience lasts for about 45 minutes so you should get home just after seven. I'll be popping down the pub after I'm finished with my work at the office. Why don't you join me? I can introduce you to some of the locals."

McSorely guessed he would need a drink after being dragged about like a rag doll by Munchkin so he accepted Buchan's invitation and asked where he could find the pub.

"It's called the Tortured Soul and it's at the opposite end of Hannibal Crescent to our office, which is very handy. Just pop into the office first and we'll go up together."

# Chapter 10:

# Baby Talk

Jimmy tried his best to concentrate on the Moristoun Gazette as he slugged from his mug of tea but it was hard to focus on anything other than the sight and sound of his wife nervously pacing around the room. This only added to a sense of agitation that had been building since alcohol last touched his lips a week ago and Jimmy reached into his left pocket to grab the stress ball that Dr Barrett had provided to help with the task of dealing with his withdrawal symptoms. Most of Jimmy's anger flowed down his arm and into the ball through his fingertips, helping to ensure that the rebuke he dished out to Brenda was free from genuine malice. Wicked words, after all, had helped send them both to Moristoun and Jimmy was keen to avoid upsetting his spouse further on what could be a momentous day for them. "Sit yourself down, Brenda," he said, with only minor irritation. "You're giving me a headache marching about like that. Buchan told us The Council would reach their verdict at ten and it's only two minutes past. Give the man some time to make his way up here. He's not an Olympic sprinter."

"I'm sorry, Jimmy, but I'm too excited to sit down," said Brenda as she continued her march between the fireplace and window. "I won't be able to relax until that baby is in my arms again. You know how much this means to me."

Jimmy knew exactly what was at stake and realised the loss of this particular baby would hit Brenda like a sledgehammer to the solar plexus. While each doomed foetus had taken a chunk of her soul to their metaphorical graves, Brenda had never cradled them and gazed into their eyes like she had with Gail. This child may not have been her own flesh and blood but that mattered not a jot to Brenda, who viewed Gail's arrival in Moristoun as a miracle akin to the Immaculate Conception. She would be inconsolable if The Council snatched that divine child from her arms and Jimmy realised nothing he could say or do would be able to repair the damage. His own love for Brenda was just as strong as the emotional bond that had formed between his spouse and their prospective child but even he would be powerless to save her from eternal despair. Jimmy quickly realised he couldn't live without Brenda as he came to terms with her suicide back on the mainland and it wasn't long before depression and guilt combined to push him towards the act that led to their reunion in the afterlife. Farqhuar had insisted that Jimmy's arrival in Moristoun, rather than one of the other 15 islands, was a mere statistical coincidence and pointed out that he would have ended up on the shores of Arbus had a jilted bride from Kirkcaldy not paused for one final Hail Mary before throwing herself off the Kincardine Bridge. But Jimmy didn't believe in coincidences and knew fate had thrown them back together for a reason, with confirmation arriving many years later when Brenda burst through the doors of the Tortured Soul sporting the smile that Jimmy feared had been lost forever.

That smile would never return if Buchan was the bearer of bad news and Jimmy was feeling every bit as apprehensive and tense as Brenda as they awaited the lawyer's arrival. He had looked at every story on the first five pages of the Gazette but not one detail had stuck in his mind as the words failed to dislodge thoughts of Gail's future. The editor could even have splashed with the story "Pub landlord unmasked as a transvestite alien: Big Jimmy's big secret" and it wouldn't have raised an eyebrow. Only one story mattered to the Mathiesons this morning and that was The Council's verdict on the first baby to land in Moristoun. Every second felt like an eternity and the tension was becoming unbearable. Jimmy tried to escape from the mental torment by focussing afresh on his newspaper and turned to the sports section for the latest gossip on Moristoun's footballing heroes. He hoped this would be United's season after five years of playing second fiddle to Athletic but the headline "Simpson goes missing again – United's fears for Hughie" suggested it would be another miserable campaign for his side. Jimmy was halfway through a story that was depressingly familiar when Brenda broke the silence by screaming: "I can see him, Jimmy! Buchan's coming – and he's pushing the pram!" This discovery sparked Brenda into an even greater frenzy and she flew across the living room like a dervish before clambering down the stairs into the bar. Jimmy set off in pursuit and finally caught up with his wife as she attempted to unlock the bolts on the pub's front door. The speed at which Brenda approached this task only succeeded in making a simple task much more difficult and Jimmy had to step in to finish the job before blocking the door with his own imposing frame. "I don't want you rushing out on to the street," he told Brenda as she bounced up and down on the spot. "This is a private matter and we need to keep it behind closed doors. Yes, Buchan appears to be pushing Gail's pram up here but we still don't know what he's going to tell us. It could be bad news and we have to prepare for every eventuality."

"Not this time, Jimmy. I just know that baby is coming home for good. I can feel it in my bones, call it maternal instincts. For once, everything is going to be alright."

Jimmy could only pray that Brenda was right as Buchan banged twice on the door to signal his arrival. He turned round to open the door and was heartened to see the lawyer sporting a grin as Buchan pushed the pram into the Tortured Soul then stood to face them.

"The Council have delivered their verdict and I'm delighted to announce that you are now the proud parents of a baby girl," said Buchan. "The official term is actually legal guardians but that doesn't quite have the same ring, does it?"

Etiquette decreed that Buchan should congratulate the new mother first but Brenda had already made a beeline for the pram and was busy extracting her adoptive daughter from the comfort of her mobile home, so he instead turned to Jimmy and offered a handshake. Placing one's hand into Jimmy's mighty mitts always carried an element of risk and Buchan feared the excitement of the occasion would ensure the landlord's grip was even more formidable than usual. That trepidation did not prove unfounded and Buchan was relieved to find none of his bones had been shattered when he finally managed to extract his hand from Jimmy's grasp.

"I'm really pleased for you, Jimmy," he said. "I know how important this was for you both, especially Brenda."

The two men then paused for a moment to enjoy the sight of Brenda cradling Gail in one of the cubicles to the left of the bar. She was lost in a trance as she gazed into the baby's eyes and the eagerly anticipated rematch between Finn McCool and Benandonner could have been raging just a few feet away without Brenda even batting an eyelid.

"I can't even bear to think about what Brenda would have been like if we weren't allowed to keep the baby," said Jimmy. "She's been through so much pain already and having Gail taken away would have broken her spirit for good. How did you manage to persuade The Council to let the baby stay? You always told us not to get our hopes up."

"That was because The Council had never heard a case like Gail's before," said Buchan. "The change in legislation after Dr Barrett's report opened the door for us but I had no idea how The Council would react because there was no precedent. Young Gail is a pioneer, she will go down in Moristoun history."

"What exactly did The Council say when they passed down their verdict?" asked Jimmy. "I can't imagine they'll just leave us to our own devices. Are there any rules we need to stick to?"

"The most important one is that Gail must be ready to return before her 18th birthday. It's our job to prepare her for life on the mainland and The Council are happy to let us proceed at our own pace. However, they have set a limit. If she's still here on the morning she turns 18 then The Council will take matters into their own hands and send Gail back themselves."

Jimmy knew his wife's heart would be broken afresh on that date as Brenda had already formed an unbreakable bond with the child that now lay in her arms. She had spent only a few hours with Gail since that fateful first meeting in Buchan's living room but was clearly deeply in love. So Jimmy could only imagine how much heartache Brenda would suffer when forced to bid the child farewell after 18 years of attachment. Most parents went through a similar torment when their offspring flew the nest but they at least had the consolation of knowing their children would return sporadically during times of celebration or extreme penury. When Jimmy and Brenda waved Gail goodbye it would be in the knowledge that they would never see her again. There was only one way for their daughter to secure a return to Moristoun and Jimmy could only pray that Gail would avoid the misery and pain that had landed her adoptive parents on these shores. He would do everything in his power to ensure that Gail never felt the need to take her own life, no matter what fate threw at her back on the mainland. She had to be mentally prepared for every cruel twist in a world of endless possibilities and Jimmy was determined to make sure his own emotions didn't get in the way of what was best for the child. Moristoun was no place for the young and Brenda would simply have to accept that, if she truly loved Gail, she would set her free. That emotional storm was for another day, though, and Jimmy was happy to let his wife remain oblivious to future concerns as she enjoyed every tender moment of Gail's first day under their roof.

While Brenda went through her songbook of lullabies as she rocked Gail to sleep, Jimmy led Buchan towards the bar and invited him to take his pick from the delights in front of him as they prepared to wet the baby's head. "That's very kind of you, Jimmy," said Buchan as he pointed towards the bottle of malt whisky that provided most of his lubrication on visits to the Tortured Soul. "Are you joining me in a wee dram?"

"Oh, I'm a changed man these days," replied Jimmy. "The demon drink is no longer my master so I'll just get wired into an orange juice instead."

Buchan saluted Jimmy on his sobriety as they raised their glasses to Gail but it didn't quite seem right to see the landlord's hand dwarfing a tiny tumbler of orange juice instead of cradling a pint of stout. The feeling was akin to peeking inside Genghis Khan's tent and witnessing the mighty Mongol dress up his dollies while waiting for a vegan quiche to brown in the oven but Buchan was glad to learn that fatherhood was bringing about a change in Jimmy's habits.

"I can't return to my old ways now the baby is here," he told Buchan. "It wouldn't be fair to both Brenda and Gail. Alkies are bad news for babies – you won't see another drop pass my lips."

Buchan was impressed to see Jimmy display such an attitude to parenthood but doubted whether he could remain sober with so many temptations so close at hand. Moristoun was home to many an alcoholic and Buchan had yet to meet someone with the necessary willpower to resist a return to the comforting bosom of their addiction. Only those willing to read The Book stood a chance of conquering the earthly urges that had accompanied them to Moristoun and alkies found this assignment particularly irksome. Reading through a magnifying glass is difficult enough with a steady hand but when the shakes associated with a lengthy dependence on the bottle are factored into the equation, it becomes almost impossible. Buchan knew this from personal experience, after trying to tackle a chapter in Sanskrit on the morning after one of the Tortured Soul's legendary Burns' Suppers, and realised Jimmy would have to fight his battle without any spiritual backup. Writing off such a formidable man in any fight was also an act of folly, however, and Buchan had to concede Jimmy's huge heart and brute strength might prove enough to send his alcoholism sprawling to the canvas.

"I'm pleased to hear you've turned over a new leaf," said Buchan as he reached into his briefcase to fetch a manuscript that he planted down on the bar. "Both you and Brenda are going to need a clear head to make sense of these guidelines The Council have laid down. I've already told you the most important rule about Gail's upbringing but there are countless others you will need to learn over the coming weeks. Everything is written down here in black and white."

Buchan recognised the look of resigned despair that flashed across Jimmy's face as he picked up the manuscript because it appeared every night when McCall strolled through the pub's front door to take his pew alongside Henderson. Just as witnessing the standard of conversation descend to several tiers below the gutter was an inevitable consequence of accepting their custom, Jimmy realised he would have to defer to The Council's rulings if he wanted to become a father. A brief look at the first page confirmed Jimmy's fears that the manuscript would require much closer scrutiny than the Dick Francis novels he borrowed from the library so he placed the hefty tome back on the table before asking Buchan to provide a summary of the main points.

"I'm afraid it remains as much a mystery to me as it does to you," Buchan said. "The Council only handed the manuscript over after passing down their verdict so I haven't had a chance to read it yet. I've asked for a copy to be sent to my office so I'll have a proper look at all the guidelines then let you know what I make of it."

"But what should we do before we read all the guidelines? It will take a couple of days at least for us to get through all of this."

"I wouldn't worry too much," said Buchan as he turned to look at the Brenda and the baby, who had both now drifted off into the world of dreams. "Your wife seems to be something of a natural when it comes to motherhood. She's certainly doing a much better job than the biological mother when it comes to keeping the baby quiet. I'd swear it was a different child to the one whose howls echoed around Princes Street Gardens."

"What are we going to do about her real mum?" asked Jimmy. "What if she suddenly turns up and asks for her back."

"That will never happen. The unfortunate Frances Barr booked a ticket for Aterstoun when she stepped in front of that bus. Had she ended up in Moriston, The Council would never have agreed to let Gail stay here."

"Well, that's a relief," said Jimmy. "But what about the rest of the people here? Do we need to keep Gail hidden away from them?"

"The guidelines will go into far greater detail but I can't imagine we'll need to keep her under house arrest. Gail is just like any other Q101 and the only difference is she will be hanging around for longer. The Council have told everyone about her and the usual rules for a Q101 apply."

"So if anyone comes round asking questions, I don't need to make up some kind of cover story?"

"Honesty is always the best option, Jimmy. And you will have plenty of visitors when tomorrow's Gazette comes out. Gail has just become Moristoun's biggest celebrity."

# Chapter 11:

# Cupid draws back his bow

Sadness descended upon Brenda as she watched Gail put the finishing touches to her history homework at the living room table. While time stood still for the majority of Moristoun's citizens, the last 17 years had flown by for Brenda as she revelled in maternal duties that once seemed but a distant dream. Watching Gail develop into the confident young woman who sat before her had been the greatest pleasure of Brenda's existence but she had to grudgingly accept such joy was a finite commodity. The magic would soon be over and Brenda felt like a child unwrapping the final chocolate bar of a selection box as she faced up to the fact Gail would be gone in a matter of months. A better life awaited her daughter on the mainland but it tore Brenda apart that she wouldn't be around to share in the moments that made mortal existence so special. This seemed like the cruellest punishment attached to her own imprisonment in Moristoun but the pain of their separation was a price Brenda was willing to pay for 18 years of bliss she never thought she would experience. Self-pity had landed her in Moristoun and she now had to conquer such feelings to ensure Gail would never come close to suffering the same anguish. A university education would provide Gail with a better chance of avoiding the same fate as both her adoptive parents and her biological mother. As a former school mistress, Brenda was perfectly placed to deliver the knowledge Gail needed to take the step into tertiary education but home schooling had proved a considerable challenge for both teacher and pupil. The Scottish education system had evolved at an alarming rate since Brenda last stood in front of a blackboard and she had to mug up on subjects that seemed as alien to a 1930s schoolteacher as the concept violence wasn't the only way to restore order in the classroom. This, combined with the inevitable sparks that fly whenever mother and daughter spend so much time in each other's company, ensured Gail's tutoring proceeded at a slower pace than Brenda would have liked. However, she remained confident Gail would be ready to pass the entrance exam before she turned 18 if they both worked hard in the coming months. That was why her daughter remained deep in study beyond the usual 6 p.m. cut-off time instead of helping Jimmy behind the bar. Gail had spent the best part of two hours documenting Hitler's rise to power but her essay was now coming towards an end every bit as abrupt as the one that awaited the Fuhrer deep inside his bunker. Brenda could always tell when Gail was about to finish one of her assignments as a satisfied smile flashed across her face and the pace of her handwriting picked up for the final flourishes. Tonight was no different and Gail's homework ended up in Brenda's hands before a minute had elapsed.

"Can I go downstairs now to help Dad out?" said Gail as she handed over the assignment. "It's Happy Hour so I'm sure the place is filling up."

"Of course you can," replied Brenda. "But let your father do most of the work. You've done a lot of studying today and deserve a wee rest. I'll come down to help you both out once I've had a look at your homework."

McSorely was still feeling the effects of his titanic struggle with Munchkin as he walked towards the Tortured Soul with Buchan. He felt like Joe Frazier after the Thrilla In Manila but that analogy was probably unkind on Smokin Joe as McSorely had lost his fight in around 14 seconds while Frazier had slugged out 14 brutal rounds with Muhammad Ali before succumbing. With Munchkin declared the undisputed champion at the start of their walk, McSorely was left to chase the consolation prize of preserving his dignity by refusing to let the Deerhound drag him to the ground. He managed to win that battle over the next 40 minutes but McSorely had to exert every ounce of energy to stay on his feet. He felt like going straight to bed when Munchkin led him back through their front door only to decide that alcohol was a better cure for his aching body than seeing if his insomnia was still being held at bay.

"You'll certainly enjoy that first drink tonight," said Buchan as he watched McSorely struggle to keep pace on the short walk to the pub. "It has been quite a day. You look exhausted."

That was an understatement to rival Donald Rumsfeld's claim that "death has a tendency to encourage a depressing view of war" as McSorely could never have envisaged the events that had unfolded after he set foot on the train to Inverness. His mind had already been frazzled by the thrill ride of his final day in Glasgow but those extravagances now seemed mundanely normal compared to the surreal nature of his new life in Moristoun. After becoming the lodger of a beast plucked straight from the darkest recesses of Tolkien's mind, McSorely wouldn't have been surprised to open the doors of the pub and witness pirates arm-wrestling with bearded mermaids while Lord Lucan belted out Don't Get Around Much Anymore on the karaoke. Instead, he was treated to the sight of hardened drinkers staring blankly into their drinks as Patsy Cline provided a fitting backdrop by singing: "Now they are gone and I sit alone and watch one cigarette burn away."

"I hope you're a fan of country music," said Buchan as he led McSorely towards the bar. "It provides an almost constant soundtrack in this place, particularly when McTavish has plenty of loose change rattling around in his pockets."

"My tastes are rather more contemporary," replied McSorely. "But I can think of worse things to listen to. At least it's not heavy metal."

"I don't think you'll ever have to worry about hearing that in here," said Buchan as they reached the bar only to find nobody standing behind it. "Jimmy isn't a fan and only a brave or stupid man would risk incurring his wrath."

McSorely was about to ask Buchan to reveal the identity of this fearsome character but he was stopped in his tracks as Jimmy emerged from the back room to take his place behind the bar. It was hard for McSorely not to feel intimidated as the landlord leaned over the bar to envelop Buchan in a bear hug. His own introduction was now only seconds away and McSorely feared his broken body wouldn't be able to survive such an embrace while it continued to recover from the punishment dished out by Munchkin. Thankfully, Buchan was thinking along similar lines so he cautioned Jimmy to handle McSorely with care as he formally introduced his apprentice to the proprietor of Moristoun's finest watering hole.

"Young McSorely has just taken Munchkin for a walk, so he's feeling rather fragile," said Buchan. "While I'm sure he would appreciate the warmth and congeniality behind your trademark greeting, perhaps a handshake would be more appropriate on this occasion."

Those words ensured that only McSorely's right hand would suffer but the appendage would have little time to recover as it soon greeted the other patrons in close proximity. Henderson was the first of the bar flies to make his acquaintance and instructed Jimmy to furnish the new boy with a drink at his expense.

"If anyone deserves a drink it's you," he said. "I saw you struggling with the Hellhound out on Hancock Green. You looked a dead cert to fall on your arse, so fair play for managing to stay on your feet."

"That's very kind of you, Mr Henderson. I'll have a lager thanks. Do you have Stella on draft here?"

McSorely's enquiry brought a laugh out of everyone within earshot and Henderson added to their mirth by telling him: "The only Stella we have here is Stella MacPherson and you definitely don't want to be drinking her. She's that 20-stone heifer sitting in the far corner knitting a jumper."

McSorely's thoughts drifted once more to Edward Woodward and The Wicker Man as the locals enjoyed a laugh at his expense but Buchan then intervened to make him feel less ill at ease.

"Such smutty asides are an unfortunate consequence of sharing a bar with Henderson and his partner in crime McCall," said Buchan as McCall took a break from demolishing a packet of crisps and raised his glass to McSorely by way of introduction.

"They mean you no harm and are just amused by the idea that Belgium's finest brewers would ever sell their wares in this establishment."

"That's right," said McCall. "It's nothing personal. We just find it funny when someone from the mainland comes here and expects to find the same luxuries behind Jimmy's bar. At least you didn't ask for one of those wanky wee bottles with a bit of fruit floating around in it."

"What beers do you have then?" McSorely asked Jimmy, fearful that the swill produced by Tennent's and McEwan's would be his only source of lubrication in Moristoun.

"Everything here is produced locally so none of the names will be familiar to you," said Jimmy. "Nobody really uses brand names anyway. They just ask for a lager, a heavy, or a whisky."

McSorely wondered if he had travelled back in time to the 1950s as he agreed to try out a pint of the generic lager. He half-expected to see miners cloaked in soot sipping from pints of Guinness as he scanned the rest of the pub. A more aesthetically pleasing sight awaited him, however, when he switched his gaze back to the bar as Gail emerged from the back room to lend Jimmy a helping hand. McSorely had never believed in the concept of love at first sight and held those who espoused the idea in the same contempt as the saps who lined the pockets of psychics claiming to have a direct line to their rotting relatives. Something definitely stirred inside him, though, when his eyes met Gail's gaze for the first time. It was a feeling far above the lust that had surged through him upon meeting Carla, his expensive gift from Argentina, and McSorely lost the power of speech for a few seconds when Jimmy introduced his daughter. He eventually broke out of the spell her beauty had cast to mouth a few platitudes but

McSorely was so enchanted that he could barely remember any details of the ensuing conversation. The idea of playing the Edward Woodward role on this mysterious island suddenly seemed more attractive as McSorely began to fantasise about being seduced by the landlord's daughter. While Woodward's God-fearing policeman had somehow managed to resist the charms of Britt Ekland, McSorely would need little encouragement to bow to the temptations of the flesh. However, the look that Jimmy cast in his direction after Gail had finished welcoming McSorely soon dispelled any notion that such an event would come to pass. If anyone had been brave enough to attempt a conquest of her then they surely now resided deep in the ground or in the depths of the Atlantic Ocean.

"Gail is our pride and joy," said Jimmy, a statement that met with no dissent from Buchan, who shared in Jimmy's paternal pride, and the two barflies, who took a less wholesome joy from her daily presence in their lives. "It's going to break my heart when she leaves us to go to university on the mainland."

"What are you going to study, Gail?" asked McSorely. "If it's anything to do with computers I can pass on some advice. I've got a degree and used to work in IT."

"I want to do a history and philosophy degree at the Highlands and Islands University," replied Gail. "Mr Buchan has promised to set up an entrance exam before my 18th birthday next February. I think I'm ready for it already but Mum says I need to do more studying."

"Your mother is right," said Buchan. "No teenager enjoys spending endless hours with their head stuck in a textbook but it will be well worth it in the end. As Shakespeare put it, knowledge is the wing whereby we fly to heaven."

Gail gazed at Buchan in devotion as he delivered his latest sound bite and McSorely cursed the fact that his own education wasn't extensive enough to quote Shakespeare at the drop of the hat. While literature and poetry were handy weapons in the arsenal of budding Casanovas, the fairer sex were less impressed by intimate details of Linux and Random Access Memory. Revealing his past as an IT drone within seconds of meeting Gail was something of a schoolboy error and one of the few quotes he did have committed to memory immediately came to mind – "It is better to remain silent and be thought a fool than to open one's mouth and remove all doubt." McSorely couldn't even use that gem when trying to impress someone as he had picked it up from The Simpsons and didn't know who first uttered those famous words. All he could do was follow the sage advice and let others pick up the baton of conversation. It was McCall who grasped the opportunity and his query about Gail's day in the classroom led to a debate about the Third Reich and their cryptorchidic leader.

McTavish, the pub's elder statesman, had remained silent since the arrival of Buchan and McSorely as he went walking after midnight down memory lane with dear old Patsy. But Gail's mention of Hitler brought him to life and he said: "A nice girl like you shouldn't be reading about an evil old bastard like him. I lived through those dark days and nobody should want to relive them."

"Oh, I don't know about that," said Buchan. "Learning from past mistakes is the only way we can hope to have a brighter future."

"Nonsense," replied McTavish. "People have been studying history for centuries but things continue to get worse. We should have learned a lesson about the Germans from the First World War but we stood back and let that maniac whip them back up into a state of frenzy. Those bloody Jerries tried to finish me off twice but I managed to see the bastards off."

This hint that McTavish had lived through the two crowning moments of humanity's inhumanity made Buchan shift uneasily in his seat. Both his outstanding Q101s were in attendance and they would have been able to deduce that something was not quite right with McTavish's story by virtue of simple mathematics. The debilitating effects of alcohol dependence had ensured that McTavish was far from a sprightly 70-year-old but it was something of a stretch to imagine a telegram from the Queen took pride of place on his mantelpiece. Letting an awkward silence drift over the bar would only lead to more suspicion so Buchan quickly jumped in and tried to change the direction of the conversation.

"What about your philosophy homework, Gail?" he said. "Did you learn anything that opened your mind today?"

"Mum just went through a bit of Thomas Hobbes," Gail replied. "We only spent an hour or so looking at his theories but I need to go to the library tomorrow to read Leviathan."

"It's an intriguing book," said Buchan. "I like his theory that life without government would lead to a 'war of all against all'. That's certainly the case here in Moristoun. One can only imagine the chaos that would ensue if The Council didn't exert their considerable influence."

McSorely was surprised to see the others agree with Buchan's assertion as local politicians were held in such disdain back in Glasgow. While the regulars at his local dive in Govanhill were too apathetic about politics to debate the burning issues from Westminster and Holyrood, they enjoyed a good moan about matters that had a more obvious effect on their daily lives. Nobody in the Tortured Soul, however, was complaining about the preponderance of "towel heids", "gypsies" and giant potholes that could only be traversed successfully if one had the keys to a Sherman tank. Living in isolation had either fostered a strong sense of community spirit or The Council had broken new ground by becoming the first collection of politicians to put the needs of the populace above ego aggrandisement and profiteering.

"Is everyone here happy with the work of The Council?" McSorely asked what seemed to be an eclectic cross-section of Moristoun society. "Back in Glasgow, it's almost impossible to find anyone with a kind word to say about politicians. Why is it so different here?"

"Most fair-minded citizens can see The Council run things for the benefit of the people but we have our fair share of dissenters as well," said Buchan. "If everything was a bed of roses then both you and I would be out of a job."

"That's right," added Jimmy. "Crime's much lower than it is on the mainland but every now and then someone steps out of line."

"We even had an attempted murder last week," chipped in Gail. "A man called Hogg came at Mr McCall with a knife when he was walking home from here. He's lucky still to be alive."

This brought a chuckle out of McCall and he wished he could tell Gail why her words were so bitterly ironic. But he didn't fancy joining his assailant on a passage to damnation by committing a Category A offence so he merely shrugged and said: "What can I say? I must just be one of life's great survivors."

McSorely asked McCall for further details about his ordeal and had little cause to doubt his claim about being a great survivor after learning that Hogg had left him with 16 stab wounds. McCall was too embarrassed by his puny physique to show McSorely the majority of his cuts, especially with Gail looking on, but rolled up his sleeves to reveal two slashes on each arm.

"They're beginning to heal a bit but Dr Barrett says I'll be scarred forever," he told McSorely. "So I'll always be reminded of what that slimy wee bawbag did to me."

"What's going to happen to this Hogg then?" said McSorely. "Is he going to jail?"

"You're going to become much more familiar with Hogg's story," said Buchan. "As the public defender, it's my duty to represent him in court when the case comes to trial. Helping me prepare will be your first duty as my assistant. I've arranged a meeting with Hogg for tomorrow afternoon. You can talk through the case with him and give me some ideas on how we can proceed."

Conversing with a cold-blooded assassin wasn't what McSorely had imagined for the first day of his new legal career as he thought Buchan would ease him in gently with some filing or essential reading. However, his apprehension mingled with pride that his new boss would trust him with such a key task. If Buchan wanted to throw him in at the deep end then McSorely was keen to prove he didn't need water wings.

"I'd be honoured to help with such an important assignment," he said, not realising that Hogg's cut-and-dried case was a waste of Buchan's time and energy. "But isn't there a conflict of interest given the fact I'm now enjoying a pint with the victim?"

McSorely's attempt to sound like a bona-fide member of the legal profession elicited more laughs from the locals and Jimmy said: "You've been watching too much TV, son. I'm sure Buchan has already told you things work in a different way here on Moristoun. The only way to maintain your privacy here is to live like a hermit and never set foot outside your house. Secrets don't stay secret for long in Moristoun."

"Where can I find this Hogg, then?" said McSorely. "Is he banged up in jail?"

"We only have a small police station on the island," said Buchan. "That's where Hogg will reside until his case comes to court. If he loses he will be banished from Moristoun forever."

# Chapter 12 –

# The Prisoner

Hogg never thought he would pine for the duty of cleaning Moristoun's toilets but it now seemed infinitely more attractive than the prospect of spending another second in his cell. A week had elapsed since his attack on McCall and the solitude of confinement was driving him around the bend. Hogg's only contact with the outside world had come with the trip to Buchan's office but that brief flash of freedom only darkened his mood further as the hopelessness of his case was laid bare. The tears that had sparked such a furious response from Farqhuar continued to flow over the next few days as Hogg handled the stress of life behind bars with the same grace under pressure as a Big Brother contestant charged with controlling the Hadron Collider as the weekly shopping task. However, that blubbering was only permitted to continue unchecked when Hogg was left alone inside the police station as such emotional outbursts were brought to an abrupt end whenever Sergeant McLeish was in earshot. His approach to prisoner relations had its roots in the Middle Ages and one expletive-laden burst of his guttural Glaswegian was enough to cow Hogg into silence. Tales of Sergeant McLeish's suppression of prisoner dissent were legendary and Hogg didn't want to test the veracity of those rumours. He may have been regarded as one of the biggest fools in Moristoun, with his attack on McCall providing the wags with further ammunition, but Hogg wasn't that stupid. Even Big Jimmy wouldn't fancy his chances in a fight with the barrel-chested policeman, an abomination who hinted at the horrors awaiting Moristoun's citizens if they ever stepped out of line. Indeed,

Hogg found it hard to imagine anything more chilling could lie in store if he lost his case. He felt the hairs on the back of his neck stand up whenever Sergeant McLeish wandered within 20 feet of his cell and on this occasion that advertised his jailer's presence a few seconds before he appeared in front of the bars.

"I've got a nice surprise for you," Sergeant McLeish told Hogg in a tone that suggested this surprise would only be nice on his own sadistic terms. This time, though, there was no malice to the policeman's words and Hogg began to realise even a request for tea and scones would sound like a spine-chilling threat when tumbling from Sergeant McLeish's lips. "Buchan has arranged for his new assistant to come down to the station for a little chat with you. He'll be here in a few minutes so get your arse in gear and make this cell look less like a fucking pigsty."

Hogg jumped off his stony mattress at that command and set about tidying his quarters with a speed that would have impressed even the most pernickety of drill sergeants. While he was engaged in the task of assembling his meagre possessions into a more appealing arrangement, Sergeant McLeish began to answer some of the questions that had popped into Hogg's head.

"Buchan's assistant goes by the name of McSorely and he's a Q101," the policeman said. "So you hopefully won't need me to remind you certain topics of conversation are off limits. You will be fucked even harder by my good friend Farqhuar in court if another Category A offence is added to your rap sheet. I will also be far from amused if you reveal any of Moristoun's secrets while you are pouring your heart out. I've been Mr Fucking Mellow in my dealings with you so far – you definitely don't want to see Mr Angry put in an appearance. Do I make myself clear, you worm-infested piece of shite?"

When faced with such aggression, Hogg always found it wise to keep his mouth shut in case anything he said led to another eruption. However, testing Sergeant McLeish's patience with a question about the forthcoming meeting was less risky than incurring his wrath by divulging any unwanted information to McSorely, so Hogg summoned the courage to quiz his jailer.

"What can I talk to this McSorely about?" he said. "Does he know anything about Moristoun?"

"Of course he doesn't, you fuckwit," said Sergeant McLeish. "He's a Q101 and, from what Buchan has told me, he has only been here for a day. So I'm pretty sure he thinks we're just a nice wee island with a few mental inhabitants. It's our job to make sure it stays that way before he returns to the mainland."

"So I can talk to him about my case, then? If Buchan thinks this guy is up to the task of being his assistant then maybe he can help me win in court."

Hogg's misguided optimism brought a snort from Sergeant McLeish and he took great pleasure in planting a boot atop the prisoner's dream just seconds after it was conceived.

"Stop talking shite," he growled. "We both know there's no chance of you weaselling out of this one. Buchan just wants to keep this McSorely occupied so his thoughts don't turn back towards topping himself. He's only letting him handle your case because it's total a waste of time."

Job satisfaction was a concept that had remained alien to McSorely during his time in the IT trade. The pleasure derived from playing with computers as a teenager had conned him into believing working with them would be the most entertaining way to make a living. By the time this idea was exposed as being hopelessly naive, McSorely was already two years into his computing degree and hurtling towards a career written out in the monochrome of binary. It was too much of an exaggeration to say McSorely hated his life in the IT sector as he was no more depressed and unfulfilled than the hundreds of other suited monkeys trapped in their corporate cages. His job was relatively easy and delivered a decent wage so McSorely was genuinely upset when that devious bastard Robert Harrington directed his computer to amputee sex orgy and set his sacking in motion. But the joy of heading to work with a spring in your step was something McSorely had never experienced back on the mainland. Genuine excitement was thin on the ground, with salacious office gossip providing the only intrigue for those whose dreams were left to decay behind computer terminals. As he set off on his first assignment as a legal assistant, though, McSorely felt a surge of adrenalin flow through him. He would soon come face to face with a man who had only avoided becoming a cold-blooded killer due to McCall's remarkable survival instincts and McSorely was gripped by both fear and exhilaration as he walked into the police station. The figure who greeted him needed no introduction as Buchan's description of Sergeant McLeish – "a granite outhouse that would survive an apocalyptic hurricane" – had already painted a vivid picture. It was clear Buchan had little time for the policeman, whom he considered an unhinged boor, and it angered him that The Council let such a vicious character play a key role in Moristoun's governance. "As the great Ghandi once said, the pursuit of truth does not permit violence on one's opponent," he told McSorely. "Unfortunately, our chief administrator Farquhar sees things rather differently and views our psychotic policeman as crucial to maintaining law and order."

McSorely could see why Farquhar held the policeman in such high esteem as just a few seconds in Sergeant McLeish's company induced a feeling of genuine terror. The sheer size of the man was enough to sow seeds of doubts in the mind of potential criminals but McSorely found his voice even more unsettling. Sergeant McLeish sounded like a man who worked his way through a cigarette machine each day before rounding off his preparations for bed by gargling with gravel. His habit of peppering every sentence with expletives added to the menace and he was particularly expressive when it came to the subject of his prisoner. "This wee prick shouldn't cause you any bother," he told McSorely as he led him towards Hogg's cell. "He might have been brave enough to have a go at McCall but he's actually a spineless shitebag. I've told him not to step out of line and he's such a fucking coward that you'll be treated like royalty."

McSorely was relieved to discover Moristoun's police station came equipped with just three cells, two of which lay empty, as he had feared running the same gauntlet as Jodie Foster in the Silence of the Lambs. However, even if McSorely had been forced to walk past a series of rabid degenerates before reaching his destination, the chances of him receiving the same repulsive face cream would have been non-existent. Nobody would have dared to indulge in self-pollution on Sergeant McLeish's watch as such a foolish act would have surely led to their member being pulverised by a truncheon. Hogg certainly didn't look like a man who was brave enough to risk the ire of his captor and McSorely found it hard to believe such a pitiful figure had come within a few centimetres of murder. The prisoner was curled up in the foetal position on his mattress when McSorely first set eyes on him but he was soon on as his feet as Sergeant McLeish rattled his truncheon off the bars and bellowed: "Get to your feet you snivelling little fucker. Your visitor is here." Hogg responded to the command like the star pupil of a canine obedience school then stood alert as he waited for his master's next call. That arrived just seconds later and Hogg followed the instruction to park his "scrawny arse" down at the table to the left of his bed. He was soon joined there by McSorely before Sergeant McLeish took his leave with an icy stare and the words: "Remember what we talked about earlier, sunshine. You better be on your best fucking behaviour."

McSorely felt like offering Hogg some sympathy over his captivity at the hands of such a sadist but decided against voicing any dissent of Sergeant McLeish's methods. Moristoun's answer to Judge Dredd may have been out of sight but he was probably still listening to every word and McSorely didn't want to make an enemy of such a powerful figure on his first day in the legal profession. It was best to keep matters on a purely professional level so he started off by asking Hogg to run him through the events of May 17.

"It all kicked off after McCall turned up at my work," Hogg said. "He always comes there to take a dump, even though he could do it at his own office or house."

Even by the strange standards Moristoun had set since McSorely's arrival, this daily deed of defecation seemed outrageously incongruous. Although most people would mark McCall down as a filthy creature within seconds of setting eyes on him, it was hard to imagine him plotting a course for an enemy's place of work whenever the turtle's head started to peek out of his bony backside. McSorely found himself relieved, therefore, when Hogg revealed he worked as a lavatory attendant.

"It's not the most respectable of jobs and that bastard took great pleasure in reminding me of that fact," he said. "Each day brought another wee dig and there's only so much a man can take."

"What did he say on this particular occasion?" asked McSorely. "It must have been pretty bad if it made you want to kill him."

"McCall started mouthing off about every man being a product of his environment. He then told me I was slowly turning into a massive shite. The exact words were: 'That giant toley I've left as a present in trap three bears more than a striking resemblance to you'."

"So what happened after he said that? Did you just go for him?"

"I'm afraid so. I usually ignore him but this time I lost the rag and flew at McCall. I managed to get a good few punches in before he started fighting back."

McSorely wouldn't have liked to wager on the winner of a bout between Hogg and McCall as they were both pitiful physical specimens. Hogg's shortcomings were of a more literal nature to his lanky nemesis as he was short and stubby, standing no more than 5ft 4in. He probably packed more power than McCall but was at a significant disadvantage when it came to reach.

"Who won the fight?" asked McSorely. "Did you come back later with the knife because he gave you a doing?"

"I'd say it was a draw," said Hogg. "We went at it for a few minutes before Big Jimmy heard all the commotion and came inside to break the fight up."

It wouldn't have taken Jimmy long to restore order and McSorely imagined him plucking Hogg away from the melee by merely gripping his collar between forefinger and thumb. With Jimmy acting as a peacekeeper there was little chance of war breaking out again so McSorely asked Hogg to expand on how the drama unfolded later that day.

"I had calmed down a little by the time I went for a drink at the Tortured Soul after work," he said. "But McCall then turned up and all that anger started bubbling to the surface."

"What did he say to set you off again?"

"It was nothing particular at first. He was just being McCall. That's enough to make me angry at the best of times. Have you met that bastard yet?"

"Only briefly. I bumped into him at the pub last night when Buchan was introducing me to everyone. I didn't speak with him long enough to form a proper impression."

"Don't worry, you'll soon find out what a lowlife he is. McCall and his pal Henderson sit at that bar every night spouting filth. They should be ashamed of themselves. Some of the things they say about young Gail are outrageous."

McSorely's ears pricked up at Hogg's mention of Gail as she had taken a firm grip of his thoughts since the previous evening. But it now seemed he wasn't the only one with a keen interest in her, a fact that became clear as Hogg continued his attack on the Tortured Soul's resident barflies.

"That poor wee lassie only turned 17 earlier this year but that doesn't stop those two scumbags from shooting their dirty mouths off whenever big Jimmy isn't around. They've been at it since she was just 14 or 15. It's shameful."

McSorely noted these details down with interest as painting McCall as a potential paedophile in court might help Hogg's case. However, he found it hard to believe McCall and Henderson could verbally defile Gail for three years without incurring the wrath of her father.

"They get away with it because they're a couple of sleekit rats," said Hogg. "But one of these days they will slip up and get skinned. I'd give anything to be there when Jimmy catches them red-handed but I'll never step through the doors of that pub again unless Buchan and your good self can pull a rabbit out of the hat."

"You must try to stay positive, Mr Hogg," said McSorely. "Buchan's a very smart man. I'm sure he'll have a few tricks up his sleeve by the time you end up in the dock."

"That's not what he told me. When I last saw him a few weeks ago Buchan seemed to think I didn't stand a chance of winning."

"Oh, I'm sure he didn't mean that. He probably just didn't want you to get your hopes up. I can assure you Buchan is taking your case seriously. That's why he hired me. You now have two people working on your case – I don't think that would happen if it was a lost cause."

Hogg was far from convinced by McSorely's words as Sergeant McLeish had made a much more forceful argument just moments before his new legal adviser breezed into the prison on a wind of optimism. However, he was unsure if pointing out the futility of McSorely's assignment fell into the category of conversation that would lead to a vicious beating and decided to keep his own counsel.

"Once I know all the details of your case, I'll be able to pass on my advice to Buchan," said McSorely. "Can you tell me what happened in the pub that night to force you into the attack?"

"It was when McCall started talking about our fight that I really saw red. He told Henderson about his theory I was turning into a turd and said he had decided to call it his Scatological Imperative. Henderson then claimed that was appropriate because I was a bit of a Kant and that left them in stitches. I didn't have a clue what they were talking about and that made me even madder."

"Did you run across and have another go at McCall then?"

"Not at first. I just sat there slowly stewing but I couldn't hold back my anger any more when he banged on about the fight itself. McCall made it sound like I was taking a pummelling until Jimmy stepped in. When he said I cried for mercy like a battered bride it was the final straw. I hurled my pint glass at the bastard."

"Did you hit him?"

"Sadly not. I didn't get enough purchase on the throw and it smashed off the bottom of the barstool instead. Jimmy was far from amused and I was soon escorted off the premises. I was determined to get that bastard back, though, so I raced home and armed myself with a kitchen knife. Then it was just a matter of waiting for closing time and surprising McCall on his way home."

McSorely may have been new to the legal profession but he had watched enough episodes of Taggart and Inspector Morse to realise why Buchan had told Hogg his chances of avoiding a long stretch at her Majesty's pleasure were slim. The motive and murder weapon were already established and Hogg had twice assailed his victim in front of witnesses before attempting to deliver the coup de grace. Still, if OJ Simpson's lawyers had managed to hurdle the considerable barriers of a bloodied glove and televised police pursuit, then all hope wasn't lost. Maybe the doomed, diminutive figure sitting in front of him could slip through the tiniest of legal loopholes.

"Well, thanks for being so honest with me, Mr Hogg," said McSorely. "It's important to get everything out in the open so there's nothing the prosecution can surprise us with in court."

"Has Buchan told you who we're up against yet?" replied Hogg.

"Not yet. Why is that important?"

"Farqhuar himself is taking charge of my case so I hope Buchan and yourself are up to challenge. He's not a man to be messed with."

Having heard Buchan mention Farqhuar in the same breath as Sergeant McLeish, McSorely had no reason to doubt Hogg's assertion. Buchan hadn't gone into further detail about Moristoun's chief administrator, though, so McSorely pressed Hogg for further details.

"He has plenty of power and influence in Moristoun," said Hogg. "Buchan told me he's the last man you want to see in a courtroom when you're standing in the dock. There's no messing around with a man like Farqhuar, he's ruthless."

Each additional piece of information was hammering another nail in Hogg's coffin and McSorely's earlier optimism was fading fast. However, he still managed to put on a brave face when Hogg asked him for an honest assessment of his chances.

"I'm not going to lie to you, Mr Hogg, your case does sound like a considerable challenge. But nothing is impossible and I'll explore every nook and cranny in search of something that can help us surprise this Farqhuar. Do you have any suggestions about where I should start looking?"

"The Book is the only thing that can save me," said Hogg. "If you speak nicely to the new librarian she might let you take a peek at it."

"The Book? What's that?"

Hogg did answer McSorely's question but his words were drowned out by the sound of Sergeant McLeish's truncheon rattling along the bars of the cell. As he met the stare of the enraged policeman and felt panic assault his senses, Hogg realised what a blunder he had made. Any talk of The Book was strictly off limits with a Q101 and Hogg was now destined to discover why Sergeant McLeish had built up such a harrowing reputation.

"Visiting time is fucking over," Sergeant McLeish shouted. "You've had your five minutes of greetin' and I'm sure Mr McSorely doesn't want to break the rules by outstaying his welcome on his first day."

"We were just finishing off when you banged your truncheon on the bars," said McSorely. "But the noise you made drowned out Hogg's answer to my final question. Can you let him answer again before I head back to the office?"

"No I fucking can't. Rules are rules, McSorely. People who break them end up behind bars like this degenerate bawbag. Now gather up your notes and sling your hook before I start to lose my temper."

McSorely was under the impression Sergeant McLeish had already lost his temper and didn't want to be around when the brooding menace on the other side of the bars shed what he considered to be a calm exterior. Hogg, unfortunately, did not have the same luxury of beating a hasty retreat and McSorely could tell his client wouldn't be able to retreat from a hasty beating when left alone with his captor. As he bid Hogg farewell and followed Sergeant McLeish out of the detention area, McSorely couldn't help but think the timing of the policeman's intervention was no co-incidence. There had been no mention of a time limit when Sergeant McLeish let McSorely into the cell so why was their meeting brought to such an abrupt end? It must have been something to do with the mysterious book Hogg had mentioned. McSorely had no idea why one tome could prove so important but maybe Buchan could shed some light on the matter back at the office.

# Chapter 13 –

# Book smarts

Buchan guessed something had gone wrong when McSorely walked back into the office just 15 minutes after embarking on his first assignment. Hogg had wasted almost an hour of Buchan's own time blubbering like a child so he found it hard to imagine a man starved of company since that meeting would dry up after a couple of questions. McSorely was either inept as an interviewer or had managed to light Sergeant McLeish's notoriously short fuse by deviating from the suggested script. If the latter had transpired then McSorely was likely to wear same haunted look as someone who had just been asked to deliver the best man's speech at Stalin's wedding but it was curiosity rather than terror that was written across his face. "You're back early," said Buchan as McSorely placed the case notes on his desk before sitting down. "I was expecting your interview with Hogg to last at least an hour. What happened?"

"Sergeant McLeish happened," replied McSorely. "Just when Hogg was about to tell me something interesting, he burst in and told me the five minutes of visiting time were over. Does he have the power to do that?"

"As a member of Hogg's legal team you were entitled to spend as long as you wanted with him so McLeish was wrong to eject you so early. Unfortunately, brutes like him believe they have the power to do anything they wish."

"Yeah, I guessed Sergeant McLeish wasn't the kind of man who took kindly to debating the intricacies of law."

"You would have more luck arguing over theological determinism with the chief torturer of the Spanish Inquisition.

The only way to deal with McLeish is to take things to a higher level by speaking to his superiors. I'll get in touch with Farqhuar and set up a longer meeting for next week. You can continue where you left off.

"Hogg mentioned something called The Book just seconds before we were rudely interrupted. He said it was his only hope. Do you know what he was talking about? I'm beginning to wonder if that had something to do with my early exit."

Buchan had been banking on Hogg's obsequiousness ensuring that McSorely would remain ignorant of Moristoun's many mysteries so he was taken aback by this mention of The Book. While there was never any danger of McSorely finding out the secrets hidden behind locked doors at the library – he came from a generation that balked at reading any book over 200 pages in their own language – trouble could only ensue if his apprentice started making further enquiries. His curiosity, therefore, had to be snuffed out as quickly as the inquisitiveness of a child who wonders what will happen if he kicks that missile-shaped appendage hanging down from the family Labrador.

"You must have misheard Hogg," Buchan said. "He probably said 'books' instead of 'book' and if that was the case I certainly agree with him. You will need to become accustomed to the finer points of law and philosophy if we are to come up with a plan to save our client. The library is stocked with some of the finest tomes ever written. The Council are determined to ensure every citizen can broaden their mind if they wish."

"I'm pretty sure Hogg was talking about just one book. He even said the new librarian might let me take a peek at it. I don't think there can be any confusion between the plural and the singular there."

Buchan could only curse Hogg's stupidity as he became charged with the task of digging his way out of an even bigger hole. He had initially thought McSorely's ejection from the police station was just another example of Sergeant McLeish's heavy-handedness but Buchan could now see why the meeting with Hogg had been brought to such a hasty conclusion. Had the buffoon been allowed to open his mouth for just a few minutes longer, he would probably have revealed all of Moristoun's secrets and Buchan could only wonder what horrors Sergeant McLeish would unleash from his bottomless bag of cruelty when dishing out Hogg's punishment.

"Well, if that's the case, I have no idea what Hogg was going about," said Buchan, trying his best to hide the panic building inside. "I've been going to that library for years and I've never heard anyone talk about this book. Hogg didn't mention it to me when we had our initial meeting and we spoke for almost an hour so I find it strange he should bring it up after just a few minutes with you. Maybe he's starting to go mad. Being held in the iron fist of Sergeant McLeish has sent much better men round the bend."

McSorely had little experience dealing with mental health issues, although some would contend he spent every Saturday in the company of those crazy enough to follow Albion Rovers religiously, but he was sure Hogg hadn't yet lost all of his marbles. Life behind bars may have broken his spirit but the lights were definitely still on upstairs.

"I still think we should at least try to find out if this book actually exists," said McSorely. "If Hogg believes it is his only salvation then I would be failing in my duty if I didn't try to seek it out."

"Very well," said Buchan. "But I think you're about to embark on a wild goose chase. You can pop round to the library now if you so wish. I was going to take you there this afternoon anyway to meet the delightful Ms McLoughlin. She's the new librarian Hogg told you about. Maybe she can help you find this mystical book."

Karen cursed the humble social standing of her parents as she grew increasingly frustrated with the Latin textbook. Had they been wealthy enough to send her to a private school then she may have already ticked off at least two of the languages needed to master to decipher The Book. One of the conditions of continuing as a librarian in her new world had been a commitment to reading the daunting tome and she was determined to complete the task in as short a time as possible. That seemed but a distant dream as she struggled to conjugate her verbs, however, and Karen was relieved when the phone rang and she was given a brief respite from her studies.

"Moristoun library, how can I help you?" she said in a weary tone that betrayed her academic toils.

"Hello Karen, it's William Buchan here. How are you this morning?"

"I've had better days, Mr Buchan. I'm still mugging up on my Latin and things are going far from smoothly."

"I'm afraid you'll just have to keep at it, my dear. As Charles Spurgeon once said, 'By perseverance the snail reached the ark.' It took me 14 years to read The Book once I started studying so you've just taken the first few steps in a marathon."

"Fourteen years? How did you summon up the strength to keep going? Most people would have chucked it after a couple of months."

"Time is irrelevant here, you'll find that out soon enough. All I can say is that the greatest waste of one's time is not even attempting to tackle The Book. It's a trap so many of our fellow citizens fall into."

"Don't you worry, Mr Buchan, I'm determined to stay at it. I like a challenge."

"That's good news because I have another one for you."

"That sounds intriguing. I'm all ears."

Buchan then informed Karen of Hogg's unfortunate slip of the tongue and stressed the urgency of feigning ignorance of the library's most precious item when McSorely started his enquiries.

"My new assistant is a Q101, just like young Gail Mathieson," he said. "Do you remember what they told you about dealing with her in your induction?"

"Of course I do, Mr Buchan," Karen replied. "It was only a few weeks ago. Gail has been here a few times already and there has never been a problem. She's here at the moment actually, leafing through Thomas Hobbes' Leviathan."

"Dealing with McSorely is likely to be more demanding," Buchan said. "Gail doesn't question her surroundings because she was brought up here but McSorely has just arrived from the mainland and is already beginning to get suspicious. You will have to tread carefully."

Karen didn't have any time to prepare for McSorely's arrival as she spotted a stranger walking through the main door just as Buchan was bidding her farewell. She was hoping the new arrival would be something of a looker as most of the men she had met in Moristoun so far made members of a leper colony look like more viable sexual partners. Indeed, the first potential suitor to introduce himself – a reptilian creature called McCall – was so repulsive that Karen felt a powerful urge to empty her stomach within seconds of setting eyes on him. McSorely was much more presentable but the overwhelming feeling was still disappointment as Karen ran a quick eye over him. Six months of toil in the gym would probably be enough to turn him into boyfriend material as he lacked any obvious deformity and had probably just let himself go in the last few years. At the moment, though, McSorely was hardly the kind of man who set feminine pulses racing.

"Good afternoon, sir. How can I help you?" said Karen. "Is this your first time in the library? I haven't seen you here before."

"It is. Let me introduce myself. My name is James McSorely and I'm Mr Buchan's new legal assistant."

"It's a pleasure to meet you. Mr Buchan told me you would be popping in at some point. Are you here to join the library?"

"It's actually a business call. One of our clients, a Mr Hogg, is up on an attempted murder charge and he told me something called 'The Book' was his only chance of acquittal. Buchan said he didn't know what Hogg was talking about so I was hoping you could shed some light on the matter."

"The Book? That's a bit vague. As you can see, Mr McSorely, this is a library. We have rather a lot of books. Wasn't he any more specific?"

"No. He just referred to it as The Book. I was hoping you would know what he meant because Hogg told me: 'If you're nice to the new librarian she might let you take a peek at it'."

With McCall and Henderson busy at their respective workplaces, the innuendo in McSorely's sentence was allowed to pass unnoticed. A blush still came to Karen's face, though, as she always became flustered when engaged in the act of deceit.

"I'm afraid I don't have a clue what he was talking about," she said. "I've only been here a few weeks and I'm still getting acquainted with all the books. My predecessor Miss Sanderson might have been able to help you. Buchan told me that she had read every book here."

"Do you know where I can find her?"

"Oh, you're a bit late for that. She passed to the other side a couple of months ago."

"Is there anyone else you can think of who might be able to help me? Finding this book could help us win his case."

"I can't, sorry. Buchan is probably the best-read man in Moristoun so if he hasn't heard of this book then I doubt if anyone else has. Feel free to have a look about the library, though. You might find something that gives you a bit of inspiration."


McSorely began to wonder if Hogg was indeed a babbling crackpot as he started to wander around the vast library. While Sergeant McLeish would no doubt take great pleasure from crushing Hogg's last hope of freedom, it was hard to see what Buchan and the librarian had to gain from lying about The Book's existence. The sanity of anyone who turned into a knife-wielding maniac also had to be called into question and McSorely realised he had painted far too positive a picture of Hogg. He wanted to think of his client as a tragic, downtrodden figure so he could emerge as a hero by helping win Hogg's freedom. Now, though, he was beginning to view the accused as a violent, delusional nutcase. The early optimism of his first day as a legal assistant was quickly fading but McSorely's mood brightened when he reached the end of the first aisle and spotted Gail deep in study at a table to the right. She looked even more beautiful with her reading glasses on and McSorely was thrilled to find her alone as it gave him the chance to repair the damage of his lame conversation from the previous evening. The smell of Gail's perfume added to McSorely's intoxication as he approached the table after grabbing a book randomly off the shelf. It had been brutally overpowered by the masculine smells of a bustling boozer when they first met but the library was thankfully free from smoke, hops and that mysterious aroma from within a packet of dry roasted peanuts that defies description. McSorely breathed in the delightful fragrance surrounding Gail before sitting down at the table and making his second attempt at forming a good impression.

"That must be a good book, Gail," he said. "You were so wrapped up in it you barely noticed me sitting down."

"Oh, hello, Mr McSorely. How are you? Sorry I didn't see you there. There's some pretty complicated stuff in the book and it's easy to get lost if you don't give it your full attention."

"Please, call me James. Mr McSorely makes me feel so old and I've only just waved goodbye to my twenties. The memory of cramming for my own exams hasn't quite faded yet. What subject are you working on today?"

"Philosophy. I'm reading Leviathan, the book I was talking about with Mr Buchan last night. It's hard going in places so I'm glad you've arrived to give me a wee break. What are you reading yourself? Can I have a look?"

Had McSorely been more practised in the art of conversing with beautiful women, he would have checked the title of the tome he had plucked from the shelf before handing it over for inspection. Unfortunately, he was still at the stage of instantly complying with every request from luscious lips without giving a second's thought to the consequences.

"The Velvet Rage by Dr Alan Downs," said Gail as she took the book from McSorely's grasp and read the title out aloud. Had McSorely picked a work that was well known within the literary community, discovering the title and author might have been enough to satisfy Gail's curiosity. The Velvet

Rage, alas, was obscure enough to force the casual reader to check the sub-heading and blurb to gain a better understanding of the text.

"Overcoming the pain of growing up gay in a straight man's world," said Gail as she read the sub-heading before flipping the book over in search of further information. "Therapist Alan Downs describes how growing up gay in a straight world contributes to shame, self-hate and internalized homophobia later in life. Downs claims this sense of rejection can lead to unloving feelings and addiction. Well, that certainly sounds like an interesting read, Mr McSorely. What made you pick this book from the thousands on offer?"

McSorely now found himself in a similar trap to the tortured teens who agonised between trying to feign interest in the opposite sex to satisfy their peer group or bowing to the raging torrents of their lust. Even though he knew telling the truth was the best way to avoid constructing a house of cards that could come crashing down at any point, McSorely couldn't live with the shame of admitting he was so desperate to join Gail that he had merely picked up the nearest book. Admitting he had sought out the Velvet Rage was the best course of action and McSorely racked his brains in search of a story that would convince Gail he wasn't personally trying to overcome the pain of growing up gay in a straight man's world.

The awkward silence that usually reins whenever middle-class parents watch their offspring clamber out of the closet descended over the library for what felt like an eternity before McSorely eventually found some inspiration.

"This book could actually prove crucial with the case I'm working on," he said. "I'm trying to gain a better understanding of Mr Hogg's psyche and I think the Velvet Rage will help to unlock a few doors."

"You think Hogg is gay?" said Gail. "He never mentioned that to anyone before. Did he confess to you in jail or something?"

"Not in as many words but I think he's just too ashamed to admit it. I have a few gay friends back in Glasgow and there's something about Hogg that makes me think he might be a closet homosexual."

"It would certainly cause a stir if that came out at his trial," said Gail. "Do you have any evidence to back up your suspicions?"

"Not yet but he does work as a lavatory attendant. If Hogg is that way inclined then he is ideally placed to pick up those of a similar persuasion. There might even be more to this attack on McCall than people think."

"What do you mean? You're not trying to suggest they were having it off with each other, are you?"

"I don't think we can rule it out. Crimes of passion have left many a man behind bars. Maybe Hogg attacked McCall in a jealous rage."

McSorely was the kind of person who usually felt uneasy engaging in deceit. Indeed, he often felt guilty when filling in the section that dealt with supporting organised crime on those irritating airplane forms one has to complete before landing in a foreign country. Having regularly handed over £2 to the ragamuffins who "mind yer car, mister" in the streets surrounding football grounds, it was clear he had been a willing participant in a protection racket. McSorely, therefore, was always plagued by minor pangs of guilt every time he ticked the box that asserted his conscience was clear with regards to Mafiosos. Any shame he felt over churning out far more blatant lies about Hogg and McCall was instantly wiped out, though, when McSorely saw how entertained Gail was by his outlandish story. She was hanging on his every word as the power of salacious gossip asserted itself over the wise words of Thomas Hobbes. There was no going back now, McSorely had to embrace his deceit with the same passion he longed to show Gail if he ever held her in his arms.

"Hogg has even admitted McCall visited him almost every day at his work," he said. "Don't you find that a bit strange?"

"I suppose it's a bit weird but McCall only does that to wind Hogg up. He spends hours dreaming up his insults with

Henderson at the pub. I also find it hard to believe McCall could be gay. He's always talking about women and never wastes a chance to flirt with me."

"Maybe he's just doing that to disguise his true sexual urges. The fact he advertises his fondness for the ladies so blatantly might suggest he has something to hide. Have you ever actually seen him with a girlfriend?"

"I haven't but that's probably because no self-respecting woman would touch him with a barge pole. He's hardly a looker and you'd get more stimulating conversation out of a mime artist."

Gail then steered this particular chinwag towards McSorely's own romantic history and the fact she asked if there was "someone" special in his life suggested the doubts raised by the Velvet Rage had yet to subside.

"Had things turned out differently, I would have been a married man by now," McSorely told her. "I was engaged to a woman called Sarah but she walked out on me about six months ago."

"I'm so sorry," said Gail. "You must have been devastated."

"It was hard but, if I'm being honest, it had been on the cards for a while. We had been drifting apart and I didn't try hard enough to patch things up."

"What was your fiancée like?"

"Sarah was nice but also quite cold. She never really opened up to anyone. I lived with her for a couple of years but even I never managed to get through her defences."

"What's she doing now? Do you still keep in touch?"

"Sarah dumped me for some high-flier at her work, a chinless wonder called Damien Jones. She lives with him now. I have her address but I don't see the point in trying to get back in touch. That chapter of my life is over – all I'm concentrating on at the moment is writing a new one here in Moristoun."

"What made you decide to come here? I can't see why someone would want to leave a city like Glasgow to live in Moristoun."

"In today's job market you can't afford to be too picky. Life on the dole is a living hell no matter where you live. Sitting on your Jack Jones watching TV and eating pot noodles feels the same if you're in Auchertmuchty or New York."

"It doesn't here," said Gail. "We're too remote to get a signal so there's no TV, internet or mobile phones."

As a former member of the IT profession, McSorely found it hard to believe anywhere could be so technologically backward in 21st century Britain and assumed Gail was just the latest in a long line of islanders enjoying a joke at the city slicker's expense. When he told her to stop larking around, though, McSorely discovered she was being deadly serious.

"What do people around here do for entertainment then?" he asked. "Time must drag like a bastard if you can't watch telly or surf the net."

"The Council ship in some of the best films and programmes from the mainland and screen them every Friday night at the cinema. For the rest of the week, most people either stay at home or go to the pub. There are two other boozers apart from our one – The Cliff and The Bleak Midwinter. But I wouldn't go in either of them alone – they're much rougher than the Tortured Soul."

McSorely could see why some of Moristoun's citizens would turn to violence as most of his fellow Glaswegians would be storming the City Chambers with rudimentary weapons and frothing mouths if deprived of the opiate delivered by their iPhones, iPads and 42-inch plasmas for more than just a couple of hours. Teenage girls such as Gail would be leading the charge with all the fervour of a Bolshevik sacking the Winter Palace so McSorely found it strange that she seemed to accept the situation without a hint of dissent.

"You can't miss what you've never known," said Gail when asked for an explanation. "I've never been outside of these islands. When I go for my entrance exam in Inverness, it will be the first time I've set foot on the mainland."

"But how do you keep up to speed on what's happening in the world if you can't log on to websites or watch the news on TV?"

"The local paper devotes three or four pages to national and international news so we're not totally ignorant of what happens away from these shores. There's also a round-up of news clips at the cinema at every week and new books are always arriving at the library. When you live somewhere like this, you soon develop a fondness for the printed word."

"But you must be curious about all the things you're missing out on. You can do some wonderful things with a phone and computer these days."

Gail then asked McSorely to describe some of these digital delights and he paused for a moment before fishing his iPhone out of his pocket and showcasing his favourite apps.

"I can't get a connection here so I won't be able to get some of these programmes to work," he said by way of a disclaimer. "But there are a few interesting ones that don't need an internet connection."

McSorely's first stop was the phone's mobile library, something that was bound to impress a keen reader. However, his demonstration was far from impressive as the only tomes McSorely had downloaded were the iPhone User Guide and the Viz Annual.

"There's only two books there at the moment but if I had a connection I would be able to download anything that was out of copyright for free," he said. "You can get all the classics and read them anywhere you go."

As Gail flirted with the early stages of a migraine while reading the tiny text on McSorely's screen, she wondered why anyone would choose this cold electronic device over the comforting feel of an actual book. But she decided to keep both her counsel and an open mind while McSorely ran through some of the phone's other uses. While some of the apps provided a brief dose of amusement, Gail found herself largely underwhelmed after spending the next 10 minutes throwing virtual pieces of paper into wastebaskets, catapulting kamikaze birds at green pigs and trying to swerve free-kicks round a defensive wall with her index figure. If this was the pinnacle of innovation on the mainland then she clearly hadn't been missing out on much.

"There are much better games available to download," said McSorely as he tried to muster greater enthusiasm from Gail. "But you have to pay for them and I could only afford the free ones when I was on the dole."

As he watched Gail become increasingly disinterested in his iPhone, McSorely cursed the fact he had failed to build on the promising start provided by his theory concerning Hogg's sexuality. Gail was no longer hanging on his every word and he could tell she would rather return to the chore of her studies than spend another minute listening to him drone on about his pathetic collection of virtual stocking fillers. If he was going to win the heart of this beautiful girl, he would need to become a man of greater substance – someone who read Homer instead of chuckling at the cartoon idiocy of the Simpson patriarch. Maybe being stuck in a place where expensive gadgets had about as much use as bullet-proof vest constructed from tracing paper was actually a blessing in disguise. He would no longer be a prisoner to the pointless pursuits that had lustily devoured such a large portion of his free time – comedy repeats on Dave, internet pornography, fantasy football and online gaming. It was time to cast aside his electronic crutches and stride forward as a real human being for the first time. McSorely would have to develop a passion for literature if he was ever going to impress Gail but he was starting from scratch as the few books he had actually read from start to finish were written from the perspective of a professional footballer. If he tried to engage in literary debate at the moment it would be like someone who counted Westlife's Greatest Hits as his only CD entering into musical combat with the editor of the NME. McSorely needed to dip his toes into far deeper philosophical waters than pondering the wisdom of deploying a sweeper system away from home in Europe so he asked Gail to recommend a book from the library's vast reserves.

"Once you're finished with the Velvet Rage you should take out a book called The Unbearable Lightness of Being," she said. "It's written by the Czech writer Milan Kundera and I adore it."

"What's it about then?" asked McSorely.

"It's basically a love story," replied Gail. "But it's much deeper than that. Kundera explores what really makes humans tick and it's a book that opens your eyes to the world around you. I can't recommend it highly enough."

"That sounds like just the kind of thing I'm looking for," said McSorely. "Maybe it can help me understand Hogg a bit better as well. Armed with The Velvet Rage and The Unbearable Lightness of Being, we might even be able to win this courtroom battle against all the odds."

# Chapter 14 –

# Friday night at the movies

Only five days had passed since McSorely's decision to embrace the intellectual life and he already found himself bored to tears. It disturbed him to discover how much he pined for TV and separation from the goggle box had even managed to induce a feeling he never thought he would experience – empathy for residents of the Big Brother house. McSorely could now understand why seemingly intelligent people such as George Galloway agreed to participate in the most degrading of tasks for the public's entertainment. Dressing up as a cat and lapping imaginary milk from the hands of a washed-up actress may have been humiliating but it probably provided a welcome distraction from the crushing boredom of sitting around scratching one's arse. McSorely had been on intimate terms with his own solitude for months, thanks to the collapse of his engagement and employment, but he now realised what an important role digital devices had played in distracting him from the mounting misery. Had McSorely been left to confront his demons without the help of his computer, DVD player, iPod, iPhone and TV then he would surely have topped himself long before Buchan's email popped into his inbox. The only thing that now stopped dark thoughts from reasserting their dominance was a certain young lady. McSorely's fascination with Gail had grown each day, mainly due to the fact visiting the Tortured Soul was his only entertainment option. While this situation had its downsides – he had been forced to endure more cowboy music and graphic sexual language than the buxom waitress of a honky tonk – the considerable plus of spending hours in Gail's company outweighed the negatives. McSorely had hoped to impress Gail by rattling through The Unbearable Lightness of Being in just a couple of days but he was finding the book unbearably heavy going. As a novice reader, McSorely lacked the attention span needed to tackle a novel that was littered with philosophical insights and had so far managed to make his way through just 58 pages. Back in Glasgow he would probably just have read the book's Wikipedia page and tried to con Gail into thinking he had pored over every word of the 305-page masterpiece. Such an option, however, was not available in the analogue world of Moristoun so he simply had to bite the bullet and read through the entire text. Spending most of his free time at the pub didn't help McSorely's cause as he was usually too pissed to focus on the page by the time he returned home. Most of his reading was done during the generous two-hour lunch break afforded to him by Buchan, who was keen to instil a passion for literature in his apprentice. Buchan didn't need to use much of his intellect to deduce the reason for McSorely's interest in Kundera's seminal work as he had spent many an hour discussing the book's merits with its most ardent fan. While he wasn't surprised to see his employee fall under Gail's spell – it seemed Jimmy and himself were the only men in Moristoun not to have a crush on her – Buchan had yet to decide if it was a positive or negative development. If McSorely fell head over heels in love with Gail and followed her to Inverness with all the devotion of Greyfriars Bobby then both his Q101s would be resolved at the same time. Buchan, though, was well aware things rarely ran smoothly with affairs of the heart, a fact amply illustrated by his own presence in Moristoun. Love and lust were equally capable of destroying lives so he would have to keep a close eye on Moristoun's only mortal residents. That was why Buchan now stood outside McSorely's door as he prepared to introduce his apprentice to the delights of a night at The Rialto.

McSorely had been full of enthusiasm at the Tortured Soul 24 hours earlier as he looked forward to his first taste of popular culture in a week. Buchan could tell that the whiskies his employee was knocking back with gay abandon had been purchased with the intention of building up enough courage to ask Gail to accompany him on his maiden trip to the cinema. Such an outcome was fraught with danger, though, so Buchan jumped in and turned the night into an office outing instead. "Everyone remembers their first trip to The Rialto and I want to make it a special evening for you," he told McSorely. "Help yourself to the biggest bag of popcorn and the juiciest of hot dogs because it's all on me."

It would have been rude for McSorely to turn down such a generous offer so he was forced to abandon his plan to form a more intimate bond with Gail. However, McSorely was still keen to discover her plans for Friday night and asked if she would also be heading to the cinema as well.

"Almost everyone in Moristoun goes to The Rialto," she said. "It's the highlight of the week. Dad even closes the pub down for a few hours because all our customers are there. The only people who don't bother going are the Goths and the hardened alkies who drink at The Cliff."

"But how do they fit everyone inside?" asked McSorely. "Surely there's not enough room to accommodate the entire town. I've walked past the building a few times and it doesn't look that big from the outside."

"As William Booth once said, 'Don't be deceived by appearances – men and things are not what they seem'," said Buchan. "The Rialto has a capacity of 2,000 so there's usually just enough room to cram everyone in. And if all the seats are taken people don't mind sitting in the aisles or standing at the back. But it's better to turn up early so you're guaranteed a seat – the show usually lasts for four hours."

The more McSorely learned about Moristoun, the stranger it seemed. If the cinema was so popular and regularly attracted crowds of over 2,000 then why did it open just once a week? The owner was sitting on a winning lottery ticket but for some reason couldn't bother his arse to walk down to the corner shop and cash it in.

"The Rialto is owned by The Council," said Buchan, when asked about this baffling lack of business sense. "They aren't concerned with making profits and the cinema's sole purpose is to educate and entertain the public."

"But it still doesn't make sense to open just once a week," replied McSorely. "The people clearly can't get enough of The Rialto so why doesn't it stay open for seven days?"

There was no way Buchan could reveal the real answer – that living in Moristoun was a punishment and the populace should be grateful for any small mercies – so he relied on the island's isolation as an explanation.

"It takes a few days for the new programmes and films to arrive from the mainland," he said. "Production companies keep raising their prices as well so The Council can only afford to buy three or four reels each week."

Although Buchan's answer seemed perfectly plausible, McSorely still couldn't understand why the islanders meekly accepted this sorry state of affairs. His thoughts turned once more to his native Glasgow and visions of angry telly addicts assembling gallows on George Square for the Lord Provost who had the temerity to limit their dosage to just four hours a week.

"Why aren't people up in arms about it?" McSorely asked. "If they put enough pressure on The Council then I'm sure they would dig a little deeper into the budget and provide funding for at least another day."

"Most of us are quite happy to do without hours of television," said Buchan. "Groucho Marx summed up my view on the matter when he said, 'I find television very educating. Every time someone turns on the set I go into the other room and read a book'."

"Mr Buchan's right," added Gail. "Going to The Rialto feels special because we only do it once a week. The magic would fade if we went there every day. You'll see what I mean when you go there for the first time. I'm sure it's unlike any cinema you ever visited in Glasgow."

McSorely had no reason to doubt Gail's assertion as he stood in the rain outside a building that looked far more impressive with its vast array of lights turned on. Even though they had arrived 45 minutes before the curtain raiser, Buchan and McSorely were still forced to stand in a queue that snaked round the corner. Although McSorely was depressed to discover it would take at least 10 minutes before they could escape from a soaking, his mood quickly improved when Brenda, Jimmy and Gail joined the queue just behind them. "There seems to be a bigger crowd than usual for this one," said Jimmy. "Let's hope The Council have something special lined up for us."

Amid all the excitement of his maiden trip to The Rialto, McSorely had forgotten to ask what programmes the cinema would be screening. Enquiring about the delights on offer would have been a waste of time, however, as Jimmy revealed The Rialto's bill always remained a mystery. "It adds to the excitement," he said. "You never know what you're going to get – The Council like to keep us on our toes."

McSorely failed to share Jimmy's enthusiasm for this policy as he always preferred to be armed with a wealth of information before handing over the king's ransom that secured entry to Cineworld in Glasgow. The combined cost of his last trip to the flicks with Sarah had been swelled to £25 thanks to the ridiculous mark-up on two giant cartons of Coke and a bag of M&Ms. Had he then sat down to discover the next 90 minutes would be spent in the company of Alvin and the Chipmunks, McSorely would have been more than a little miffed. Even though Buchan was footing the bill for The Rialto's magical mystery tour, McSorely still felt agitated at his ignorance of the running order.

"Someone must have an inkling of what will be shown," he said. "Isn't there an insider at The Council who can tell us what programmes they have each week?"

"They're very secretive down at The Council buildings," said Brenda. "Buchan works quite closely with some of the administrators but even he doesn't find out what will be shown at The Rialto."

"I wouldn't want to find out anyway," said Buchan. "You need a bit of mystery in your life. Besides, the Council are usually spot on with the programmes they pick. I've never returned disappointed from a trip to The Rialto."

When they arrived at the ticket booth and Buchan offered to pay not only for McSorely but the entire Mathieson family, the chances of this particular trip ending in disappointment increased markedly. Footing the bill for a party of five back in Glasgow would have relieved Buchan's wallet of at least £50 and McSorely now anticipated having to limit his snacking to a small packet of popcorn when they reached the lobby. Any guilt about exploiting his employer's generosity soon evaporated, though, when the cashier rang up the total and demanded just £10 to grant them access.

"They only charge £2 for a ticket?" said McSorely with incredulity as he walked through the main doors into the lobby.

"As I told you before, The Council's motivation isn't turning a profit," said Buchan. "It's all about educating and entertaining the people. Even those in the lowest-paid jobs, like our unfortunate client Mr Hogg, can afford to come along to The Rialto. It's very egalitarian."

Egalitarianism wasn't the first word that sprang to McSorely's mind as he looked around the lobby and spotted crystal chandeliers, marble sculptures, Persian rugs and a couple of water fountains. Opulence was the overriding characteristic of The Rialto and the fact lowly peasants were allowed to wander around for less than the price of a pint seemed unbecoming of the place.

"So what are your first impressions of The Rialto?" asked Gail as she watched McSorely gaze at his surroundings in wonder. "Didn't I tell you it was a special place?"

"You're not wrong there," he replied. "I can now see why they only open up once a week. You wouldn't want to run the risk of letting the place get run down. It's almost like a museum."

"The Rialto has plenty of history behind it," added Brenda, who had wasted no time in acquiring a hot dog from the oak-panelled concession stand. "It was built in the 19th century as an opera house before The Council converted it into a cinema in the 1930s. It's the most beautiful building in Moristoun – they just don't make cinemas like this anymore."

The soulless skyscraper that housed most of Glasgow's movie-goers certainly paled in comparison with the majestic Rialto and McSorely was also impressed by the absence of marketing materials inside the lobby. No giant cardboard cut-outs made a pitch for his future patronage and McSorely's ears weren't being assaulted by the anodyne pop of an official Hollywood soundtrack album. Even the concession stand was untouched by the grasping hands of big business as McSorely failed to find the brands that usually fattened themselves off the gluttony of consumers. Their gaudy colours and logos were replaced on the shelf by transparent bags sporting handwritten tags advertising products such as McArthur's Fudge, Hector's Liquorice Allsorts and Moristoun Midget Gems. The most popular items – the hotdogs and popcorn – seemed to be produced in-house at The Rialto as they lacked any form of branding and were available for just £1 each. This helped ensure Buchan's total outlay for his employee's night at the movies stood at £4, something that made McSorely feel much more comfortable as he munched from his hotdog on their walk up the marble staircase to the main auditorium.

McSorely was keen to see if the auditorium could live up to the lobby's sartorial standards and his sense of wonder only increased as he stepped into a room that was even more impressive. He had emerged into the heart of an arena that boasted three tiers of seating and each level was fronted by lavish panelling with the most intricate of decoration. The three boxes across to McSorely's right on the first level were particularly luxurious, with velvet curtains flanking vast leather armchairs that were illuminated by miniature chandeliers. This was clearly the VIP section and McSorely asked Buchan to identify the luminaries dressed in tuxedos who were arriving in dribs and drabs. "Those boxes are reserved for The Council's administrators," said Buchan. "You will soon become familiar with that gentleman sporting the bushy moustache in the first box. That's the esteemed Farqhuar, our courtroom adversary."

McSorely began to realise why Moristoun's citizens rarely voiced any dissent about The Council as he stared into the cold, cruel eyes of Farqhuar. Thoughts of Stalin immediately came to mind and it wasn't just because of the moustache. Farqhuar also seemed capable of breaking a man with one withering glance and the fact this brooding figure was gazing down from his own private box hinted that some animals were more equal than others in Moristoun. The governors of this strange outpost had been painted as the benign rulers of an almost utopian land by Buchan but McSorely started to wonder if his boss was just toeing the party line out of fear. What if Buchan was like one of those poor North Koreans who continue to tell outsiders life is peachy while trapped in their totalitarian nightmare?

"Isn't it a bit off that the administrators dress up in tuxedos and distance themselves from the plebs in private boxes?" McSorely asked Buchan after they had sat down in less luxurious surroundings. "Maybe they'd have enough money to screen more programmes if they didn't live in such opulence themselves."

"You seem to have forgotten what I told you earlier about being deceived by appearances," replied Buchan. "A tuxedo is compulsory if you are one of The Council's administrators, it is part of the island's traditions. I'm sure Farqhuar and his colleagues would like to slip into something more comfortable from time to time but they are duty bound to wear one while on official business. It adds a bit of class to proceedings."

McSorely couldn't help but think it only added to a class divide as he looked around at his fellow citizens. While Buchan was impeccably dressed as usual and the Mathiesons had pulled on their finest threads, most of the audience had turned up in their familiar attire of jumpers and tracksuit bottoms. For many Moristounians, this weekly trip to The Rialto had lost most of its magic and they couldn't even be bothered to dress up for a night out anymore. Going to the cinema still provided a welcome distraction from the drudgery of their daily existence, however, and the auditorium was packed to the rafters by the time the curtains parted and the show began.

Having grown accustomed to sitting through endless adverts and trailers, McSorely was taken aback somewhat when programming instantly began at The Rialto. His brain would not have the luxury of warming up by deciding whether to process or ignore marketing messages of varying degrees of subtlety. It would have to come flying out of the traps instead and tackle the weighty subject matters covered by BBC Four's World News Today. The economic crisis in Greece provided a highbrow start to proceedings and it wasn't just the Greeks who were plagued by torment and fear as patrons of The Rialto were soon treated to harrowing stories from almost every continent. Two Tibetan monks had set fire to themselves in a protest against Chinese rule, a Texan was up in court after killing a man who had raped his five-year-old daughter, Turkey had mounted air strikes against Kurdish rebels and brutal tribal conflicts in Libya had left over 100 dead. Things got a little cheerier when Jackie Bird appeared on screen to give Moristoun's populace the lowdown on more humdrum events back on the mainland but the overall message after 40 minutes of news clips was clear: life on earth was unremittingly bleak.

"That was hard going this week," said Brenda as the screen went blank for a few minutes before the next programme. "Why didn't they put in a couple of light-hearted clips to give us all a wee break from the misery?"

McSorely doubted if stories about a physic hamster or piano-playing cat would have been able to erase the memory of those charred Libyan corpses but understood where Brenda was coming from. Those little rays of hope can save everyone from throwing in the towel and McSorely had come within inches of being engulfed in total darkness himself. Gail was providing almost all of the illumination as he tried to plot a course out of the pits of despair and he was keen to find out what emotions the news clips had stirred inside of her.

"Does all that bad news put you off life on the mainland?" he asked. "Moristoun might be a bit dreary but it seems like a safe haven compared to some places."

"You can't live your life in fear," said Gail. "Just because bad things happen in the world, it doesn't mean you will also suffer. One of the philosophers I was reading about today summed it up when he said, 'There are more things to alarm us than to harm us. We suffer more in apprehension than reality'."

"We would all do well to heed the wise words of Seneca," said Buchan. "But I wonder if the great philosopher had cause to doubt his own sentiments when Nero ordered him to kill himself."

"It didn't mention anything about that in the book," said Gail. "What did he do to upset Nero?"

"Seneca found himself entangled in the tentacles of an unfortunate affair known as the Pisonian Conspiracy. He probably had nothing to do with the plot but Nero wasn't taking any chances and instructed Seneca to take his own life."

"It might have been one of those tests of loyalty," said McSorely. "The Romans always did weird things like that to see if they could rely on someone."

"Sadly for Seneca, nobody rushed to his aid when he slit his veins. His wife also tried to kill herself at the same time but legend has it that Nero ordered her to be spared. There was no reprieve for the man himself, though, and it was a slow and painful death. Seneca's friends had to carry him into a bath to speed up the sorry process."

Buchan's gory story darkened the mood of the group further but Brenda and Gail took on a sunnier disposition when the projector kicked back into action and one of David Attenborough's Frozen Planet documentaries flashed up on screen. "Oh, I love these programmes," said Brenda. "They show the earth in all its glory. The Council haven't shown any Attenborough for months so it's about time we got to see him in action again."

Gail also voiced her approval before asking McSorely if he was also a fan of nature documentaries. "I am indeed," was his reply. "Nobody does these programmes better than Attenborough. He's the silverback of the documentary jungle."

Although McSorely had exaggerated his enthusiasm in a bid to curry favour with Gail, he did actually enjoy witnessing the animal world in all its glory. The glacial expanses of Antarctica looked even more awe-inspiring on the big screen and the wonders of creation entranced everyone in the audience for the next hour. Barbarism returned in the form of killer whales picking off defenceless seals for their supper but this brutal sight seemed to induce fewer feelings of disgust than the cruel demonstrations of human power picked out by the news editors at BBC Four. Brenda was the only one who voiced any sympathy for "those poor wee seals" at the end of the programme and the general consensus was that Attenborough had produced another masterpiece. The next item garnered less universal approval as The Rialto screened 30 minutes of highlights from the group stages of the European Championships. While McSorely and Jimmy were thrilled to see some of the world's greatest footballers in action, Gail, Brenda and Buchan were less enamoured. The wonders of the beautiful game were lost on Buchan as he had departed the mortal realm a few decades before the putative pastime asserted its dominance over society. Brenda, meanwhile, was the archetypal football widow while Jimmy's hopes of turning his daughter into a fervent fan had evaporated when Moristoun United played out a dreary stalemate with Athletic on Gail's first visit to a windswept Moyne Park. However, varying political considerations ensured that the trio retained an interest in the matches on screen, with Buchan backing the Poles out of sympathy for their geographical location betwixt Germany and Russia. "They deserve a bit of happiness after being bludgeoned by two of history's biggest bullies," he told McSorely just seconds after celebrating Poland's spectacular equaliser against the Russians. Brenda's loyalties were more familiar to McSorely as most Scots held the same philosophy at major international tournaments: anyone but England.

Having been raised by Irish immigrants, Brenda hated the English with much greater passion than McSorely, whose antipathy was largely fuelled by the arrogance of St George's flag bearers in the media. She had clearly passed on tales of her family's oppression to Gail as both of them were out of the seats when France netted their equaliser in the first group game. They were not alone as almost the entire audience let out a roar as that daisy cutter nestled in the bottom corner of the English net. McSorely had yet to discover which party controlled the all-powerful Council but he now seemed certain most people in Moristoun voted SNP. The highlights package had a disappointing end for the electorate as England secured passage to the quarter-finals by virtue of a fortuitous victory over Ukraine. "Those jammy bastards will probably end up winning the whole thing," said Jimmy with a sigh. "I don't know if I can bear turning up next week in case I have to watch their victory parade."

If The Council had wanted to play to their crowd then Braveheart would have been the logical choice for the weekly movie. The nationalistic fervour was allowed to subside, though, as Ingmar Bergman's The Seventh Seal returned the audience's thoughts to far deeper matters than the outcome of a game of football. The match played out between Max Von Sydow and Death on a chess board held much greater significance and McSorely couldn't help but think about his own brush with the reaper as he watched the drama unfold. Instead of trying to postpone his departure like the noble Swedish knight, McSorely had pondered speeding things up by taking matters into his own hands. While the hooded figure in Bergman's film seemed happy to wait a little longer before leading the knight into the next realm – with the Black Death spreading across Sweden there was plenty to keep him occupied – his reaction to suicides was probably less philosophical. This was a man who took great pride in his work and he wouldn't take kindly to amateurs such as McSorely cutting his grass with their own pitiful excuse for a scythe. It was best to leave the job to the master and McSorely was glad he had accepted Buchan's job offer instead of his giant catapult. The hero of The Seventh Seal had used the extra few days granted to him constructively, helping a young family temporarily elude the clutches of his cunning opponent on the chess board. Now McSorely was determined to make the most of the time he had left before death finally got round to chapping on his door. He wanted to join the knight in acting selflessly to aid his fellow man and McSorely vowed to pursue Hogg's case with even more vigour. But he also promised to treat himself with more respect to ensure there would be no repeat of the misery that had pushed him to the brink of suicide. One look at Gail provided McSorely with all the motivation he needed to whip himself into shape. If he could make this beautiful and intelligent girl fall in love with him then it would prove beyond doubt he wasn't such a worthless specimen. That challenge seemed every bit as difficult as the one he faced in his professional capacity but McSorely was fuelled by a determination he hadn't felt since that epic two-hour struggle to untangle his Christmas tree lights in 2009. His refusal to give up when all seemed lost had paid off on that occasion, with the colours of his lights shining extra brightly after the tortures endured during their assembly. Winning Gail's heart would also be far from straightforward but McSorely was determined to illuminate his emotional landscape with the eternal light of love. He would cling to any ray of hope and one arrived within seconds of The Seventh Seal coming to its conclusion when the Mathiesons invited McSorely and Buchan to The Rialto's bar to discuss the film's merits.

"It's only fair I treat you and your apprentice to a drink after you paid for our tickets," said Jimmy. "I'd normally invite you back to the Tortured Soul but I think young James here would appreciate seeing the bar of The Rialto."

"What an excellent idea," said Buchan. "It lacks the warmth and atmosphere of your own establishment but I'm sure McSorely will be impressed by the lavish surroundings. What do you say, squire, shall we join them?"

"It would be a pleasure," replied McSorely. "But the first drink's on me. I want to thank you all for making my first night at The Rialto so special."

"What a nice gesture," said Buchan. "Make mine a Gin Fizz. With apologies to the present company, nobody makes them better than The Rialto."

# Chapter 15:

# A Night At The Opera

Buchan gazed into the dying remnants of his third Gin Fizz at the bar as the rest of The Rialto's patrons continued to drink in the delights of The Magic Flute in the auditorium. He had been in Moristoun for three months now and the hopelessness of his situation was starting to register fully. Visions of Jane swinging from the gallows continued to haunt his dreams and Buchan's waking world was now becoming every bit as bleak. Landing in Moristoun had been a pleasant surprise at first as Buchan had assumed his suicide would lead to far graver consequences. His hopes were then raised further by Farqhuar's revelation the library contained a book with the answer to all of his questions but that optimism was crushed when he set off in search of enlightenment. After returning home from the library in frustration that day, Buchan began to wonder if The Book was the cruellest of all Moristoun's jokes. What if he spent years learning those seven languages only to discover the text contained no answers and merely led the reader deeper into an elaborate maze from which was there was no escape? Buchan wasn't willing to take that chance and decided he would attempt to discover life's true meaning without the help of the library's most cherished item. The first few months of that quest had been far from illuminating, though, as his existence in Moristoun was painted in shades of grey. Establishing his legal practice had kept Buchan busy initially and he now had a few cases to occupy his mind. However, there was still far too much time to think about the misery that had ended his mortal existence, especially in the evenings when trips to The Bleak Midwinter were the only alternatives to curling up at home with a less intimidating book from the library. The Rialto shone like a beacon in the darkness for Buchan, who was an opera buff and aficionado of classical music, but this week's show conjured melancholy instead of magic. Mozart's music had cast a spell over Jane and this particular opera was her favourite so Buchan couldn't help but think of the maestro's biggest fan as he watched three other lovely ladies kill the serpent that had been pursuing Tamino. Had he known The Magic Flute would be performed, Buchan would have spent the night finishing off The Merchant of Venice and the bottle of whisky sitting next to his bed. But The Council's policy of secrecy had lured him to the opera house as usual and he was forced to endure the emotional torment in front of his fellow citizens. By the end of the first act it had become too much for Buchan to bear and he remained in situ at the bar after the intermission when the rest of the audience returned to their seats for the second instalment of Mozart's masterpiece.

The thunderous applause that now floated down the hallway from the auditorium told Buchan he wouldn't be alone for much longer. Unlike himself and Jane, Tamino and Pamina had successfully endured their many trials, thereby ensuring the audience would return to lift a selection of spirits from the Rialto's crystal glasses with their own spirits lifted. Buchan wasn't in the mood for company, though, so he decided to take his leave while the cream of Moristoun's artistic community was taking a curtain call. However, just as he was draining the remainder of his Gin Fizz, Miss Sanderson breezed into the bar and ordered a new drink for both of them, thereby ruining his plan of escaping unnoticed. Had it been anyone else, Buchan would have politely declined the drink and taken his leave but the librarian was the one person he had managed to befriend since his arrival and he didn't want to add to his loneliness by alienating her. "What are you doing hiding away in here?" Miss Sanderson asked him. "The opera wasn't that bad, was it? Our singers might not be as professional as the ones who used to entertain you in Edinburgh but they try their best."

"No, it's not that," replied Buchan. "Although the fact you didn't see fit to stay and applaud them seems to suggest you were far from impressed yourself."

"Even if we were in La Scala, I wouldn't have hung around to massage their egos. It has been two hours since a gin last passed my lips and that's far too long. I had hoped to be the first person at the bar but it appears you have beaten me to that honour."

"You never stood a chance of getting here before me. I've been sitting here since the intermission."

"Why's that? I know they make a good Gin Fizz here but surely the only morsel of culture and entertainment we are thrown each week should be more appealing?"

"When The Magic Flute is playing it leads my emotions in a danse macabre. Too many bad memories come flooding back. I managed to make it to the interval somehow but there was no way I could go back out there."

"It sounds like you need a shoulder to cry on. They've finally stopped clapping through there so it's about to get rather busy in here. Why don't we sit down in one of the booths and you can tell me all about it?"

Buchan had yet to open his heart to anyone about his doomed romance but decided he now had little to lose from revealing the details of his deepest torment. Indeed, as he relived the pain of his final few months in Edinburgh, Buchan felt a weight lift off his shoulders. Lugging around such a shameful secret was turning him into an emotional hunchback but the sympathy of Miss Sanderson helped to lighten his burden. "I can see why you found The Magic Flute so hard to handle," she said after Buchan had ended his story. "That would be painful viewing after a couple of decades here, never mind just a few months. You did remarkably well to make it all the way to the interval."

"As soon as the music started, I couldn't get Jane out of my head," Buchan said. "It was as if she was playing every character on stage. Each time I looked at one of the actors I saw Jane's face. Maybe it was all planned by The Council. Could they have set this all up just to punish me further?"

"Now you're just being paranoid," said Miss Sanderson. "The only punishment for a law-abiding citizen of Moristoun comes from within. The Council doesn't need to hurt us because we're perfectly capable of ripping ourselves apart. That's why you failed to turn up for the second act and why I still can't seem to resist the urge to drain the contents of a gin bottle."

"You've probably got a point there but maybe it's just The Rialto. Wasn't it Judith Drake who said: 'Going to the opera, like getting drunk, is a sin that carries its own punishment'?"

"It was Hannah More actually," replied Miss Sanderson. "We have most of her works down at the library. You should check them out sometime. The Search After Happiness might be quite apt given your current frame of mind."

"I'm sure one book wouldn't be able to deliver the answers one needs to complete that particular quest."

"Not Miss More's effort, certainly. But, at the risk of repeating myself, there is one book we have that can provide you with all the answers."

"You're persistent, Miss Sanderson, I'll give you that. However, my stance on The Book remains the same. I just don't have the patience, not to mention the talent, to tackle it."

"I'm sorry to hear you haven't changed your mind. If you want to understand Moristoun then it really is essential reading. My eyes only became truly open when I finally finished The Book."

"But why are you still battling your own demons if you're now so enlightened? You've just admitted you still can't resist the urge to demolish a bottle of gin."

"The Book can only provide you with knowledge and a better understanding of life's mysteries. It's still very much up to you to put its teachings into practice and make that journey to enlightenment. The agony of my own earthly existence can't be erased that easily. I still have plenty of penance to serve."

Although Buchan had enjoyed many a literary and philosophical discussion with Miss Sanderson at her place of work, he remained totally ignorant of her personal life. It was hard to imagine such an intelligent and grounded person taking her own life so he was intrigued to discover how she had arrived in Moristoun. Asking such a personal question of someone who should still have been regarded as an acquaintance rather than a genuine friend probably transgressed the etiquette of civilised conversation. Having revealed his own darkest secrets just moments earlier, however, Buchan felt entitled to pry into Miss Sanderson's past a little. So he took another sip from his Gin Fizz before asking his drinking companion for the story behind her journey to Moristoun.

"We're not so different, you and I," said Miss Sanderson. "I also had the misfortune to fall in love with someone who had married another. He was a lawyer, just like yourself, and was well respected in Glasgow's legal circles."

"What was his name?" asked Buchan. "The Scottish legal community is tightly knit so our paths may have crossed."

"That's highly unlikely," replied Miss Sanderson. "It's almost a century since I arrived in Moristoun so John Miller has also long since departed the mortal realm. You might have read about him from case studies but even that's a long shot because he was never handed any high-profile cases. Defending a necrophiliac was about as glamourous as it got.

"How did you make his acquaintance? Was it love at first sight?"

"Not really. It took time for our passions to enflame. My father was in charge of the university library so I spent most of my time there, reading and helping him out. We still had legal deposit status in those days so people of your ilk were always floating around. I could tell by the look in his eye that John found me attractive but the ring on his finger provided a strong deterrent at first."

"What happened to change things?"

"It was mostly down to John. He became more and more flirtatious and after about six months he finally plucked up the courage to ask me to dinner. I knew married men were bad news but I just couldn't resist and after that first dinner I was hooked. Conducting an illicit affair gave me a thrill I had never experienced before."

Buchan knew exactly what Miss Sanderson was talking about because he had also experienced the intoxicating surge of sensual energy generated by a clandestine romance. But he also realised toying with such dangerous power could create a monster every bit as destructive as the one he had read about in Mary Shelley's Frankenstein as a teenager. Buchan's own horror story had ended with two people swinging from the gallows and he braced himself to hear a tale of similar heartache as Miss Sanderson continued with her narrative.

"Our romance became more frenzied over the next few months and I longed to spend every day with John. But he was soon consumed by guilt and tried to cool our passions by becoming more distant. Instead of meeting two or three times a week, we started to see each other just a couple of times a month and I couldn't handle the rejection."

"Was that when you started to hit the bottle?"

"I'd always enjoyed a drink but I started to hit the gin more and more," replied Miss Sanderson. "The alcohol made things even worse with John. I can't really blame him for wanting to keep his distance because I turned into an emotional wreck. When I was drunk I always threatened to expose him and John often broke down in tears. He was quite a pious man and people like that usually find their own hypocrisy the hardest thing to deal with."

"Did you ever push ahead with your threat to expose him? You must have been tempted to pay his wife a visit."

"With the benefit of hindsight, that probably would have been the wisest course of action. But alcoholics tend not to think so clearly. I told John I would kill myself if he didn't come clean to his wife and leave her. I could tell he didn't think I was brave enough to do it but I wanted to give him a scare and prove I was willing to give up my life for him. So I drew a bath just a few minutes before our next meeting then wrote a suicide note and climbed into the tub. When I heard

John climbing up the stairs, I slit both of my wrists and waited for him to open the door and rush to my rescue."

"But he didn't jump in and save the day, did he?" said Buchan.

"Sadly not. My foolish actions gave John the escape route he had been yearning for. I hadn't told another soul of our affair and the only thing that incriminated him was the note I had left on the sideboard. That was what he rushed for after surveying the scene and he took a quick scan of its contents before scrunching the paper into a ball and depositing it in the oil lamp. Tears welled up as I watched the dying embers of our romance burn away and John turned to me in disdain and said: "You really are a stupid woman, Julia," before striding out of the room."

"Did you try to jump out of the bath and run after him?" asked Buchan, whose own suicide now looked rather dignified in comparison to Miss Sanderson's botched attempt to save her doomed romance.

"I made too good a job of slashing my wrists, unfortunately," she said. "I couldn't summon up the power to clamber out of the bath and I was hurting so much inside that I couldn't see the point in going on anyway. So I just lay back in the bath and cried my heart out until darkness descended. When I woke up I was sitting fully clothed and dry inside Farqhuar's office."

Buchan didn't need Miss Sanderson to tell him what an unsettling experience that had been, having felt disorientation and dread when faced with Farqhuar for the first time. But he was keen to discover whether the administrator was more sympathetic to members of the fairer sex.

"What were your first impressions of Farqhuar?" he asked. "I found him rather terrifying but maybe he was less cantankerous a century ago."

"Sympathy was certainly in short supply," said Miss Sanderson. "Farqhuar branded me a 'supine, hysterical concubine' and claimed a woman of my intellect should never have allowed such a louse to ruin my life."

"He's a charmer, isn't he?" said Buchan. "I incurred his wrath for having the 'arrogance and temerity' to end my own 'miserable existence'."

"The worst thing about a put-down from Farqhuar is that he's always right," replied Miss Sanderson. "He knows all your secrets and weaknesses so you'll never earn his sympathy. The best you can hope for is to win some respect back."

"How do you do that? He looks like a hard man to impress."

"Farqhuar is an administrator so he likes people who stick to the letter of the law. If you do things by the book you won't have a problem with him. He also has a great respect for intellect. I heard you managed to impress him with your three questions. That was a good start."

"I just got lucky. Farqhuar said he was in a charitable mood so he told me the cautionary tale of Hogg. That saved me from wasting at least one of my questions. The rest was just down to my courtroom experience. You soon learn the value of open questions in that environment."

"I hope Farqhuar's answers shed some light on the mysteries of Moristoun. It took me years to figure out how things worked in this place."

"Why's that? Did you waste your own questions?"

"I'm afraid I did. I used up the first by asking the whereabouts of John and Farqhuar told me he was 'fornicating with his good lady wife on the matrimonial bed'.

"That couldn't have been good for your frame of mind," said Buchan. "You need to remain calm and composed to make sure you come up with the right questions."

"Indeed. I flew into a rage and shouted: 'What's he doing with that frigid bitch?' a query that met with the answer: 'True love will always conquer lust'. Farqhuar then stepped in to advise me only one question remained, which was fortunate as I was about to say: 'You're not trying to tell me he was actually in love with that cold, manipulative harridan?'"

"So what did you finally ask him about?"

"I was still clouded by rage unfortunately, so I couldn't think straight. I racked my brains for a minute or so then just gave up. So I turned to Farqhuar and said: 'I need a bloody drink. Where's the nearest pub?'"

Buchan couldn't help but laugh as Miss Sanderson recalled the moment that encapsulated her mortal failings with a smile. It heartened him to see people could still see the funny side after almost a century on this accursed island. Maybe his own mood would start to lift once he became more attuned to his surroundings. He was stuck in Moristoun for perpetuity but that didn't mean he couldn't enjoy the little moments that sometimes made life so precious. He was enjoying a drink in lavish surroundings with a woman who was proving to be fascinating company. That was a splendid Friday night by anyone's standards and the pain he had suffered earlier in the evening was washed away by each Gin Fizz that passed his lips. Buchan wanted to know how Miss Sanderson had bounced back from that inauspicious start to life in Moristoun so he pressed her for further details.

"I remained a lost cause for at least a decade, I'm afraid," she said. "Farqhuar told me I would have to commit to reading The Book if I wanted to take the job The Council had in mind for me at the Moristoun library but I reacted in the same way as you did when I first set eyes on it. I told him it was an impossible task so Farqhuar insisted I would have to find another job.

"Did it take you a while to find something?"

"I wish it had – that would have saved me from further heartache. Unfortunately, I took the first offer that came my way."

"And where was that?"

"The Cliff. That's where Farqhuar directed me when he answered my third and final question."

Buchan winced at that mention of The Cliff as he recalled his one and only visit to the den of iniquity a few days after arriving in Moristoun. His arrival had initially gone unnoticed as most of the patrons were entranced by the cockfight raging in the middle of the pub. Having worked his way around the outside of this circle of bloodlust to reach the bar, Buchan then tried to attract the attention of the barman. This proved to be far from easy as the bloated, red-eyed ogre was also keeping a keen eye on the poultry pugilists and Buchan had to beckon him five times before he jumped down off his stool and stormed across to take his order. "What the fuck do you want?" bellowed the barman, leaving Buchan unsure if it was a genuine enquiry about his tipple of choice or one of those violent rhetorical questions that should always remain unanswered. After tearing this demonic character away from a bantamweight contest that seemed to be providing so many thrills, Buchan decided it was best not to waste any more of his time. So he pointed at the bottle of whisky sitting behind the bar and said: "Give me one of those". As the barman collected Buchan's money and turned round to fetch the bottle, a huge roar went up from the crowd, hinting that one of the cockerels had just delivered the coup de grace. This did not go down well with the barman, who slammed Buchan's whisky down on the bar and raged: "You made me miss the end of the fight, you fucking Mary. Couldn't you have waited just a minute longer for your bloody drink?" Buchan feared the publican would try to make amends for failing to witness that killer blow by leaping over the bar and letting his own fists provide the entertainment. Thankfully, though, the barman's attention was soon diverted away from Buchan as the owner of the winning cock held his bird up in triumph and marched towards the bar for a celebratory drink. "I'll have the usual, Charlie," said the grinning figure, who looked like a cock handler in every sense of the term. "And give me some ale for The Duke. I'll need to keep his strength up because he's back in the ring tomorrow night." As the barman walked back towards the centre of the bar to serve the heroes of the hour, Buchan decided it was time to make his exit. So he downed his whisky and scarpered before he could make any more enemies, pausing only to take a brief look at the broken man cradling his deceased gamecock on the blood-soaked floor. That sight was enough to confirm The Cliff was a place to be avoided at all costs and Buchan found it hard to comprehend the demure lady now sitting in front of him had worked behind the bar there for a decade.

"How did you manage to survive so long in such an awful place?" he asked. "I was only in there for a couple of minutes and it chilled me to the bone."

"When you're drowning in a sea of alcohol, you tend not to worry too much about the beauty of your surroundings," said Miss Sanderson. "The only thing I cared about was getting my daily dosage of gin and the landlord was happy to oblige so long as I helped around the place and provided certain other services."

Buchan shuddered at the thought of Miss Sanderson being defiled by the loathsome toad who had afforded him the kind of hospitality usually reserved for a malodorous leper with rabid dog in tow. He could only hope the barkeep was another employee and not the actual proprietor of the inn.

"Please tell me you're not talking about that abomination who goes by the name of Charlie," he said. "He wanted to inflict grievous bodily harm on me just because I had the temerity to order a drink while a cockfight was raging."

"Of course I'm not talking about him," said Miss Sanderson. "Give me some credit. Alcohol may dull one's senses but no amount of drink could force a woman to bow to Charlie's sexual advances. That's not to say he didn't try but I can put up quite a fight once I have few gins inside me. Charlie is just an employee. He had a similar arrangement with the landlord to me, although probably without the added extras. Still, with a man as twisted as William Hughes you can't rule anything out."

The name of William Hughes had popped up a couple of times in conversation since Buchan's arrival but he remained a mysterious figure. None of Buchan's Moristoun acquaintances had ever actually met the man but it seemed Miss Sanderson had an intimate knowledge of him.

"I didn't know William Hughes was landlord of The Cliff," said Buchan. "That's a bit low rent for him, isn't it? I thought he was an entrepreneur."

"Billy has fingers in plenty of pies," replied Miss Sanderson. "I can't see the point of it myself, seeing how all the profits go to The Council anyway. I think he just likes to feel important. He was a big shot back on the mainland and finds it hard to give up that power and influence. But those things mean nothing here and it's destined to end badly for him. He hasn't committed a Category A offence yet but it can surely only be a matter of time."

Buchan had committed those offences to memory within hours of his induction and wondered which one would eventually trip Hughes up – attempted murder, rape, arson, burglary, perjury, embezzlement, gnostical turpitude and speaking out of turn to a Q101. From what Miss Sanderson had revealed about him, it seemed to be a toss-up between rape and embezzlement. The odds then shorted on rape as the librarian continued with her psychological profile.

"Some of the things Billy used to do in the bedroom would have made the Marquis de Sade blush," she said. "He's a very handsome man and emits this powerful sexual energy that just drags you in. Most women are happy to go to bed with him but only the desperate and the depraved keep coming back. I'd like to think I fell into the former category."

"How did you managed to escape from that hell?" said Buchan. "I'd never have guessed you went through such misery during your first decade in Moristoun."

"When you live that kind of life it all becomes too much eventually. I reached such a low I just couldn't continue anymore. After one particularly debauched evening, my nightmares were even more vivid than usual. All my miseries combined into a perfect storm and I woke up screaming at four in the morning. I then ran out of the pub and kept going until I reached the actual cliffs. After stopping to catch my breath for a second, I took a few steps back then ran at full tilt before flinging myself into the sea."

Buchan had yet to meet a Moristounian who had attempted suicide for a second time so he asked Miss Sanderson to describe what happened after she had taken such drastic action.

"When my body hit the sea, I was consumed by the cold," she said. "It was the most unpleasant feeling I had ever endured. I was hoping the fall would knock me unconscious but it was a good five minutes or so before I finally blacked out. Peace then returned for a few fleeting moments but that soon disappeared when I opened my eyes and saw Farqhuar scowling at me.

"So you just ended up back in his office again?"

"Yes, it was just like my arrival in Moristoun, except this time Farqhuar was even less courteous. He ranted for a good 10 minutes and cursed his bosses for failing to add suicide to the list of Category A offences."

"I must admit, I've always wondered why it's not on there," said Buchan. "It would certainly help keep the population down."

"Thankfully, The Council believe we all deserve two chances to redeem ourselves," said Miss Sanderson. "When he finally stopped shouting at me, Farqhuar revealed their initial job offer still stood, so long as I committed to reading The Book. I was more than happy to accept their terms this time as the thought of heading back to The Cliff filled me with dread. But Farqhuar told me in no uncertain terms I was destined for damnation the next time I tried to pull off such a 'moronic and selfish act'."

The chances of Miss Sanderson performing such a deed now looked even more remote than the possibility of Farqhuar pursuing a new career as a wet nurse. Although she had yet to win her battle with the bottle, the librarian had clearly conquered the emotional demons that had twice pushed her into the abyss. That gave Buchan hope as he faced up to the considerable challenge of trying to recover from the damage wrought by his own ill-fated affair.

"The key to escaping from Moristoun is learning to let go," she told him. "That's perhaps the biggest lesson I have learned from my time here. Clinging to the past and the things we loved in the mortal realm will only lead to perpetual torture. Enlightenment comes when you're willing to give up everything."

# Chapter 16:

# Match of the Day

"We're going to have to tell her everything. You do realise that, don't you?" said Jimmy as he sat back in bed flicking through Saturday morning's Gazette. "It's not fair to send Gail away without letting her know the truth."

Brenda looked rather irritated at having her own attention diverted away from marking Gail's essay on the Third Reich and placed the papers down on her lap before turning towards her husband. "You don't have to tell me that," she snapped. "You didn't think I was just going to let The Council throw her down the portal without saying a word, did you?"

"Of course not," Jimmy said. "But we need to make it clear that once she goes to the mainland she will never see us again. It's going to hurt all three of us more than we could ever imagine but it's the only way to make sure Gail can move on. We can't let her believe she will be able to come back and see us whenever she wants because that will only hurt her even more when she finds out there's no way back."

Brenda's irritation had now risen from level one (akin to defending your picnic from a persistent wasp) to around level three (being cornered by a garrulous gobshite who has strung the handful of noteworthy incidents from his miserable existence into one interminable bar-room anecdote). If her husband continued to assail her with obvious facts she had faced up to years ago then it would only be a matter of time before she reached level five (the aforementioned gobshite being either Henderson or McCall).

"Stop talking to me as if I'm some kind of idiot," she said. "I know fine well what we have to do. I just want to make sure we tell her in the right way and at the right time. It's not easy explaining to someone her whole life has been a fabrication. And how do we even go about trying to explain the reality of Moristoun? Gail might be our daughter but she's still a Q101. If we tell her the truth about this place then we'll be committing a Category A offence."

"Buchan has come up with a way to get round that," said Jimmy. "He thinks we should take Gail down to The Council buildings and have one of the administrators explain Moristoun fully to her. Then we can talk things through with Gail and try to answer the thousands of questions that will come flowing through her mind."

Brenda had to admit Buchan's plan made sense but she doubted whether they would be able to provide adequate answers for any of Gail's questions. How could such a warm and caring child comprehend the fact fate had thrown her into a place as cold and desperate as Moristoun? And how could she accept a second cruel severance of the maternal cord was the best thing for her welfare? Was life on the mainland really so hot that it was worth abandoning everything she loved? If it was such a wonderful journey then why had both her parents, not to mention a man as intelligent as Buchan, jumped overboard while still at sea?

"I'm just worried Gail will be too fragile for the mainland," said Brenda. "We both know how scary life can be and she will have to face it all by herself. Gail won't have anyone to look out for her in Inverness."

"That's not entirely true," said Jimmy. "There is one person here who can help her out."

"Buchan won't be able to interfere once Gail goes back through the portal," said Brenda. "He's only allowed to deal with matters that relate to new cases. Unless Gail becomes a Q99 herself, he won't be able to do anything. And the last thing we all want is for that to happen."

"I wasn't talking about Buchan," replied Jimmy. "I was referring to his assistant, McSorely. He's a Q101 as well, remember, so he could be heading back to the mainland soon. Maybe he can help look after Gail in Inverness. He seems like a decent enough guy."

Brenda's early impressions of McSorely were mostly positive but she didn't know enough about the new arrival to place her trust in him. The look in McSorely's eyes whenever he was in Gail's company also set a few alarm bells ringing. While not as lascivious as the essence of sheer lust emanating from Henderson and McCall, that look betrayed the fact McSorely's intentions were not entirely pure. Jimmy's intimidating physique and manner were doing an admirable job of protecting Gail at the moment but he would not be around to defend his daughter's honour on the mainland. That would leave her open to the inevitable advances of a broad spectrum of lowlifes and Brenda was still unsure if McSorely numbered among this subspecies.

"It's a bit dangerous to pin our hopes on someone we've only known for a week," she told Jimmy. "McSorely's a Q101 so he's not exactly a well-balanced human being. If Buchan hadn't stepped in to intervene, he would have killed himself. The man obviously has issues."

"That might be true but he's our only hope at the moment," replied Jimmy. "I think McSorely's a decent man deep down. He probably just fell on hard times like the rest of us."

"I don't know, there's something about him that I find a bit creepy. You must have seen the way he looks at Gail."

"She's a good-looking girl, Brenda. Almost every man in Moristoun acts like that around Gail. Looks never hurt anyone, it's when those looks turn into actions you have to act. And, don't you worry, if McSorely steps out of line I'll make sure he never thinks about doing it again."

"But you won't be around to protect Gail when she goes to Inverness. What if this McSorely just bides his time before having his dirty way with her when they arrive on the mainland?"

"McSorely doesn't look like a sex pest to me – he seems pretty harmless. But you're right when you say it's too early to judge him. We need to find out a lot more about him. That's why I've asked him along to the game today. It will give us a chance to get better acquainted."

Jimmy took shelter under his umbrella as the rain battered down outside a windswept Moyne Park and tried to pick McSorely out from the heaving mass of bodies approaching the ground. He now realised it had been mistake to meet McSorely at the stadium as the glamour of the Inter Island Cup always attracted a bigger crowd than usual. The rivalry between United and Athletic was bitter enough to keep plenty of punters flowing through the turnstiles every week but even Jimmy, who never missed a match, had to admit watching the same two sides battle for local supremacy often became rather wearisome. The Cup provided some much-needed variety as it pitted 16 teams from all of the islands into one annual fight for the right to acclaim themselves as the kings of suicidal football. United had won the tournament just three times since Jimmy's arrival in Moristoun – a golden spell in the mid-1980s when their mercurial manager masterminded three successive victories after temporarily managing to conquer his alcoholism – but the misguided optimism that flowed through almost every football fan made him believe this might be the year when the long wait finally ended. Deep down, Jimmy probably knew that drought only stood a chance of ending if poor Hughie could remain dry himself and the latest report in the Gazette did not make for encouraging reading. "The Cup is half-empty," read the back-page headline, with the sub deck confirming: "Simpson still AWOL as United prepare for Arbus test."

Jimmy didn't let that worrying news dull his enthusiasm, though, as football's inherent unpredictability kept a glimmer of hope alive. Even without their talismanic leader, United still stood a chance as players often rallied in times of adversity and Arbus were far from the strongest team in the competition. Home advantage might just inspire this rag-tag bunch of losers to victory and Jimmy couldn't wait to get inside and sample what promised to be a memorable Moyne Park atmosphere.

For that to happen, however, McSorely would have to turn up and Jimmy's frustration increased as he glanced at his watch and learned his companion was 10 minutes late. Jimmy's eyes were then diverted from his watch as a figure wearing a giant yellow raincoat and sou'wester approached from his right. As this strange apparition came closer, Jimmy discovered the man trapped inside was actually McSorely. It was strange to see him in such bizarre clothing as McSorely had always seemed to dress so smartly, coming a close second to Buchan in sartorial standards.

"What in the name of God are you wearing?" said Jimmy as he burst into a laugh. "Are you planning on going fishing after the game?"

"Sorry I'm late," replied McSorely. "But I had to stop off in town to buy a raincoat. I haven't done much shopping since I came here and I didn't want to ruin my suit in this downpour."

"Why didn't you just buy an umbrella? That way you could have kept dry and kept your dignity."

"In case you haven't noticed, it's blowing a bloody gale," said McSorely. "You might be strong enough to avoid flying into the air like Mary Poppins but I didn't fancy my own chances. I looked around for a more fashionable jacket but most of the shops were closed. I was already running late and this abomination was the only thing I could find. Does it look as bad as I think it does?

"I'm afraid so. A giant banana is the first thought that springs to mind. We should stand behind whatever goal Arbus are shooting at because you might just put their strikers off."

"I thought you said you had got us tickets for the stand?"

"Don't worry, I'm only joking. We will indeed be sitting in the stand. At least that will give us some protection from the elements. I'm sure you'll look much less ridiculous once you take that sou'wester off. Shall we make our way inside?"

McSorely had set off for Moyne Park with low expectations as he believed the footballers of Moristoun would struggle to match even the low standards set by Coatbridge's finest. The last campaign had actually been a season of triumph for his beloved Rovers as their successful fight against relegation to the bottom tier had included a 7-2 win over Airdrie, the team McSorely liked to call "those knuckle-dragging troglodytes from down the road". The euphoria of such an historic triumph was only fleeting, though, as it failed to save McSorely from the bleak reality of his personal hell. Further proof that Bill Shankly was way off the mark with his claim football was much more important than life and death arrived when Rovers were pitched into the relegation play-offs. McSorely shared in the ecstasy of his fellow fans at Cliftonhill when a penalty kick saved them from the drop but that triumph wasn't enough to save McSorely from bidding his own farewell just a few weeks later when he jumped on the train to Inverness to meet his destiny. He thought he would never set foot in a football ground again but here he was, stepping through the gates of Moyne Park with Jimmy to sample the delights of Moristoun United v Arbus.

"You've picked a good game for your first trip to Moyne Park," said Jimmy as they walked up the stairwell to reach their seats. "These Inter Island Cup ties always attract a capacity crowd. There should be a cracking atmosphere."

"How many people can fit in here?" asked McSorely, who was impressed by an old-fashioned ground that, even in such inclement weather, felt far warmer than the soulless plastic boxes which house many a game in Scotland's top flight. "It looks like there's close to a thousand in already and there's still 15 minutes to kick-off."

"It holds about one-and-a-half thousand. Arbus will bring less than a hundred fans with them so I'm hoping our backing can inspire the boys to victory."

"I didn't realise football was so popular on Moristoun. Almost half of the town is packed in here."

"The only people who aren't here are those who hate football and Athletic fans, peas from the same pod as far as I'm concerned. If you really love the game and everything it should stand for then I can't see how you can lower yourself to support a team like Athletic."

McSorely was then given an introduction to Moristoun's fiercest sporting rivalry as Jimmy provided an extensive, albeit slightly biased, history.

"Both teams were set up in 1880 and it soon became clear which one was the force for evil and which was the force for good," said Jimmy. "They were pub teams initially, with United representing The Bleak Midwinter and Athletic playing for The Cliff."

"Why didn't the Tortured Soul have a team?" said McSorely. "It would have made things more interesting if the town had three sides."

"This was in the days when Moristoun only had two pubs," replied Jimmy. "The Tortured Soul didn't open until the 1950s when The Council agreed to grant another licence. Drinkers back then only had two choices and it took a brave man to step through the doors of The Cliff. It's still pretty rough these days but back in the 19th century it made a Tijuana tavern look like a Kensington tea room. It was owned by a gangster called William Hughes and he was the one who founded Athletic. He was captain, manager and benefactor so the whole team revolved around him."

"I'm guessing the first Athletic side wasn't a paragon of fair play and Corinthian spirit then," said McSorely.

"Exactly. United had the better players at first and won the first five games quite comfortably. But Hughes then turned to the dark arts and an increasing number of United players ended up at the infirmary. Referees didn't give you much protection in those days so the dirtiest team often came out on top. United tried to fight fire with fire but they were no match for the reprobates who drank at The Cliff and Athletic were soon the dominant force. They opted for a win at all costs mentality and it bore fruit unfortunately."

McSorely wanted to find out if football in this far-flung outpost was disfigured by the same scar of sectarianism that blighted the game back on the mainland. Jimmy had admitted to being a Celtic fan before moving to Moristoun so maybe United were the Catholic team while Athletic represented the Protestants. This concept was soon shot down, however, as

Jimmy responded to his enquiry with an answer that hinted this was an island inhabited by pagans.

"Organised religion never really took off here," he said. "I was brought up a Catholic but after arriving in Moristoun I soon began to see things differently. When you live in a place as remote as this you find yourself much closer to God so there's no need for a middle man. Haven't you noticed the lack of churches?"

The absence of places to worship hadn't really registered with McSorely as the Glasgow he had left behind was becoming increasingly secular. The spire he could spy from his living room window in Govanhill now sat atop some swanky apartments instead of a spiritual home for the local community. While many fundamentalists would consider that an act of sacrilege, at least the conversion guaranteed the building a more dignified future than the churches that had been turned into pubs and nightclubs. Most Glaswegians now worshipped at the altar of Bacchus and Mammon, no matter how much they pretended to be defenders of their faiths when clad in the green and blue of their respective tribes at Celtic Park and Ibrox. That phoney allegiance seemed much more sacrilegious than shunning organised religion completely like the people of Moristoun. Indeed, Jimmy's assertion that one felt closer to God on this rugged island had struck a chord with McSorely. He had only been in Moristoun for a matter of days but the absence of TV, the internet and other distractions had led him to ponder more ethereal matters. Such thoughts would be put on hold for 90 minutes, though, as the beautiful game cast its spell on McSorely once more. Jimmy's brief history of Moristoun's football rivalry had whetted his appetite and McSorely was keen to learn about the current balance of power.

"Who's the dominant team these days?" he asked. "Are Athletic still a shower of dirty bastards?"

"Things improved a little when Hughes' tentacles loosened their grip on their team but his legacy still remains. Athletic have always been the dominant side but I'd rather lose and play the game the right way than resort to their tactics. Our manager is something of a purist thankfully but I'm not sure what to expect from the lads today because he has gone missing again."

"Missing? That's a bit vague. What do you mean?"

"I'm afraid dear Shug is one Moristoun's many alkies. There are spells when he manages to keep things together but they don't last for long. He usually vanishes at least once a season. The landlord of The Bleak Midwinter sometimes hides him away but he mostly just heads off for the caves with a clinking bag of bottles."

"Why don't United find a new manager if he's so unreliable?"

"Shug's a football genius. When he's focused on the task in hand there's no finer manager. You can't just discard someone with a talent like that. Besides, there's not much at stake here. When your league only contains two teams you are guaranteed runners-up spot at least. And nobody really expects us to win the cup."

McSorely was given cause to doubt Jimmy's last statement as a huge roar greeted the arrival of the teams. If these fans didn't genuinely believe their heroes stood a chance of lifting the trophy, they were doing a good job of hiding it. Their hopes were then raised further when United took the lead midway through the first half with a low shot from the edge of the box, a development that sent a roar echoing around the stadium. McSorely had the misfortune to be sitting next to the man with the loudest voice in Moristoun but the assault on his ears soon paled into insignificance as Jimmy enveloped him in a trademark bear hug. His body was still recovering from that embrace when the referee brought 45 minutes of frenetic cup football to a halt, with United still holding their slender advantage. "What did you make of that?" asked Jimmy. "It was a bit of a battle but you have to expect that in a cup tie. I thought it was pretty exciting."

Although Jimmy's claim that United were football purists was clearly the stuff of fantasy, McSorely had to admit the fare on offer had been no worse than the usual guff he watched each week. Some of the players on display would have more than held their own in the Rovers team, particularly the striker responsible for edging United's noses in front.

"I'm quite impressed by the standard," he told Jimmy. "What's the name of the wee guy who scored the goal? He's the best player on the pitch."

"That's Jimmy Smith. He played Junior with Cumnock before coming here. He's only 20 so he gives the older defenders a hard time with his pace."

"He could probably do a job for a First Division side," said McSorely. "What are the chances of him winning a move? Do you get many scouts coming to games here?"

Many a senior side had in fact been sniffing around when Jimmy Smith was in his Cumnock pomp but their interest died along with the troubled striker when he filled his Vauxhall Capri with exhaust fumes in 1986. Furnishing a Q101 with that explanation was not an option, however, so Jimmy merely told McSorely that Moristoun was too remote to register on most clubs' radar. That mention of the island's isolation also gave Jimmy the opportunity to fish for further details about the man who could be charged with the task of looking out for Gail on the mainland. McSorely had done little to suggest he was a potential rapist but true deviants were experts at displaying a veneer of respectability, with William Hughes the perfect example.

"How are you finding Moristoun so far?" said Jimmy. "You've been here long enough to get a proper feel for the place."

"It was a real shock to the system at first," said McSorely. "Finding out there was no TV or internet would have sent most people scurrying back to the mainland."

"What made you stay then? Buchan would have understood if you wanted to quit."

"I guess I just wanted to give this place a chance. There was also very little to tempt me back to the mainland. I was broke, unemployed and lonely back in Glasgow. Moristoun may be a bit boring but here I have a job, a house, a dog and some company."

"So you're planning to stay with us a while then?"

"I can't see any reason to leave at the moment. The place is beginning to grow on me and Mr Hogg's trial is keeping me busy at work. It's nice to have a sense of purpose again after years on the Nat King."

"But you'll have to head back to the mainland eventually," said Jimmy. "Moristoun is no place for the young. That's why we're so desperate for Gail to pass her university entrance exam. Living here is like serving a long stretch at one of those cushy open prisons. You find yourself settling into a routine that's comfortable and warm but deep down you know you're not free."

Having experienced so much misery in his supposedly free world, McSorely didn't necessarily agree with Jimmy's analogy. Wasn't it better to be a caged parrot who amused his owners by spouting profanities well into his 90s than a wild chick who served as lunch for a sparrow hawk within days of leaving the sanctuary of his egg? McSorely knew from bitter experience how cruel and arbitrary mainland existence could be so he asked Jimmy if Gail was ready to deal with a world that was far removed from Moristoun.

"You can't prepare for every possibility," said Jimmy. "But Gail's a smart cookie so I'm sure she'll be able to cope. She also needs to be around people of her own age. It's not healthy for a teenager to spend so much time alone. Going to the mainland will help her make more friends."

"Aren't you worried she will also attract unwanted attention?" said McSorely. "Gail seems like a very innocent girl and teenage boys have a one-track mind these days. You wouldn't believe some of the filth they watch on the internet. I was on a bus to the city centre a few weeks ago and the two neds sitting in front of me were watching an orgy on their phone."

McSorely had touched on Jimmy's greatest fear but even this most formidable of men was powerless to prevent such a scenario from unfolding if fate decreed it. It wouldn't be fair to lock Gail up like a shamed nun whose faith hadn't been strong enough to resist the advances of a church organist who found himself in thrall to one particular organ. Jimmy would just have to let her fly the coop and take his chances, no matter how much it pained him.

"Of course I'm scared about things like that," said Jimmy. "But I'll just have to let fate decide what happens to her. Gail's first boyfriend might be a right bastard but there's also a chance she could meet the man of her dreams within days of arriving in Inverness. You can't predict what happens in life, that's what makes it so exciting. Football is exactly the same. When the teams come back out we don't know what we'll be served up. It could be the worst 45 minutes of football we've ever seen or one of the players might score a beautiful goal we will never forget."

As McSorely watched United's captain take one final drag from his cigarette before leading the team back on to the pitch, he hazarded a guess that the first of those scenarios was far more likely. However, both actually came to pass as 43 minutes of attritional warfare – enlivened only by a punch-up that reduced both sides to 10 men – were followed by a moment of magic from the precocious Jimmy Smith. He picked the ball up at the centre circle and skipped past four increasingly desperate challenges on a run that took him to the edge of the Arbus box. A blasted shot that sails over the bar usually provides a disappointing climax to such rare moments of technique and skill in the lower reaches of the Scottish game. Composure reigned for once, however, as Smith shaped for a piledriver before clipping a delightful lob over the bemused keeper and into the net. With the clock edging towards 89 minutes it was 2-0 to United and game over. Moyne Park duly erupted and Jimmy's joy was unbounded. "What a fucking goal!" he screamed as McSorely disappeared into an embrace that was at least two times more powerful than the one that greeted the opening goal. "That's us in the quarter-finals now, only two games from glory. All we need now to cap the perfect day is for those bastards to lose away to Aterstoun."

McSorely didn't need to ask who "those bastards" were but he was curious to find out how news of Athletic's fortunes would reach Moristoun in such a technologically backward place. Was a carrier pigeon winging its way towards Moyne Park with the final score or would they have to wait for tomorrow's Gazette to find out who would join United in the hat for the draw?

"All we need to do is look at the faces of McCall and Henderson when they come into the pub tonight," said Jimmy. "Those glory-hunting bastards are Athletic diehards and follow them home and away. Let's hope their ugly coupons are painted with the bitter colours of defeat. Drinks will be on the house if we've won and Athletic have been dumped out."

# Chapter 17:

# Cell mates

Buchan's distaste was palpable as he picked up the Moristoun Gazette and saw William Hughes' slimy face grinning back at him from the front page. Many newsworthy events had taken place on August 6, 1978, with the death of Pope Paul VI the most notable. However, the heart attack that had spirited this spiritual leader towards the next world, thereby sparking worldwide mourning in the realm left behind, was worthy of just a wing on the Gazette's front page. The Pope's passing was considered a trifling matter in comparison to Moristoun Athletic's 70th victory in the Inter Islands Cup, with the Gazette hailing Hughes and his players as "LEGENDS" in 75pt type above a giant bull picture of the triumphant captain holding the trophy aloft. This was sadly indicative of the slump in editorial standards since Henderson had replaced Nicholas Barraclough at the helm of this once-proud paper. One hundred and fifty years of objective and honest journalism had brought Barraclough the reward of a passage to the other side nine years ago. Buchan's knowledge of this dimension remained sketchy as it had been patched together by the few nuggets of information extracted from Miss Sanderson when gin had lowered her guard. But he sincerely hoped a copy of the Gazette wasn't thrown on Barraclough's celestial doorstep every morning as the great man would be dismayed to see the damage wrought by Henderson's populist brand of journalism. Barraclough had arrived in Moristoun well over a century before Buchan so he was even more resistant to the powerful sporting opiate that now left millions in desperate need of their weekly fix. The idea of allowing what he termed this "cretinous cancer" to spread from the back pages towards the front of the book would have been anathema to Barraclough but Henderson was a football fanatic and the importance of yesterday's game in his eyes was summed up by the fact the editor himself had assumed responsibility for writing the match report. Buchan usually skipped past any sporting stories but this time he read on in a bid to see if there was even the tiniest glimmer of logic behind Henderson's decision to grant a mere football match pride of place on the front page.

William Hughes and his Moristoun Athletic players entered the pantheon of sporting greats yesterday when they comprehensively dismantled local rivals United to make history in the Inter Island Cup, writes Alan Henderson.

This proud club's 70th victory in the tournament every team wants to win underlined their status as the region's true superpower. The scoreline may have been just 2-0 but the chasm in class between Moristoun's bitter rivals was evident as Athletic toyed with the opposition at times as they eased to victory at Moyne Park. It was a day every Athletic fan will cherish forever and a personal triumph for the mastermind behind the victory, William Hughes. It was fitting that the man who moulded this great sporting dynasty scored the goal which capped their victory. Manager, captain and inspiration, Hughes is Mr Athletic and he confessed to an enormous sense of pride as he reflected on another momentous day for his club. "I'd like to dedicate this win to the fans," he said, wiping a tear away with the sleeve of a shirt caked in mud after another 90 minutes of boundless effort. "We are the pride of Moristoun and I'm thrilled we are able to bring so much joy to so many people."

Buchan was only two paragraphs into what the Gazette had proudly advertised as their "10-page analysis of the biggest day in Moristoun's sporting history" but Henderson's sycophantic eulogy to Hughes was already making him feel sick. Football had allowed the perverted sadist responsible for Miss Sanderson's second suicide to transform himself into some kind of local hero, a masterpiece of propaganda that would have shamed even the most brilliant exponent of agitprop. The dubious business practices and disturbing sexual proclivities of Hughes were swept under the carpet thanks to the increasing success of his sporting empire. Anyone who brought up the issue of his salacious private life was quickly shouted down by a growing band of apologists. "He's a single man," was the oft-repeated cry. "What two consenting adults get up to behind a bedroom door is none of our business." The Council clearly seemed to agree as they were content to sit back and let Hughes go about his dirty work. "Our records suggest he hands over all his profits, so there's nothing we can do with regards to his business enterprises," said Farqhuar when Buchan first quizzed him about Moristoun's most eligible bachelor. "I agree he's an incredibly distasteful character but until he breaks the law there's very little we can do. Someone has to file a complaint before we can act on any act of sexual misconduct. The ladies and gentlemen who jump into bed with Mr Hughes are clearly happy to consent to the many degradations he puts them through."

Buchan believed Hughes had many a metaphorical body buried deep in his back garden and guessed anyone willing to excavate to an archaeological standard would eventually find the evidence. Barraclough had shared this view during Hughes' rise to prominence and charged his most senior reporter with the task of investigating the man whose name was on everyone's lips. But that reporter was a certain Alan Henderson and he soon became seduced by the charm and celebrity of the very person he had set out to bring down. If Henderson did discover any secrets during the course of his two-year investigation, he kept them to himself. When the time came to report his findings to the editor, Henderson insisted there was little to sully the reputation of this upstanding sportsman except the colourful details of his bedroom conquests. Barraclough trusted his chief reporter enough to take that assertion at face value and came from a long-lost generation of newspaper editors who believed the private lives of the rich and famous should remain private. He therefore decided to limit his reportage of Hughes to the business and sports sections, helping the entrepreneur avoid any unfavourable coverage as his Athletic dynasty went from strength to strength. When Henderson assumed the editor's chair after Barraclough's exit, it was like manna from heaven for a man keen to cement his rise to the top of Moristounian society. Hughes was now the puppet master and Henderson was happy to dance to his tune. Athletic's exploits took on far greater prominence in the pages of the Gazette and Hughes tightened his grip on power by using the paper to denounce his business and sporting rivals. The alcoholism of United's manager soon became laid bare in print, sending poor Hughie Simpson into a deeper spiral of darkness. He had recovered sufficiently to lead United to this year's Inter Island Cup final but yesterday's defeat was sure to lead to another destructive bender, particularly with Hughes and Henderson using the Gazette to gloat about their "comprehensive dismantling".

Alcohol had also been flowing freely at The Cliff last night as Buchan could hear the raucous victory party of the Athletic players on his walk home from the Tortured Soul. Hughes' narcissism was so virulent that drinkers at his pub had to be subjected to his singing at least three or four times a week. The glamour of being a football icon wasn't enough to satisfy an ego that soared high into the stratosphere; he wanted to be a pop star as well. While nobody could deny Hughes had some talent when it came to kicking a ball about, God had been less generous when crafting his vocal chords. That much became obvious to Buchan as the chorus of Burning Love assaulted his ears. Even from a distance of around 200 metres, Hughes' rendition was a painful experience, as if Elvis was trying to coax yesterday's double cheeseburger and fries out of a bowel left maddeningly constipated by his latest cocktail of pharmaceuticals. Buchan could only imagine how unpleasant it would be to have a front-row seat when Hughes was living out his musical fantasies but the captive audience inside The Cliff seemed unbowed by their leader's vocal limitations. Indeed, they were enraptured by his tribute act, with thunderous applause filling the air when Elvis was finally given the chance to take a break from spinning his considerable frame in its Graceland grave. Buchan could only wonder at the obsequiousness of this braying mob as he picked up his pace to escape the first few bars of Hughes' next number. How could a mere game induce such a sense of devotion and adoration in so many people? The folly of worshipping false gods had been laid bare to every citizen of Moristoun but they now seemed happy to confer the status of a deity on to one of their own. It just didn't make sense, especially as the demigod in question seemed to possess less moral fibre than the capo di tutti capi of the Cosa Nostra. Maybe the esteem Hughes was now held in by almost half of the island's population was the prime example of press power. Most Moristounians relied on The Gazette to stay informed so it was hard to blame these poor fools for admiring the man acclaimed as a legend on today's front page. Buchan was too smart to fall for Henderson's propaganda, though, and was preparing to toss the paper away when a small story at the bottom of the front page caught his eye.

Under the Late Extra section reserved for news breaking close to the Gazette's 1 a.m. deadline was a story headlined: "Woman attacked on Albinus Street".

It read: A YOUNG woman was last night the victim of an alleged sexual assault on Albinus Street in Moristoun. The incident took place at around 11.30 p.m. and police are asking witnesses to come forward. The victim, 23, is helping police with their enquiries. Sergeant Hector McLeish said: "Our investigation is still at early stage. Further information will be released when we have it."

Buchan guessed he was in for a busy day as he read the story and that suspicion was confirmed a few minutes later when the phone started to ring. "Have you read today's Gazette?" said the voice at the other end. "Our putrefied community has taken another step into the cavern of criminality." Buchan could tell within seconds he was speaking to Farqhuar as the chief administrator only introduced himself once to every citizen of Moristoun. If you failed to recognise his dulcet tones after that initial meeting then it merely provided confirmation of your inferior mental capacities.

"The report in the Gazette was pretty brief," said Buchan. "Do you know anything more about the case?"

"Of course I do, you cretin," replied Farqhuar. "It's my job to know what goes on with you miserable louses. The victim was one of our new arrivals, Moira Clarke. You probably haven't had the pleasure of meeting her yet. She only arrived here three days ago."

"Raped within three days of setting foot in Moristoun," said Buchan. "What a wonderful welcome. She must be devastated."

"Indeed, I'm afraid she hasn't been of much use to us thus far. She has spent most of her time crying and hasn't furnished us with much information."

"What about her attacker? Did she manage to identify anyone?"

"All we could get out of her last night was a sketchy physical description. She told us the attacker was a man in his late 30s, with an athletic build and green eyes."

"That's hardly a definitive description," said Buchan. "It won't exactly help you narrow it down."

"Thankfully, we had a breakthrough this morning when Ms Clarke burst back through the doors of the police station waving a copy of the Gazette in the air. She slapped the paper down on the front desk, pointed at the giant picture of our town's sporting hero and said: 'That's the bastard there!'"

The words Miss Sanderson had muttered about William Hughes a century ago now came flooding back to Buchan: "It's destined to end badly for him". Rape was a Category A offence and if Farqhuar could muster enough evidence then Hughes was indeed set for an infernal finale.

"A rather large fish has fallen into my pan and I intend to fry him up," said Farqhuar. "But every citizen of Moristoun is entitled to due process, which is where you come into the equation. Mr Hughes has requested your services so your presence is required post haste down at the police station."

"How can I defend someone like that?" said Buchan. "I despise the man. It would give me greater pleasure to lose the case."

"You are the public defender, Buchan," replied Farqhuar. "This comes with the territory. You don't have a choice in the matter and The Council expects you to act professionally. After all, the man might even be innocent."

"I very much doubt it. His grubby fingerprints are all over this case. I'm just surprised it has taken this long for his rapacious libido to land him in trouble."

"That may be so but Hughes still needs someone to defend him at the trial and that pleasure is reserved for you. So kindly shift your posterior down to the police station before I have to kick it there myself."

Buchan could tell this was no ordinary case when he arrived at the police station and caught sight of Sergeant McLeish. The look of sadistic delight that usually burned behind the policeman's eyes whenever a prisoner was at the mercy of his fists was absent for once. It had been replaced by a mien of sheer devastation and the man standing in front of him seemed to be on the brink of tears. "Thank God you're here, Mr Buchan," said Sergeant McLeish. "A terrible mistake has been made. Billy Hughes is a hero not a criminal."

"That will be for the court to decide," replied Buchan, who now realised Sergeant McLeish was one of the many fools who worshipped Hughes and his cohorts at their Moyne Park temple each weekend. "If Mr Hughes is indeed innocent then he has nothing to fear. But a very serious allegation has been made and we need to keep him under lock and key until the matter is cleared up."

"You don't believe that lying bitch, do you? Why would a great man like Billy want anything to do with her? She's hardly a looker and Billy could have any woman in Moristoun."

"I've heard your so-called hero is far from picky when it comes to matters of the flesh," said Buchan. "An American clergyman called Douglas Horton once said: 'Beauty is variable, ugliness is constant.' That sums things up rather nicely as far as I'm concerned. An ugly crime has been committed and we have a duty to make sure the perpetrator is brought to justice. I would have thought a man of the law such as yourself would have been able to appreciate that."

"Of course I appreciate that," said Sergeant McLeish. "I'm just saying this stupid woman has accused the wrong man. Billy was celebrating in The Cliff all night so he has a cast-iron alibi. Hundreds of people could back it up."

"If that's the case then you have nothing to worry about. But I can't make any judgments until I've spoken to everyone involved and looked at the evidence. Can you take me to Mr Hughes now so I can start my enquiries?"

Buchan received another reminder of Hughes' celebrity when he arrived at the cells and spotted the accused warming himself in front of the portable gas fire that usually resided in Sergeant McLeish's office. The footballing hero had also been afforded the luxury of two extra pillows and a selection of chocolate biscuits to accompany the mug of tea clasped in his hands. "You've certainly rolled out the welcome mat for our esteemed guest," Buchan told Sergeant McLeish. "Will I have enough time to speak with my client before the masseuse arrives?"

"Very amusing Mr Buchan," replied the policeman. "I just want to ensure Billy is looked after while he's under my roof. He's an innocent man so it would be wrong to treat him like the scum we usually have here."

"You've certainly created a nicer ambience than usual. This particular visit to your cells might not be as objectionable as I first thought. It actually looks quite cosy in there. If it's not too much trouble, do you think you could rustle up a cup of tea for me as well?"

Buchan took particular pleasure in making that enquiry as Sergeant McLeish would normally rather place his genitals in a vice than show even a glimmer of hospitality towards the man who tried to help the "scum" held captive in his cells. On this occasion, though, he had no choice but to accede to Buchan's request for a hot beverage. The fate of his hero lay in Buchan's hands and Hughes would not be impressed if his lawyer wasn't afforded due respect. "It would be a pleasure," said Sergeant McLeish, although the hostile look he fired at Buchan suggested it would be anything but. "Why don't you two get yourself acquainted while I make that cup of tea?"

Although Buchan had been in Moristoun for over a century, he had yet to meet the redoubtable William Hughes face to face. The men Buchan usually encountered in Sergeant McLeish's cells were broken and pitiable characters but Hughes was cut from a different cloth. He carried himself with grace and confidence and certainly didn't seem like someone overwhelmed by fear. Even when the uncharacteristic hospitality of Sergeant McLeish was factored into the equation, Buchan was astounded to see the accused maintain such a calm exterior. He was either totally convinced of his innocence or held Buchan's legal expertise in far greater esteem than it merited.

"William Buchan, we meet at last," said Hughes as he greeted his lawyer with a hearty handshake. "I can't believe our paths have never crossed before."

"That very thought had crossed my own mind," said Buchan. "I guess I'm not really a man you want to meet. If you end up needing the services of the public defender it usually means you're in deep trouble."

"You're quite right. That young lady has made a serious allegation and the consequences will be severe if I'm found guilty."

"So you're aware that the charge against you is a Category A offence?"

"Yes, the charming Mr Farqhuar paid me a visit earlier this morning and outlined all the grisly details."

"If that's the case then why are you looking so relaxed? I would have thought a man facing such a punishment would be riddled with nerves and apprehension."

"Only the guilty have cause to fear for their future," said Hughes. "And I'm an innocent man. There's no way I could have committed that attack."

As Buchan supped from the cup of tea that had been thrust through the bars by Sergeant McLeish, Hughes started to expand on his alibi, providing detailed information of his movements on the night in question and a lengthy list of witnesses who could vouch for his whereabouts. It all seemed rather contrived for Buchan, though, as crystal-clear recollection rarely went hand-in-hand with boozy football celebrations. When he put this point to Hughes, however, the reply was defiant.

"Alcohol never touched my lips during the entire evening," he said. "I've been teetotal ever since I started up the football team. That's why we've enjoyed so much success and United have been such a shambles under their degenerate manager."

Hughes' case for acquittal was becoming stronger by the minute but Buchan couldn't shake off the suspicion that he was a guilty man. Miss Sanderson had painted such a vivid picture of his sexual degeneracy and Buchan could easily imagine him preying on poor Moira Clarke just for the hell of it. Escaping from a rape charge would also give Hughes the clearest indication yet of his increasing power in Moristoun. He could then throw down the gauntlet to the opposite sex by reminding them: "It's my word against yours and I have an army of acolytes to back me up. Accuse me of rape and I'll make sure we destroy you."

Before Hughes could make that declaration, however, he would have to see off a far more formidable foe in the shape of Farquhar. Buchan had no doubt that the chief administrator would relish frying his "big fish" and warned his client about the capabilities of the prosecution.

"Farquhar will find out every dark secret," he told Hughes. "And from what I've heard, you certainly have a colourful past. Things will get rather ugly in court."

"I'm the first to admit I was rather wild in the past," said Hughes. "But I'm a changed man these days, a respectable businessman. You do believe me when I say I didn't commit this terrible crime, don't you?"

"If a client tells me they are innocent then I always believe them," said Buchan. "I just need you to be aware Farqhuar is equally convinced of your guilt. The murky waters of your past will provide him with fertile ground for digging up dirt. Even I've heard plenty of stories about you and you're a man I've taken very little interest in, despite your increasing celebrity."

Hughes looked shaken for the first time after learning that Buchan was far from impressed by his achievements in the sporting and business world. This was clearly a man who enjoyed having his ego massaged and Buchan guessed he would pick ignominy over anonymity every time. Hughes relished being the talk of the town and asked Buchan to expand on what he had heard about him.

"I'm a close friend of one of your former employees, Julia Sanderson," he said. "Do you remember her?"

"You never forget a woman like Julia," replied Hughes with a lascivious chuckle. "We had 10 passionate years together before her unfortunate accident."

"What happened on the cliffs that night was no accident, Mr Hughes. Living in sin under your roof drove that poor woman to suicide for the second time. Don't you feel any remorse about that?"

"Why should I feel any remorse? I gave that woman a job and a roof over her head when nobody else would give her the time of day. Julia's many problems were entirely of her own making. It wasn't me who thrust a gin bottle into her hands."

"Maybe so, but you certainly didn't need much encouragement to take advantage of a vulnerable woman."

"I think you'll find Julia was the one who first initiated any sexual contact. She might be all sweetness and light these days but Julia was quite the harlot when she first started working at The Cliff. I could tell you plenty of sordid stories."

Anger welled up inside Buchan as Hughes besmirched the character of his friend but he tried his best to keep a level head. It was his duty to defend the man sitting in front of him, no matter how distasteful he found him to be, and there was little to be gained from losing the rag.

"I'd rather you didn't, Mr Hughes," he said calmly. "I prefer to think of Julia as the sweet and chaste woman she is now."

"You wouldn't be saying that if you knew her back then. Julia was a blast when she had a few gins inside her but she's a crashing bore these days. All she does now is sit in that library and read. What a criminal waste of time."

"Julia would contend that you're the one wasting his time," said Buchan. "You're not on the mainland any more, Mr Hughes. What's the point in building up an empire in a place like this? The main goal for every Moristounian should be engineering their exit in the quickest time possible. How long have you been here now?"

"I'm coming up for the triple century and have no intention of cutting my stay short. I'm not like everyone else in Moristoun, you see. I view being trapped in this rather fine body for eternity as a reward, not a punishment. I'm in perfect physical shape and at the top of my game. Why would I want to bring that to an end?"

"But if you love yourself so much then how did you end up in Moristoun in the first place? Perfectly contented human beings don't commit suicide."

"I only killed myself because I didn't want to give others the satisfaction of carrying out the act. Back on the mainland I made my money from smuggling whisky and, as you can imagine, it was a cut-throat business. I made the mistake of treading on the toes of a particularly powerful competitor and he decided to wipe me out. I managed to evade his men for a while but they eventually managed to track me down. I could tell by the look of sheer evil in their eyes that they had been looking forward to killing me for the duration of their pursuit. So I took out my knife and slit my own throat to deny them that pleasure."

Buchan wasn't surprised to discover Hughes had quickly managed to thrive in his new environment, swapping whisky smuggling for the more legitimate pursuit of establishing the island's second public house. Drive and ambition were characteristics alien to most Moristounians so Hughes had little competition as he set about crafting a dynasty in his own image. He now considered himself lord and master of all he surveyed, with Moira Clarke nothing more than an irritating insect that would soon be swatted. The very idea he could be found guilty, thereby destroying everything he had built over the last three centuries, seemed anathema to Hughes. Buchan had never met anyone so sure of himself and began to wonder if his services were actually needed in court. After all, nobody could present a better case for the defence than the man himself because Hughes had total faith in his own infallibility. If he was being tried by a jury then Hughes would have little trouble charming them into delivering a verdict of not guilty; even Farquhar at his brilliant best would be powerless to prevent such an outcome. Members of The Council were less easily fooled, however, and it would take hard evidence to secure Hughes' freedom in front of one of the Lords. That probably explained why Hughes didn't want to shoulder the burden of defending himself in court, no matter how much the idea must have appealed to his ego.

"I enlisted your services mainly because I was keen to finally make your acquaintance," said Hughes. "I've been watching you from afar and consider us to be peas from the same pod, no matter how much you like to consider yourself my moral superior. Your lecture about the true meaning of life in Moristoun would carry more merit if you actually practised what you preached."

"What do you mean by that?" said Buchan. "Helping those accused of crime is hardly the same as running a pub, a football team and several other businesses."

"I beg to differ, Mr Buchan," replied Hughes. "We both started out with nothing on this island and devoted our time to progressing professionally. I remember the days when you were just a two-bit lawyer dealing with petty domestic disputes. But look at you now – the exulted public defender. That rise is every bit as impressive as my own. If Moristoun is all about spiritual advancement, as Julia insists, then we have both taken our eye off the ball."

# Chapter 18:

# Date With Destiny

From the instant Jimmy swaggered towards the bar with a smug grin on his face, Gail could tell events at Moyne Park had been played out to her father's satisfaction. Further evidence of this rarest of occurrences wasn't required but it arrived anyway when Jimmy told McSorely to put some "party tunes" on while he sorted out the celebratory drinks. Jimmy's latest convert to the United cause dutifully set off to carry out this request but finding upbeat songs to laud their footballing heroes was to prove much more difficult than he imagined. Jimmy's jukebox seemed to have been plucked from the lounge of the Grand Ole Opry and the troubadours of Nashville took their inspiration from tragedy far more readily than triumph. Had he plunged coins into the jukey at his local dive in Glasgow, McSorely would have been able to treat his fellow drinkers to uplifting ditties such as We Are The Champions, What A Wonderful World, I Feel Good and Walking On Sunshine. As he trawled through the fare on offer at the Tortured Soul, however, McSorely was taken on a harrowing journey through an American netherworld inhabited by incestuous, trigger-happy alcoholics and their suicidal spouses. Charming numbers such as The Little Box Of Pine On The 7.29, She Broke My Heart I Broke Her Jaw, Mama Get The Hammer (There's A Fly On Daddy's Head) and They're Hanging Me Tonight numbered among the more positive offerings and McSorely turned to Gail for help as he tried to find a chink of optimism amidst the malaise. "I'm afraid that jukebox is better suited to those who want to drown their sorrows," she told McSorely. "Try some Willie Nelson – he can sometimes be a bit cheerier than the others."

"Don't you have anything more contemporary on here? It must drive you mad listening to this hillbilly music all the time."

"I don't mind it actually," said Gail. "I enjoy listening to the lyrics. There's a dark poetry to some of the writing. When you start analysing the words you find country music can actually be quite beautiful."

McSorely failed to see the beauty in an enraged husband shattering the jaw of his promiscuous wife but he was so smitten with Gail that he was now at the stage of agreeing with everything she said. So he vowed to pay closer attention to the savage poetry of the prairie, a promise that met with an enthusiastic response from Jimmy as he plonked a pint of lager down on the bar for McSorely.

"You can learn everything about life from country music," he said. "But I'm talking about the real stuff – not that pish churned out by pretty boys in fucking Stetsons. You should listen to your man Willie Nelson – he's as wise as any of those philosophers Buchan bangs on about. How about this for a lyric: 'The years have passed so quickly as once again fate steals a young man's dreams.' You don't get much more profound than that."

McSorely had to admit those 15 words provided a pretty expansive assessment of his own existence but if such introspective lyrics were typical of Willie Nelson's output then his quest to find some celebratory music was set to drag on even longer. "That's all very well," he told Jimmy. "But we're looking for songs to get us in the party mood. Does he have any more up-tempo numbers?"

"Willie does a good version of Sunny Side Of The Street," said Jimmy. "You can make that your first selection. After that, you should go for On The Road again. We could get an away tie in the next round so that would be pretty apt."

"There's also a song on here called The Party's Over," said McSorely as he punched the first two numbers into the jukebox and acquainted himself with the Red Headed Stranger.

"That could be a good one to wind up McCall and Henderson if Athletic have lost."

"I like the way your mind works," said Jimmy. "It would be brilliant if that was playing when those two bastards walked in after a depressing journey back from Aterstoun. But you should save that for your last selection. They probably won't get here for another 45 minutes or so."

"That leaves me with two songs to pick," said McSorely as he continued to work his way through the jukebox. "What about this one called 'Little Buddy' by Hank Snow? That sounds a bit cheerier. What's the song about?"

"It's about a wee dog," replied Gail.

"Well, there you go," said McSorely. "Just what we all need to cheer us up."

"Not when the wee dog in question ends up being kicked to death by an alkie," countered Jimmy. "That one's a guaranteed tear-jerker. If you're not bawling your eyes out after Hank sings 'Then he stroked the fluffy head but his little pal was dead' then you're one cold-hearted bastard."

McSorely's detachment from the world of domesticated animals probably would have helped to ensure that he remained stony-faced while Little Buddy elicited water works from those suddenly reminded of long-lost furry friends. Although he was now a dog owner of sorts himself, the prospect of anyone kicking Munchkin to death remained so incredulous that it was difficult to imagine what emotions such an act would stir inside him. Anyone foolish enough to volley a Scottish Deerhound in the ribs would soon be rendered a monoped, with the associated benefit of halving one's sock bill providing little in the way of consolation. Had McSorely been patient enough to trawl through the jukebox's entire catalogue, he would have found a song to match his train of thought, Steve Goodman's Three-Legged Man. He was destined to miss out on the tale of the man who stole both Peg Leg Johnson's wife and his artificial limb, however, as McSorely's desire to get wired into his pint ensured he merely punched in A11 and M9 at random before re-joining Jimmy and Gail at the bar.

"Where's your mum tonight?" McSorely asked Gail after draining the first few mouthfuls from his glass. "Isn't she joining us for the big celebration? From what your father has told me, victories don't come around very often for his team. This is a momentous occasion."

"She's upstairs doing her homework," replied Gail. "Mum's trying to learn Greek so her head has been in a textbook all afternoon."

"That seems a rather strange language to tackle," said McSorely. "Most people usually opt for Spanish, German, French or Italian. What made her go for Greek?"

"She's been obsessed with classical languages for the last couple of years. Mum has already mastered Latin and now she's determined to get her head around ancient Greek. I can't make head nor tail of it myself."

"Your mother's just trying to educate herself," said Jimmy, who knew he couldn't reveal the real reason behind her studies. "You would do well to follow her example as you set about your own work. It's not long now before that entrance exam."

Gail rolled her eyes in the trademark "heard it all before" manner teenagers have perfected throughout their evolution then reminded her father somebody had to take care of the bar while the landlord and his good lady were otherwise engaged. This excuse met with a large measure of derision from Jimmy, though, as he looked around the bar and spotted only Moira with her omnipresent bottle of vodka for company. "Oh yeah, it looks like this place has been jumping this afternoon," he said. "Aside from Little Miss Sunshine over there, has anyone actually been here since I left for Moyne Park?"

"Karen from the library popped in for a quick half during her lunch break," Gail said. "Mr Buchan also paid a visit before heading off to the Council buildings. He said Farqhuar had called him in to discuss important business."

"That sounds ominous," said Jimmy. "Farqhuar is rarely the bearer of good news. Did Buchan give you any more details?"

"He didn't. Buchan just said Farqhuar was keeping his cards close to his chest as usual. Do you have any idea what it might be about, Mr McSorely?"

Although McSorely had now spent a week under the employ of Buchan, his boss remained something of an enigmatic figure. While Buchan was happy to discuss the finer details of Hogg's case with his assistant, all other business matters remained off limits. Such secrecy seemed like a wise modus operandi for someone who ran an illicit sideline in despatching desperados to the afterlife. McSorely doubted whether the Mathiesons were aware of Buchan's dark secret, particularly as Gail seemed to hold him in almost messianic esteem, so he opted against offering up the hypothesis that The Council may have found out about Scenic Suicides. "I've been concentrating pretty much exclusively on Mr Hogg's case since I started working for Buchan," he told Gail. "I really don't have a clue what else he has on his plate at the moment. Your guess is as good as mine."

"Well, this is turning into an evening of mystery, isn't it?" said Jimmy. "We're now waiting with bated breath to discover two pieces of news. I wonder who will come through those doors first – Buchan or the gruesome twosome?"

"Why don't we have a little wager to make it a bit more exciting?" said McSorely. "If Buchan comes in first then you have to buy me a pint and if it's McCall and Henderson then I'll splash out on another lemonade for you?"

In purely monetary terms, it was far from a fair wager as Jimmy had much more to lose than gain. But his dormant passion for gambling, which had lain undisturbed under three or four duvets in a land devoid of bookmakers, was tempted out of its pit as McSorely's proposition floated tantalisingly through the air like the smell of buttered toast wafting up from the kitchen table. "Ok, you're on," said Jimmy. "The odds are stacked in your favour because McCall and Henderson are probably still making their way back from Aterstoun but if Farqhuar and Buchan are debating the finer points of law then I may just stand a chance."

Gail was disappointed to see Jimmy take on the bet as she knew how much damage the twin evils of alcohol and gambling had wrought before she came into his life. Her mum often spoke about those "dark days" whenever Gail fell out with Jimmy, hammering home the point it was love for his daughter which enabled him to conquer those demons then keep them at bay. Although the bet with McSorely seemed relatively harmless it was still a form of gambling and Gail feared it would send her father spiralling down a slippery slope that would eventually lead to him wagering the deeds of the Tortured Soul on one turn of a card. She was also saddened to witness further evidence of McSorely's development into a protean version of McCall and Henderson. The new arrival had intrigued Gail initially as something seemed to set him apart from most of the hopeless causes who wandered into the Tortured Soul. He may have shared the slumped posture and defeated air of those around him but there was also an aura that suggested a reservoir of untapped potential. It looked like McSorely would set about discovering those hidden depths when he agreed to tackle The Unbearable Lightness of Being but it was now six days since he took the book out and he was still only a few pages in. He seemed to be more interested in knocking back pints as all but one of McSorely's nights in Moristoun had been spent propping up the bar. It was depressing to see him lapse into the routine that snared so many of the Tortured Soul's patrons and if he kept on attacking the bar snacks with such zeal then it wouldn't be long before McSorely had a waistline to rival Henderson's. Gail wasn't the only female on the island to make this observation as Karen had made the same point earlier in the afternoon. The librarian's lust was in desperate need of sating and she had hoped a week of punishing walks with Munchkin would have started to transform McSorely into someone capable of arousing a glimmer of sexual desire. The early portents were not good, however, with McSorely's daily diet of lager and crisps wiping out the benefits of his daily exercise while adding the grease of McCall and the girth of Henderson to his appearance. "It's a good job you're heading off to the mainland in a few months," Karen told Gail. "Finding a decent lumber on this manky piece of rock is tougher than the 12 tasks of Hercules. Even the gargoyles I had to fend off in Kirkcaldy look like Greek gods in comparison to the men here. There's not one decent candidate."

"That's a bit harsh," said Gail. "What about Mr Buchan? I've always had a bit of a crush on him. He's handsome, well dressed and well read."

"You're not wrong there but I'm pretty certain he's gay," said Karen. "I tried all my best moves on him a few days after arriving in Moristoun and fell flat on my face. All he would say was that his heart belonged to another."

Karen's revelation made Gail feel better about her own failed attempts at flirtation and it would certainly explain a lot if Buchan was indeed gay. He had always sidestepped any questions about his romantic dealings and this mention of a beloved offered the first glimpse into that aspect of his life. It seemed impossible to keep such affairs secret in a place like Moristoun so Gail assumed the lucky person in possession of Buchan's heart resided on the mainland.

"He must have a lover stashed away in Inverness," she told Karen. "Buchan claims to go there regularly for business trips but maybe they're romantic liaisons instead."

Gail's theory brought a laugh out of Karen, who realised the poor girl standing behind the bar would be in for a rude awakening when she arrived in the Highland capital. "I don't think it's possible to have a romantic liaison in Inverness," she said. "Grubby sex in a Travelodge is probably as good as it gets."

"But Buchan's always telling me how beautiful it is in the Highlands," said Gail.

"That's only out in the countryside. The city itself has about as much charm as a skunk's scrotum. Don't get me wrong, though, it's still a million miles better than Moristoun. You'll also have your pick of vibrant young men down at the student union instead of the bloated old degenerates that populate this place on a Saturday night."

"I take it you're not holding out much hope for tonight then?"

"Not unless your father has hired The Chippendales as the evening's entertainment."

"The Chippendales? Who are they? They sound like a folk group."

"That couldn't be further from the truth," said Karen as she finished off her half of lager before standing up to take her leave. "Folk music would be even less appealing if the old fogeys on stage started taking their clothes off and smearing themselves with baby oil. What a hideous thought."

Gail doubted whether even the most accomplished of erotic artistes would be capable of conjuring feelings of genuine arousal inside the Tortured Soul as Willie Nelson took a bow and handed the microphone to Buck Owens for McSorely's first random jukebox choice. Tear-soaked sawdust made its reappearance as Buck belted out the song that matched its number on the jukebox – A11. "It's good job Mr Owens isn't with us tonight or you would have really pissed him off," Jimmy told McSorely. This cryptic reference flew right over McSorely's head and it wasn't until the chorus kicked back in that he realised what Jimmy was talking about – "I don't know you from Adam but if you're going to play the jukebox, please don't play A11."

"Very clever," said McSorely. "To hear the song you have to go against the singer's wishes. I doff my cap to your sense of irony."

"I'd like to take the credit but it was nothing to do with me," said Jimmy. "The jukebox was already set up when The Council gave it to us as a present to mark 10 years of business. It's one of their subtle little jokes."

McSorely couldn't imagine the bureaucrats at Glasgow's City Chambers having the imagination to come up with such a clever reference. They had reached their creative zenith in the late 1980s with the realisation the phrase "Glasgow smiles better" could be turned into a null comparative with a carefully placed apostrophe. The marketing department had been dining out on that triumph ever since, lapsing into such a state of complacency that an urban sprawl plagued with knife-wielding rats in shell suits had been branded "the friendly city" and "Glasgow: Scotland with style". If such slogans cut little ice with most Glaswegians, then the inhabitants of Moristoun would be even less impressed with their taxes being squandered on brainstorming sessions in marketing suites. Handing out free jukeboxes was a much more effective way of getting the voters onside and McSorely now realised politicians back on the mainland were missing a trick when it came to their campaign strategies. David Cameron and his corporate puppet masters had spent £16million in their bid to drag Gordon Brown kicking and screaming out of Downing Street as he clung to the radiator in the hall at No.10 with his chewed fingernails. That wad of cash was easily enough to install a new pool table, dart board and jukebox at every pub in the land and had the Tories spent their money more wisely, they would have been able to shaft the country without taking their wee Lib Dem brothers out for ice cream first. McSorely had yet to learn which political party ran the show in Moristoun, though, so he asked Jimmy who had won the last Council election.

"We don't have the same political parties out here," Jimmy said. "The Council is run by independent councillors and administrators. Trust me, it's a much better way to do things. We don't have any of that party political squabbling that goes on back on the mainland. The Council can also make their decisions without having to worry about any interference from above."

That much became clear as McSorely looked across at the jukebox as it was difficult to imagine Tory or Labour party HQ sanctioning the purchase of the world's most depressing music collection for a humble village pub. The machine whizzed into action again as Buck Owens reached the end of A11 and all eyes turned towards the front door when the first few bars of The Party's Over started to play. It looked like McSorely's plan would pay off as the doors swung open but it was Buchan, not the returning Athletic diehards, who walked towards the bar. McSorely's disappointment was only fleeting, however, as he realised Buchan's arrival had secured him a free pint as the victor of his wager. "What are you drinking, Mr Buchan?" said McSorely as he welcomed his boss to the bar. "Jimmy's just about to buy me a drink and I'm sure he won't mind dipping into his pocket for you as well."

"Such generosity must be the consequence of a rare victory for your brave boys on the sporting battlefield," said Buchan as he turned towards Jimmy. "How many did you win by?"

"It was a fully merited 2-0 victory but that's not the reason why I'm buying young McSorely a drink."

"That's right," said McSorely. "We're waiting on McCall and Henderson arriving with news of the Athletic score and I bet Jimmy you would get here before them."

"I hope you're not lapsing into your old ways Jimmy," said Buchan. "As the wise William Inge once said: 'Gambling is a disease of barbarians superficially civilised.'"

"There's no need to lecture me. It was just a harmless little wager with your boy here. He was the one who proposed the bet and I didn't want to be a killjoy by turning it down."

"Jimmy's right," said McSorely. "It was all my idea. Why are you taking things so seriously? We were just having a little fun."

"Perhaps I was over-reacting a little," said Buchan. "It's probably down to spending the last hour in Farqhuar's company. It takes one a while to lighten up after a meeting with him but I'm sure the whisky Jimmy is about to pour will help take some of the starch out of my collar."

As Jimmy turned round to fill a whisky glass from the optics, Gail seized the chance to quiz Buchan about his meeting with the chief administrator. Mention of his "important business" down at the Council buildings had left her intrigued all afternoon and she was keen to discover just what had been on the agenda at Buchan's summit. "It was about Mr Hogg's case," revealed Buchan. "The Council have finally set a date for his trial so I had to go through all the preliminaries."

McSorely's ears pricked up at this news as he had spent almost as much time pondering Hogg's fate over the past few days as he had lapsing into fantasies about Gail that alternated between the romantic and pornographic. Although he had worked tirelessly on gathering information for Hogg's defence, it remained very much a work in progress and McSorely feared the worst when he asked Buchan how long they had before the case went to trial. "We only have two weeks," replied Buchan. "So I'm afraid we're going to have to pick up the pace somewhat. Your first job is to break the news to the man himself. Farquhar has already spoken to Sergeant McLeish and he has agreed to grant you access to the accused tomorrow morning."

"Will I be allowed to speak to Hogg for more than just a few minutes this time?" said McSorely. "I hope you told Farquhar about the unacceptable way I was ejected during my first trip to the police station."

"I did, but Farquhar just laughed it off. He has something of a blind spot when it comes to our sadistic sergeant. Farquhar has told him to let you stay for longer this time but you will still be at the mercy of his unpredictable whims. For your sake, I hope McCall and Henderson arrive here in a cheery mood."

That last sentence left McSorely a little puzzled so he asked Buchan what McCall and Henderson had to do with the policeman's frame of mind. It was Jimmy who jumped in with the answer though as he said: "Sergeant McLeish is an even bigger Athletic fan than those two saps. If his team have been knocked out of the cup I wouldn't like to be your shoes tomorrow morning."

"Jimmy's right," added Buchan. "Approaching a hungry, pre-menstrual bear whose foul mood has just been soured further by an unsuccessful raid on a surprisingly well-defended beehive would present less of a risk."

It was with a sense of trepidation, therefore, that McSorely turned his gaze towards the front door when it opened again a few minutes later. He feared the worst initially as McCall and Henderson made a rather solemn entrance instead of skipping

233

to the bar in song like the stars of a 1950s musical. But as they came into sharper focus McSorely searched in vain for the look of utter devastation that betrays the inner torment of a grieving football supporter. McCall and Henderson knew Jimmy was waiting anxiously for the score so they kept him hanging on by maintaining total silence as they removed the coats and Athletic scarves that had protected them from the elements throughout their trip to Aterstoun. McCall then decided to open their lines of communication with a request for two pints of heavy but the landlord refused to comply until "one of youse bastards tells me the score". The Athletic fans then finally dropped their poker faces and broke into a smile as Henderson revealed they had progressed via a penalty shoot-out. "Our brave boys refused to relinquish their grip on the trophy, no matter how hard that bastard referee tried to stamp on their fingers," he said.

"I take it your rough-and-ready approach to the beautiful game didn't go down well with the man in black?" said Jimmy. "How many did you have sent off this time?"

"The cheating bastard dished out three red cards," said McCall. "One in the first half then another two in the last 15 minutes. It was a miracle we managed to hold on for a 0-0 draw."

"Another triumph for the kings of expansive football," said Jimmy. "At this rate you might even beat last year's record. What was it again? Two goals scored and none conceded during the entire cup campaign. The fans really get value for money when they turn up to watch your boys, don't they?"

"We're just saving all the goals for the next time we meet your diseased plague of amateurs," Henderson replied. "I hope we get you in the next round. Watching Athletic knock United out of the cup is one of life's great pleasures."

"You're destined to feel pain instead of pleasure if you draw us this year," said Jimmy. "After pumping Arbus 2-0 we fear nobody. The lads were brilliant today. Just ask McSorely – I took him along to Moyne Park with me."

McSorely felt obliged to back up Jimmy's boasts with a positive assessment of United's prospects for silverware, especially as his own cup had just been filled with a complimentary pint of lager. But his glowing reference prompted McCall to accuse Jimmy of brainwashing the newcomer, a claim that was vehemently denied. "If that's the case then I haven't done a very good job," Jimmy said. "Young McSorely was desperate for your lot to march into the next round as well. Isn't that right, Buchan?"

"Never has a truer word been said," said Buchan. "Beads of nervous sweat were dripping down the head of my apprentice as you approached the bar. Had you been less busy torturing Jimmy with news of your team's triumph you would have noticed the relief oozing out of McSorely's pores."

Henderson was perplexed as to why McSorely should care so much about Athletic's fortunes, especially after spending the afternoon cheering on their bitter rivals. Civic pride was the only explanation for backing both of a town's football teams but Henderson struggled to comprehend how anyone could view Moristoun through such rose-tinted spectacles.

"Why did our result in Aterstoun mean so much to you?" he asked McSorely. "I thought you had already nailed your colours to the United mast."

McSorely paused for a few seconds as he tried to come up with an answer that wouldn't portray him as spineless coward living in fear of Sergeant McLeish's long and muscular arm of the law. He was powerless to avoid such a fate, though, as Buchan stepped in to furnish Henderson with the answer.

"McSorely has a meeting with Sergeant McLeish at the police station tomorrow," he said. "He's not the easiest of people to deal with at the best of times, never mind when his mood has been soured by defeat on the football field."

"That's the understatement of the year," said Henderson. "He was standing next to us at the game and you could see the rage building up with each red card. He was practically frothing at the mouth as he hurled insult after insult at the ref. Losing the penalty shoot-out would have pushed him over the edge."

Henderson then revealed McSorely wasn't the only one with a vested interest when Athletic's players stepped up for their latest 12-yard test of nerve. "One can only imagine what would have happened to Hogg back at the police station had we lost the shoot-out," he said. "There would have been no need for that trial of yours – Sergeant McLeish's boots would have kicked Hogg all the way to a meeting with his maker."

# Chapter 19:

# Death row

Sergeant McLeish's size 14s sat atop his desk as he leaned back in his chair and read about his beloved Athletic in the Gazette. Every kick of ball and shin from his side's act of defiance remained fresh in his mind but he was keen to see what Henderson had made of the cup tie. Although the Gazette's editor had remained defiant about Athletic's cup chances in the Tortured Soul, the tone of his back-page piece was more cautionary. Under the headline "Red Alert" was a story that outlined the fears of Athletic's manager ahead of the quarter-final draw:

Moristoun Athletic manager Paul Robertson last night blasted card-happy referee Titus Shaw and claimed the blundering official could have ruined his side's chances of defending the Inter Islands Cup, writes Alan Henderson. Shaw dismissed three Athletic players – star striker Marcus Johnston, midfielder Paul Jones and full-back Gordon Sheddon – as the holders bravely battled through to the quarter-finals with a shoot-out win away to Aterstoun. All three will now be suspended for the last-eight tie and Robertson believes his heroes were the victims of a grievous miscarriage of justice. "The red cards were scandalous," he said. "Referees these days don't seem to realise tackling is an art. If you can get man and ball at the same time then it's a thing of beauty. But football is turning into a game for nancy boys thanks to refs like Titus. The Council should strike him off their list."

Sergeant McLeish agreed with Robertson's assessment of football's degeneration into a pastime for pansies. He fondly recalled the days when Billy Hughes snapped and snarled his way around the pitch; now that was a real man. But Moristoun's sporting landscape had changed forever on the day Billy was banished from its shores and the game he now watched was becoming increasingly emasculated. Letting an opponent know he was in a game by raking one's studs down the back of his calf was no longer considered an acceptable tactic. That had been one of Sergeant McLeish's signature moves in his own playing days and he was glad that, at 46, he was too old to step back on to a football field. The frustration of not being allowed to kick fleet-footed wingers with impunity would have driven him insane but the uniform he pulled on in a professional capacity thankfully provided a more effective outlet for his pent-up anger. Nobody was on hand to dish out a red card when he volleyed scumbags like Hogg in the ribs and it was impossible to beat a prisoner to death in Moristoun, thereby ensuring there was no repeat of the unfortunate incident that kicked off the events leading to his own arrival on the island. That dishonourable discharge by the City of Glasgow Police had robbed Sergeant McLeish of his identity and reason to live. Resuscitation arrived before his body had even washed up on the banks of the Clyde, however, as Farquhar added Sergeant McLeish's mighty frame to Moristoun's thin blue line. Fear and respect returned to the eyes of those he walked amongst, providing Sergeant McLeish with the oxygen he needed to breathe again, and the air was especially pure as McSorely stepped through the doors of the police station and made his way towards the front desk.

"So Buchan's bum boy is back for more," said Sergeant McLeish as he looked up from his newspaper in response to the cough that had signalled McSorely's arrival. "I take it you're here to see the Cunt of Monte Cristo?"

Had this charming welcome been delivered in a more threatening tone, McSorely would have been given reason to doubt Henderson's assertion that Athletic had actually won their penalty shoot-out. But there was a jocular air to Moristoun's most feared law enforcer that gave the casual observer cause to think he might be in a cheery mood for once. Sensing this, McSorely briefly pondered firing a cheeky aside back at the policeman, who looked far less imposing than usual in his horizontal position. Common sense soon intervened, though, as he knew any perceived insubordination would lead to his second meeting with Hogg coming to an even speedier conclusion than the first. "If you mean Mr Hogg, then that is correct," McSorely said. "I have some important news to tell him."

"Important news?" replied Sergeant McLeish. "I wonder what that could be? Have The Council found someone to scrub the shite off their lavvies in his absence? Surely not – it must take years to train someone up for such a complicated job."

"It's to do with his trial," said McSorely. "The Council have finally set a date so I'm afraid you won't be able to torture the poor man for much longer."

"Well that is a shame," said Sergeant McLeish. "We were just beginning to build up a wonderful rapport. How many weeks do we have before our tearful farewell?"

"Just the two. The trial is on Friday July 6 so time really is of the essence. As much as I'd love to spend the morning chatting with you, I really must see my client as a matter of urgency. Can you take me to his cell now?"

"It would be a pleasure. I can't wait to see the look on that fucker's face when he finds out he's just two weeks away from going down."

Had McSorely been caged up under the charge of Sergeant McLeish for the past couple of weeks, the overwhelming emotion upon learning the date of his trial would have been one of relief, not trepidation. Wherever Hogg was heading after Lord Bane delivered what was looking increasingly like a guilty verdict, it was hard to imagine how his daily routine could get any worse. As Hogg hauled himself off the filthy mattress to greet his legal counsel, he cut a figure of total defeat. It had been just days since their first meeting but the accused seemed to have aged by decades. Arthritic pensioners on industrial-strength tranquillizers showed greater agility and vibrancy than the figure who grimaced with every step of his short walk to the table McSorely had sat down at. It was clear Hogg had taken the kind of savage beating the boys in blue usually reserved for bearded gentlemen whose internet history revealed a keen interest in the Quran, applied chemistry and flight simulators. When faced with this accusation, though, Sergeant McLeish responded with fury and threatened to throw McSorely out of the police station before he had even spoken to his client.

"How dare you make such an unfounded allegation!" he said. "I haven't laid a finger on this pitiful creature."

"If that's the case then how do you explain the sorry state he's in? The poor man can barely stand up."

"Hogg has become so desperate that he's turned to self-harm. I've tried to protect him by removing any potential weapons from his cell but I can't stop him from throwing himself against the walls."

This was one of the most pitiful excuses for police brutality McSorely had heard but Hogg was now so scared of his jailer that he was happy to back up Sergeant McLeish's ridiculous claims by admitting to self-harm. Pointing an accusative finger at his assailant would have only led to more suffering and Hogg had decided to see out the rest of his time in cowed compliance. It was with a sense of great relief, therefore, that he greeted the news of his impending trial, much to the disappointment of Sergeant McLeish. Deprived of his expected dose of sadistic pleasure, the policeman made do with a menacing look that left Hogg in no doubt what would transpire if his conversation with McSorely strayed into restricted areas once more. Sergeant McLeish then took his leave, giving McSorely the chance to cajole his client into making an official complaint.

"It's not right what that beast is doing to you," he said. "He's trampling all over your human rights – it's outrageous. If you make an official complaint then I'm sure Farqhuar and The Council would do something about it."

"I'm touched by your concern, Mr McSorely, but it's for the best if we just let things lie. I'll be out of here in a couple of weeks and kicking up a fuss might postpone my trial. That's the last thing I want."

"But don't you want to see that monster punished for what he has done to you?"

"Oh, he'll be punished eventually," said Hogg as he started to smile for the first time in days. "Don't you worry about that. Sergeant McLeish might think he's the law around here but we're all being judged by a far higher power. He'll have to pay for his crimes one day, just like me."

Those words seemed to suggest Hogg had come to terms with his fate and held little faith in his legal team conjuring up a miracle. Any remaining hope had clearly been trampled by Sergeant McLeish's jackboots, with philosophical resignation mounting a bloodless coup d'état over the blind optimism that had been clinging to power in his psyche.

"I take it you're not expecting us to win in court then?" said McSorely. "What has changed from our last meeting? You seemed to think some book at the library could help earn you a reprieve."

"I was just clutching at straws," said Hogg. "The last act of a desperate man. It looks like nothing can save me now, unless yourself and Buchan can find some legal loophole in the next fortnight."

"But does this book actually exist? I mentioned it to Buchan and the librarian and they didn't have a clue what I was talking about. I also find it strange Sergeant McLeish turned up with his truncheon flying when you started to talk about it. Are they hiding something from me?"

Hogg cursed his stupidity anew as he tried to think of a way to dodge McSorely's enquiry. The pain that still coursed through his body provided a salient reminder of what would happen if he mentioned The Book again but McSorely had a look of determination in his eye that suggested he would not accept a throwaway answer. "That was just a slip of the tongue," he said. "I actually meant to say..."

Hogg then desperately racked his mind for a word that rhymed with book. Rook was the first he stumbled upon and Hogg foolishly decided to take the conversation down a surreal cul de sac by claiming there was a talking bird that dished out words of wisdom to desperate men in their hour of need.

"So let me get this straight," said McSorely as he started to wonder if Sergeant McLeish had knocked more than just a few screws loose while using Hogg as a human punch bag. "You're telling me the library has a talking rook that people turn to for advice when they've run out of hope?"

"That's right," replied Hogg, who now realised far too late that "cook" would have been a much easier rhyme to explain. "His name's Gerald and the people of Moristoun have come to think of him as a great sage."

Even though his new home had thrown up many surprises over the past week, McSorely found it difficult to believe avian philosophy could be added to the seemingly unending list of baffling local curiosities. Hogg had clearly lost his mind, the only question was how deep he had fallen into the pit of insanity.

"A great sage?" McSorely said. "That's quite a title to bestow on a bird. Do you have any examples of Gerald's extraordinary wisdom?"

Hogg had been anticipating this question from the moment the word "rook" had tumbled from his lips so he was able to answer relatively quickly, helping to mask the fact he was making everything up as he went along.

"Have you been to visit McCauley's restaurant since arriving in Moristoun?" Hogg asked McSorely, who took this sudden change of direction as another hint that his client would soon be placing underpants on top of his head and a couple of pencils up his nose.

"Not yet but Buchan has told me to try their lobster. He says it's divine."

"Divine doesn't even begin to describe it. People travel from miles around to have a taste of it – and it's all down to Gerald."

"So he's the one who came up with the recipe?"

"Exactly. McCauley's might be Moristoun's finest restaurant these days but it came within days of going out of business. Poor Dan McCauley tried everything to turn things around but fewer and fewer people came through the doors. He was down to his last few quid when he turned to Gerald as a last resort. Gerald told him to try his secret sauce with the lobster and it worked a treat. Within a year Dan was rolling in it."

"This Gerald sounds like a remarkable bird," said McSorely. "Are you sure you don't want me to ask him anything on your behalf? If he's as wise as you say then he might be able to find this legal loophole that could get you off the hook."

"I'm afraid Gerald is a bit of a nomad so he probably won't be at the library right now. He flies around all the islands and only turns up here from time to time."

"That's a shame. I was hoping he could sort me out with the lottery numbers or give me some pointers about my love life."

"Gerald only deals with the desperate, remember. Surely your love life can't be that bad?"

Hogg would have realised just how desolate McSorely's sexual landscape had become if his legal counsel had admitted his only lumber in the past six months had come at a significant cost to his bank balance. McSorely decided against disclosing this information, though, as it would have been too depressing to receive the pity of such a desperate madman. Instead, he decided to confide in Hogg and reveal his infatuation for Gail.

"I've fallen head over heels in love with someone but my chances of winning her heart are slim to none," he said. "She's too beautiful and smart to be interested in someone like me, not to mention too young."

Hogg didn't need to ask who the object of McSorely's affections was – he was merely the latest in a long line of lovelorn insects caught in Gail's web of charms. Affairs of the heart were hardly a specialised subject for stubby, dim-witted lavatory attendants but Hogg had seen enough in his 440-year existence to realise McSorely's pessimism was warranted. There was little in McSorely's appearance, personality or demeanour to suggest Gail would fall for him but Hogg didn't want to add to the gloomy atmosphere by voicing these crushing home truths.

"Don't sell yourself short," he said. "I've only met you a couple of times but I can already see you're a decent, caring man. You're the only person in this entire town who has afforded me any respect. Everyone else sees me as a tragic joke but you've been working your arse off trying to win my case. I'll never forget that. If Gail gets to know you properly then you might stand a chance."

"But she won't get the chance to know me properly. She's heading to Inverness in a couple of months so there won't be enough time. I need at least another year to get myself in shape both physically and mentally."

"Then why don't you turn your attentions elsewhere? There are plenty of other fish in the sea. You might enjoy better luck if you set your sights a little lower."

"It's not just about looks, there's something special about Gail. When I set eyes on her for the first time it felt like a lightning bolt was coursing through my body. I'd never experienced that with any woman before. Everything seemed just so perfect – I wanted to preserve that image forever."

Hogg was so touched by McSorely's outpouring of emotion he considered telling him one simple act of suicide would achieve this indefinite preservation he longed for. But the condemned man still retained the tiniest glimmer of hope and wasn't ready to ruin his slim chances of acquittal by adding another Category A offence to his rap sheet. Hogg also had a keen interest in avoiding another trip to Sergeant McLeish's chamber of horrors, with the policeman providing a reminder of his anthropoid aggression by emitting a roar of "Yaassssss!!!!" just seconds after McSorely had finished pouring his heart out. The floor of Hogg's cell then began to shake as Sergeant McLeish bounded down the corridor to share the news that had left him in such a frenzied state. "Ya fucking dancer," he roared as he banged his truncheon off the bars in celebration. "It's Athletic v United in the next round of the cup! And the game's just one day after this bastard's trial so we can toast a glorious double – fucking over Hogg and United in the same weekend."

# Chapter 20:

# Memories are made of this

Buchan tried his best to concentrate on the case notes for his latest Q99 – a train spotter who was pondering taking his relationship with the machines to a physical level by throwing himself in front of them – but was powerless to stop his mind drifting towards Jane. Even after all these years she was never far from his thoughts, with the memories proving particularly powerful when the calendar on his desk displayed June 26. Today was Jane's birthday and Buchan wondered what his beloved was doing back on the mainland to mark the occasion. Instead of tumbling towards Farquhar's office when the noose squeezed the last drop of life out of her, Jane had continued on the cycle of rebirth and Buchan spent many an hour daydreaming about the adventures she had been on since that day on the Mercat Cross. He pictured her as a rotund tabby cat being spoiled beyond belief by the daughter of its aristocratic owners, a chimpanzee finding new and inventive ways to pleasure itself on a lazy summer's day in the Amazonian jungle, a majestic eagle looking down on the wonders of creation as it soared across America and a powerful tigress hunting down prey for the cubs she tended with loving care. Buchan had even more fun dreaming up stories for Jane's human incarnations, painting vivid pictures of virtuoso musicians, brilliant poets, pioneering scientists and visionary artists. She was certainly due some enjoyment after all the misery he had put her through and Buchan hoped Jane would sup from the deep well of life's pleasures before attaining the wisdom that would spirit her to the other side. His own trip towards enlightenment had been far more arduous, a morale-sapping trek through the dense jungle of classical languages interrupted regularly by bouts of intellectual dengue fever, but Buchan was edging ever closer to the promised land. Securing the safe return of McSorely and Gail to the mainland would be a huge step in the right direction and Buchan's thoughts shifted back towards the Q101s as his assistant returned from the police station.

"How did Hogg react to the news of his trial?" said Buchan after McSorely had sat down at his desk to begin the debriefing. "I hope he didn't break down in tears again."

"He seemed relieved more than anything and I can hardly blame him," said McSorely. "It's disgusting what that brute is doing to Hogg. The poor bastard could hardly stand up. The Council need to do something about it."

"They can only act if Hogg makes an official complaint. I take it our client was too brutalised to voice any dissent?"

"It was even worse than that. Sergeant McLeish came up with some ludicrous story about Hogg self-harming and he was more than happy to back him up. What could bring a man to completely abandon his dignity like that?"

"Never underestimate the persuasive power of Sergeant McLeish's fists. Trust me, I've seen plenty of prisoners submit to much greater acts of degradation. Nobody has ever been brave enough to make an official complaint."

"But doesn't that just prove the system needs to change? It's the 21st century; we can't have a tyrant like him ruling with an iron rod."

"I've made that very point to Farquhar many a time but he refuses to budge. And I'm afraid the local statutes back him up. If the prisoners are happy to remain under Sergeant McLeish's care then there's nothing we can do."

"But what if we can prove Hogg has lost his mind? Surely they would have to transfer him to a mental hospital instead?"

"The Council might agree to let Dr Barrett visit him at the police station but I don't think Hogg has lost his marbles – he's just a broken man."

"With the greatest of respect, I beg to differ. That beating by Sergeant McLeish has sent him headlong into insanity.

247

Hogg has just tried to convince me that there's a talking rook called Gerald who acts as Moristoun's unofficial oracle."

Buchan, having guessed this talking rook might have been Hogg's attempt to explain his unfortunate mention of The Book, viewed the story of Gerald as proof that the prisoner's mental faculties were actually sharper than ever. If Hogg could come up with such an inventive excuse for the looseness of his lips then perhaps he wasn't the imbecile everyone took him for. The stupidity of his crime still remained beyond doubt but allowing McSorely to proceed with a plea of insanity would be equally demented. Such a circus would send Farqhuar flying into one of his rages and Buchan was keen to stay in the administrator's good books with his own freedom seemingly close at hand.

"The only talking bird I know of in Moristoun is a foul-mouthed parrot who amuses drinkers at The Cliff by describing female genitalia in the most graphic of terms," he told McSorely. "If there's a rook dishing out words of wisdom then it is news to me. Maybe Hogg was just spouting an old wives' tale. People from outposts like this are more susceptible to legends and fables."

"Hogg's story was no legend, it was far more contemporary," said McSorely. "According to him, the secret of Dan McGregor's culinary success is a lobster recipe dreamed up by Gerald. Moristoun's master chef was apparently on the brink of going under before Gerald stuck his beak in."

Buchan sifted through his vast library of knowledge for something to counter this compelling evidence of Hogg's insanity but soon realised he would have to admit defeat. The notion of a rook perching on the handle of a saucepan, while stirring in the spices of the secret sauce with his beak, was simply too ridiculous to comprehend. Even if Gerald assumed the role of head chef and had his minions carry out the actual cooking, it was still a stretch to imagine him barking out: "It needs more oregano, you fucking halfwit" while his terrified staff clattered around the kitchen.

"It sounds like Hogg is beginning to lose his grip on reality a little," said Buchan. "I have a meeting with Dr Barrett this afternoon so I'll ask him to pop down to the police station and check out Hogg at some point."

With Dr Barrett likely to conclude Hogg was no madder than the average Moristounian, it was imperative his legal team pushed on with preparing for his big day in court. Even though Buchan knew his client stood about as much chance of acquittal as an unrepentant psychopath who has just told the jury "I'm coming for you bastards next", he was determined to put on a professional façade for the benefit of McSorely. It was clear his assistant's sense of worth had increased tenfold since being handed the responsibility of preparing Hogg's defence. His work would ultimately count for nothing but it was important McSorely realised he had left no stone unturned in his attempt to pull off a minor miracle.

"Did Hogg return from his fantasy world long enough to let you know how he wanted us to proceed in court?" Buchan said. "It would save us a lot of time and energy if he just accepted his fate."

"I think he now realises there's little chance of a reprieve but he told me to keep looking for a loophole. The intricacies of law aren't my strong suit so it's over to you. Any ideas?"

"I've read every book on these shelves, not to mention the vast legal collection they have down at the library, and nothing I've come across seems to offer us much hope. There might be something relating to mental health that can help Hogg but that will depend on what Dr Barrett has to say. The wisest course of action is probably to plead guilty but ask for mercy when it comes to sentencing."

"What can I do while you're checking up on the small print? Are there any books you want me to read through?"

"Your talents are better suited to plotting court-room performances. If you look in that filing cabinet to your left you will find a list of names. They are the witnesses Farqhuar plans to call if we take what he deemed 'the diabolical liberty' of pleading not guilty. I don't think it will come to that but it's best to be prepared for all eventualities so I'd like you have to a quiet word with all of these witnesses to find out what they plan to say in court."

"What if they don't want to speak to me? Don't prosecution witnesses have a right to stay silent?"

"Getting them to shut up will prove a more difficult task than persuading them to talk. You seem to be confusing our humble community with South Central LA. A diminutive lavatory attendant is unlikely to induce the same level of fear in witnesses as a 24-stone gangster accused of running a prostitution ring and peddling hard drugs. On our mean streets the people are addicted to gossip, not crack cocaine. I'm sure everyone will be more than happy to speak to you."

As McSorely pulled open the filing cabinet to fish out the list of witnesses, his attention was caught by a bottle hiding towards the back of the compartment. It sat just in front of a rag that shielded its label from prying eyes but one quick flick of the index finger soon revealed what was inside the bottle – chloroform. This discovery added to the air of macabre mystery surrounding his boss and McSorely lapsed into his own dreamlike state as he wondered what devious uses Buchan had for the anaesthetic. Buchan's voice acted as the smelling salts that brought McSorely back into reality, though, as he made the perfectly reasonable observation that fetching a piece of paper was not a task that should have devoured more than 10 seconds of time.

"What's taking you so long?" he said. "I thought I put the list of witnesses right at the top of the pile. It should be staring you in the face."

"It is staring me in the face," replied McSorely. "I'm just having a quick scan of it before I take it out. I want to see if there are any familiar names on it."

"All of those names should be more than familiar to you by now. Most of the drama was played out at the Tortured Soul and I gather that has become something of a second home to you. Poor Munchkin will be feeling rather neglected with the amount of time you spend at Jimmy's watering hole."

"What can I say? I'm a social animal, someone who prefers the company of people to canines," said McSorely as he returned to his desk with the list. "But don't you worry about Munchkin, she gets more than her fair share of attention from me. Two punishing walks every day is above and beyond the call of duty. And what I lack in devotion, I make up for with a steady supply of dog biscuits. Winning a dog's heart is much easier than I expected."

Although McSorely had delivered that last line with a smile, Buchan could tell from the wistful look in his eyes that he was thinking about the far more daunting path to Gail's affections. One look at the bookmark wedged between the pages of The Unbearable Lightness of Being provided confirmation McSorely's attempt to embrace the intellectual life was faltering. It had failed to move for three or four days now and seemed destined to stay in a state of stasis like the thousands of fallen comrades struck down midway through the first chapters of Finnegans Wake, Phenomenology of Spirit and Swann's Way. If McSorely thought perpetually perching himself at a barstool just a few feet away from Gail like a lapdog could make up for this cerebral sloth, he was in for a rude awakening. Such pitiful devotion cut little ice with Gail; she was looking for a soul mate who could challenge and inspire her, not someone who merely worshipped at her altar. That was why she continued to make passes at Buchan, the one potential suitor who seemed immune to the physical charms that left her many admirers in a trance. If McSorely was to stand any chance with Gail back on the mainland, he would have to shed the cloak of slavering desperation he pulled on every time he walked through the doors of the Tortured Soul. Such attire would also be ill-befitting of a legal professional conducting important business so Buchan would have to make sure his apprentice was well briefed before sending him off to quiz potential witnesses.

"It's probably best if you start your enquiries with Jimmy," Buchan said. "He witnessed the lavatorial combat as well as Hogg's bar-room attack so I'm sure Farquhar would use his testimony as a key part of any case. Gail and Brenda were also behind the bar on the night in question so you can interview them after you've finished with Jimmy."

Brenda could only stand back and marvel at the puerility of the male species as she opened the living-room door and watched her husband leap about in celebration. Had a stranger witnessed such scenes of unbridled emotion, they would have been well within their rights to assume Jimmy had just received news of a lottery win or an imminent addition to his family. Brenda knew her man far too well to jump such a conclusion, however, especially as he had been talking about the cup draw with feverish anticipation all morning. "I take it the draw was kind to you?" she said after Jimmy had reacted to her presence by racing over and lifting her into the air.

"It couldn't have gone any better," replied Jimmy. "We drew the bastards – this is our chance for revenge! Didn't I tell you it was going to be our year?"

"I don't see what you're getting so excited about. You play Athletic every week in the league – wouldn't you rather draw one of the other sides for a bit of variety?"

"But this is the cup, the one tournament every team wants to win. We're not good enough to win the league but anything can happen in a one-off game. They also have three guys suspended so we'll never have a better chance to beat those dirty animals."

"Aren't you worried about losing again? Henderson and McCall give you enough grief as it is. They'll be 10 times as smug and unbearable if Athletic knock you out of the cup."

"Don't you worry, my dear. Those two wallopers will have nothing to crow about this time. They're already running scared – I could hear the fear dripping from McCall's voice when he broke news of the draw on the radio."

"He should have more important things to worry about, with Hogg due up in court a week on Friday. Buchan has sent young McSorely round to speak with you about what you saw on the day of the attack. He's downstairs at the bar now. Do you want to talk with him there or shall I send him up?"

"It's probably best if I speak to him up here. That way we can avoid any distractions. Will you be alright opening up the bar without me?"

"I'm sure I'll be able to cope with such a Herculean task," replied Brenda. "If I'm washed away by a flood of punters when the doors open I'll just scream your name and you can run to my rescue."

Jimmy had little time to stew about his wife's sarcastic scorn as he was soon forced to open the doors of the Mathieson family home and welcome McSorely inside. He underlined his impeccable hosting credentials by offering the visitor a whisky from the private reserve that had remained untouched since two became three in their household. McSorely was touched by Jimmy's generosity but, mindful of the lecture he had just received from Buchan, insisted he needed to keep a clear head while on official business. "A wee cup of tea would hit the spot better," he told Jimmy, who returned from the kitchen moments later with two steaming mugs and a plate of biscuits.

"Who needs drink when you can sit back and savour a good brew, eh?" said Jimmy as he placed the tray carrying their bounty down on the coffee table. "But I'm impressed with your level of restraint – most of my regulars would sell their mammies into slavery for a sip of my private reserve."

"You couldn't possibly be referring to Henderson and McCall, could you?" said McSorely before taking his first sip of tea from a mug that bore more than a passing resemblance to a soup bowl.

"Those two bastards probably suckled on a wolf like Romulus and Remus," replied Jimmy. "They have that feral look you can see in almost every Athletic fan. Once you drape that scarf around your neck you cease to be human."

Having witnessed Sergeant McLeish react to the cup draw like a hungry, sexually frustrated primate who has just spotted the zookeeper heading towards his cage with a heavily sedated Carmen Miranda as a birthday present, McSorely was in no position to disagree. Professional pride stopped him from voicing agreement, however, and he told Jimmy any sporting antipathy would have to be cast aside if he stepped on to the witness stand.

"You don't need to tell me that son," said Jimmy. "This is a Category A trial and if I lie under oath then I'll be standing in the dock myself just a few weeks later. I feel sorry for Hogg but I'm not going to put my own head in a noose just to help him out."

"So this case is as hopeless as Buchan seems to think it is then?"

"That would be my assessment. I didn't actually see the attack that landed Hogg in jail but I had a front-row seat for their two earlier spats."

McSorely then asked Jimmy to describe the two incidents in a bid to learn if there were any discrepancies with Hogg's versions of events. Jimmy's take on the hostilities was almost identical to that of the condemned man but there was one crucial difference. Hogg had neglected to mention his parting words to McCall as Jimmy escorted him off the premises were: "This isn't over you lanky streak of pish. I'll fucking get you later." Those damning words shot down McSorely's Plan B, which he was considering offering up to Buchan in the unlikely event of Dr Barrett giving their client a clean bill of mental health. Although Hogg was going to admit to his savage attack, McSorely wanted him to claim it was an act of self-defence. Instead of waiting patiently to exact revenge on McCall, he was set on as reprisal for the pint glass hurled in his direction. Hogg was merely fortunate enough to have a kitchen knife on his person – McSorely had yet to come up with plausible explanation for this but still had a few days to think something up – and acted to save himself from McCall's fists of fury. That defence might have stood a slim chance had it been a simple case of Hogg's word against McCall's but the verbal outburst seemed to ruin any hope of painting the victim as the initial aggressor.

"Is there any chance I could persuade you not to reveal what Hogg said if he decides to plead not guilty?" McSorely asked Jimmy in desperation. "Those words are almost as bad as a signed confession."

"Like I said earlier, I'm not going to risk my own freedom to defend Hogg. If Farquhar brings it up then I'll have to tell him what Hogg said. Besides, I'm not the only one who heard it. It was happy hour and he shouted so loud that he drowned out Patsy Cline."

"So every witness I speak to will tell me they heard Hogg make a clear threat?"

"I'm afraid so. Farquhar won't have to work very hard to get the testimony he needs."

"If that's the case then I can see why Buchan wants us to plead guilty. You can't win when almost every witness is against you."

"Oh I wouldn't be so sure about that," replied Jimmy as he broke into a smile. "Do you remember that William Hughes fella I was telling you about…?"

# Chapter 21:

# Moristoun v Hughes

The words of the man sitting in the dock continued to eat away at Buchan as he watched Farqhuar quiz Miss Sanderson at the witness stand. No matter how much he tried to convince himself otherwise, Buchan had to admit deep down that he did share some of William Hughes' repugnant characteristics. The pursuit of professional success had consumed him so much over the past century that spiritual contemplation had rarely been given a look-in. Although Hughes had stretched credulity a little when he described them as "peas from the same pod", Buchan had also let pride and ego guide him since arriving in Moristoun. He loved the limelight that accompanied his courtroom jousts with Farqhuar and it was now shining particularly brightly with Moristoun's most celebrated sportsman in the dock. All the evidence seemed to suggest Buchan would score his most notable victory over the town's sharpest legal mind, a feat that would lift his prestige to new heights. But he found himself filled with shame, not pride, as he prepared to cross-examine Miss Sanderson. She had tried her best to guide Buchan down the right path but he had refused to heed her advice and devote his free time to deciphering The Book. Now he was set to deliver another slap to her face by bringing up sordid details of a past Miss Sanderson no doubt preferred to forget. The fact she had been so reasonable about this when pre-warned during Buchan's preparations for the trial – "you're just doing your job, William, there's no need to apologise" – made the task even more painful. As Farqhuar had pointed out, however, such hardships came with the territory as the public defender. He had little choice, therefore, but to bite the bullet and act in his client's best interests.

"Thank you for providing Mr Farqhuar with such extensive, not to mention graphic, testimony," said Buchan as he greeted Miss Sanderson at the stand. "For those of us who have lived a rather sheltered sexual existence, your vivid descriptions of my client's boudoir proclivities have acted as an education. My eyes have certainly been opened to a world I never knew existed, although the unfortunate consequence of this is that I will never be able to eat a chocolate éclair again or look a donkey in the eye without being filled with feelings of overwhelming disgust."

Buchan's joke brought a raucous laugh out of the public galleries, which had been filled to bursting point for the trial of the century, but Lord Bane was less amused.

"May I remind the public defender this is a court of law, not a music hall," he raged. "Stop acting like a bloody harlequin and start treating this court with the respect it deserves."

Buchan apologised to Lord Bane then set about trying to repair the more significant damage wrought by Miss Sanderson's testimony against his client. Farqhuar had done an excellent job of deconstructing the image Hughes presented to the public through acolytes like Henderson. The carnal excesses of this footballing god could no longer be written off as harmless fun after hearing what Miss Sanderson had to say. The leap from Romeo to rapist now seemed perfectly plausible and Buchan was charged with the task of sowing fresh seeds of doubt in Lord Bane's mind.

"Your testimony has shocked and reviled almost everybody in this court," Buchan told Miss Sanderson. "But we can't lose sight of the fact Mr Hughes has been accused of rape, not indecency. As a woman of words, I'm sure you can understand the difference between those two terms."

"I certainly can," replied Miss Sanderson. "But I'm not the one making the accusation here. I just tried to answer Farqhuar's questions as honestly as I could."

"Not to mention exhaustively," said Buchan. "I find it hard to believe you can describe incidents from 200 years ago in such graphic detail, especially as you were a renowned alcoholic at the time."

"Some of the things Billy asked me to do were so shocking I will never be able to forget them. No matter how much you drink, you can't escape those memories – the shame will haunt me for the rest of my days."

"If these alleged degradations were so disturbing then why did you agree to take part? All you had to do was say one simple word – 'no'."

"I was a desperate woman. The only thing that mattered was feeding my addiction and Billy was my supplier. He provided a steady stream of booze and a roof over my head so I felt obliged to give him something in return."

"So it's safe to say every physical act between you was consensual? Remember, that word matters the most when it comes to deciding the fate of my client."

"Consensual might be stretching it a bit because I hated myself every time I climbed into bed with Billy. But I never voiced any dissent so I couldn't accuse Billy of raping me."

"My client would also contend it was you who first initiated any sexual congress. Is that correct?"

Buchan's question caused Miss Sanderson to shift in her seat as memories of her first night under The Cliff's roof made an unwelcome return. Her embarrassment soon became evident in a blush and Buchan was overwhelmed by self-loathing as he watched his friend suffer.

"I appreciate the pain you are feeling as we delve into your past but a man's fate is a stake here," he said. "Could you please tell the court if Mr Hughes forced himself on you at first or if you were the one who did the initial chasing?"

"I'm ashamed to admit I made the first move," said Miss Sanderson. "I don't think anybody could dispute Billy is a handsome and charismatic man. I had just arrived in Moristoun with a broken heart so I was an emotional wreck. I needed someone to console me and Billy seemed the perfect fit. He emitted this raw sexual energy and it made me take leave of my senses."

"You have nothing to be ashamed of, Miss Sanderson. Countless women have also been swept away by my client's charms. He is Moristoun's most eligible bachelor after all, the jewel in our sporting crown. That's why I find it hard to believe he would attack a young lady like Miss Clarke. My client was basking in the glory of a cup victory and plenty of girls would have been more than willing to accompany him to bed. Why risk it all by raping Miss Clarke in the street?"

"You wouldn't have to ask that question if you knew Billy like I do. He gets these urges and if you're in the wrong place at the wrong time then God help you."

"I'm not sure if you're qualified to make such a character reference any more. Isn't it true you've stayed away from Mr Hughes ever since that night you threw yourself off the cliffs?"

"I don't think anyone could blame me for trying to avoid Billy after all I went through. Giving him a wide berth has allowed me to piece my life back together."

"And what an excellent job you've made of that, Miss Sanderson. You stand as a shining example of what someone can achieve if they put in the effort to turn their life around. As Mahatma Gandhi said: 'You must be the change you wish to see in the world.' I can only commend you for the way you have recovered from those dark days. But if you can transform from a hopeless alcoholic into an upstanding member of our community then why can't my client change from a perverted purveyor of liquor into a clean-cut sportsman and entrepreneur?"

Miss Sanderson paused for a moment then delved deep into her own reservoir of knowledge for something to shoot down Buchan's theory. "I would have thought a man as educated as you would have been too smart to fall for Billy's public relations exercise," she said. "The image he presents to the public is just a façade. Was it not Herman Wouk who said: 'Illusion is an anodyne, bred by the gap between wish and reality'? The reality is Billy hasn't changed one iota, no matter how much he wishes he was this pillar of society. The fact he now stands accused of rape clearly shows that."

Miss Sanderson had expressed exactly what Buchan thought about his client but this was neither the time nor place to commend her for such an excellent summation of Hughes' artifice. Nothing would have given him greater pleasure than standing in Farqhuar's shoes as he would have relished sullying the reputation of Moristoun's most odious hypocrite. Fate had cast him as the public defender, however, and Buchan had no choice but to pour scorn on the words of his oldest friend.

"It sounds like your testimony is driven by revenge," he said. "You clearly blame my client for your second suicide and you're not going to waste this chance to hammer some nails into his coffin."

"That's nonsense," said Miss Sanderson. "Anyone who has read The Book understands the futility of revenge. I don't need to explain the stupidity of your theory to the likes of Farqhuar and Lord Bane but I appreciate such matters are still a little beyond your own intellect. I know for a fact you've read a little Francis Bacon, though, so I'll let him sum it up for you: In taking revenge, a man is but even with his enemy; but in passing it over, he is superior."

Buchan couldn't help but think Miss Sanderson's withering put-down was laced with irony as it was clearly her own revenge for his nasty line of questioning. He had to admit he deserved to feel her wrath, though, so Buchan decided against sharing this observation with the rest of the courtroom. Miss Sanderson had proved herself his intellectual superior and Buchan could only curse his ego as he reflected on the folly of trying to work out Moristoun's many mysteries without deciphering The Book first. He now realised allowing Miss Sanderson to spend any more time at the witness stand would only endanger his client's freedom. Buchan therefore quickly wrapped up his cross-examination and handed the floor back to Farqhuar, who was waiting to introduce his star witness.

From the moment Moira Clarke ghosted her way towards the witness stand, everyone inside the courtroom could see what a terrible toll her ordeal had exacted. The craters that sat underneath her haunted eyes underlined the fact sleep had proven particularly elusive while Moira's reddened cheeks and nose suggested alcohol was responsible for the precious few moments she had managed to escape from her conscious torment. Food had clearly been limited to no more than a cameo role as well and Buchan doubted whether the poor woman would have enough strength to finish what was a journey of no more than 50 paces. This awful sight would have made Buchan's task far more difficult had his client's fate been decided by a jury. Only those with a heart of stone would have failed to be moved by Moira's suffering, so it was to Hughes' advantage that Lord Bane was the sole arbiter inside this courtroom. As a member of The Council he was freed from the emotional shackles that often restrain reason when humans are charged with the task of ruling on matters of law. This ensured Hughes' case would be decided purely on hard facts, something the accused must have been extremely grateful for as Farqhuar expertly led Moira through her testimony. Nobody could dispute Moira had been the victim of a wanton crime after she had poured her heart out to Farqhuar. Even the accused himself freely accepted this; Hughes merely maintained the wrong man had been fingered and the real rapist was still prowling Moristoun's streets. This made the cross-examination far more palatable for Buchan, who would have found the task of painting Moira as a lying harlot even more distressing than digging into the salacious past of his closest friend. He still felt rather dirty and devious as he approached Moira, however, as casting doubts on her reliability was a key part of Hughes' defence.

"I'd like to start off by thanking you for having the courage to face this court," said Buchan as he met the glazed gaze of Moira for the first time. "Nobody should have to be subjected to the suffering you have endured and it's only right the man responsible for this terrible crime receives a fitting punishment. But we have to make sure it is the right man and, as a host of witnesses will testify later today, William Hughes could not have committed this crime. What makes you so sure that it was my client who raped you?"

"I never forget a face," said Moira. "When I picked up the paper on the morning after my attack and saw that same sleazy grin on the front page I just froze in terror."

"But if you never forget a face then why was your initial description to the police so sketchy? I think the exact words were: 'A man in his late 30s, with an athletic build and green eyes.' That's hardly what one would expect from someone with a photographic memory."

Buchan's dig at Moira brought Farqhuar to his feet as the prosecution voiced their first objection to the public defender's conduct.

"The witness never said she had a photographic memory," Farqhuar said. "The public defender is putting words in her mouth."

Lord Bane concurred with Farqhuar's assessment and Buchan accepted the warning that flew his way with a bow of the head. He was surprised Farqhuar had taken so long to slap him down but the administrator's silence during the cross-examination of Miss Sanderson was maybe down to his faith in the witness possessing sufficient intelligence to win any verbal jousts on her own. Moira needed more protection but her fighting qualities soon became evident as she tore into Sergeant McLeish, a man who could have crushed her between forefinger and thumb.

"With the way I was treated down at the police station, they were lucky to get any kind of description out of me," Moira said. "Sympathy was in short supply and that brute of a sergeant just wanted to get rid of me as quickly as possible so he could get back to his kip. I was treated even more shabbily the following morning when I came back and told him William Hughes was the man who had attacked me. That shaved ape didn't actually call me a liar but it was clear he didn't believe me. He told me Hughes was a hero, not a rapist."

"Surely you can appreciate why he viewed your accusation with such incredulity? My client is indeed a sporting hero, not to mention a successful businessman. What could motivate him to attack you and put his empire at risk?"

"The same thing that motivates every man. It's currently swinging between your legs, Mr Buchan."

Buchan couldn't stop himself from blushing a little as the public galleries made the most of this light relief after half-an-hour of testimony that made a public beheading seem like end-of-the-pier entertainment. It was a mistake for Moira to lead the conversation down this seedy alleyway, however, as it gave Buchan the chance to delve into her grubby past.

"I gather that is something of a specialist subject for you, Miss Clarke," he said. "Would you mind telling the court what your profession was back on the mainland?"

Farqhuar was off his seat before Buchan had even finished the question but Lord Bane sided with the defence and invited Moira to answer the query.

"I'm not ashamed to admit I was a prostitute," she said. "We all have to earn our keep somehow. At least it's an honest profession, unlike some I can think of."

Moira's jibe at members of the bar further decimated Buchan's sense of self-worth but he put his growing ethical crisis to one side and continued to probe on behalf of his client.

"Your job may have been honest but it was hardly conducive to a healthy existence, both physically and emotionally. If life was a bed of roses you wouldn't have ended up in Moristoun. Can you tell us what forced you to take your own life?"

The expected objection arrived within a matter of seconds as Farqhuar once more implored Lord Bane to censure Buchan. "The past of Miss Clarke has nothing to do with the matter at hand," he said. "We are here to establish the guilt of the accused. How Miss Clarke arrived in Moristoun is totally irrelevant."

Farqhuar's point seemed perfectly valid but Lord Bane kept an open mind and invited Buchan to explain the reasoning behind his intrusive line of enquiry.

"Miss Clarke was attacked just hours after arriving in Moristoun," he said. "Ending up on this island is a traumatic experience in itself but the manner of one's passing can often make things even worse. Miss Clarke may have been in an intensely emotional state at the time of the alleged attack. If that was the case then her recollection of the incident would have to be regarded as unreliable at best."

Buchan's argument was convincing enough for Lord Bane to instruct Moira to reveal the circumstances behind her arrival in Moristoun. This command caused Moira's fingers to twitch nervously. Those bony digits usually wrapped themselves around a comforting vodka bottle in such times of psychological crisis but such an option wasn't available in Lord Bane's courtroom. They were therefore left to drum out a beat on the wood of the witness box before Moira broke the silence and revealed her torment.

"I had a bad experience with a punter," she said. "He was an evil, sadistic bastard – cut from the same cloth as that fucker over there if what the last witness told us was true."

Moira's outburst provided further amusement for the public galleries but it also earned her a rebuke from Lord Bane, who said: "Such disgraceful language may be the patois of a Glasgow streetwalker but it has no place in a court of law. If you continue to use such profanities you are in danger of contempt."

This left Moira in something of a pickle as describing the myriad of debauched degradations to her body without resorting to such base language was almost impossible. Miss Sanderson's testimony had provided Moira with a few more socially acceptable terms for some of her professional practices – she was particularly impressed by the mysterious term "fellatio" that seemed to describe a blowey – but even William Hughes had failed to plunge the same depths as her final customer. Moira explained her predicament to Lord Bane, who paused for a few seconds before instructing the witness to whisper the crudest terms into the ear of Farqhuar for a pre-watershed translation. This provided the chief administrator with a courtroom challenge far greater than any of his battles with Buchan and it took him several minutes to describe the full extent of Moira's ordeal.

Buchan was amazed her battered body had survived such a perverted attack and summoned enough strength to walk in front of the No.66 bus just 30 minutes later. That fate had then thrown her into a headlong collision with William Hughes seemed an even greater insult and Buchan couldn't bring himself to heap any more pain on the poor woman. After forcing Moira to relive that agony for the benefit of a lowlife like Hughes, Buchan hated himself almost as much as the beasts who had lustily drained every last drop of life out of her. He now realised this job was slowly extinguishing the flame that burned inside him and if he continued down the same path it wouldn't be long before the oxygen ran out. Buchan was nothing if not professional, however, and vowed to see out the remainder of the trial before starting to plot his strategy for a far more important case: William Buchan v Moristoun.

Moira's candid and heart-breaking words had left Buchan even more convinced of his client's guilt but he had little faith in justice being done as the defence of William Hughes started in earnest. Buchan still had the option of sabotage but this would have been futile as Hughes was bound to appeal, citing the professional incompetence of a lawyer who had managed to lose the legal equivalent of a 10-2 lead on the football field. Someone else would then be charged with the simple task of leading the 10 defence witnesses through their fawning eulogies and alibis for Moristoun's sporting deity before Lord Bane finally freed the Moyne Park One. There was little to gain, therefore, from any attempt to help Farqhuar snare his client, no matter how much that would have helped to appease his conscience. The genius of the chief administrator was all that could save the day now and Buchan was disturbed to see Farqhuar rarely move out of second gear during his cross-examination of the defence witnesses. Even knuckle-dragging simpletons like The Cliff's barman Charlie escaped relatively unscathed during their encounters with Farqhuar, much to Buchan's dismay. It was as if the administrator suddenly regarded the case as a waste of his time and energy, something Buchan struggled to comprehend. Although the evidence in support of Hughes was strong – it was hard to see how 10 citizens would put themselves at risk of perjury out of a simple sense of loyalty – there were enough holes in the testimony for someone of Farqhuar's undoubted abilities to exploit. Only two of the witnesses, Charlie and Athletic's vice-captain Tommy Sloan, claimed to be in the accused's company at the estimated time of attack. They couldn't account for every second of their pool tournament, however, so it wasn't too fantastical to imagine Hughes slipping out for a spot of fresh air while his two chums were engaged in combat on the baize. Yet this theory was only given a passing mention by Farqhuar, who seemed to accept their assertion it was impossible for Hughes to prey on Moira in such a short space of time without attracting any unwanted attention. Buchan wasn't alone in wondering why Farqhuar was now conducting his enquiries in such an apathetic manner as most of the crowd had been expecting fireworks from the chief administrator in perhaps the most incendiary case ever brought before a Moristoun court. Something had to be up his sleeve but Farqhuar was running out of time to pluck out his ace as witness after witness departed the box.

Buchan could only hope Farqhuar was saving that ace for a grand finale as he handed the floor over to his adversary for the final time after allowing William Hughes to regale the court with countless tales of his propriety and benevolence. By the time Farqhuar had finished with the conceited braggart sitting in front of him, however, Buchan could only reproach himself for ever having doubted him. From the moment Farqhuar held up a ledger adorned with the Moristoun Athletic club badge, the smug grin that had been etched across Hughes' face for the last hour was wiped away. It was replaced by the look of a rabbit caught in the headlights, a rabbit that then revealed itself as an albino when Farqhuar said: "Have you seen this book before Mr Hughes? It won't be familiar to Miss Sanderson as they don't stock it down at the library but I'm sure every citizen of Moristoun would find it an interesting read. It certainly provided me with a great deal of illumination."

The accused could only sit there in silence as Farqhuar and the rest of the courtroom awaited an answer. When quizzed once more about his knowledge of the ledger, Hughes made a half-hearted denial of its existence, a lie Farqhuar took great pleasure in debunking. "I find that rather hard to believe Mr Hughes," he said. "After all, it's written entirely in your hand. But maybe this is just another unfortunate case of mistaken identity. Perhaps this look-a-like rapist you insist still roams about our streets also shares your calligraphic capabilities?"

As Buchan stared into the eyes of his client, he could tell Hughes was a doomed man. Unbridled anger was laying siege to the cold calculation that had served Hughes so well and the advancing armies soon prevailed. "Which one of those fucking Judases gave you that book?" he raged, causing shocked gasps to echo all over the courtroom. "We're supposed to be a team but one of those jealous bastards has sold me down the river."

Having already chastised Moira for her coarse method of communication, Lord Bane had no option but to issue a grave warning to the accused.

"Any more language like that and I'll have no hesitation in sending you down for contempt. This court has been turned into a burlesque house far too often today and I won't stand for it any longer."

Lord Bane then turned his ire on Farqhuar and demanded to know what that "bloody ledger" had to do with the accusation of rape he was being asked to rule on.

"This ledger proves beyond doubt William Hughes is a devious, conniving liar," Farqhuar said. "What is written on these pages shows this man has defrauded The Council on a grand scale for over a century and simply cannot be trusted. Ultimately, it's one person's word against another's when it comes to deciding the veracity of a rape accusation. And who should we believe on this occasion – poor Moira Clarke or the biggest liar ever to step foot on these shores?"

# Chapter 22:

## Back on the couch

The short jaunt from the Tortured Soul to Buchan's office had become a well-trodden path for McSorely and he usually found himself in high spirits whenever he headed in either direction. This was mostly down to the intoxicating effects of alcohol and Gail, a heady mix that blew away the clouds in his emotional landscape, but McSorely had only received a minor dose of one of those drugs on his latest trip. His regret at missing out on a dram from Jimmy's private reserve would have been rendered but a piffling inconvenience had McSorely then been allowed to spend some quality time alone in Gail's company. This pleasure was also denied him, however, as Brenda insisted on being present when her daughter was recounting the events that had led to Hogg's incarceration. "Gail's still not 18 yet," she told McSorely, a statement designed to remind him she was determined to protect her daughter's chastity as much her legal rights. "It's only right I sit in on the interview as she's technically a minor. I don't want her dragged into any controversy just a few months before going to university."

Gail responded to Brenda's plea with the trademark flounce of a teenager who has just found their maturity called into question by an authority figure.

"If I'm old enough to leave home and live in Inverness then I'm pretty sure I'll be able to cope with a few simple questions," she said while darting her mother an affronted look.

Brenda, though, remained insistent and eventually won the battle of wills, ensuring that the interview was played out under the cloud of inter-familial animosity. McSorely, therefore, learned little from the Mathieson women that Jimmy hadn't already imparted, although the feminine eye for detail admittedly furnished him with a more elaborate picture. Learning the colour of Hogg's jumper and what McCall had ordered for his dinner that night was unlikely to be of much use in the courtroom, however, so McSorely was as well tossing his notes into the bin when he returned to the office. Any notion of an impending romance with Gail also seemed destined for waste disposal as the small talk was pained once McSorely's professional duties had come to an end. Gail had initiated the switch to social conversation by enquiring about McSorely's progress with The Unbearable Lightness of Being but all he could offer was a pathetic "I'm getting there slowly but surely". This led to a follow-up question about what stage he had reached, a query that left McSorely squirming as it had been three days since he last picked up the book. All he could remember was the two female characters engaging in a nude photo-shoot but flagging up that chapter would only lead to the kind of embarrassment that manifests itself in a family living room when the BBC's flagship Sunday night drama sets the poisoned pens of Points of View devotees into overdrive by revealing a bit of nipple. Admitting he hadn't made any progress with the book would have left him with a face every bit as red, however, so McSorely was forced to recount the naked photoshoot in language suitable for his audience.

"I've just reached the bit where the two female characters get better acquainted," he said. "It's an intense and stimulating chapter."

"Oh, the chapter where Sabina takes naked pictures of Tereza," said Gail, who failed to share McSorely's reluctance about referencing such erotic subjects in front of her mother. "You're right, it is quite an intense chapter. But that's still quite early in the book, you've got a long way to go."

"Like I said earlier, slowly but surely," replied McSorely, who decided it was time to save himself from any further embarrassment by revealing a pressing need to return to his workplace. "This case is consuming most of my time at the moment but it will be over soon. Then I can give the book more of my attention."

McSorely could see the disappointment in Gail's face as she received confirmation of his intellectual sloth but helping to secure Hogg's freedom might just win back some of her admiration and respect. As he trudged down the road, however, such a scenario seemed as far-fetched as the Faroe Islands plotting the next terrorist attack on America with suicide puffins. All that could save Hogg now was convincing Dr Barrett of the prisoner's insanity, a task that seemed impossible in a place as demented as Moristoun.

"A talking rook?" said Dr Barrett with a shake of his head. "That's certainly a new one. I've seen many a condemned man embark on a flight of fantasy in a bid to prove their insanity but Hogg has broken new ground by inventing Gerald the Great Sage."

"Indeed, it's an impressive feat of creativity," said Buchan. "I didn't think our humble toilet attendant had it in him. Hogg was so convincing that my protégé is convinced he has lost his marbles."

"But you know as well as me it's impossible to lose your mind in Moristoun. That is perhaps its cruellest punishment – you can never escape into the comforting world of pure delusion. Your mind remains fully aware of every act and thought that brought you here."

Buchan didn't need Dr Barrett to remind him of that fact as visions of Jane swinging from the gallows made their inevitable return and caused him to shudder. But McSorely remained oblivious to the unfortunate mental fortitude of Moristoun's permanent residents and Buchan pleaded with Dr Barrett to give Hogg a cursory examination in a bid to aid the rehabilitation of his assistant.

"Very well," said the psychiatrist. "It will give me a chance to say goodbye to Hogg. Believe it or not, I'm actually going to miss my sessions with him. There's a gormless innocence about the man that is quite refreshing. It will be like

270

watching a vet administer the lethal injection to a senile family Labrador when Lord Bane sends him down."

"I think most people feel sorry for him, with the obvious exception of McCall," said Buchan. "Hogg has been here for so long it's hard to imagine Moristoun without him. I'll try my best to plead for clemency when it comes to sentencing but even Hogg admits he's guilty as sin."

"He has committed a Category A offence, I'm afraid," said Dr Barrett. "There is nothing you or I can do to save him. Hogg was handed his second chance in Moristoun but eventually fell victim to his rage and has to accept the consequences. There's a lesson there for every Moristounian."

Buchan doubted if any of his fellow citizens would heed that lesson as trials usually sparked just a few days of introspection before minds were diverted back towards more simple, if ultimately pointless, pursuits. Indeed, it had taken the downfall of William Hughes to focus Buchan's own mind on gaining the enlightenment that would help end his exile in Moristoun. How could others be expected to ponder such weighty matters in detail if the public defender, a man armed with extensive knowledge of every doomed client, had remained trapped in his own bubble of self-importance for so long? Following the departure of Miss Sanderson, he was now the only person on the whole island who had managed to decipher The Book. That statistic was unlikely to change soon, with Karen and Brenda still at the early stages of their linguistic apprenticeship, and Buchan saw little evidence of intellectual prowess in the new generation of suicidal Scots. McSorely was the perfect example as he seemed to be treating The Unbearable Lightness of Being – a book Buchan had found both stimulating and easy to read – as a text every bit as challenging as a Flemish treatise on astrophysics. If 300 pages of Kundera's sparkling prose were proving so arduous then Buchan could only imagine how his apprentice would react when handed The Book and a magnifying glass for the first time. He was as ill-equipped for the long journey ahead as a bare-chested holiday maker setting off from the foot of Ben Nevis in his gutties with just a packet of fags and a bottle of whisky for company. Guiding McSorely away from a precipitous path that would see him freefall into a permanent stay in Moristoun was of paramount importance, something Dr Barrett was also keen to stress when conversation turned towards how the new arrival was adapting.

"I'm glad young McSorely has settled in well but you have to make sure he doesn't grow to like this place too much," Dr Barrett said. "Building up his confidence and self-esteem is all very well but the ultimate goal is returning him to the mainland. You can't lose sight of that."

"I'm hardly likely to forget that, given McSorely's fate is linked to my own," said Buchan. "But it would be hard not to blame him from wanting to stick around when you consider what he has left behind. People have become so isolated and apathetic on the mainland that their quality of life arguably improves when they arrive here."

Dr Barrett could see Buchan's point, having watched from afar over the past 100 years as human civilisation went into reverse with each supposed step forward in their technological advancement, but his patient had failed to see the wider picture, something of a recurring theme in their sessions.

"This is still a place of punishment," he reminded Buchan. "Moristoun might have all the benefits one would associate with an open prison but if you delve a little deeper you eventually realise living here is actually more like solitary confinement. You will always be a prisoner to your psyche."

"But isn't that also the case on the mainland?" replied Buchan, who relished these philosophical debates with The Council's most sympathetic member. "The many misfortunes to befall McSorely will always prey on his mind."

"Only in this life," said Dr Barrett. "If he tries his best to master those demons and leads a reasonably virtuous existence then there's every chance the next chapter in his story will be much more pleasant. I don't know why I need to explain this to you, Buchan. You have read The Book, haven't you?"

"Yes, I didn't just flick through it and look at the pictures. But my point here is McSorely hasn't read The Book. How is he supposed to know everything will get better next time around? As far as McSorely is concerned, he only gets one hand in the great game and God has dealt him the two of spades and three of diamonds. You can hardly blame him for wanting to throw in his cards."

"Of course not. It's perfectly understandable. That's why Farqhuar has enlisted you to help persuade him otherwise. You seem to have made a decent start but, although McSorely seems to be finding life far more agreeable in our little community, he can't stay here for more than a couple of months. The Council won't stand for it."

"But if we send him back too early there's every chance McSorely will end up back here for good. Re-joining the working world has restored his self-belief and pride while drinking at the Tortured Soul has ended his social isolation. If both those pleasures are taken away and he's thrown back on the mainland then McSorely could easily turn suicidal again. What should I do?"

"You seem to be forgetting that I'm a psychiatrist. I'm here to ask questions, not answer them. I'm sure Farqhuar would be more than happy to issue some orders to you on this matter but it's not part of my remit. All I can do is enquire about what you think is the right course of action."

Buchan would rather breeze into The Cliff during one of their bare-knuckled boxing nights and boldly declare: "Which one of you benders fancies a fight?" than creep into Farqhuar's office and admit to his professional shortcomings. He was left with little option, therefore, but to outline one of his own hastily assembled plans and gauge Dr Barrett's reaction.

"McSorely has developed quite a crush on young Gail Mathieson," he said. "That's not an entirely unexpected development given Gail's looks and personality but it's something we can perhaps use to our advantage."

Buchan's words elicited a concerned look from Dr Barrett but the psychiatrist maintained a professional air and invited his patient to expand on his theory.

"Gail will be leaving us in a few months and I'm hoping her presence on the mainland will help persuade McSorely he

273

should return there as well. That would wrap up both of my Q101s at the same time – I could kill two birds with one stone."

Dr Barrett shuddered at Buchan's use of that awful metaphor, a phrase which only a species as cruel and barbaric as man could dream of using to convey a positive development. The inherent destructiveness of the people Dr Barrett had to deal with on a daily basis also made him doubt the wisdom of Buchan's plan. Tempting McSorely back to the mainland using lust and desire as the bait was destined to end in tears.

"Don't get too wrapped up in your own concerns," he said. "Success with a Q101 isn't measured by the simple act of returning them to the mainland. You have to make sure they are ready to cope with the challenges ahead. Throwing Gail and McSorely together is unlikely to do either party any good."

"I'm not so sure about that," said Buchan. "Gail needs somebody to look out for her on the mainland so it might help to have a familiar face around."

"I'm more of the opinion she needs to have a clean break with Moristoun. Gail is the only person on this island who remains undamaged and we should strive to keep it that way. She needs to be with people who grow and develop at the same pace as her instead of kicking around with the living dead. Surely you can appreciate that?"

"But McSorely isn't one of the living dead. He's a Q101, just like Gail. The best way to keep him away from these shores is to give him something to live for. At the moment, Gail seems to be providing that."

"If you follow that line of thought then the only way to keep McSorely alive is to sacrifice Gail. She's an innocent 17-year-old girl so I doubt she has much of an interest in a damaged man of 30. I take it the doe-eyed devotion you have witnessed in McSorely is far from reciprocal?"

Buchan had to admit Gail had shown little interest in McSorely's neglected body and she now seemed to hold his assistant's mind in equally low esteem. This added weight to Dr Barrett's argument that their potential pairing would only lead to disaster so Buchan vowed to come up with a more reasoned solution to the dilemma of his Q101s.

"It's for the best," said Dr Barrett. "If McSorely is as besotted with Gail as you claim he is then it would make sense to put some distance between them. Lust can send a man down dangerous paths."

# Chapter 23:

# The Penny Drops

Jimmy felt like handing out party hats and streamers before leading his customers in a conga line but the sight of Buchan brooding at the bar forced him to postpone the celebrations, at least until the arrival of McCall and Henderson. It was disconcerting to see the public defender in such a despondent state as Buchan was his most personable customer, a man whose erudite take on life both entertained and informed. On this occasion, though, there was little to distinguish Buchan from the other lifeless lumps who stared intensely into their drinks as if they were pondering the next move in a game of chess with a grand master. Jimmy had never seen Buchan react so badly to courtroom defeat and it was a disappointment he should have been inured to after seeing so many clients lose the limited freedom life in Moristoun accorded them. This was no ordinary case, however, and Jimmy knew many Athletic fans would never forgive Buchan for failing to haul their hero back from the abyss. From what Jimmy had learned about the verdict from McCall's almost tearful radio report, only the most myopic of critics could have held Buchan responsible for William Hughes' demise. Football fans rarely let the facts stand in the way of their prejudices, however, and many were bound to hold a perpetual grudge against Buchan. As far as they were concerned, the equation was simple. Buchan was Hughes' lawyer and he had lost the case. That made him guilty of a crime against their club, even though Hughes had made a rope for his own neck with his greed and stupidity. Jimmy knew Buchan possessed the mental strength required to deal with such idiotic antipathy but also felt it was important to lend some emotional support when he was in such a fragile state.

"Don't beat yourself up about it," he told Buchan as he refilled his customer's whisky glass for the third time inside an hour. "You did the best you could. How were you to know that Hughes was fiddling The Council for all those years? It's no shame to lose a case under those circumstances."

"I'm not ashamed about losing," Buchan said. "In fact, I couldn't be happier about that particular development. The fetid stench of William Hughes' menace no longer hangs in the air and that is something everyone should celebrate."

"Then why do you look as happy as someone who's just stepped in one of those massive shites laid down by Miss Sanderson's dug?"

"Look deep into my soul and you'll find something even more disgusting than that which is embedded on the soles of those unfortunate shoes. What kind of man defends a monster like Hughes? If Farquhar hadn't found that ledger, I would have played a key role in helping a rapist roam the streets of Moristoun with impunity."

"But Farquhar did find the ledger. Justice was done in the end and that's what matters most, isn't it? You shouldn't be too hard on yourself – you were just doing your job."

That was the mantra Buchan always repeated to himself whenever his conduct in court sparked a crisis of ethical confidence but those words now seemed more hollow than a skyscraper constructed from Polo mints. The shudder that ran through his body as he took another swig from his glass had nothing to do with the acrid taste that characterised Moristoun's amateurish attempts at malt whisky production. Instead, it marked his recollection of the moment Moira Clarke had approached him outside of court and delivered a slap that was fully merited. The fact she made this riposte to his intrusive line of questioning in total silence before storming off only served to increase the severity of the blow. Moira was telling him: "I don't need to explain why I'm smacking you in the puss, you know fine well what forced me to do it," and Buchan was left reeling from an emotional haymaker that made the pain of her slap seem trifling in comparison. He then braced himself for a second bout of flagellation when he spotted Miss Sanderson approaching but his friend remained impassive in the wake of her courtroom embarrassments. She greeted Buchan's grovelling apology with a smile that lacked its usual warmth but still contained enough tenderness to suggest their friendship hadn't been irrevocably damaged. "I'm not going to pretend I wasn't hurt by our skirmish at the witness box but it's for the best if we just try to put this unwholesome episode behind us," said Miss Sanderson. "There's nothing to be gained from hanging on to the past. The only way for us both to prosper is to move on."

This gave Buchan the chance to inform Miss Sanderson of his decision to write a new chapter in his own story by finally attempting to tackle The Book. Buchan's revelation returned the librarian's smile to something approaching full beam and she said: "I'm glad to hear Billy's banishment wasn't the only good thing to come out of this awful business. You've taken the first step towards enlightenment but it's a long road. You will need all your mental strength to reach the end."

"If I don't succeed it won't be through a lack of effort," said Buchan. "I can't take many more days like this one. Like most lawyers, I had deluded myself into thinking I was one of the good guys, a crusader for justice. But I now see what a terrible fallacy that is. There's no way you can be the public defender and maintain a clean conscience when that very public encompasses degenerates such as Hughes. The only way I can truly find peace of mind is to leave this rotten job and Moristoun behind."

"You've already won half the battle if you've managed to grasp that concept," replied Miss Sanderson. "Maybe you'll be able to finish The Book quicker than I expected. When do you plan to start your studies? Do you want me to give you a Latin refresher course tomorrow?"

"You'd better make it Monday," said Buchan with a wry smile. "I plan to erase the memories of this harrowing day by draining at least one of Jimmy's whisky bottles."

Buchan had set an impressive pace in his bid to achieve alcoholic amnesia but the first three drinks had only washed away a tiny portion of his shame. Spending time in Jimmy's company was helping to lift some of his gloom, however, and the publican was left in a state of rapture when Buchan revealed the full details of what Farqhuar had found inside that Moristoun Athletic ledger. Jimmy then fetched a bottle of champagne from upstairs and placed it in an ice bucket before eyeing the gleaming glass with the same feverish anticipation as a child glancing across the dining-room table at the ice cream that awaits him once the last of his Brussels sprouts is successfully dispatched. Buchan didn't need to ask why the bottle remained unopened for the time being as he knew Jimmy was saving that pleasure for the moment Henderson and McCall walked in. But he was curious to know how Jimmy had acquired the bottle in the first place. If creating a whisky that didn't taste like the urine of farmyard animals was beyond the ken of Moristoun's alcoholic artisans, then how in the name of God had they managed to concoct some champagne?

"This is the finest French champagne!" said Jimmy in outrage as he responded to Buchan's query about the origins of the bottle. "You can't produce something as classy as this in Moristoun. The Council gave it to us as a gift when we first opened. I've been saving it for a special occasion and today certainly qualifies. I can't wait to offer those two bastards a glass. They'll be dying to drink some champagne but won't be able to bring themselves to accept it given the circumstances."

Buchan found it hard to understand how sporting loyalty to a convicted rapist could force anyone to forego their first taste of champagne in decades but Jimmy soon furnished him with a detailed picture of the football fan's warped mind.

"This is the darkest day in Athletic's history," he said. "Not only has their best player and manager been banished forever but we now have proof they've been cheating for the last 100 years. Each and every one of their triumphs has been tainted for eternity. The dark cloud of shame hangs over everyone associated with the club."

"But why should the actions of one man make everyone guilty? William Hughes is the villain here. I don't see what Henderson and McCall have to be ashamed about."

"Don't turn into an apologist for those arseholes. They're supposed to be journalists, the eyes and ears of the local community, but they sat back and did nothing as Hughes went about his dirty business. Any reporter worth his salt would have uncovered the fraud decades ago. Look how quickly Farqhuar managed to get to the bottom of it once he started probing."

"You're not trying to suggest they both knew Hughes was paying his players on the sly, are you?"

"Of course they knew! But they turned a blind eye to it because they wanted their team to keep winning. All the best players signed for United because they were getting backhanders. That's why they humped us year after year. But that's all going to change now – especially if all their players get sent down as well."

"I wouldn't build your hopes up too much. Technically, it was only Hughes who defrauded The Council because he was paying the players with cash that should have been handed over. The players will probably escape with a warning."

Jimmy responded to Buchan's objective assessment with a five-minute rant that saw the words "injustice" and "sporting integrity" make regular appearances. Buchan was impressed by the landlord's passion for his cause and started to wonder if Jimmy's talents would have been better suited to a different kind of bar. He would have made for a formidable courtroom opponent back on the mainland simply by virtue of his sheer size and booming baritone. Few witnesses or juries would have dared to disagree with Jimmy had he addressed them with the same ferocity shown when attacking Athletic's "shameless mercenaries". This made Buchan wonder if Jimmy might be the ideal man to replace him as public defender once he had gained enough knowledge to earn a ticket out of Moristoun. But it took more than physical presence, passionate presentation and a thirst for justice to triumph inside one of The Council's court rooms. Their judges were made of far sterner stuff than your average juror and considered such qualities to be superficial compared to intelligent, informed argument. However, as Jimmy continued to vent his spleen and demand Council action over Athletic's "corrupt regime", his own argument began to look less and less astute. If The Council came down as hard on Athletic as Jimmy wanted them to, then the club would be left with no players. Football in Moristoun would subsequently grind to a halt as Jimmy's own team would have nobody to play every weekend, limiting their own involvement to a handful of games every year in the Inter Islands Cup. Buchan made this point when Jimmy finally took a brief hiatus from his sermon to pour himself another pint of stout but he merely batted away the inconvenient truth and continued to proselytise.

"They need to be punished for cheating," he insisted. "If that means starting from scratch with no players then so be it. I'm sure Athletic would be able to scrape together a new side in a few months. I'd be happy to wait until they're ready to play us with a team that hasn't been assembled illegally. The Council need to hold an inquiry into the last 100 years of football on the island. I want Athletic stripped of all their honours – each and every trophy was won dishonestly."

Buchan knew The Council had far more important matters to deal with than interceding in what was essentially a petty sporting squabble. The crux of Jimmy's argument was football had to be treated as an amateur sport in Moristoun and that was exactly what The Council would do by paying it no more than lip service. Once they had censured the Athletic players for taking Hughes' illicit payments they would wash their hands of the matter and leave the two clubs to resume hostilities on the field. In the meantime, though, a far uglier battle was set to rage in the pubs of Moristoun as diehards on each side of the football divide fought their corner ferociously. That much became clear when McCall and Henderson finally made their entrance, thereby kicking off the first of a thousand tiresome debates on Athletic's allegedly tainted triumphs. Jimmy greeted their arrival with a cheer and made a beeline for the bottle of champagne after releasing the balloons he had hidden behind the bar.

"You must have had quite a dilemma with the front page headline tonight," he said to Henderson after handing him a champagne flute. "What did you go for in the end – Bye Bye Rapist or Cheating Bastards?"

Henderson ignored Jimmy's taunt as he was far more interested in the glass he had just been handed. "Is this champagne?" he asked after sniffing it suspiciously. "Where in God's name did you manage to get this?"

"Oh, we've had it hidden away for years," replied Jimmy. "Like I said to Buchan earlier, we were just saving it for a special occasion."

"If you classify a rape case as a special occasion then you're even more perverted than I first imagined," said McCall, who was less impressed by the champagne as he had tasted it just five years ago at his mother's fourth wedding, a catastrophic coupling that had helped contribute towards his arrival in Moristoun.

"But today's about much more than the demise of your dear friend William Hughes," said Jimmy. "This is the day when we can celebrate the truth, the joyous confirmation that Moristoun Athletic cheated their way towards every trophy. I'm sure, as journalists, you'll join me in raising a glass to truth and justice."

"Only an idiot would say we cheated our way to all those trophies," said Henderson after choosing to drain his champagne flute rather than raise it. "They were won fair and square on the field of play. Athletic never once broke the rules of association football."

"But they did break The Council's rules," said Jimmy. "Football is an amateur sport here, you're not allowed to pay your players. All the best players in Moristoun signed for your lot because Hughes was giving them backhanders. How on earth were we supposed to compete? Of course it's bloody cheating."

"Players don't sign for Athletic because of the money," added McCall. "They do it for the prestige, because they want to win trophies."

"Exactly," said Henderson. "It's not as if Billy was paying them a fortune. These so-called wages only amounted to a few quid a week. That's hardly going to make a massive difference when it comes to choosing your club."

Jimmy was perfectly placed to rip Henderson's argument to shreds as 40 years behind the bar had provided him with irrefutable evidence of Scotland's stereotypical stinginess. Punters had responded so enthusiastically to the introduction of Happy Hour back in 1959 that Jimmy was hastily forced to impose some restrictions in order to avoid financial ruin. Drinkers now had to present an empty glass before receiving their next cut-priced drink and no individual was permitted to make more than four trips to the bar, a restriction many tried to circumvent by ordering doubles. Jimmy's policy of providing complimentary bar snacks also had to be abandoned when it became clear some regulars wolfed down these peanuts and crisps in lieu of their evening meal. It was nonsense, therefore, to suggest a few quid mattered little in Moristoun, something Jimmy illustrated further once McTavish had taken his regular pew.

"McTavish can back me up on this one," said Jimmy. "Tell these two bastards why you drink here instead of The Bleak Midwinter, with the obvious exception of securing your daily Patsy Cline fix."

"You serve a good pint of heavy son and it's 10p cheaper," said McTavish. "That's enough to keep me away from The Bleak Midwinter."

Jimmy took a bow as he proclaimed himself victor of the first verbal skirmish in this battle to revise Moristoun's footballing history. He then fired the first shot in the next round of hostilities by demanding punishment for the players who had accepted their thirty pieces of silver. "They were taking money from The Council and that's embezzlement as far as I'm concerned," he said. "Then there's the small matter of perjury. At least four players provided Hughes with an alibi and they have to be hammered for lying in court."

Jimmy's demand met with a predictably outraged response from Henderson and McCall, who had also acted as character witnesses for Hughes. "How dare you accuse anyone of perjury," said McCall. "I stand by every word I said and I'm sure all the other witnesses were telling the truth."

"Of course we were telling the truth," added Henderson. "That's an outrageous allegation. Billy wasn't even found guilty of rape, it was the fraud charge that did for him. Isn't that right Buchan?"

"The word Lord Bane used was 'unproven', although he did offer the opinion Hughes had in all probability carried out the attack," said Buchan. "That doesn't mean my witnesses were perjuring themselves, though. Henderson's right, it's an outrageous allegation to make. To the best of my knowledge, everyone in that court was telling the truth, with the obvious exception of the accused."

Jimmy was reluctantly forced to apologise but continued to show Henderson and McCall little respect as he addressed their professional shortcomings. "Don't tell me you're going to give these players an easy ride," he said. "They've been exposed as money-grabbing cheats – it's all there in that ledger."

"The players themselves haven't been called before a courtroom yet," replied Henderson. "We need to be careful we don't prejudice their trial before it begins. If we ripped into them now then I would be at risk of contempt."

"I take it Radio Moristoun's taking the same cowardly line?" Jimmy said to McCall. "You spineless bastards are still frightened of rocking the boat even though the captain is now baw deep in an iceberg."

"Like Henderson said, we need to tread carefully until the trial begins. If the players are found guilty in court then we'll have no hesitation in criticising them. Until then, we can only report them as allegations. Our hands are tied."

Buchan could only hope those players were hauled before a court in the next few days as he had already grown tired of a debate that made Hogg's musings on the best way to banish a resilient skid mark seem like sparkling conversation. The footballing foes were still raking over the coals of fires that had been extinguished decades ago by the time Buchan had reached the bottom of his whisky bottle. Although he was bored beyond comprehension and yearned for some decent conversation, their mindless meanderings at least provided Buchan with a small measure of consolation. Studying seven classical languages now seemed infinitely less depressing than the prospect of hearing another word about Moristoun's fatuous footballing rivalry.

# Chapter 24:

# University Challenge

Gail regretted bringing her history books down to the bar as she found her concentration broken for the umpteenth time by the debate raging to her left. She had relocated from the living room to escape the din caused by her mother's antiquated hoover, which sounded like an elephant receiving an enema when it roared into life, but even that was less irritating than the noise of a footballing feud in full flow. Five days had elapsed since Athletic and United were paired in the Inter Islands Cup draw but it still remained the hottest of topics for her father and his Moyne Park enemies. One league game had been played in the interim and Athletic's 3-0 victory had given Henderson and McCall plenty to crow about ahead of the cup engagement. Jimmy was having none of it, however, and insisted the outcome would be different when the sides next met. "We're just lulling your lot into a false sense of security," he insisted. "And three of your top men will be suspended in the cup after their animality in the last round. That will make a massive difference."

Henderson then made the mistake of claiming such a handicap had failed to hinder his heroes in some of their most famous cup victories, handing Jimmy the chance to preach about his specialist subject, Athletic's tainted trophies. Gail knew this would spark at least another hour of mindless verbal sparring so she gathered up her books and prepared to head back upstairs. She was soon stopped in her tracks, however, as Buchan made his entrance and sat down at the booth Gail had appropriated for her studies. "I hope you're not abandoning your homework already," said Buchan as he took a pew opposite her. "You will have to hit the books with renewed vigour after the news I've just received."

"Does that mean what I think it does?" said Gail. "Have you heard back from the university?"

Buchan responded with a nod and said: "Your interview and entrance exam are booked for July 17. The door to a brave new world is now ajar – all you need to do is kick it down."

Gail greeted this news by throwing herself across the booth to envelop Buchan in a hug. She actually wanted to thank him with a passionate kiss but her subconscious thankfully activated a defence mechanism, thereby saving Buchan from being thrown through the window by Jimmy. Even the innocent hug aroused her father's suspicions sufficiently for him to cut short his deconstruction of Moristoun Athletic's history and direct his attention towards Gail and Buchan. "What's going on here?" Jimmy said as he came out from behind the bar and approached the booth. Gail was still too emotional to present her father with an adequate explanation so it was left to Buchan to pass on the good news. "I've just heard back from the university," he told Jimmy. "They've agreed to give Gail an interview and exam – they're booked for July 17."

It was now Jimmy's turn to be overwhelmed by emotion and he plucked his daughter out of the booth before throwing her in the air in celebration. He repeated this act three times, returning Gail to the wonder of her youth when such trips into the stratosphere were a regular occurrence. The fall from the sky seemed far more precipitous now Gail was four or five times heavier, however, so she instructed her father to halt the thrill ride before it ended in tears of pain instead of joy. Jimmy reluctantly concurred but as he placed Gail back on the deck he told her: "Even though you're heading off to university, you'll always be my little girl. Never forget that."

While few could doubt the sincerity of Jimmy's statement, there was someone else under the Tortured Soul's roof who could lay greater claim to such a sentiment. Gail would always be Brenda's little girl first and foremost but the Mathieson matriarch had missed out on hearing the momentous news thanks to the voluble dissent of the contraption she was dragging across the living-room floor. The hoover's growl had even succeeded in drowning out Jimmy booming voice as he beckoned his wife downstairs to join in the celebrations. Gail was therefore despatched to deliver the news that left both woman in tears as they embraced on the side of the carpet which still remained sullied by the detritus of more subtle bodily secretions. They were mostly tears of joy but every third or fourth drop was mustered from despair as both woman realised Buchan's news had taken them a step closer to separation. This brutal truth was particularly hard to take for Brenda, who knew she would never set eyes upon her daughter again if Gail aced her exam and interview, but she did a good job of hiding the hurt gnawing away at her.

"That's wonderful news sweetheart," she said. "I just know you'll make us proud."

"But what if I make a mess of the exam?" said Gail. "I'll be shaking like a leaf when I step into the room."

"Don't worry, you'll be fine. All you need to do is remember everything I've taught you and be yourself in the interview. If they don't want someone as smart as you at their university they need their heads examined."

"You're just saying that because you're biased. I'm sure all the other candidates are much more intelligent than me. After all, they've gone to a proper school."

Brenda couldn't help but feel a little hurt at the slight on her teaching talents but this was not the time to take Gail to task for being an ingrate. What she needed was a confidence boost so Brenda said: "Believe me sweetheart, you have nothing to worry about on that score. You're the most intelligent teenager I've ever met. From what Buchan has told me, kids on the mainland have too many distractions these days. They spend most of their time fiddling about with phones and rotting in front of computer screens. Picking up a good book has become an alien concept."

Having witnessed McSorely's pathetic attempt to showcase his iPhone, not to mention his laborious progress through The Unbearable Lightness of Being, Gail could see the wisdom in her mother's words. If someone as intellectually limited as McSorely could not only secure entry to university but emerge with a degree, then what did she have to fear from a mere entrance exam? The prospect of leaving Moristoun's shores for the first time still remained daunting but Gail took succour in the fact her parents would surely accompany her for such a momentous trip.

Brenda couldn't bring herself to disabuse Gail of this notion and mouthed the comforting words expected of a mother when the subject was brought up. There was no way The Council would agree to let all the Mathiesons through the portal so it would be left to Buchan to provide the emotional support when Gail took the first step in her great adventure. Furnishing Gail with this upsetting information would serve little purpose at the moment, however, as it would only distract her from cramming for the entrance exam. Brenda's final maternal duty, therefore, was to ensure the only emotions preying on Gail's mind were the doubt and anxiety that assault most teenagers in the build-up to a big exam. There was no way Gail would be able to secure entry to university if her head was awash with thousands of questions about the mysteries of Moristoun so the truth would have to be concealed from her until she returned from Inverness with a letter of acceptance tucked into her back pocket. Pulling off such a trick was fraught with difficulties but Brenda believed Buchan and The Council were astute enough to plot safe passage through a road strewn with mines and broken glass. The challenge for Brenda and Jimmy was far less daunting – coming up with a convincing excuse for their absence on the trip. Feigning serious illness was the best Brenda had mustered thus far but she still hoped to come up with something better as that would also sow seeds of worry in Gail's mind. With three weeks remaining until her daughter ventured forth to Inverness, there was little point in fretting unduly on what was supposed to be a day of celebration. Jimmy certainly seemed oblivious to such concerns when his arms wrapped themselves around his two "special ladies" on their return to the bar. Brenda hadn't seen her husband in such a good mood since

William Hughes' demise and that day sprang to mind when Jimmy proposed a toast to "the smartest girl in Moristoun".

"We should be breaking out the champagne in honour of your achievement," she told Gail. "But your father decided to waste the one bottle we had on some petty footballing matter."

"I can only offer my humblest apologies," said Jimmy. "That was long before you were born my dear, in the days when alcohol was clouding my judgment. I now realise some things are more important than football."

Those words stirred Henderson into action and he said: "I hope you will take some comfort from that statement when you watch your rag-tag ensemble get systematically dismantled at Moyne Park next weekend. As the fifth goal flies past the cack-handed clown who masquerades as your goalkeeper, just keep telling yourself it's only a game."

"I'm sure Jimmy's already well acquainted with such emotions," added McCall. "After all, it's the mantra of losers the world over and United fans are experts when it comes to dealing with the pain of defeat."

Jimmy's face became redder with rage as each word spewed forth but he was stopped from venting that steam as Brenda stepped in to nip yet another exasperating argument in the bud.

"If I hear another word about bloody football I'm going to kick the three of you out into the street," she said. "This is Gail's big night and I'm not going to let you spoil it by squabbling about a stupid game. Can you not call a truce for one bloody evening?"

Brenda's rant left the three men suitably ashamed and Henderson led the apologies after they had agreed to put a temporary halt to hostilities. "Please forgive us, Gail," he said. "We were just enjoying a little mischief at your father's expense. Although his choice of football club would suggest otherwise, your father is a man of great wisdom. He hit the nail on the head by claiming some things were more important than football and I would gladly trade a victory in next week's game for the answers to your exam."

"I'll second that emotion," said McCall. "We're all hoping you pass with flying colours – even though it will break our hearts when you leave. It just won't be the same without you here."

Gail was touched by the first compliment she had received from the debauched pair that remained unsullied by innuendo or lecherous undertones. Beneath all the grime and filth she would probably find two hearts capable of genuine generosity and Gail had to admit she would miss her daily dose of Henderson and McCall.

"For all your bluster, you two are just a couple of big softies, aren't you?" she said. "Don't worry, I'll come back to see you as often as I can. I'm only going to Inverness, it's not the other side of the world, is it?"

Every pair of eyes drifted towards their drinks in a bid to escape Gail's gaze as they tried their best to hide the sadness her words had stirred. Inverness would be every bit as remote as the offices of the National Hermit Association in Outer Mongolia once Gail stepped through the portal, a sobering thought for those who had just raised their glasses to the budding émigré. Some of the darkness that had descended over the party was soon blown away, though, as McSorely breezed through the doors to provide a welcome distraction.

"What are you having son?" said Jimmy. "The drinks are on me – we're having a wee celebration."

"That's very kind of you, Jimmy," replied McSorely. "I'll have a lager. What's the occasion?"

"My wee girl's moving up in the world. Buchan's just had word back from the university about her entrance exam. It's lined up for July 17."

McSorely raised his glass towards Gail in congratulation once Jimmy had finished pouring the pint and wished her all the best for the impending grilling. Like so many of those gathered around the bar, however, those words of encouragement were delivered through gritted teeth. He still retained hope of becoming intimately acquainted with the girl who had brought some light back into his dingy world but such a scenario could only unfold if Gail remained in Moristoun. McSorely was not a vainglorious man but he had spent long enough in his new surroundings to realise he was actually one of the island's most eligible bachelors. If McSorely needed any assurance such a belief wasn't pure braggadocio, it arrived when he made a visual sweep of the Tortured Soul. Had The Council decided to improve the standard of their stock by introducing a policy of eugenics, most of McSorely's fellow drinkers could have few complaints about being rounded up for sterilisation. Not since his last trip to New Broomfield had he witnessed such a grotesque collection of gargoyles and even PT Barnum would have baulked at putting some of the poor creatures on public display. If this was the standard of competition, it was not unreasonable to expect Gail would eventually consider him as a potential partner, especially if he managed to undergo a gradual intellectual transformation. Just two men in Moristoun made McSorely look like the sexual inadequate he truly was and they were the only ones who had no carnal interest in Gail – Jimmy and Buchan. It would be a different story on the mainland, however, and McSorely would stand little chance once Gail started associating with the cocky, athletic young men who were bound to gravitate towards her on campus. This realisation saw a familiar fog of depression engulf McSorely and he took refuge in alcohol, downing the complimentary pint within a minute before investing in another drink.

Buchan could sense the despair that accompanied each gulp from his assistant's glass and realised his second Q101 had been booted backwards by the giant stride taken towards a successful conclusion of Gail's case. He now understood it had been sheer folly to think Gail and McSorely could tread the same path towards the mainland as each step one took would ultimately hinder the other from safely reaching their destination. Keeping them apart, as Dr Barrett had suggested, was the best way of assuring they both had a happier future, no matter how much McSorely would beg to differ as he gazed at Gail lovingly through the slivers of lager that clung to the inside of his second empty pint glass. Buchan was best served focusing most of his energy on finishing the labour of love that had consumed more than 17 years of his life before turning his attention back towards McSorely. He would just have to hope his assistant possessed the mental fortitude to endure the heartbreak in the interim, which was admittedly something of a gamble as the collapse of his engagement had edged the poor man towards suicide. This time, though, McSorely had gainful employment to distract him and Buchan was hoping the excitement of going to court for the first time would take his assistant's mind off Gail's departure. Hogg's trial was destined to be an anti-climax, as it would simply be a matter of sentencing once Buchan had entered a plea of guilty, but it was for the best if McSorely retained a sense of purpose. He had to believe there was still a chance of getting Hogg off the hook, so Buchan moved across the bar to his apprentice and informed him that the prisoner was scheduled to receive his mental MOT from Dr Barrett tomorrow morning.

"If poor old Hogg is as batty as you believe he is then we might just have a chance," said Buchan. "But feigning insanity is the oldest trick in the book for those awaiting the vengeance of a public thirsting for blood. If Hogg is faking it then there's no way he will be clever enough to outsmart Dr Barrett."

"It seemed pretty real to me," said McSorely. "After all Hogg has suffered at the hands of that animal McLeish, I'd be more surprised if he wasn't crazy. There's only so much a man can suffer before he breaks down completely. Hogg should be in a hospital bed instead of a cell."

"I totally agree but unfortunately those in charge of our penal provisions think otherwise."

"But surely The Council will have to move Hogg into a mental hospital if Dr Barrett rules that he has gone insane. It must go against European law to keep him banged up with that maniac."

Given that sanity was an incontestable permanence for the populace, Buchan was able to give McSorely the comforting assurances he sought, safe in the knowledge he would never have to back up his claims. "If Dr Barrett rules that our client has gone round the bend then Hogg will be tucked up in a hospital bed this time tomorrow," he said. "All we can do is sit back and pray. His fate lies in the healing hands of Dr Barrett."

# Chapter 25 –

## The patient is a virtue

Almost a year had passed since Dr Barrett's last visit to the police station but the memory of Alan Gallagher's tear-stained face was still fresh in his mind. The fire that once burned within Moristoun's most notorious arsonist had been stamped out within 24 hours of his captivity by Sergeant McLeish's savagery. Gallagher's transformation into a wet blanket was complete by the time Dr Barrett came calling three weeks later and it saddened the psychiatrist to see one of his most intriguing patients reduced to a quivering excuse for a human being. He had hoped to delve deeper into the mind of a man whose burning desire to become the island's finest restaurateur had led him to torch the premises of every competitor on one infamous night. That fiendish mind became an empty shell, though, after Gallagher had been left alone in Sergeant McLeish's company. The policeman took particular relish in dishing out his trademark brand of tyranny as he was one of the diners forced to abandon their expensive dishes when smoke started to spread through McCauley's. His choice of flame-grilled steak was rather prophetic but Sergeant McLeish failed to appreciate the irony as he was forced to head back to the station and make do with a humble plate of pie and chips instead. "You should be taking this fucker straight to the gates of hell because he deserves to burn," he told Farqhuar upon receiving delivery of the accused the following morning. Sergeant McLeish then turned towards Gallagher and roared: "And whatever Beelzebub dreams up for your punishment it will seem like a fucking picnic compared to what I have planned for you." Gallagher soon discovered Sergeant McLeish's bite was every bit as fierce as his bark and within a couple of days he did indeed begin to view Satan's dwelling of the damned as something of a safe haven in comparison to his cell. The accused barely had enough strength to string a coherent sentence together when Dr Barrett visited but there was one phrase he managed to repeat three or four times between repeated bouts of sobbing and it was "Get me out of here".

Dr Barrett expected Hogg to be in a similar state of torpor after almost two weeks of Sergeant McLeish's hospitality but the man who extended a warm handshake inside the cell seemed to be bearing his punishment far more stoically. Hogg had clearly suffered considerable physical pain during his confinement as he moved rather gingerly around the cell. The prisoner's mind, however, had proven far more resistant to the tortures inflicted on it. From what Dr Barrett could gather from the small talk that preceded their official business, Hogg remained very much the same man he had examined every month for the last four centuries – an amiable, seemingly harmless buffoon. That "seemingly" qualifier had been added to Dr Barrett's assessment of his patient in the wake of Hogg's attack on McCall, a sudden burst of violence that had shocked the psychiatrist. He never thought the lavatory attendant would be capable of such a horrific assault but the one thing Dr Barrett had learned from his work was that man would always remain an unpredictable beast. Indeed, there remained an open book in The Council offices as to how earth's most destructive species would ultimately engineer their own downfall. Dr Barrett was one of many who had wagered on nuclear Armageddon in the wake of Hiroshima and Nagasaki being razed but almost 70 years had passed without one of those infernal devices being detonated in aggression. It was still far too early to tear up his betting slip as the threat of atomic annihilation would remain very much real until man had the wisdom to put each and every nuclear warhead out of commission. But Dr Barrett had to admit the horse he had backed was no longer the odds-on favourite in the 2,000

Guineas You've Only Got Yourselves To Blame You Stupid Bastards Stakes. The only safe bet seemed to be that man would blast his brains out long before that well-deserved asteroid arrived or the sun started to spew out fatal levels of radiation. Humans seemed incapable of looking at the bigger picture and failed to appreciate the long-term harm associated with acts that satisfied more immediate needs. Hogg was the perfect example of such idiocy, a man who had wasted the second chance of life in Moristoun by carrying out the act that guaranteed him damnation. He knew fine well repeatedly plunging a knife into McCall would hurt himself much more than his victim but opted for the instant opiate of sating his rage. Hogg had already paid a heavy price for such short-sightedness but the blows inflicted by Sergeant McLeish were nothing compared to the terrors that awaited him in the next realm. There was little to gain, however, from divulging such information to his patient now his crime had been committed. If Hogg was to take some measure of enjoyment from his last few fleeting moments in Moristoun then he would have to remain ignorant of future torments, just as Alan Gallagher had. Dr Barrett had comforted the arsonist by assuring him the intense physical pain he was feeling would soon be over and that was indeed true. He had merely neglected to mention far greater spiritual suffering awaited him, something Hogg would also soon discover.

If Hogg's feeble mind had managed to grasp that concept, he was doing a remarkably good job of hiding his anguish. Indeed, the prisoner even managed to break into a laugh when Dr Barrett revealed his presence at the police station was down to Gerald the talking rook.

"I had a feeling that story might have a few consequences," said Hogg. "It was just the first thing that popped into my head when I tried to cover my tracks after mentioning The Book. What can I say? I guess I'm not very good at thinking on my feet."

"On the contrary," said Dr Barrett. "I regard Gerald as a wonderful creation. It's just a shame your tale isn't true. It would save me a lot of time if people turned to your winged philosopher for therapy instead of darkening my doorstep."

"People probably wouldn't need therapy if we could all talk to the animals like that Dr Doolittle fella. I remember thinking he was the luckiest man in the world when that film was shown at The Rialto all those years ago."

Dr Barrett had considered that frivolous movie a grievous waste of his Friday evening back in 1968 but was nevertheless keen to learn why it had made such a lasting impression on Hogg.

"You'd never be lonely if you could have a chinwag with your animal friends," said Hogg. "That's the worst thing about being stuck in this cell, the isolation. It's far more painful than anything that ape in a uniform can inflict on me. Wee birds perch on those bars up there all the time and I'd love nothing better than to have a natter with them, just to break the monotony."

"So you've not been overwhelmed by visitors since landing here, then?"

"You're only the second one who has bothered their arse to come and see me. I'm like a ghost to everyone now, they want nothing to do with me."

"I wouldn't take it too personally. Prisoners have always been viewed as pariahs round here, with the exception of William Hughes. I'm still amazed by the level of devotion such a repugnant character managed to inspire in people. You weren't one of those weak-minded fools who kowtowed to him, were you?"

"No. I know people regard me as an idiot but I was smart enough to see right through that bastard. He brainwashed people through football but I never had any interest in the game. I'm a child of the 1600s, remember. The national sport when I was growing up was Hunt The Jesuit. I was there when they hauled John Ogilvie through the streets of Glasgow then strung the poor bastard up and disembowelled him. When you've seen things like that, it's hard to get excited about 22 men in shorts kicking lumps out of each other."

"It's a shame the rest of our citizens don't share your sense of perspective. Moristoun's two tribes are engaging in cup battle on the day after your trial and it has left some in a state of feverish anticipation. I'm afraid you will be forgotten by most of the populace within hours of discovering your fate."

The prisoner greeted this news with a resigned shrug but Dr Barrett could tell his patient was hurting more inside. Hogg was leaving no legacy from his 400 years in Moristoun and the only real mark he had made in all those years was found on the chest of McCall. His mainland existence had been equally inconsequential with Hogg devoting most of his adult life to caring for his sick mother. When his only social companion finally departed for a better world, Hogg was robbed of his raison d'etre and slumped into depression. Far from being liberated by the loss of the woman who had burdened him for so long, Hogg felt utterly lost and it wasn't long before he joined his mother in bidding farewell to their world. Arriving in Moristoun gave Hogg a chance to rediscover himself but he blew it almost instantly, wasting the three questions that could have helped guide him along the right path. Now his journey had ended in a prison cell and this time there would be no instant shot at redemption. He would soon join all the murderers, rapists, pederasts, necrophiliacs, warlords and marketing managers in the darkest recesses of hell and the penance of a 400-year stint in Moristoun would seem like an hour of after-school detention by the time Hogg was finally allowed to return to a more agreeable realm.

Dr Barrett was usually employed as a mere shoulder to cry on when he met men condemned to such a fate but all Hogg's tears seemed to have dried up. Indeed, the man widely regarded as Moristoun's most intellectually challenged resident was now impressively philosophical about his destiny. Dr Barrett found this change in Hogg's bearing fascinating and started to probe for the reasons behind his new outlook.

"I must say, you seem to be dealing with your predicament remarkably well," he said. "From what Farqhuar and Buchan told me, you were a babbling wreck when you first arrived here. Why are you now so calm?"

"I've finally found some inner peace," said Hogg. "I now realise all suffering comes from within."

Dr Barrett pressed for further details about this moment of clarity and found it ironic that Hogg's inspiration came while Sergeant McLeish was booting him in the ribs.

"Instead of flinching and fighting against the pain I just relaxed and let my body go limp," Hogg said. "I shut my mind down and that was when I discovered he could no longer hurt me, no matter how hard he kicked."

"I take it Sergeant McLeish didn't react particularly well to that development?"

"No, he went fucking crazy. He feeds off your fear and it drove him mental when I just soaked up every punch and kick. He kept hitting me harder and harder until he eventually realised it was utterly pointless and stormed off. It was brilliant – my body was beaten to a pulp but I had never felt so powerful. It felt like I was the one in control, as if I was untouchable. He hasn't laid a finger on me since then."

Dr Barrett couldn't help but smile as he listened to Hogg's story. His patient had understood one of life's most important lessons, a feat that often proved beyond even those who had managed to decipher The Book. This illumination had sadly come too late to be of any use to Hogg in Moristoun but it would certainly serve him well as he underwent what would feel like an interminable penance for his crime.

"Mastery of the mind is perhaps the greatest gift you can bestow on yourself," Dr Barrett said. "If you had managed to blank out all that anger and bitterness a few weeks earlier you wouldn't be facing such a terrible fate."

"I've always been a bit slow I suppose but I usually get there in the end. That's not going to happen this time, though, is it? I'll be stuck in hell for all eternity for what I've done."

"No soul is ever completely lost. It might seem like an eternity when you're down there but there is always a way back. If you repent and learn from all your punishments then you will get there in the end. But there won't be any short cuts

– that easy path is cut off the second you are banished from Moristoun. Your journey will take far longer."

Dr Barrett's words brought tears back to the prisoner's eyes but this bout of weeping was borne by feelings of relief, not trepidation. Although Hogg's immediate future was even bleaker than that of a bridegroom who has awoken from his Eastern European stag night in a crack den operated by the Serbian militia, he now realised he would eventually emerge from the darkness. Armed with this knowledge, he would be able to endure whatever miseries awaited him. Hogg had already learned how to master physical pain so the task of dealing with hell's psychological assault now seemed far less daunting. As for his impending trial, it was now relegated to a minor inconvenience. Hogg's sins would be laid bare before the people of Moristoun but why should he care about what they would think of him? The only genuine friends Hogg had made in his 400 years on the island had long since departed and he felt no connection with the current crop of citizens. Empathy for those who had joined him in taking their own lives was also in short supply. Indeed, the one person in Moristoun whom Hogg did feel sorry for hadn't even committed suicide and it was to McSorely that his thoughts turned when Dr Barrett started to talk about the trial.

"I know I have to plead guilty and accept the punishment for what I have done," said Hogg. "But I feel bad for young McSorely after all the work he has put into my case. He was the only one who genuinely believed I had a chance and I don't want him to feel like a failure. He's a Q101 and losing his first case might darken his mind again."

"I'm sure Buchan knows what he's doing," said Dr Barrett. "He let McSorely take charge of your case in the knowledge it was destined to end in failure. The job was designed to give him a sense of purpose and make him feel important. If you let McSorely know how much you appreciate all his hard work then I'm sure everything will be fine."

"I'm not sure if I can deal with another one of his visits. He keeps asking awkward questions and my stupid answers only create more problems. It's probably safer if I avoid seeing any more visitors until the trial."

"It seems like you're on something of a roll when it comes to words of wisdom. Why don't you write McSorely a letter instead? That way you can tell him how grateful you are while avoiding any difficult follow-up questions."

"There's no way that bastard McLeish will let me have a pen and paper," replied Hogg. "He hates giving anything to me. It's like he's handing over diamonds and rubies every time he grudgingly pushes the food tray through the bars."

"It's a good job I came prepared then," said Dr Barrett as he delved into his jacket pocket and produced a notepad. "I always carry this about in case I have to jot something down. There's still 45 minutes before my next meeting so knock yourself out. Just make sure your letter contains nothing controversial."

Although Dr Barrett had to correct several grammatical and spelling mistakes when Hogg handed back his pad 15 minutes later, there was little within the actual content that needed any censorship. Hogg had merely expressed his sincerest thanks for all McSorely's efforts and warned him against the folly of throwing his own life away, advice that could actually prove helpful in the Q101's rehabilitation. There seemed little danger, therefore, in delivering his note to McSorely as promised, an assumption that would ultimately prove Dr Barrett was every bit as fallible as his patients.

# Chapter 26:

# Guilt trip

Buchan stifled a yawn as he surveyed the news Henderson had seen fit for public consumption, with proof of the editor's corruptive influence evident in the strap that informed readers: "Big cup countdown – only five days to go." To be fair to Henderson, there was little else in Moristoun to get excited about and Buchan gave only a cursory glance to the Gazette's banal selection of local stories before reaching the section he always found most interesting – mainland and world news. The preceding day, Sunday July 1, had been relatively inconsequential in terms of global incident, with only the Mexican general election, continuing turmoil in Syria and a distressing attack on two Kenyan churches attracting Buchan's attention. One major international event had kept millions glued to their TV sets, computers and radios but Buchan had no interest in that as it was a mere game of football, the concluding match of the European Championships. Had he wished to discover whether Spain or Italy had emerged victorious, all he had to do was turn a few more pages. Buchan rarely wasted his time sifting through the sports section, however, and decided remaining in a state of ignorance would make sitting through the highlights less of a chore when he took his usual seat at the Rialto on Friday night. Avoiding the score for the next four days would be nigh on impossible, though, given how often football came up in conversation at his favourite watering hole. Even his own office was no longer a sanctuary, thanks to the presence of McSorely, and his assistant gave the game away within seconds of Buchan deciding to keep the outcome of the final a mystery. "Are you reading about last night's game?" McSorely asked. "That was some doing the Italians took, wasn't it? Who would have thought the Spanish would hammer them 4-0?"

"There are far more important things than football to read about," replied Buchan. "Don't you think the 15 people killed in cold blood at those churches in Kenya deserve more attention than 22 prima donnas running about a football field?"

"I didn't see that story," said McSorely. "I only had a quick skim through the paper and I always start from the back."

Buchan wasn't surprised McSorely had failed to read about the atrocity, given Henderson had only allocated three paragraphs to a tragedy that needed to be extensively dissected if any lessons were to be learned about religious intolerance. Such an editorial oversight enraged Buchan as he could remember the days when the Gazette would delve far deeper into such important issues under Barraclough's leadership. But with Henderson at the helm, the paper now pandered to populism, delivering the pap that satisfied imbeciles who read the paper from the back inwards and give up once they reach the cartoon page.

"If you want to become the kind of man who can impress an educated woman, then I suggest you start reading newspapers from the front," said Buchan, who had noticed McSorely returning to The Unbearable Lightness of Being since learning of Gail's impending departure. "The Indian philosopher Chanyaka held the view that education beats beauty and youth – that's certainly the case when it comes to matters of the heart."

Although McSorely had to admit there was some merit in Chanyaka's words, he doubted if they held much resonance in modern society. The only thing that seemed to beat beauty and youth in the world he had grown up in was money, not education. How else could one explain the preponderance of crusty intellectuals doomed to a life of celibacy while fat-headed footballers and C-list celebrities were beating beautiful women off with a stick? McSorely made that observation to Buchan in the hope it would prove he was no dunce when it came to reasoned debate but it merely acted as further proof of his myopia.

"If you are jealous of those idiots then you truly are a lost cause," Buchan said with a sigh. "You don't want to be yearning after the kind of women who find themselves drawn to such characters. You need someone who engages your mind as much as your loins. Outer beauty is ephemeral but inner beauty is eternal."

Gail possessed both of those qualities and Buchan's bid to steer the conversation towards the object of his assistant's affection had all the subtlety of a pest-control officer whose preferred option for disposing of mice was death by sledgehammer. This made McSorely feel uneasy as he had never felt comfortable talking about his emotions. Indeed, he had only opened his heart to one person about the collapse of his engagement and that was the woman he hoped would eventually fill the void created by Sarah's departure. Although McSorely got on well with the man who was now his boss, he still didn't know Buchan well enough to confide in him about such delicate matters. It was with a great sense of relief, therefore, that McSorely greeted the arrival of Dr Barrett, as it aborted what would have been an embarrassing conversation.

He was also pleased to see the psychiatrist from a professional perspective as McSorely's hopes of winning his first case would hinge on what Dr Barrett had to say in the next few minutes.

"What news do you bring from our mutual friend behind bars?" asked Buchan as he invited Dr Barrett to take a seat. "Has Hogg really lost his marbles, as my assistant insists, or is it all just an act?"

"As far as I can ascertain, it's neither of those things," replied Dr Barrett. "Hogg certainly isn't insane but I'm also far from convinced his bizarre tale about the talking rook was one last desperate bid for freedom."

"How do you explain it then?" said McSorely. "Why would he come up with such a surreal story?"

Dr Barrett knew he couldn't tell McSorely the real reason for Hogg's flustered prattling and tried his best to come up with an explanation that would arouse the fewest suspicions. This was the first time Dr Barrett had met Buchan's assistant since chemically inducing his amnesia but he made the sensible assumption that McSorely was the kind of person who failed to question the complex terms thrown at him by members of the medical profession. "My conclusion is Hogg suffered from what is known as Sokal's Illusion," said Dr Barrett, naming his fictional ailment in tribute to the American professor who once duped a journal into publishing his nonsensical paper by virtue of its grandiloquence.

"It's a temporary form of hallucinatory hysteria that usually strikes patients who have undergone a Salpingo-oophorectomy. Hogg has yet to receive such intrusive treatment but in rare cases it can also affect those with underlying Diffuse Idiopathic Skeletal Hyperostosis or Visceral Leishmaniasis if they are subjected to bouts of extreme violence."

"Of course!" said Buchan, as he joined Dr Barrett in having some fun at McSorely's expense. "I knew there had to be some explanation. I forgot that Hogg was one of the unfortunate few who suffered from Visceral Leishmaniasis. I didn't know it could spark a bout of Sokal's Illusion but that's why I'm just a humble man of the law and the health of our good citizens is placed in your hands."

"It's the first time I've actually seen such a case first hand," said Dr Barrett. "Sergeant McLeish must have triggered it when he was manhandling your client. It's just a shame I never got to observe Hogg when he was in his delusional state. You witnessed a piece of Moristounian medical history when you visited Hogg, Mr McSorely. Is there anything you can tell me about his behaviour that might prove useful for my notes?"

McSorely paused for a few seconds as he tried his best to recall details of Hogg's physical and psychological deportment. After hearing Dr Barrett and Buchan bandy such complicated terms about, he didn't want to sound like an ignoramus but his knowledge of medicine was largely drawn from episodes of Holby City and ER. To him, Visceral Leishmaniasis sounded like a condition that forced sufferers to belt out spontaneous stanzas of poetry about Dunfermline FC. He didn't want to admit this to Dr Barrett, though, and pressed ahead with his own flowery description of Hogg in a bid to mask his ignorance.

"Physiologically, he was in a state of great distress," said McSorely. "It was clear that he had suffered many fractures and lesions from Sergeant McLeish's attack. You said that bouts of extreme violence could spark Sokal's Illusion and I would have to conclude Hogg had been the victim of such an assault."

"I don't think anyone could dispute that," said Dr Barrett. "He's still in quite a poor physical condition and it's now almost a week since the attack took place. I'm more interested in Hogg's mental state, though. What can you tell me about that? Was he manic or quite calm?"

"I'd say he was remarkably calm, given what he had suffered. The only sign of any mental instability came when he started talking about the rook. He was totally convinced of Gerald's existence and talked about the bird's exploits as if they were entirely natural."

Dr Barrett knew McSorely would only start to view Hogg's ramblings as natural if he played a part in confirming the diagnosis of Sokal's Illusion. So the psychiatrist was effusive in his praise as he thanked McSorely for his analysis.

"Your input has proven invaluable," said Dr Barrett, before telling Buchan it was easy to see why he had snapped up such an intelligent young man for his legal practice. "From what you have told me, I'm now certain Hogg suffered from Sokal's Illusion. I wasn't sure before I came here because I didn't get the chance to see the patient while he was ill but your description was spot-on. He fits the profile exactly."

"Where does that leave us then?" said McSorely. "If this condition was brought on by an attack from Sergeant McLeish then surely it affects his trial. Is there any chance we can have the case thrown out?"

"I'm afraid not," interjected Buchan. "The best we can hope for is to bring a separate action against Sergeant McLeish for assaulting a prisoner. And, as I've explained before, that can only happen if Hogg decides to make an official complaint. That now seems unlikely from what Dr Barrett has told us. You have to remember what Hogg has suffered behind bars doesn't affect his guilt. He will still have to pay for his assault on McCall."

McSorely looked across to Dr Barrett in hope of a more positive prognosis but none was forthcoming. "Buchan's right," the psychiatrist said. "I share your pity for poor Hogg but he will have to be judged for his own crimes. He even accepts that himself. In fact, Hogg asked me to inform you he wants to plead guilty and accept his punishment without any appeals for clemency."

Such news came as little shock to Buchan and he was relieved to hear Hogg had now come to terms with his fate. For the sake of McSorely's future, though, it was best to put on an air of disappointment and curse the collapse of a case his assistant had pursued so rigorously. That was McSorely's instinctive reaction and he viewed Hogg's decision to throw in the towel as something of a slap in the face.

"He can't just give up after all the work I've put in," McSorely said. "His case has been a labour of love ever since I started working here. It can't just count for nothing."

"It's a disappointment you will have to get used to in this line of work," said Buchan. "We are here to represent those who choose to accept our services and must let them choose their own path. The worst thing a lawyer can do is become too attached to a client and consider themselves a potential saviour. Samuel Johnston perhaps summed it up best when he said: 'He who seeks happiness by changing anything but his own disposition will waste his life in fruitless efforts.' This is merely a job my dear boy. Please don't make the mistake of viewing it as some kind of calling."

McSorely had to admit his heightened sense of self-worth since leaving the mainland had been linked to viewing himself as some sort of messiah for the broken man behind bars. Although he had stopped short of donning vestments and offering absolution for Hogg's sins, McSorely had come to think of himself as an avenging angel engaged in a battle against forces of darkness expertly marshalled by the demonic Sergeant McLeish. That was why Hogg's lack of faith had come as such a blow and Buchan had now delivered the equivalent of a follow-up volley to the midriff by further debunking his deification. Fortunately for McSorely, a medical professional was on hand to tend to his wounds and Dr Barrett helped to soothe some of his pain.

"You couldn't have done any more to help Hogg," he said. "He admits that himself. Hogg knows he was lucky to have you fighting his corner when everyone else had given up on him. You've brought a small measure of happiness to a condemned man and for that you should be proud. Defeat is never truly a defeat if a man can hold his head high at the end of the contest."

McSorely could only wish those in charge of compiling the Scottish league tables held a similar view when it came to deciding Albion Rovers' position in the grand scheme of things. He had also rarely subscribed to the view held by Dr Barrett, preferring to wallow in the pity associated with being a luckless loser in almost every sphere of society. As far as he was concerned, Hogg's decision to give up the ghost provided further proof of his glaring inadequacies and Dr Barrett's words of consolation seemed hollow. Besides, how was he to know Hogg had even paid him a glowing tribute? Dr Barrett could have just been making it all it up in a bid to make him feel like less of a failure. McSorely made this point to the psychiatrist, forcing Buchan to make an apology for the insolence of his assistant, but Dr Barrett took no offence and fished into his pocket to pluck out Hogg's letter.

"Hogg asked me to deliver a letter that summed up his feelings," he said. "I sat there and watched him write it inside the cell. I took the liberty of correcting the errors that littered his prose but you can rest assured the sentiments expressed come from the bottom of his heart."

McSorely apologised to Dr Barrett for questioning his integrity as he took the letter from his hands. He then returned to his desk, placed the letter in front of him and started to read:

Dear Mr McSorely,

I'm not an educated man so please excuse the poor quality of this letter. I'm lucky to have Dr Barrett sit by me as I write these words so at least that will save me from looking like an even bigger idiot. If I had my time all over again I would try to learn a lot more as I now see it's a waste to spend so much of your life in ignorance. You are a much smarter man than me so I hope you have already realised this and are always trying to improve your knowledge. But that can only take you so far in life and it's much more important to have a big heart. I've known plenty of clever clogs over the years and some of them were right bastards. McCall is the perfect example and while I regret knifing him 16 times he can't say he didn't have it coming. You don't want to turn into an arsehole like him and I'm sure you won't. When I first saw you, I knew you were one of the good guys. I might not know much but I like to consider myself a good judge of character and there's a kindness in your eyes that puts people at ease.

You're probably not very happy with me after learning I want to give up without a fight but please don't take it personally. I truly appreciate all the work you have put into my case. You were the only one who believed in me and never gave up but it was wrong of me to ask you to take on a fight you stood no chance of winning. I committed a terrible crime and now I must pay. We all have to face up to our actions one day and my time has come. But I'm no longer scared and I'm ready to receive my punishment with dignity. Justice is always served in the end and that's something I can't wait for Sergeant McLeish to find out. I know you want me to make a complaint about him but there really is no point. Every time he attacks someone like me he's moving another step towards hell himself. We shouldn't be scared of people like him – we should pity them.

I now have just a few days left in Moristoun and would like to spend them alone. Please don't be insulted when I ask you not to visit. I have finally found some calm in my life and want this peace to last. Seeing visitors now would be an unwelcome distraction. I need to keep a clear head as I try to face the challenges ahead so I will use these last few words to say goodbye and offer you some advice. I'm glad you have settled in well to our little community but you have to realise Moristoun is no place for a bright young man like you. Once you have got your head straight you should head back to the mainland and try for a fresh start there. Don't waste your life rotting away here like I've done. You're still young but I can tell you that every minute of life is precious. Try your best to make sure you have no regrets and let your heart guide you. I can't think of anything else to write so it's probably best if I just say goodbye. It was a pleasure to know you and I'll never forget everything you have done for me. If you still remember me with the same fondness many years down the line then I guess I wasn't such a bad man after all. Keep smiling and I'll see you in court.

Your good friend
Robert Cameron Hogg

# Chapter 27:

# Moristoun v Hogg

McSorely's mind had been in a state of flux ever since he set eyes on Hogg's letter and confusion continued to reign as he watched the accused make his courtroom entrance. Although the emotions expressed in the prisoner's letter had seemed heartfelt enough, McSorely couldn't shake the feeling it was a fabrication. He could accept Hogg coming to the realisation his case was a lost cause but found it hard to see why the prisoner would refuse to see visitors. If McSorely was facing the prospect of a life behind bars he would want to see as many people as possible before the shame of his status as a common criminal became official. Like a politician who has just learned the Sunday papers will unmask him as a serial sodomite with fiendishly inventive uses for every item in his fruit bowl, McSorely would want to enjoy one last Saturday night basking in the warmth of his friends and family before the tabloids extinguished those flames by flooding through his letter box like a raging torrent. Something seemed fishy about Hogg's plea for solitude and the foul stench of Sergeant McLeish's involvement lingered in the air. McSorely could easily imagine Hogg being forced to write his letter under duress but this theory was put in doubt by the sentences that provided a withering critique of his captor. Had Sergeant McLeish been a cunning manipulator, he would have told Hogg to insert these cutting barbs in order to fool the reader into thinking there was no way he could have been involved in the letter's creation. From what McSorely had learned from his meetings with Moristoun's dim blue line, however, such a plan seemed beyond the policeman's limited intellect. Sergeant McLeish's approach to law enforcement was more Wyatt Earp than Sherlock Holmes; this was a policeman who got results through fear not forensics. That made him a powerful ally for those who did possess an adroit mind and McSorely suspected Sergeant McLeish was working in tandem with either Farqhuar or Dr Barrett. When he voiced this theory to Buchan, however, it was met with cynicism. "Do you really think Farqhuar would put a certain victory at risk by getting involved in something as stupid as that?" Buchan said. "He has nothing to gain from Hogg maintaining a dignified silence. If anything, Farqhuar will be disappointed Hogg isn't trying to plead his innocence as it robs him of the chance to perform in court."

"But what about Dr Barrett?" said McSorely. "Don't you find it strange Hogg changed his tune after just one visit from him? And we only have his word for it that the letter is genuine. How do we know Dr Barrett didn't write it himself?"

"Because it's clearly in Hogg's childish scrawl," said Buchan. "Besides, Dr Barrett is a man of the highest integrity. If there's one man in Moristoun you can trust implicitly it's him. I'm not surprised it took just one visit for Hogg to come to his senses as Dr Barrett has a gift for making people see things clearly."

The psychiatrist's intervention in the case had only muddied McSorely's waters further but he was hoping to gain a clearer picture from Hogg's behaviour in court. If the defendant twitched about restlessly in the dock then it would be hard to believe Dr Barrett's diagnosis of spiritual calm. But McSorely had to admit there was a sense of serenity about the man being led towards the dock by Sergeant McLeish. Hogg even broke into a smile as he took a look at his surroundings and spotted McSorely sitting next to Buchan. The defendant wanted to embellish this visual contact by waving at his defence team but further evidence of his enlightenment arrived when he decided against such an act on the grounds it would probably lead to Sergeant McLeish attempting to break his wrist. He settled for a respectful nod, therefore, before coming to a rest in the dock as he joined the rest of the courtroom in waiting for Lord Bane's arrival.

"First impressions can often be misleading but I'd say Hogg looks a little too cheery for your conspiracy theory to gain any credence," said Buchan. "I'm no psychiatrist or expert on body language but I'd say he seems like someone who has found inner peace. What do you think?"

Having suffered more emotional crises than the grizzled matriarch of a soap opera's most dysfunctional family, McSorely found inner peace rather difficult to quantify. How could he tell if the toilet attendant had flushed away every mental turd when so many dreadnoughts were still clogging up his own psychological latrine? What McSorely could say with some degree of certainty, though, was Hogg had undergone a physical transformation since their first meeting. He no longer cowered like an abused canine and stood upright in the dock, adding an inch or two to his miniscule frame. His chest was also puffed out in pride so Hogg was clearly primed to face his fate with courage and, from what Buchan had told McSorely, the defendant wouldn't have to wait long before his permanent incarceration was rubber-stamped. "These cases rarely take longer than a few minutes," Buchan said. "The longest part is usually waiting for the judge to arrive. It's a good job Hogg's case isn't being heard first thing in the morning because Lord Bane always treats himself to a monumental breakfast. I've known cases to start an hour behind schedule if he wakes up with a ravenous hunger."

Given that the courtroom clock was now edging towards 4.35 p.m. – too late for afternoon tea and too early for dinner – it was safe to assume Lord Bane wouldn't keep them waiting for much longer. Indeed, it was just nine minutes past the scheduled start of proceedings when the judge finally opened the door to his realm. The speed with which Lord Bane then approached his chair suggested he wished to conclude matters with similar alacrity and he pushed straight ahead with business once the court had risen to acknowledge his presence.

"I'm here to pass judgment on case QM345966, The People of Moristoun v Robert Cameron Hogg," said Lord

Bane. "The charge before the court is that Robert Cameron Hogg attempted to murder Steven Valentino McCall on the night of June 27. How does your client plead to this charge, Mr Buchan?"

The public defender had to wait for a few seconds before the laughter McCall's middle name drew from the public galleries finally subsided. Buchan considered this public embarrassment of McCall a minor victory for his client but the answer he gave to Lord Bane confirmed the victim would soon have the last laugh.

"My client pleads guilty, your honour," he said. "Mr Hogg acknowledges he has committed a terrible crime and is ready to accept his punishment."

"I'm pleased to hear he has come to that realisation and spared us the tiresome charade of a trial," replied Lord Bane. "Is there anything the prosecution wishes to add before I decide what sentence to pass?"

"There isn't really much more to say with regards to this episode," said Farqhuar after all eyes had turned his direction. "The defendant has admitted to a Q45 offence and the statute books clearly state the punishment for such a crime. I merely wish to see the law respected."

"How about you, Mr Buchan?" said Lord Bane. "Would you like to make a plea for clemency on behalf of your client?"

"Although I'm sure Mr Hogg would contend anyone unfortunate enough to be well acquainted with our good friend Valentino could appreciate the motive for his attack, my client understands there is no excuse for stabbing him repeatedly. We have nothing further to add."

With that brief exchange, McSorely's first foray into the world of legal affairs was brought to an abrupt conclusion. The anti-climactic denouement was in keeping with the narrative of his life thus far, with courtroom battle joining sex, marijuana, pop tarts, countless World Cup Finals and The Phantom Menace in the big binder marked "Is that fucking it? I've been looking forward to this for ages and this is how God mocks me?" The familiarity of the feeling failed to lessen McSorely's

315

disappointment, however, and guilt gnawed away at him as Lord Bane passed judgment on Hogg.

"It is to your credit, Mr Hogg, that you accept full responsibility for your actions and await your punishment with dignity," the judge began. "While that has gained my respect, it won't succeed in rousing any feelings of mercy. As the chief administrator has pointed out, you have committed a Q45 offence and the laws are clear on what must happen to those found guilty of such a transgression. I have no option, therefore, but to impose the full penalty. You will be taken away from these shores tomorrow evening to start your sentence and I can only hope the journey away from Moristoun also marks the beginning of your long road to rehabilitation. Do you have anything to say before I return you to Sergeant McLeish's care for your final night in Moristoun?"

Hogg informed Lord Bane he did wish to share some final thoughts with the courtroom and brought a smile to the judge's face by claiming the only advantage to being a condemned man was getting to deliver what was effectively the eulogy at one's own funeral. The address that followed was far from maudlin, though, as Hogg signed off with an unexpectedly philosophical flourish.

"Plenty of people would have taken the chance to settle some old scores when stood in front of everyone for the last time," Hogg said. "And I've been in Moristoun for such a long time that there are plenty of skeletons waiting to be dragged out of your closets. But I'm going to resist the temptation because I've learned the hard way just how destructive revenge can be. Even though almost every person here has treated me like the shite they leave behind in my lavvies, I'm going to rise above it and try to forgive you. It's not your fault that I'm standing where I am now. I'm leaving Moristoun because I lost my self-control and there's nobody else I can blame for that, no matter how much I try to convince myself that McCall is the real villain. We're all on this island because we let ourselves down and I hope you can realise this much faster than I did. That way you can maybe make a much happier exit than me."

Hogg was only halfway through the address he had composed before arriving in court but Lord Bane was growing increasingly concerned by the dangerous subtext of its content. Gail and McSorely were among those listening to the condemned man and Lord Bane intervened before Hogg enlightened the Q101 further about the reality of their surroundings.

"This is not a pulpit for you to preach from," he told Hogg. "I expected far greater brevity when I offered you the chance to say some farewell words. This is a court of law with important business to attend to and I won't allow you to waste any more of our precious time. Take him away, Sergeant McLeish."

The policeman took great pleasure in following Lord Bane's instruction and clasped Hogg's right arm in his giant left claw before hauling him out of the dock. McSorely's gaze was fixed firmly on Hogg's face as he made this ugly exit, desperate to find the desolation that would prove his projection of inner peace was a sham. The condemned man remained calmness personified, however, as his eyes met McSorely's for what he thought would be the last time. Buchan also jumped to that incorrect assumption as he said: "Well, that's the last we'll see of poor Hogg, a simple soul who was outsmarted by the burning rage Satan sends to test every man. Will you join me in raising a farewell glass to our client back at the Tortured Soul?"

# Chapter 28:

# Waking life

Barely half-an-hour had passed since Lord Bane's judgment but word from the courtroom had passed quickly to the Tortured Soul. As Buchan and McSorely made their entrance it was hard not to notice the "Victory for Valentino" banner that took pride of place above the bar. Although it seemed to have been constructed crudely from one of Brenda's bedsheets and a box of felt-tipped pens, there was much to admire in Jimmy's creation. The effeminate nature of McCall's middle name was alluded to in the giant pink love hearts that flanked the text while a bloodied knife protruded through the "O" in Valentino. If this was what Jimmy could cobble together in just a few minutes, one could only wonder what kind of masterpiece he might have produced given a few hours.

"I didn't know you had an artistic side," said Buchan as he complimented the landlord on his handiwork. "Have you ever tried your hand at painting?"

"Only with emulsion," replied Jimmy. "I quite enjoyed art at school but never really took it seriously. I like doodling when I'm stuck behind the bar on a quiet night but that's about it."

McSorely was also impressed by Jimmy's banner but found it hard to believe one man could have completed the arts and crafts project in such a short space of time. That Jimmy had even learned of McCall's embarrassing secret was incredulous enough, given Buchan and McSorely were the first two patrons to arrive back from the courtroom. But Moristoun's antiquated mass media had succeeded in relaying the news just as quickly as the 24-hour outlets that bombarded mainland dwellers with information. With McCall ruled out of the equation due to the most blatant conflict of interest, the burden of reporting from court fell solely on the shoulders of his assistant at Radio Moristoun, a goth by the name of Caitlin McCorry. Having been subjected to four years of low-level sexual harassment at the busy hands of her boss, Caitlin wasn't going to miss out on the chance to exact a small measure of revenge. McCall was therefore referred to by his full name every time he was mentioned in her report, providing confirmation that Jimmy's ears were not playing tricks on him. "It sounded too good to be true when the reporter said Valentino for the first time but she kept plunging in the knife, just like Hogg," said Jimmy. "McCall's never going to live this one down, he'll be called Valentino for the rest of his days."

By the time the bold Valentino arrived to quench his thirst, he was already fed up with the taunts about his middle name. Almost every person he had passed on the short walk from the courtroom had either sniggered or cried out his new moniker and McCall stopped Jimmy mid-sentence before the landlord could join the fun. "My fucking grandma was a fucking fan of Rudolph fucking Valentino," he raged, before apologising for his coarse language as he spotted Gail making her return from court. "My parents were stupid enough to let her choose my middle name and there's nothing I can do about it."

Had McCall's granny known the cute little baby cradling in her daughter's arms would turn into such a visually repugnant specimen, she would probably have thought twice about naming him in honour of the Latin Lover. That thought immediately crossed the mind of everyone old enough to have seen one of Valentino's films at The Rialto but it was Henderson who voiced the observation out loud. Still, Valentino had starred in The Four Horsemen of the Apocalypse so maybe the old bird was more prescient than he was giving her credit for. Henderson's mention of the film snapped McTavish out of the trance that usually rendered him speechless while the jukebox was delivering on his £2 investment in Patsy Cline. "I remember going to see that movie with Bella Barnes at the Eglinton Electrum," he said.

"Your man inflamed such a passion within wee Bella that I got my jollies three times that night. I'm sure I wasn't the only punter in the audience to reap such a reward so you shouldn't feel ashamed about having the name Valentino. The man was a legend."

Buchan was quick to second that emotion, having read an exhaustive biography of the screen star at the library just a few years ago. "Plenty of people considered Valentino a dandy but that was far from the case," he told McCall. "He once trained with the great boxer Jack Dempsey who branded him the 'most virile and masculine of men'."

Gail couldn't help but laugh at Buchan's quote as they were the last words anyone would think of when setting eyes on Moristoun's very own Valentino. The only connection one would make with McCall and virility was that he resembled the used prophylactic of a sperm whale. As for masculinity, the fact he had been overwhelmed and stabbed repeatedly by Hogg – a man who would have only been able to audition for a part in Snow White and the Seven Dwarves had he followed the more fabled Valentino into the acting world – said everything about McCall's shortcomings.

It was to the condemned man that Gail turned the conversation as she tried to make amends for the laughter that wounded McCall just as deeply as Hogg's knife.

"You must be glad the trial is finally over," she said. "How did it feel when you watched Lord Bane send Hogg down?"

"Bloody brilliant," replied McCall. "Hogg thought he was the big man taking a pop at me but I survived and now he's the one who's doomed."

"Justice was served," added Henderson. "People like Hogg have to learn there's no excuse for trying to take the life of another."

"I think he has learned that lesson already," said Buchan. "You heard what Hogg said in court. They might not have been expressed with great flair but they were wise words nonetheless."

Having spent the past two years studying philosophy, Gail found herself in agreement with Buchan's assertion. She had witnessed a handful of citizens suffer the same fate in the dock but none had expressed themselves with the honesty and sapience of Hogg. One matter continued to perplex her, however, and she turned to her philosophical mentor for enlightenment.

"What was Hogg going on about when he said: 'We are all on this island because we let ourselves down'?" Gail said. "It was the only part of his speech that didn't make sense."

McSorely was also intrigued by that pearl of wisdom, particularly as it had provided the cue for Lord Bane to cut Hogg's address short. It reminded him of Sergeant McLeish's hasty intervention when Hogg had started speaking about The Book and it seemed like Moristoun's law enforcers were trying to hide a dark secret. Buchan could sense this suspicion seeping out of both his Q101s and decided to rely on an intellect far greater than his own to find a convincing excuse for Hogg straying off script once more.

"Hogg was dipping his toe deeper into philosophical waters with that observation," Buchan said. "He was alluding to something that was perhaps expressed most eloquently by Oscar Wilde when he said: 'Ambition is the germ from which all growth of nobleness proceeds.' In essence, Hogg was saying we can never reach our full potential living in a backward place like this. That's why it's of paramount importance you pass that entrance exam and start a new life in Inverness."

Playing the Wilde card seemed to have satisfied Gail's curiosity, although that was perhaps to be expected given she rarely questioned any utterance from Buchan. McSorely's mind wasn't clouded by a teenage crush, however, and the conspiracy theorist in him deemed Buchan's explanation far too flimsy. He also viewed the claim that life on the mainland was a huge step forward with a large measure of cynicism. Moristoun may have been something of a backwater but it was the one place where he wasn't drowning in a sea of depression. That was subject to change, however, as Gail was preparing to take a sniper rifle to his water wings by upping sticks to Inverness. Although he had a vested interest in hoping she would remain in situ, McSorely was also genuinely concerned for Gail's welfare. Her intelligence was beyond doubt but there was a naivety to Gail that suggested mainland life would come as something of a rude awakening. Moving to Inverness was a clear sign of ambition but McSorely doubted if that characteristic was as noble as Oscar Wilde insisted. The careerists and social climbers he had come across in Glasgow were reprobates who would have had no compunction in pimping out their grandmother to clamber just a few more inches up the ladder. They were also just small fry in the grand scheme of things and he could only imagine what reprehensible acts the big boys of global business had committed on their rise to the top of capitalism's pile of ill-gotten goods.

From what McSorely had gathered from his brief stay in Moristoun, no tycoons or megalomaniacs lorded it over the rest of the islanders. The closest approximation seemed to be the William Hughes character Jimmy had spoken about with such disdain. But he was long gone after paying the ultimate price for attempting to swindle the all-powerful Council. It was the local politicians who wielded all the power in this far-flung outpost and Moristoun reminded him of some Eastern European satellite state positioned deep behind the Iron Curtain. Dissidents had been brutally suppressed in these so-called people's paradises and McSorely was beginning to wonder if Hogg was being sent to the gulag for speaking out of turn instead of his attack on McCall. He even started to doubt if the stabbing had actually taken place but this idea was quickly dismissed after one glance along the bar, where McCall was tilting a packet of crisps in the air to ensure every last shard dropped into his mouth, although several fell to rest in his beard instead. While that sight caused McSorely's stomach to churn a little, it didn't come close to the revulsion he had felt when McCall revealed the wounds Hogg's knife had made on his emaciated frame. Life's seemingly endless selection of cruel tricks had taught McSorely to be suspicious but even he had to admit the only dark force behind this assault had been Hogg himself. Things had become far murkier since his incarceration, however, and McSorely's mind retrospectively conjured images of cloaked Council employees following his every move as he reflected on his own dealings with the prisoner. Moristoun's meritocracy were clearly trying to stop Hogg from blurting something out before he took his leave and McSorely was determined to discover what was causing them such concern. Only one man could tell him, though, and he would set sail for a high-security prison on the mainland in less than 24 hours. McSorely was determined to hold one final meeting with Hogg but the most formidable of barriers stood in his way.

Buchan had already informed him Sergeant McLeish would treat a visitation request with the same disdain as the latest United Nations directive on the ethical treatment of prisoners. "Once a captive is found guilty here, he goes into total lockdown," said Buchan. "If you turn up at the police station seeking an audience with Hogg then Sergeant McLeish will take great pleasure in drop-kicking you back out the door. I could show you the bruise that proves it but etiquette decrees my backside should remain hidden in the presence of ladies."

McSorely's only hope, therefore, lay in gaining access to the police station while the ogre that guarded its gates was otherwise engaged. He started to hatch plans for a daring midnight raid while the beast was dormant but a more simple solution dropped propitiously into his path within a matter of seconds.

Heartened by successfully plucking the last crisp from his beard, McCall indulged in a rare act of charity as he told everyone to take their pick of Jimmy's drinks. "Part one of what promises to be a momentous weekend has come to a successful conclusion," said McCall as he led his fellow drinkers in an attempted toast. Only half of the bar was destined to follow him in raising their glasses, however, as he concluded by saying: "Here's hoping part two will go equally as smoothly and Athletic give those United bastards the gubbing they so thoroughly deserve."

McCall's speech was met with a mixture of raucous cheers and boos, with the latter winning the battle for supremacy thanks to Jimmy's peerless vocal power. That booming voice was soon reduced to a whisper, though, as Jimmy invited McSorely to join him behind the bar for a private meeting. He then walked towards the duffel coat hanging in the hallway and plunged a hand inside that re-emerged with two tickets for the big game. "These things are like gold dust so don't let on that I've managed to get you one," said Jimmy as he explained the reason for moving far from the prying eyes of the rest of his customers. "Plenty of people who drink here would think nothing of mugging you on the way home if they heard you had a ticket."

McSorely regarded that claim as rather over-dramatic but Jimmy insisted he should never underestimate the depths Moristounians would plumb when it came to a derby in the Inter Islands Cup.

"Actually, it's probably safer if I keep your ticket here and we meet an hour before kick-off tomorrow," he said. "One of those guttersnipes might put two and two together and have a pop at you on the off chance."

"Wouldn't that be a bit stupid in a community as close-knit as this one?" said McSorely. "If I told the police who attacked me then I'd get the ticket back before the game and the culprit would be in deep trouble."

"Don't expect any help from Sergeant McLeish if it's a United fan who tries to rob you," said Jimmy. "He's far more loyal to those cheating shower of bastards than he is to the law."

With those words, Jimmy prised open a window of opportunity in McSorely's bid to unravel the grand Hogg conspiracy. Although Buchan had claimed Hogg was in "total lockdown", there was no way Sergeant McLeish would miss out on Moristoun's biggest derby for years. For the best part of two hours, Hogg would be left in total isolation behind the bolted doors of the police station. All McSorely had to do was find a way to get inside.

# Chapter 29:

# Prison Break

The folly of taking a Scottish Deerhound along for an act of criminality became clear to McSorely as he tried to remain inconspicuous while waiting for Sergeant McLeish to leave the police station. He had foolishly thought Munchkin might prove a useful ally in securing a meeting with Hogg as the beast had enough power to batter down any door. McSorely had also believed Munchkin's height would come in handy when trying to gain access to any windows beyond his reach but he now realised advanced dog handling was missing from his CV for a good reason. While dog biscuits proved a sufficient form of bribery to maintain a semblance of order in their co-habitation, they were unlikely to persuade Munchkin to batter her head off a door or let McSorely trample all over her back. The mutt was rendered useless, therefore, and was actually something of a hindrance as her vast frame drew attention to McSorely's supposedly covert operation. That left him exposed on two fronts as, in addition to staying off Sergeant McLeish's radar, McSorely would also have to avoid Jimmy if the enraged landlord came looking for the ingrate who couldn't be bothered to collect the ticket he had fought tooth and nail for. With this in mind, McSorely decided it was best to put as much distance between himself and Munchkin as possible. There wasn't sufficient time to drag the hound all the way back home so he made do with tethering her to a tree that sat about 500 metres away from his outlook post. It seemed sturdy enough to avoid being uprooted if Munchkin felt the urge for a change of scenery and provided enough shelter from another miserable Moristoun day to make the dog feel relatively comfortable in her new surroundings. All McSorely had to do now was buy her silence and he hoped the smorgasbord of canine treats sprinkled on the grass would ensure a bark-free ambience until he returned from the police station. It was hard to imagine Sergeant McLeish showing the same courtesy towards Hogg as he prepared to abandon his own duty of care, although it was certainly possible to envisage him tying the prisoner's neck to one of the bars with a dog lead. McSorely felt sure the policeman would treat himself to one final beating before parting ways with Hogg and could only hope he was saving that delight for after the game. Such a scenario seemed likely as it would allow Sergeant McLeish to unleash his anger in the event of a defeat or to round off a perfect day if his heroes prevailed in the derby. The spring in Sergeant McLeish's step as he bounded out of the police station hinted that he believed Hogg would receive a celebratory pounding upon his return from Moyne Park. His enthusiasm to reach the stadium as soon as possible had also ensured the back door to the police station remained unlocked. It took McSorely a while to capitalise on this outrageous stroke of good fortune, however, as he didn't believe Sergeant McLeish would be stupid enough to leave his fortress unsecured. It was only after fruitlessly trying to prise open every window with his hands, and sourcing the rocks that would complete the job more crudely, that he tried out the back door as a last resort before turning to violence. McSorely could barely believe his luck as the door knob turned in his hand but decided it was best to tread carefully as he made his way inside. It was not beyond the limits of Sergeant McLeish's cruelty for him to leave the door unlocked on purpose so he could trap potential burglars and subject them to unimaginable horrors for having the audacity to impinge on his manor. With that in mind, McSorely popped his head inside first and looked down to check if a bear trap was lying in wait. Seeing only a bare floor, he then turned his eyes towards the top of the door in search of some string that would link it to a shotgun, cross bow or one of the many other weapons in Sergeant McLeish's no doubt impressive arsenal. But there wasn't even a relatively harmless bucket of water waiting to give him a drenching, although if Sergeant McLeish had opted to use this time-honoured practical joke he would probably have filled the receptacle with acid instead. That meant McSorely could put his best foot forward with a measure of confidence and it wasn't long before he was standing before the prisoner.

For a man who wouldn't see another friendly face for at least the next couple of decades, Hogg didn't look particularly pleased when McSorely materialised as if by magic. Indeed, the greeting he accorded his visitor was: "Oh, for fuck's sake! What the hell are you doing here?" When McSorely pointed out that wasn't the warmest of welcomes, he received confirmation Hogg still reserved a measure of fear for his captor. "That maniac only left a few minutes ago," he said. "If he comes back and finds you here there will be hell to pay."

"I don't think we have to worry too much about that," said McSorely. "There's only one thing on his mind for the next couple of hours and that's football."

"But what if he's forgotten his scarf or wants to come back for his cosh in case there's any crowd trouble? You could have given it at least half an hour before trying to break in here. And how did you manage to get inside anyway?"

Condemned men rarely find the humour in anything, which is hardly surprising given most of them remain preoccupied with the conundrum of how to preserve their anal chastity in prison. Hogg, though, couldn't help but laugh upon learning Sergeant McLeish had forgotten to lock the back door and jokingly told McSorely to check if he'd left the keys to his cell hanging on the wall as well. McSorely dutifully set off to search for those keys but was stopped in his tracks by Hogg, who informed him the comment was made in jest. "The last thing I want is for you to break me out of here," he said. "That wouldn't achieve anything except landing you in big trouble. There's no point in running away and hiding, I need to face up to what I've done. Didn't you read that letter I sent you?"

McSorely then told Hogg of his suspicion the letter had been composed by Dr Barrett as part of a grand Council conspiracy. This brought another laugh out of Hogg but McSorely insisted he was deadly serious and revealed he had broken into the police station to learn the truth straight from the horse's mouth.

"This is the first time I've been able to talk to you without Sergeant McLeish listening in," McSorely said. "You can finally speak freely. I know there's nothing I can do to save you now but I just want to hear the truth."

"I'm sorry to disappoint you but there's not really much else to say," said Hogg. "The truth of the matter is I stabbed McCall and now I must pay. I said everything I needed to say in that letter, that's why I told Dr Barrett I didn't want to see any more visitors. As much as you want to believe in a conspiracy, my case is really quite simple."

Like most conspiracy theorists, McSorely wasn't about to abandon his belief that darker forces remained at play. He still harboured too many doubts about Hogg's case, most notably the abrupt manner in which the prisoner had been halted whenever he started to talk about more mysterious matters. "How can you call it simple when the people in power seemed so determined to silence you?" McSorely said. "Don't you remember Sergeant McLeish going off his nut when you mentioned that book in our first meeting? And what about the judge cutting short your farewell speech? They were trying to hide something and I want to know what it is. You can tell me now – there's nobody here to shut you up this time."

"Trust me, you don't want to know," said Hogg, words that only made McSorely even more desperate to uncover the big secret. "They only shut me up because they wanted to protect you. I never used to understand that phrase 'ignorance is bliss', probably because I was too stupid to grasp it, but I now see how wise those words are. I've not muttered many pearls of wisdom myself but I hit the nail on the head when I told you Moristoun was no place for a young man like you. The best thing you can do is head back to the mainland and forget about everything and everyone here."

McSorely stood in silence for a few seconds as his mind tried to register what Hogg had said. Although he was pleased to receive confirmation The Council were indeed involved in some form of conspiracy, the overwhelming emotion was fear upon learning it was him, not Hogg, who was the central figure in the great intrigue. This panic then intensified when McSorely reconsidered the circumstances behind his arrival on the island. He had no recollection of the journey itself and now harboured serious doubts over Buchan's explanation of his sudden black-out and airborne dash to Dr Barrett's surgery. Hogg's courtroom speech also began to resonate as McSorely mulled over his claim that "we're all here because we let ourselves down". There was a dark mystery to Moristoun and McSorely hoped some additional probing would force Hogg to reveal the exact details. "What are they protecting me from?" he said. "I can't see what your case has to do with me. All I did was help out a little with your defence."

"They're protecting you from Moristoun itself," replied Hogg. "You won't be able to move on in your life until you leave this terrible place. Nothing good can come of staying here – and I'm the perfect example."

"But how can the town itself harm me? That doesn't make any sense. I feel much better here than I did in Glasgow. This is a real community and I feel like one of the locals already."

"There's only one way you can become an official citizen of Moristoun and that's not a road you want to go down. When your name goes down on that Council register it's written in indelible ink."

"What way is that then? Is there any chance you can give me a straight answer this time instead of talking in riddles?"

Had Hogg not already been convicted of one Q45 offence, he would have been more reticent about putting McSorely out of his misery by revealing the one secret everyone in Moristoun was duty bound to keep from outsiders. All he had to fear now, though, was an extended period of penance, a punishment Hogg was glad to accept in return for making what he naively considered to be one final good deed. "It's a method you should be more than familiar with," said Hogg. "From what I gather, you were about to go ahead with it just before Buchan stepped in to save the day."

"Suicide?" said McSorely. "That's how you become a permanent resident of Moristoun?"

"I know it sounds a bit strange but it's true. We're sent here as a punishment for taking our own lives and aren't allowed to leave. We stay in the same state until we learn to accept and better ourselves. That's why I look rather sprightly for a 412-year-old."

"Are you seriously asking me to accept you were born in the 1600s? You only look about 50."

"I was actually just 41 when I killed myself but, to use a more recent phrase, I had a tough paper round. You shouldn't be fooled by appearances here. That old duffer McTavish is actually one of our younger residents – he came here about 20 years ago."

Every good conspiracy theorist is primed to expect the unexpected but Hogg's revelations left McSorely in a state of disbelief. There was definitely something fishy about the fact he had been directed to Buchan's Scenic Suicides website on the very night he was set to take his own life. But it was stretching the boundaries of McSorely's credulity to accept Hogg's claim that every person in Moristoun was there as punishment for pushing ahead with that very act. "Why should I believe you?" he asked Hogg. "The last time I was here you tried to make me believe there was a talking bird acting as the town's unofficial shrink. You're hardly the most reliable of witnesses."

"I only came up with that story about Gerald because I was trying to cover my tracks after telling you about The Book."

"So there is some magical book that contains the answers to everything? What's it about?"

"Only a handful of people have ever read it. The Book is written in seven different languages and the writing is so small you need a magnifying glass read it. I gave up after about 30 seconds and never went back. It's a shame I never put in the effort to study it – that could have saved me from ending up in this cell. It's not as if I didn't have enough time to learn the languages. It only took Buchan 14 years."

McSorely wasn't too surprised to learn his boss was one of the few citizens to have deciphered The Book as he seemed to have read everything committed to page. This feat was less impressive now McSorely had discovered Buchan was far older than his perceived 42 years. As Hogg revealed Buchan was closer to a double century in age, McSorely began to wonder if spending eternity in Moristoun should actually be considered such a punishment. Just think of the knowledge he could accrue if given the same time to wade through the library's vast reserve of books. Inside a few decades he would also be able to drop philosophical quotes casually into conversation, turning beauties such as Gail into putty in his hands. But as McSorely's thoughts drifted back to the object of his affection, he was assailed by conflicting feelings of dread and exhilaration. If what Hogg had told him about Moristoun was true then Gail was one of the waking dead herself. It pained him to think such an innocent and tender girl had suffered the same maelstrom that pushed him to the edge during that darkest of nights in Glasgow. On the other hand, though, McSorely was excited by the thought suicide had preserved Gail's youthful beauty for eternity. He was still relatively young himself and only needed to take his own life to join Gail in attaining the holy grail of the vain – eternal youth. He would then require just a physical and mental tune-up – a task he was confident of completing inside a decade – before Gail would fall head over heels in love with him. Centuries of bliss were being mapped out in his mind but he wanted to check a few things first before commencing with the technical drawings.

"So what happened when you committed suicide then?" he asked Hogg. "Did you land in Moristoun the moment you took your last breath?"

"Pretty much," said Hogg. "I decided to bow out by hanging myself but it wasn't exactly a textbook suicide. I found myself swinging in agony for about an hour before I finally passed out. When I woke up I was sitting in Farqhuar's office and he explained everything."

"So Farqhuar's been here for centuries as well? I just can't imagine someone like him taking his own life. How did he end up here?"

"Oh, members of The Council aren't like the rest of us. They're here to run things and keep an eye on the citizens. Farqhuar and the rest of The Council have been here since the beginning of time and will never leave. Think of them as guardian angels."

No matter how much McSorely tried, he just couldn't envisage Farqhuar as a guardian angel. If the big boss upstairs truly was a creator of unending compassion he would have tossed Farqhuar's CV into the bin without even granting him the courtesy of a job interview. But McSorely had always suspected God subscribed to the school of tough love, with evidence arriving each time he switched on the TV news to learn of the latest catastrophes to befall mankind. It wasn't too big a stretch, therefore, to accept Farqhuar as a stern but ultimately equitable authority figure, like the headmaster of a public school who permits character-building thrashings but draws the line well before buggery in the faculty's big book of discipline. As McSorely started to think in greater depth about the administration of law and order in Moristoun, however, a shudder ran through him as he realised Sergeant McLeish must also be on the celestial payroll.

"Don't tell me the monster who tortures people in these cells is also part of The Council?" he said. "You've told me Moristoun is a place of punishment but a demon like Sergeant McLeish surely only belongs in the darkest recesses of hell."

"Don't you worry, that's where he's bound to end up," said Hogg. "And he won't be the one dishing out the punishment when he gets there. Sergeant McLeish is just like the rest of us. He's here because he took his own life. The Council only made him the island's policeman because that's what he did on the mainland."

"But why would he commit suicide? He takes so much pleasure from his job that it's hard to imagine him being unhappy so long as he's in that uniform."

"That's another one of Moristoun's secrets. Nobody's been brave enough to ask him how he ended up here. Farqhuar and Dr Barrett know but as Council employees they're sworn to secrecy. Some people are quite happy to talk about how they ended up here but others still see it as something to be ashamed of."

McSorely would have probably been one of the latter had he followed through with his own suicide and joined Hogg as a permanent resident. But witnessing Moristoun through eyes that still retained the faintest glimmer of hope had taught him there was nothing to be ashamed about when it came to taking one's life. Those around him had shown tremendous courage when leaping into the unknown as they had no proof of the afterlife's existence. Although McSorely had planned to make the same brave step, he had to admit fear may have forced him to pull out at the last minute. That trepidation had now been banished, though, as McSorely knew a second chance awaited him in a realm that seemed a distinct improvement on Glasgow in the early 21st century. Indeed, Moristoun would become positively heavenly if he could persuade Gail to abandon her jaunt to Inverness and remain with him on the island. McSorely was only allowed to savour this tantalising possibility for a few seconds, however, as the words "Inverness" and "jaunt" roused his rational mind out is slumber.

"Hang on a second," he said. "If nobody is allowed to leave Moristoun then how come Gail is preparing for university in Inverness? What makes her so special?"

"Gail's not like the rest of us," replied Hogg. "She's mortal just like you and isn't protected from the ravages of time. She has been here since she was a baby and we've all watched her grow up."

While most men would have been relieved to learn the girl they lusted over wasn't effectively a zombie, McSorely found himself reacting with disappointment to this latest revelation. He was convinced both their lives would be enriched by everlasting union in Moristoun, a feeling that was strengthened when Hogg furnished him with the full story behind Gail's upbringing. Having lived a sheltered existence for the last 17 years, he knew there was no way Gail would be able to cope with the cruelty of the mainland, cut off from her friends and family forever. Someone had to save Gail from that harrowing fate and return her to the loving arms of the community that had nurtured her. A hero had to step forward and make the ultimate act of sacrifice; it was time for McSorely to pull his Y-fronts over his trousers and assemble a cape from one of his bin bags.

# Chapter 30:

## Lust for strife

Sweat seeped out of every pore as McSorely summoned up one last mighty effort in a bid to drag Munchkin through the back door. Moving the mutt was proving even more difficult than usual as Munchkin and McSorely had differing viewpoints on what constituted an acceptable form of afternoon exercise. A five-minute stroll to the police station, followed by half-an-hour of spirited but fruitless tugging at her tethered lead, simply wouldn't suffice for a dog of Munchkin's calibre, no matter how much McSorely attempted to buy her off with biscuits. She was determined to stretch those gargantuan legs for at least another 20 minutes and McSorely had been forced to call on hitherto undiscovered reserves of strength to haul her this far. Now all he needed to do was shift the dog two or three more feet before he could slam the door shut and let his aching body go wonderfully limp. The thought of spending the next few centuries exploring every inch of Gail's beautifully preserved body provided McSorely with the adrenalin shot he needed to complete this task and he collapsed in exhaustion as the door clicked into place behind him. There was little time for McSorely to recover his strength, however, as one glance at his watch relayed the fact half-time was fast approaching in the Battle of Moyne Park. McSorely still had to make a brief stop at the office before heading to the Tortured Soul and his mission needed to be completed before the final whistle blew. Jimmy remained the greatest threat to his grand plan but if both Gail and McSorely had transformed into permanent residents by the time he arrived back at his pub, even that most mighty of men would be rendered powerless.

That was one of the important details McSorely had checked with Hogg before taking his leave from the police station. "It's impossible to kill a fellow citizen in Moristoun," Hogg had told him, in response to a query that was vague enough to hide his own dark intentions for Gail. "How do you think that bastard McCall survived 16 stab wounds? If we were still in the land of the living it would only take one or two plunges of a knife to drain the life out of his puny body." This knowledge reduced McSorely's fear of the consequences that would arise out of his one-sided suicide pact. Although Jimmy would expend every last ounce of energy trying to kill McSorely for the crime of taking his adopted daughter's life, there was no way he could actually succeed. Furthermore, once that initial surge of savage anger had died down, McSorely believed Jimmy would come to realise he had actually done him a favour. After all, what father would want to wave goodbye to his daughter forever? Wouldn't it be better to keep the family unit together in perpetuity? Brenda certainly seemed to be thinking that way, no matter how much she pretended to be enthused by Gail's university prospects. She was more inclined to view McSorely as the knight in shining armour he considered himself to be. Deep down she didn't want her daughter to leave and that overwhelming emotion could prove enough to ensure Brenda's complicity in his scheme if she presented a barrier to Gail upon his arrival at the pub. The only other danger to McSorely's mission came from the very man who had introduced him to Moristoun. Buchan was the driving force behind Gail's university application and when he spoke to her about mainland living it was with an almost evangelical zeal. If he found out about his assistant's plan he would do everything in his power to halt it and McSorely knew enough about his boss to realise he would be a cunning and formidable foe. Success would only be guaranteed if Buchan remained ignorant of his plot but Moristoun was such a claustrophobic community that steering clear of someone even for just an hour or two often proved impossible. Had Buchan been one of those in thrall to football, events at Moyne Park would have provided all the distraction McSorely needed. Having voiced such contempt for the beautiful game, however, there wasn't even the slightest chance Buchan was now using those same vocal chords to belt out terracing ditties, hurl obscenities at the opposition or question the parentage of the referee. His whereabouts remained uncertain and that caused McSorely to feel decidedly uneasy as he approached the office to pick up an item essential to his quest.

Self-help books were an entirely new phenomenon for Gail, who had always preferred turning to history's deepest thinkers for advice rather than some fly-by-night psychologist who probably worked out of an airing cupboard somewhere in lower Manhattan. However, the likes of Aristotle, Heraclitus and Plato had never been forced to suffer the indignity of applying for a place at the University of the Highlands and Islands. Indeed, the latter would no doubt have failed his entrance exam had he replied "That man is wisest who realises his wisdom is worthless" to the question "What qualities do you think you would bring to our Hospitality and Tourism course?" Gail, therefore, was forced to rely on the infinitely inferior mind of "lifestyle guru" Chip Hoffenberger III to prepare for the grilling that awaited her inside the university's admission office. Although Chip had boasted about his credentials in the book's introduction – bragging how his advice had turned around the careers of three washed-up actresses, two New York Mets who had turned to substance abuse and a lion tamer with a crisis of confidence – there was little in the chapter on interview technique that suggested a brilliant mind at work. A straw poll of the souses who gathered every night beneath Gail's family home would have garnered greater wisdom than the trite phrases and observations cobbled together by the latest member of the Hoffenberger dynasty. Those regulars were nowhere to be seen at the moment, however, as the big match had lured almost everyone to Moyne Park, including both of her parents. Brenda rarely bothered with football matches but had decided to accompany her husband out of pity after watching Jimmy skulk around the house bemoaning McSorely's "shameful" snub. That left Gail with only Moira for company and it was with a large measure of relief that she spotted the ghostly figure gliding towards the bar once more, as it gave her the excuse to stop reading Chip's vacuous book. Moira planted her empty vodka bottle down on the bar and Gail prepared to head for the cellar as the phrase "time for another tall, handsome Russian to come into my life" received its latest airing. That unpleasant journey into the coldest depths of the Tortured Soul always sent a shiver through Gail's spine but she received a more tangible shock upon her return to the bar as McSorely had suddenly appeared.

"If you're here for that ticket you're a bit late," said Gail rather sourly as McSorely apologised for startling her and ordered a shot of whisky to calm his own nerves. "My dad went off his head when you failed to show up and rightly so. Do you have any idea the strings he had to pull to get his hands on that ticket?"

"Believe me, the last thing I wanted to do was hurt Jimmy's feelings," said McSorely. "I was looking forward to watching the game with him but sadly found myself unavoidably detained."

Gail wasn't impressed by McSorely's excuse as the words "unavoidably detained" could have jumped straight off the pages of Chip's book. Indeed, had she managed to persist for just a few more paragraphs Gail would have found it offered up as one of the "most effective explanations for tardiness" alongside car trouble, leaping to the aid of an epileptic and news of a family bereavement. McSorely's use of the phrase had only succeeded in irritating Gail and she pressed him for details about this unavoidable delay. "I was down at the police station, visiting a former client and dear friend for the last time," he said. "It all became rather emotional and I'm afraid I lost track of the time.

"That's impossible," said Gail. "Hogg's supposed to be in lockdown – how did you persuade Sergeant McLeish to let you in?"

"I didn't," replied McSorely. "I waited until he went to the football then tried to find a way to get inside. After a few minutes of valiant effort I finally managed to break my way in."

Gail could barely believe what she was hearing as she had assumed McSorely lacked both the intelligence and the balls to pull off such a daring raid. Had McSorely admitted all it took to breach the island's high-security fortress was a mere turn of the back door handle then Gail's estimation of his character would have remained suitably low. He was in no mood to remove the mask of a master criminal, however, and the embellishments he added to his story ensured Gail started to view him in a more glamorous light.

"Nobody here has ever been brave enough to pull off a stunt like that," she said. "What drove you to it? Don't tell me you wanted to break Hogg out of jail?"

"Even though such a plan would have placed my own future in great peril, I was prepared to make that sacrifice had Hogg been the victim of a great injustice," replied McSorely. "Too many people were trying to keep him quiet and I wanted to discover what he really wanted to say."

"And what did he have to say? Did Hogg tell you about this great injustice?"

"Not exactly but he certainly opened my eyes to a few things. I know everyone makes fun of Hogg but he can really be quite perceptive at times."

"What did you talk about then? Did he tell you anything important?"

No matter what answer McSorely gave to that question it was destined to be the greatest understatement of his life, finally knocking his diplomatic critique of the Sex And The City episode Sarah had forced him to sit through off the lofty position it had held for so long. McSorely, therefore, merely informed Gail they had talked about a great number of subjects, including her childhood.

He had planned to broach this matter with Gail in a bid to gather some empirical evidence for Hogg's claims, which were possibly still just the ramblings of a madman. If time did indeed stand still for those who tumbled into Moristoun, the family pictures commemorating each stage in Gail's development would pay testament to that. Although rather embarrassed by McSorely's request to see the Mathieson family album, Gail agreed to fetch the item her mother would soon cherish more than anything else in her world. Talking McSorely through her childhood was still an infinitely better way to pass the time than reading Chip's book or counting the seconds until Moira would calm her latest nervous twitch with a large gulp of vodka. Gail even found herself starting to enjoy the stories behind each picture as it had been several years since the album had been given an airing. McSorely, though, wasn't really interested in what Gail had to say as he was preoccupied by the search for visual clues. By the time he had inspected three or four of the snaps in greater detail, McSorely was convinced Hogg had been telling him the truth. The Jimmy who balanced a two-year-old child on his shoulders looked no different to the man who stood back and watched as Gail attempted to blow out the 12 candles on her birthday cake. While middle-aged men can often hide the passage of a decade through clean living and a disciplined exercise regime, women of a similar age find it much more difficult to mask their degeneration. It was to Brenda that McSorely paid particular attention and he failed to spot a single difference in a face that seemed to have been fixed in a permanent smile for the last 17 years. A grin then appeared on his own coupon as Gail turned the page once more and revealed a veritable rogues gallery.

"You'll like this one," she told him. "It's the night mum and dad showed me off to the customers for the first time as proud parents."

All of the Tortured Soul's regulars stared back at McSorely and they all looked not a day younger, with the possible exception of McCall, whose haircut, sunglasses and oily complexion brought to a mind a cheap waxwork rendering of Liam Gallagher. As he peered into the background of the picture, McSorely could see Moira was even sitting in the same pose she now struck, staring blankly into the distance as her right hand gripped a half-empty vodka bottle. That was all the validation he needed to push ahead with his plan but Moira ironically remained the one obstacle standing in his way. He couldn't proceed until she was otherwise engaged and McSorely could only pray that such a tiny body contained a bladder of fitting proportions. Those prayers were answered within five minutes as Moira stood up, retaining her fierce grip on the bottle of vodka, and walked towards the bar. "I need to go for a pish again," she told Gail after planting the bottle down on the bar. "Keep an eye on this for me, will you? Your friend here works for that bastard Buchan so he's not to be trusted. All lawyers are lying, deceitful fuckers. Never turn your back to one of them – they'll plunge a fucking knife right in it." Gail could only laugh at Moira's outburst after the foul-mouthed spectre had disappeared into the ladies but it was a warning she should have heeded. Seizing his chance, McSorely ordered another whisky, forcing Gail to turn towards the bar. As she moved his glass towards the optics, McSorely produced a spirit of his own from his jacket pocket and hastily swabbed a handkerchief in chloroform. Within a matter of seconds, Gail was sprawled unconscious on McSorely's shoulder and setting off on a journey towards the cliffs.

# Chapter 31:

# M for Murder

While most Moristounians considered one of the island's three watering holes to be their sanctuary, Buchan found his refuge behind the doors of the library. The wonders of the written word had preserved his sanity for the last two centuries and Buchan could always be found in his favourite spot – reclining in a tattered leather armchair that looked out towards the sea – of a Saturday afternoon. He often managed to work his way through an entire novel before heading to the Tortured Soul late in the evening for a helping of Brenda's steak pie and a wee dram. But this voracious appetite for literature had now ensured something of a famine when it came to finding fresh morsels to savour. Having wolfed down all of the classics within the first few decades, Buchan found himself relying on more contemporary fare to sate his hunger. This didn't prove too much of a problem to begin with as he feasted on the Russian greats then lapped up the works of writers such as Franz Kafka, TS Elliot, F Scott Fitzgerald, Ernest Hemingway and Vladimir Nabokov. But society started to leave Buchan behind from the 1950s onwards and he found it harder to identify with the characters that graced the pages of the library's latest additions. Miss Sanderson had helped to ease this growing sense of alienation by steering him towards some of the more intelligent modern writers but her recommendations steadily reduced in number with each passing decade. That forced Buchan back towards books he had already read and he took a measure of comfort from retreating into a world that made much greater sense. He missed the thrill that came with the discovery of an exciting new talent, however, and decided to give modern literature another chance when Karen stepped into Miss Sanderson's shoes. The new librarian was particularly effusive in her praise of Irvine Welsh and urged Buchan to check out his seminal work, Trainspotting. It was to this tome that Buchan now turned for his Saturday afternoon entertainment but he was finding Trainspotting harder to decipher than The Book itself. Indeed, the paragraph he currently found himself stuck on was even more mystifying than the extract on meditation which had tested Buchan's knowledge of ancient Mayan to the limit. From what he had managed to piece together from the narrative, Trainspotting's hero had burst into the toilet of a turf accountant seeking emergency relief, only to be confronted by one of the customers. The exchange that followed proved totally mystifying, however, as it contained several words – peeve, radge, keks, wide-o and shunky – that Buchan had never encountered during his four decades in Scotland's capital. The characters in Welsh's novel may have been born in the same city as Buchan but it felt as if they came from a different planet, living an alien lifestyle and speaking in an unintelligible tongue. Karen had provided a bridge between these two worlds by acting as his translator but Buchan felt bad about pestering her for the third time in less than 10 minutes. So he popped Trainspotting back on the shelf and bid the librarian farewell before heading off to the Tortured Soul for some liquid refreshment.

With the big game tempting most of his fellow drinkers to Moyne Park, Buchan wasn't expecting much in the way of company when he walked through the doors of Jimmy's pub. But his heart sank as he looked around the empty room and spotted just Moira in her usual place in the corner. Things had remained frosty between them since William Hughes' trial and while Brenda had never repeated the slap she delivered outside the courtroom, there was violence in every look she shot at him. Barely a word had been uttered between them in the last three decades so Buchan took no offence as his entrance met with silence and opted for quiet decorum himself as he sat down at the bar then waited for Brenda or Gail to appear. Having painstakingly worked his way through The Book, Buchan had every right to regard himself as a man of great patience but even he became frustrated as three minutes passed without a presence behind the bar. He assumed the Mathieson women had retreated upstairs during the afternoon lull and decided to register his presence by ringing the bell Jimmy sounded every night to signal the advent of chucking out time. Even this failed to bring someone scurrying down the stairs, however, and Buchan found himself reaching for the bell once more after another 60 seconds of silence. His hand never reached its target, though, as Moira screamed: "Ring that bell one more time and I'll fucking kill you. You're wasting your time, there's no cunt here." Buchan was in no mood to rattle Moira's cage further so he slipped his hand back into his jacket pocket before enquiring about the whereabouts of Brenda and Gail in the politest possible terms. That failed to ensure an equally civil response, though, as Moira stared at him coldly for a few seconds before saying: "Why should I tell a fucking lowlife like you?"

Upon hearing that it was "the decent thing to do", Moira snorted and shot back: "Decent? What does a fucking lawyer know about decency? You didn't show any decency towards me in that courtroom, did you?"

Buchan had to admit Moira had him bang to rights and offered up his humblest apology in a bid to find out why the bar had been abandoned. Moira took great pleasure in watching a man of such airs and graces shamelessly grovel and prolonged his indignity for a few more seconds before finally giving Buchan the information he was seeking.

"Brenda fucked off to the football with Jimmy and left Gail in charge," she said, news that came as something of a surprise to Buchan as he had assumed McSorely would accompany United's biggest fan to the stadium. When he relayed this information to Moira, it met with a shrug but she added: "Your glamorous assistant definitely isn't at Moyne Park. He was in here just a few minutes ago nattering away to Gail."

"Where are they now?" said Buchan. "They can't just have disappeared."

"That's exactly what happened," replied Moira. "I went to the toilet and when I came back out they had vanished. If you ask me, your boy is up to no good. He looked shifty as fuck when he came in here and I warned Gail not to trust him."

"Did you hear what they were talking about before they disappeared? That might give us some clues."

"Of course I did. I hear everything that goes on in this place. It might look like I'm in a dream world when I'm sitting there drinking but there's not much that escapes my attention. Your boy was telling Gail how he broke into the police station and paid Hogg a wee visit."

Dread started to bite into Buchan as Moira revealed further details of McSorely's conversation with Gail. Buchan knew Hogg had let the cat out of the bag upon learning his assistant had been examining the Mathieson family album in forensic detail. It was now just a question of whether the feline's head was merely poking out of the sack or if its legs were enjoying the freedom they had longed for. With Gail and McSorely nowhere to be seen, it was safe to assume said moggy was now running amok somewhere in Moristoun. Buchan had to catch it before its claws did some serious damage so he thanked Moira for her help then dashed off in pursuit. As he burst out of the pub in a blind panic, Buchan found his thoughts turning towards Miss Sanderson and her final exit from The Cliff all those years ago. She had headed straight for the sea in her time of crisis and Buchan found himself drawn in a similar direction as he tried to track down his rogue assistant. If his old friend was trying to guide him from the next realm then her navigational skills were spot on as Buchan spied a dot on the horizon within seconds of setting out towards the cliffs. Buchan's superior physical conditioning, allied to the fact he wasn't forced to carry a fully grown woman on his shoulder, allowed him to close the gap on McSorely with impressive speed. The dot soon came into sharper focus in the driving rain and Buchan's concern gave way to anger as he spotted Gail sprawled unconscious over McSorely's shoulder. This caused him to opt for violence instead of diplomacy in his bid to halt McSorely's progress towards the cliffs. Buchan may have known little about football but he executed a brutal sliding tackle from behind that William Hughes would have been proud of. It brought McSorely and Gail crashing to the ground some 100 metres short of their destination and Buchan then switched sporting themes to the Big Daddy era of British wrestling as he sat down on top of McSorely in a bid to subdue him. It was a crude manoeuvre yet wonderfully effective as McSorely was incapacitated as he lay face down on the mud. Buchan was tempted to pound McSorely's head into the turf until his body became limp but the knowledge he had gleaned from The Book steered him away from such animalistic retribution. Only one person could tell him what had happened to the poor girl lying supine just a few yards away so it was best to keep him awake for questioning.

"What in God's name have you done to her?" Buchan said, while satisfying some of his bloodlust with a slap to the back of McSorely's head. "Please tell me she's just unconscious. You haven't killed her, have you?"

McSorely was still reeling from the shock of being halted by Buchan's last-man foul just as he was about to roll the proverbial ball into an empty net, so he let the rain wash over him for a few seconds before revealing Gail was merely sedated.

"What do you mean sedated? You don't know a thing about medicine. Dr Barrett had you believing Hogg was suffering from a fictional ailment."

"I might not know much about medicine but I've seen enough ropey detective films to know what to do with a bottle of chloroform."

Buchan could only curse his failure to find a better hiding place for the bottle as the gravity of Gail's situation became clear. Chloroform could be deadly in the hands of an amateur and it was clear McSorely's grasp of chemistry didn't stretch much beyond sourcing a remedy for the common cold.

"Chloroform isn't something you can mess about with, you idiot," said Buchan. "If you put too much on the cloth it can end up killing someone."

"You didn't seem too worried about the dangers of chloroform when you used it on me. That was how you got me here, wasn't it?"

"I didn't have any choice. I had to knock you out to take you through the portal."

"I came here through a portal?" said McSorely, who could only laugh at the latest absurdity to fly his way. "This place is fucking bonkers. Hogg opened my eyes to Moristoun but I guess he only had time to outline the basics. Are there any other important details I need to know?"

"I'd say there's plenty he missed out, judging by the idiocy of your actions since finding out about our rather warped reality. Would you care to explain the reasoning behind your journey towards the cliffs?"

"I'm just seeking what every man truly desires – eternal youth and happiness. If I jump off these cliffs with Gail in my arms we'll both stay young and free in Moristoun forever."

It was now Buchan's turn to break into laughter as he marvelled at the idiotic naivety of the figure trapped under him. Although Hogg was probably the last citizen he would have trusted to deliver a definitive account of Moristoun's mysteries, Buchan knew he wouldn't have lied to McSorely, especially in his new enlightened state. The madness Buchan had only just succeeded in stopping, therefore, was all down to McSorely's moronic interpretation of affairs. "Neither of you would have remained in Moristoun had you pushed ahead with such a hair-brained scheme," he told McSorely. "Suicide is the act of taking one's own life; what you had planned was cold-blooded murder. You had to knock Gail out with chloroform so I can quite confidently jump to the conclusion she wasn't a willing participant in this. And even if you had persuaded Gail to take leave of her senses and jump off the cliffs with you, there's no way you would have ended up in Moristoun together."

348

"Why not?" said McSorely, whose defiant tone suggested he still believed his plan was fundamentally sound. "I thought this was the place where all suicide victims ended up?"

"Do you have any idea how many people kill themselves every year?" said Buchan. "Go on, take a guess."

"I don't know but I'm sure it can't be that many. About ten thousand?"

"Try adding a couple of zeroes to that figure – it's actually over a million. In fact, a person takes their own life roughly every 40 seconds. You have no idea how many lost souls find themselves swept up when despair spreads its dark cape across the continents. Quite how you could believe they all end up here is beyond me. Does Moristoun look like the kind of place that could house a new resident every 40 seconds?"

"So who does end up in Moristoun?" said McSorely, who was now starting to realise his plan wasn't quite as brilliant as first thought. "Is it only for Scottish people?"

"It is but we're still far too small to cope with the depression dear old Caledonia stirs in the populace. Almost 800 people topped themselves last year and there's no way The Council could have dealt with so many new residents here. We're one of the smaller islands in The Council's network so we only get about 10 new arrivals each year."

"Where do all the others go? How many islands are there?"

"There are 15 in total. The biggest one is Aterstoun and that awful place makes Moristoun seem like a holiday camp."

"So if I managed to find a way out from under your massive arse and threw myself off those cliffs, I could end up on any one of those 15 islands?"

"Exactly. I'm glad to hear you're beginning to think with a bit of clarity at last. Keep this up and I might release your body from under the weight of said arse."

"Why do you care what happens to me anyway? This is the second time you've stopped me from killing myself. I can understand why you want to save Gail but what makes me so special?"

Buchan then told McSorely the story behind his work for The Council and revealed how his own fate was linked to the safe return of both his Q101s to the mainland. As he touched on Gail's role in this convoluted tale, the thoughts of both men shifted back towards the girl laying just a few feet away. She clearly needed attention as quickly as possible and Buchan decided it was safe to let McSorely loose, having witnessed a semblance of sanity return. "I don't think the chloroform has done too much damage," said McSorely as he picked himself up from the mud. "I could hear Gail's heart beating while I was lugging her out here."

That provided Buchan with a measure of comfort as he started to examine Gail because he knew cardiac failure presented the gravest danger. Buchan was far from an amateur when it came to assessing the health of those anaesthetised by chloroform, having sedated a handful of clients since beginning his work for Farqhuar. Gail, thankfully, seemed to be in the same state as everyone else he had knocked out so there seemed little immediate danger to her, save another burst of murderous delirium from McSorely. But his assistant appeared to have escaped the insanity that had pushed him so close to such a despicable act. Shame had become the dominant feature in his emotional landscape, although relief briefly shone through the clouds when Buchan gave a positive assessment of Gail's prospects.

"How the hell am I going to explain this when she wakes up?" said McSorely as he watched Buchan throw Gail over his own shoulder before leading the march back towards town. "She'll think I knocked her out because I wanted to have my dirty way with her. Gail's never going to forgive me. And what about Jimmy? He's already pissed off with me for missing out on the game. How's he going to react when Gail tells him what happened?"

"He'll probably try to remove your arms from their sockets and rightly so," said Buchan. "This girl has a wonderful future in front of her and you almost robbed her of it. The one crumb of comfort you can take is that I stopped you from committing one of the most despicable crimes this island has ever seen."

Terror then descended on McSorely as he considered the prospect of Buchan reporting his attempted murder to Sergeant McLeish. Moving into the cell that Hogg would soon abandon was a fate to be avoided at all costs and he even considered running back towards the cliffs to buy a ticket for the Suicide Island Lottery. This idea was soon abandoned, though, as Buchan reassured McSorely his earlier lunacy would remain a secret.

"I'm the only one who knows about your little plan and I have nothing to gain from divulging your secret," he said. "Besides, it would be rather hypocritical of me to take the moral high ground, given the circumstances behind my own arrival in Moristoun. My own lust managed to cause even more disastrous consequences."

After Buchan had revealed the full details of his dark past, McSorely found himself in the unusual position of pitying his boss. He had always been rather envious of Buchan, especially as Gail seemed to hang on his every word, but he now realised the torment that raged beneath his calm exterior.

"You must have loved this Jane a lot," said McSorely. "Do you still think about her after all these years?"

"Not a day goes past when I don't think about her," said Buchan. "But we are all parted from our loved ones at some stage so we need to learn how to let go. It's the same for you and Gail, unfortunately. If you truly love her then you will realise you can't be together. It just wasn't meant to be, the same as my relationship with Jane. Please don't repeat my mistake and cause the same misery. The only way you can both move on is to return to the mainland and go your separate ways."

"But will our lives be any better back there? I know exactly how dismal life can be. A million people don't just kill themselves every year for a laugh. It's the bleakness and hopelessness of our existence that drives us to it."

"Life may be bleak and hopeless at times but it's still life and that's the greatest gift of all," he said. "You can't just throw it away."

"But you don't really throw it away, do you?" said McSorely. "You end up here or on one of the other islands so it's more like moving house."

"It may appear that way to you but nothing could be further from the truth. Moristoun is a dwelling of the dead, we all stop living the moment we land here. It truly is a curse to be trapped here."

"I don't know about that. You've just admitted your life on the mainland was a disaster but you seem to be doing quite well for yourself here. You're a successful lawyer and all that free time has helped you amass quite an intellect."

"Time becomes a curse when you're trapped in the same body and mind for over a century. That's why so few of us ever get into treble figures and fewer still reach such a landmark while retaining a firm grip on their marbles. It's unnatural. Being denied a proper death is one of cruellest punishments imaginable. It stops you from moving on and you never progress. You may have noticed I like to pepper my conversation with quotations and there's a good reason for that. I no longer have a proper life so I have to stay alive through the experiences of others. The wonders open to mortals such as yourself are now denied me; I can merely read about them on the page."

"But what about this book that holds the answers to all life's questions? You wouldn't have been able to read that if you hadn't been stuck in Moristoun."

"There's not a single thing in The Book you won't learn eventually if you return to the mainland and accept your place in the great cycle. What would you rather do – savour thousands of different lifetimes and amass the experience that way or work your way laboriously through a book for 14 years? I know what I would pick if I had the choice again."

"What do you mean thousands of lifetimes? I was under the impression we only had one shot at it. That's what they taught us in church."

Buchan would have thought conversing with a man who had hung himself back in 1862 would have provided McSorely with all the evidence he needed to take the pontificating of his preachers with a pinch of salt. But his mind clearly needed a bit of help when it came to processing the screeds of information it had received in the last few hours.

"Religion is too dogmatic to get a proper grasp on reality," Buchan said. "The universe continues to evolve and true understanding only comes when you allow your mind to evolve with it. I don't profess to have all the answers myself. I can only go on what I learned in The Book and even that is only a guide, the reader needs to make the journey to enlightenment himself. That's why I'm still stuck here."

"So you have no idea when you will finally be allowed to leave Moristoun?"

"No, it could be weeks, months, years, decades or centuries. All I can do is lead as virtuous an existence as possible and hope my good deeds are rewarded."

"Will it help much if you manage to bring me back to the mainland?"

"That's certainly what Farquhar has told me but Dr Barrett views things a little differently. He says it will count for little if my greatest motivation for securing your return is self-interest."

Finding out that even members of The Council couldn't agree on the exact dynamics of Moristoun left McSorely's mind in an even greater muddle. Although he was far from Mastermind material, McSorely considered himself relatively intelligent in relation to most of his peers but he now realised what he had learned in the last 30 years was mainly inconsequential. Two conversations in the space of a couple of hours had proven more enlightening than two decades of formal education, although this perhaps shouldn't have come as too great a surprise given the combined age of the Moristounian duo he had conversed with was nearing 700. Asking McSorely's brain to come up to speed with such lofty subjects was akin to pushing a rusty Lada Riva on to the grid at the Monaco Grand Prix. While a man of greater humility would have remained lost for words as he pondered the many invariables of his new reality, McSorely rather cheapened the moment by opting for profanity when he answered Buchan's query about his plans for the immediate future.

"Fucked if I know," he said. "This place is way too bloody mental for me to get my head around at the minute. Let's just say I need some time to gather my thoughts."

Chief among his immediate thoughts was concern for Gail's welfare and McSorely asked Buchan how his attack would affect her own destiny.

"I'm hoping it will have no effect," he replied. "The plan remains exactly the same. The University of the Highlands and Islands beckons for the only precious thing this terrible place has ever produced."

"But how are we going to explain what happened to her?" said McSorely. "What plausible explanation can I have for knocking her out with chloroform? Gail will never want to speak to me again."

"I wouldn't worry too much about that," said Buchan with a smile as they reached their destination and he invited McSorely to open the door to The Council offices. "I know a doctor who performs wonders with chloroform victims. By the time he's finished with Gail she'll be convinced you're the hero who saved her from a potentially deadly fit."

# Chapter 32:

# One for the road

McSorely felt a little ashamed as he entered the Tortured Soul for the final time and was greeted by a banner that proclaimed: "Home James! – Moristoun bids farewell to a hero." This was Jimmy's follow up to his Victory for Valentino triumph and it hinted further at his hidden talent. The banner would have looked even more impressive had Jimmy been granted more time to rustle it up but Buchan had only broken news of his assistant's impending departure just a day previously. He had done this against the wishes of McSorely, who would have preferred to slip away without any fanfare. This was mainly down to the guilt he still felt over his brush with homicide, with Buchan's cover story merely ladling on the self-loathing as it forced him to play the role of Gail's saviour. While this charade was not without its advantages – the most prominent being a kiss on the cheek from the woman he loved – living a lie over the past six weeks had become unbearable. Returning to a world where nobody considered him special now seemed infinitely more appealing and McSorely was angry that Buchan's loose lips had ensured the hero-worshipping would be cranked up a level for his final night in Moristoun. That much became clear as he inspected the banner and Jimmy provided further confirmation as he welcomed McSorely by saying: "Make sure you keep that wallet in your pocket, son. All your drinks are on the house."

McSorely had never doubted that would be the case, given he had only been forced to dip into his own pocket for alcoholic refreshment once or twice since the day he had flirted with disaster. While McSorely had plummeted several tiers in Jimmy's estimation by snubbing his ticket for the biggest Moristoun derby in decades, he soon jumped miles beyond his initial station when Buchan used all his wiles to relay news of Gail's fictional fit. McSorely was then elevated to the status of a demigod a few weeks later when Gail departed for her university entrance exam and returned to Moristoun clutching a letter of acceptance. "I always knew you were sent here for a reason," Jimmy told McSorely. "Without you, our Gail would have been struck down just weeks before fulfilling her destiny."

Jimmy then pointed in the direction of Moira and added: "That bag of bones over there would have been our only hope had Gail been left alone that day. Can you imagine her having the strength to lug poor Gail all the way to Dr Barrett's office? She couldn't even carry a bag of crisps back to her table. Having you walk in was divine intervention. That's why fate made you miss the match."

It was to the eagerly anticipated derby that McSorely's thoughts now turned as he remembered this was the day when the Inter Islands Cup Final was scheduled to be held.

"Why have you gone to the bother of organising a farewell party for me?" he asked Jimmy. "I thought you would all be too busy listening to the cup final on radio. Who's winning?"

The grimace that appeared on Brenda's face as she poured McSorely's first pint suggested that he had strayed on to dangerous ground by talking to her husband about a topic that had been off-limits in the Mathieson household for weeks. Jimmy then left him in no doubt by growling: "Who gives a fuck? They're two shitey teams and neither deserves it."

This response brought McCall and Henderson to life and it was the printed media who first tried to coax another angry soundbite from the landlord.

"I'm guessing the subtext here is that your beloved United were the ones who truly merited getting their hands on the trophy this year," said Henderson.

"Too bloody right we were," said Jimmy. "And we would have won the cup had we not had the misfortune to come up against the Devil's 11 in the last eight. Solnus wouldn't have beaten us in the semis if your lot hadn't crocked our two best players."

"So the three suspensions had nothing to do with it then?" said McCall as he entered the debate. "Maybe if your boys had kept their discipline you would have stood a better chance of winning the cup."

"Every one of those bloody red cards was for retaliation. It was Athletic who brought shame on football and this town again that day, not us."

"The only thing that shames this town is the fact your last Inter Islands Cup win was decades ago," said Henderson. "You might have knocked us out the cup but you will still end the season without a trophy while we will remain league champions."

McSorely feared his final few hours in the most fascinating town he would ever set foot in would be soundtracked by the petty footballing squabbling that had been given far too much airplay in both his mainland and island existence. However, Buchan was there to save him yet again as he appeared from behind the bar clutching one side of a giant cake. Gail was handed the task of propping up the other end and the care she took in making sure the cake arrived safely in front of McSorely hinted at the primary role she had played in its creation.

Like the fruits of her father's imagination, Gail's farewell gift also came equipped with a message as the frosting on the cake wished McSorely well in his new job. This revealed a second betrayal of trust by Buchan, who was the only one who knew of the new posting in Edinburgh, but McSorely was less upset this time as it gave him a proper excuse for leaving his new friends in Moristoun behind.

Gail was the first to ask what job could possibly be exciting enough to halt McSorely's apprenticeship at the hands of a genius such as Buchan and he felt he was letting her down somewhat by revealing he would be returning to the world of IT. "I'm not really cut out for this line of work," McSorely added. "There's too much deception and sleight of hand for my liking."

Buchan couldn't help but be a little offended by McSorely's dig at his profession and felt like reminding him one particular deception was the only thing preventing Jimmy from strapping his bloodied corpse to the ceiling fan. But he decided to let it slide and praised his assistant for coming to a sage conclusion that he himself had only reached once it was far too late to change career direction.

"The words of Confucius sum things up rather nicely in regards to this matter," Buchan said. "He claims there are three ways to acquire wisdom. Reflection is the noblest, imitation is the easiest and experience is the bitterest. By refusing to imitate one whose experience has left him bitter, on reflection I would say you have made the wisest choice of all."

McSorely knew Buchan was referencing matters far more important than his choice of career with that sentiment and it reminded him of the huge debt of gratitude he would forever owe him. In addition to twice saving McSorely from suicide, not to mention the indelible stain of taking someone else's life, Buchan had also set the stage for his reintroduction to mainland society by sourcing a new job. One of Buchan's former Q99s, Robert Falkingham, had blossomed to such an extent that he was now in charge of Edinburgh's fastest-growing software development company. When reminded of the fact that his personal development wouldn't have been possible had Buchan not stopped him from ending it all with an asphyxiwank during the lowest point of his sexual degeneracy, Falkingham was only too happy carve out a role for McSorely in his empire. The salary was a generous £35,000 and he had even agreed to stump up a £2000 "signing-on fee", allowing Buchan to rent out a flat within walking distance of Haymarket Station ahead of their arrival tomorrow afternoon.

As Gail expressed interest in the interior design of his new pad, McSorely yearned to invite her to stay when she decided to tick off Edinburgh Castle and the capital's other delights on her sightseeing list. However, a desire to start repaying Buchan for all his good deeds prevented McSorely from doing so as he was reminded of the plea to stay as far away from her as possible. That meant this was probably the last night he would ever set eyes on Gail, although he was actually the only person inside the Tortured Soul who stood even the slightest chance of seeing her again on the mainland. Jimmy and Brenda still seemed to be coming to terms with that and McSorely guessed his farewell party was just a dress rehearsal for the real tear-jerker that lay in wait come the advent of Fresher's Week.

Although Gail had learned a great deal about her hometown's macabre nature when Buchan had been forced to explain why their journey to Inverness for the entrance exam would be conducted via a toilet cubicle rather than a passenger ferry, she remained ignorant of the fact that her second voyage to the mainland would be on a one-way ticket. Her parents had yet to summon the courage to inform her that trips home for the holidays would be off limits, mainly because they didn't want to ruin the few precious weeks they still had in her company. That was why Gail's eyes retained the sparkle evident in almost every budding student as they prepare to set off on their first solo expedition. It was to those eyes that McSorely gravitated every few minutes as his party raged on late into the night, although the image he hoped to carve deep into his mind became increasingly blurred with each pint and whisky that passed his lips. But McSorely had anticipated the steady advance of inebriation and taken precautionary measures to ensure Gail's beauty remained captured for the rest of his days. While his iPhone would effectively remain an expensive paperweight until he returned to the connected world, it was still capable of taking pictures within the analogue confines of Moristoun. That was why McSorely pestered his fellow drinkers to pose for photo after photo before he became too pissed to operate the camera, with one particular subject taking up the vast majority of his phone's memory.

When Munchkin woke the fully-clothed McSorely from the makeshift bed he had constructed in the hall – with his suit jacket providing the duvet and an empty bottle of whisky acting as a pillow – he instinctively thrust a hand into his left trouser pocket to see if his phone had survived. To his horror, the pocket was empty and a search of the right receptacle revealed only the keys to the front door. The phone proved equally elusive as McSorely scoured the rest of the house, although he was hardly in the best shape to play hide and seek given the epic status of his hangover. A heady mix of physical and emotional agony duly accompanied McSorely's breakfast and he could manage just a few spoonfuls of cereal before both his hands became engaged in the task of burying his head. This comforting darkness provided a tiny dose of opiate but McSorely wasn't allowed to savour it for long as the doorbell sent another agonising bolt of pain coursing through his head. He ignored the first three shrill assaults before coming to the conclusion that dragging his body to the door would be less distressing than suffering these repeated jolts to the head. It proved to be a wise decision as Buchan was waiting behind the door when McSorely finally opened it.

"I have a special delivery for a James Patrick McSorely," said Buchan as he held up the cherished iPhone. "I don't think you want to be returning home without this."

Given that McSorely was still half pissed from his exploits the previous night, it all became too emotional for him and he broke into tears of joy as he hugged Buchan on the doorstep.

"I don't know how I'm going to survive without you back on the mainland," he said. "You're a life-saver in every sense of the word. Every time I do something stupid, you're there to bail me out."

"I'm sure you'll get by fine without me," replied Buchan. "That you've been reunited with your beloved device is actually down to your own ingenuity."

"I very much doubt that. I can't even remember losing the bloody thing in the first place. What happened?"

"Just after midnight, upon declaring me the best friend, boss, teacher, lawyer and confidant in the world, you granted me custody of your phone and told me to guard it with my life. I think the exact phrase was 'I'm fucking steamboats, so gonnae look after this for me.' Having watched you take so many pictures of young Gail, I knew how much the phone would mean to you. Securing its safe return was the least I could do."

As Buchan handed the iPhone back over for inspection, McSorely quickly searched through its contents to make sure all the photos had survived. To his intense relief, the phone's memory remained full of snapshots that would remind him of everyone he had grown to love during his time in Moristoun. That great adventure was now coming to an end, though, and flicking through the photos on the walk to Farqhuar's office proved a bittersweet experience. While each face smiled back at him – with the exception of Moira whose gaze refused to shift from her bottle of vodka – McSorely knew everyone in Jimmy's pub truly was a tortured soul. They would be stuck in Moristoun for centuries to come, sinking further into its deep sand with each passing year.

"What's going to happen to them all?" McSorely asked Buchan as they sat in Farqhuar's waiting room upon their arrival. "If someone like you is still trapped here then what hope do the likes of McTavish, McCall and Henderson have of leaving?"

"That's a question beyond my ken," replied Buchan. "Enlightenment comes to us all at some stage and it just takes longer for some than it does for others. I'm by no means there myself. To serve my own ends, I threw you and Gail together and the consequences were almost disastrous. I'm afraid I still have a long way to go."

"So if I decide to top myself in my late 90s when I grow tired of having to summon someone to wipe my backside, you'll still be here waiting for me?"

"I hope that's a joke. Take no offence when I heartily wish this is the last time I see your ugly mug."

# Epilogue

Revulsion paid Buchan another visit as he emerged from Waverley Station and spotted the gaudy sign that welcomed visitors to the Wonga.com Princes St Gardens. Had the giant Technicolor letters merely formed part of the Christmas decorations that adorned the city centre at this time of year, Buchan would have been able to accept this latest commercial rape of his fair city more readily. But the monstrosity had been molesting the skyline for three unbroken years, causing a shudder to run through Buchan no matter the season. Distaste had become almost his constant companion on trips to the mainland in recent years, with Scotland failing to buck the prevailing global trend for intellectual vegetation. The one upside to this mental decay was people spent less time pondering the perceived futility of their existence, leading to a drop in the suicide rate. With so many distractions so close at hand, a large section of the populace remained stuck in an electronic trance. The hypnotic glare of these myriad computer screens failed to work its magic on everyone, however, and Buchan's services were still in demand. His second jaunt to Edinburgh inside six months was merely a reconnaissance mission, though, as Harry Scott's unhappiness had yet to reach the heights Farqhuar believed would push him towards suicide. "Harry is one of those transvestite types so he should be fairly easy to spot," Farqhuar had told him. "Working out what makes him tick will be rather trickier. We've had a few of these confused young chaps in Moristoun but I've always found them a bit of a mystery. There's seems little immediate danger to him, though, so just spend some time following him around to see if you pick up any clues."

Farqhuar's file on Harry revealed that his predilection for tube tops, Technicolor tights and purple mascara had made relations with his parents rather strained. Some unfortunate physiognomic quirks had also fended off any potential partners so Christmas was bound to be a particularly testing time for the 19-year-old. Harry's impending visit to the Traditional Christmas Market (sponsored by 888 casinos) was bound to stir some powerful emotions and that made it the perfect place for Buchan to begin his observations. But as he wandered through the festive shoppers, trying to spot a flash of luminous material between thigh-high boot and skirt, all thoughts of Harry disappeared as he glanced across at the Merry Go Round and saw a face from the past.

Over 17 years had passed since their tearful farewell in Inverness but the passage of time had been remarkably kind to Gail. She was still a wondrous sight to behold and age had even added to her beauty by bringing dignity and grace to the table. Buchan yearned to race across and hug Gail but knew such an act would not go down well with The Council, who had ruled a complete break from all matters Moristoun was the only way to ensure the former Miss Mathieson would be able to move forward with her life. Having only just returned to The Council's good books following the McSorely-inspired catastrophe that came within a whisker of claiming Gail's life, Buchan was in no mood to damage his standing any further. He was edging back towards an exit door that had once seemed so maddeningly close and nothing would stop him from bursting through this time. That plan would lie in ruins if Gail recognised him so Buchan took shelter behind a hot dog stand before continuing with what he thought was a covert surveillance operation. His peeping was far from discreet, however, as within seconds a voice from behind him said: "Is spying on glamorous blondes a habit of yours, or is this just a one-off?" Buchan was preparing to turn around for an awkward discussion with a policeman but the identity of his new companion then became clear as he added: "I can hardly blame you. She looks just as good now as when I first set eyes on her at 17 in the Tortured Soul."

Old father time had treated the 48-year-old McSorely more barbarously, abusing him like the bastard child who only received scraps from the table and remained locked in the coal cellar at social gatherings. The hinted girth of his Moristoun frame had blossomed into borderline obesity and he sported a hairline that was receding so quickly it would surely vanish before seeing a sixth decade. Men who let their body degenerate into such a state of disrepair usually fell into two camps – those whose waistlines grew at an exponential rate to their bank balances and lonely desperados who had long since abandoned any attempt to make themselves presentable to the opposite sex. Buchan knew nothing of McSorely's recent affairs as The Council had decreed him "no longer a viable risk" two years after his return to the mainland. From what he had gathered from their brief working relationship, however, it seemed safe to assume McSorely now swelled the ranks of those who could only sate their sexual appetite via professional purveyors of filth. That realisation caused dread to well up inside Buchan as he considered McSorely's appreciation of Gail's current shape. They were both appraising her from the same furtive vantage point and Buchan could only hope his companion's hand wasn't engaged in a sordid act through a hole in his trouser pocket. This thought soon gave way to a fear that filled Buchan with even greater panic as he began to wonder if McSorely had spent the last 17 years stalking Gail. Such a scenario certainly seemed plausible and Buchan feared the worst as he enquired about the reason for his proximity to Gail.

"There's no need to look so concerned," McSorely told him. "I'm not breaking a restraining order if that's what you're worried about. That our paths have crossed again is just one of life's little coincidences."

"Are you sure?" said Buchan, who was far from reassured by McSorely's flippant tone. "You were so infatuated by the poor girl that you once tried to take both your lives. Do you really expect me to believe there's nothing suspicious about the fact you're now ogling her from behind a hot dog stand?"

"You can believe what you want but my conscience is clear. And you're the one who's hiding away, not me. The only reason I'm standing here is because I want to eat this delicious slab of processed meat."

"So your presence at the Christmas Market has nothing to do with Gail?"

"Only in a vague sense," replied McSorely, who then instructed Buchan to fix his gaze on the Merry Go Round. "Do you see that little girl with the blonde hair sitting on the brown horse? That's Gail's daughter Heather and she goes to the same nursery as my wee boy Callum. The nursery's only about five minutes' walk from here and I've agreed to meet Callum and my wife Jenny here for a spot of Christmas shopping."

The relief wrought by McSorely's brief summation of affairs left Buchan close to tears and pride coursed through him as he reflected on his own role in the creation of two new lives.

"That's wonderful news," he told McSorely before extending his hand in congratulation. "I'm glad things have turned out so well. You were certainly due a break after everything you went through."

"Well, life's not exactly been a bed of roses since I came back from Moristoun but it all seems to be coming together now. Jenny's my third wife and this one's definitely a keeper. Once you have a wee one it changes everything."

"I'm afraid I'll just have to take your word for it on that one, having been deprived of such a pleasure myself. But you're in good company making such an assertion as the great Cicero once said: 'Of all nature's gifts to the human race, what is sweeter to a man than his children?'"

Roman philosophers were rarely referenced as Scotland hurtled towards the fourth decade of the new millennium and most people of McSorely's age would have assumed Buchan was talking about a washed-up pop star from their youth when he mentioned Cicero. But two crazy months in Moristoun had left quite a mark on McSorely and the high-brow reference warmed his soul on a typically inclement December afternoon.

"I'm glad to see you're still as educational as ever when it comes to the old sound bites," he told Buchan. "I take it the library in Moristoun remains as well stocked as ever?"

"Oh, nothing much changes in our world," replied Buchan. "Seventeen years in Moristoun is the equivalent of about a week down here. With the exception of a few new arrivals, the island is exactly the same as when you left it."

"How are Jimmy and Brenda coping without Gail? It must have hit them hard when she had to leave. Their home will seem so empty without her."

"Empty?" said Buchan. "That's the last word you would use to describe the place now. Gail's void was filled by your furry former landlord so space is rather at a premium."

"Don't tell me Munchkin is still going? She must be well over 20 by now and dogs never live to that age."

"That might be true down here but you of all people should realise things are rather different in our little world. It's not just humans who end up in Moristoun if they take their own life."

Surreal surprises such as suicidal canines had been de rigueur during McSorely's time in Buchan's employ but two decades back in dreary Scotland had restored a healthy measure of his scepticism. As he questioned a dog's mental capacity to purposely end its life, though, McSorely knew he was destined to lose the argument.

"Canine suicide is more common than you think," said Buchan. "There's one bridge alone in Dumbarton where it's thought 50 of the poor beasts have thrown themselves to an early grave in the last 50 years."

"But what drives them to it? It seems like most of them have a pretty stress-free existence."

"I've always believed you can judge somebody by the company they keep," replied Buchan. "And dogs have the misfortune to be man's best friend. As James Thurber once said: 'The dog has seldom been successful in pulling man up to its level of sagacity but man has frequently dragged the dog down to his.'"

"So you're saying Munchkin killed herself because her owner also committed suicide?"

"Miss Sanderson never told me the full story of how she came to be Munchkin's owner but I think that's what happened. It was one of her failed Q99s so she preferred not to talk about it."

"How old is the beast then? It sounds like she's been in Moristoun for a while."

"Munchkin must be nudging 50 so it hopefully won't be too long before The Council agrees to let her move on. That's a long time for an animal to serve its penance and her good work with Jimmy and Brenda wouldn't have gone unnoticed."

As Buchan elaborated on Munchkin's role in healing the broken heart of Gail's adoptive parents, he realised Brenda would be cursing him for failing to probe McSorely for details about her daughter's fortunes over the past two decades. When he turned the conversation back towards Gail, however, Buchan learned McSorely knew relatively little about the woman standing just 100 yards away.

"When I came back from Moristoun I didn't set eyes on her again for 16 years," he said. "I thought about Gail a lot, especially in the first few years when I was struggling to piece my life back together. I even thought about heading up to Inverness and seeking her out but I could never pluck up the courage to do it. I gradually began to forget about her as the years dragged on and then fate threw us back together at the gates of the nursery."

"That must have been a bit strange. Did you recognise her straight away?"

"Of course I did. Just look at her – she's hardly changed. Sadly, you can't say the same about me so I had to introduce myself before the penny dropped."

"How did she react? It can't have been easy for her seeing someone from Moristoun suddenly pop after all those years."

"It was weird to begin with but things were actually pretty civil. We went for a cup of coffee and swapped stories."

"How have things been for her? Brenda will be desperate to find out what her wee girl has been up to."

"She didn't give that much away. Apart from wee Heather, the only other things I know is that she's married to some rugby player called Todd and she works as a lecturer at Edinburgh University. Gail wanted to talk about Moristoun most of the time. She was desperate to find out how Jimmy and Brenda were getting on and we also talked about you a lot. Why don't you go over and say hello? It would mean a lot to her."

"You have no idea how much I want to do that but, as I told you back in Moristoun, learning how to let go is something we all have to master. The Council have barred me from making any contact and I need to keep them onside if I'm to find a way out of Moristoun."

"So you're still no closer to finding out what it's all about then?"

"Let's just say it remains a work in progress," said Buchan, who knew it was time to bid McSorely farewell as he spotted Harry Scott's green tights make their way towards a stall bursting at the seams with Hello Kitty paraphernalia. "Duty calls I'm afraid but I'll leave you with wise words of Albert Camus: 'There is but one truly serious philosophical problem – and that is suicide.'"

THE END